M000167029

HUNTER SHEA

MISFITS

This is a **FLAME TREE PRESS** book

Text copyright © 2020 Hunter Shea

All rights reserved. No part of this publication may be reproduced, stored in
a retrieval system, or transmitted in any form or by any means, electronic,
mechanical, photocopying, recording or otherwise, without the prior written
permission of the publisher.

FLAME TREE PRESS
6 Melbray Mews, London, SW6 3NS, UK
flametreepress.com

US sales, distribution and warehouse:
Simon & Schuster
simonandschuster.biz

UK distribution and warehouse:
Marston Book Services Ltd
marston.co.uk

Publisher's Note: This is a work of fiction. Names, characters, places, and
incidents are a product of the author's imagination. Locales and public names
are sometimes used for atmospheric purposes. Any resemblance to actual
people, living or dead, or to businesses, companies, events, institutions, or
locales is completely coincidental.

Thanks to the Flame Tree Press team, including:
Taylor Bentley, Frances Bodiam, Federica Ciaravella, Don D'Auria,
Chris Herbert, Josie Karani, Molly Rosevear, Mike Spender,
Cat Taylor, Maria Tissot, Nick Wells, Gillian Whitaker.

The cover is created by Flame Tree Studio with
thanks to Nik Keevil and Shutterstock.com.
The font families used are Avenir and Bembo.

Flame Tree Press is an imprint of Flame Tree Publishing Ltd
flametreepublishing.com

A copy of the CIP data for this book is available from the British Library
and the Library of Congress.

HB ISBN: 978-1-78758-499-0
US PB ISBN: 978-1-78758-497-6
UK PB ISBN: 978-1-78758-498-3
ebook ISBN: 978-1-78758-501-0

Printed and bound in Great Britain by Clays Ltd, Elcograf S.p.A.

HUNTER SHEA

MISFITS

FLAME TREE PRESS
London & New York

In the American folklore of Michigan, Ohio, North Carolina, and Connecticut, *Melon Heads* are beings generally described as small humanoids with bulbous heads who occasionally emerge from hiding places to attack people. Different variations of the legend attribute different origins to the entities.

Clarissa: I hear they're having an open-casket funeral for Jamie. I think that's in bad taste.

Tony: It is in bad taste. This whole episode is in bad taste. You young people are a disgrace to the human race. To all living things, to plants even. You shouldn't be seen in the same room with a cactus.

– River's Edge

For the Chiller Theatre posse, misfits in every amazing goddamn way – Amy, Sam, Star, Jack, Norm, Jerry, Mike, Tom and everyone else brave enough to spend a day with us.

CHAPTER ONE
MILBURY, CT – 1977

"Can I please go outside and ride my bike?"

Chris eyed his brand-new Ross three-speed in the corner beside the Christmas tree. Around it were boxes of unopened presents, all forgotten the moment he saw his dream bicycle.

"We're still opening gifts," his mother said, her irritation on the disruption of tradition clear enough to be heard from Saturn. She had her hair tucked into a plastic cap and her eyes looked small and bloodshot. It was her morning-after-drinking face, what Chris privately called Rude Mom. There was very little point pressing Rude Mom for anything, even on Christmas. So he turned his attention to his father, who was all smiles in his ratty robe and bed head.

"Please?"

His father flicked his gaze out the window. It had been a very warm December with nary a snowflake on the ground.

"Why don't you wait just a little while longer, bud? The best part of Christmas isn't over yet."

Oh, but it was. There was nothing Santa could have brought that would top the Ross. A long oblong box could have been the electronic football game he'd asked for. Hopefully the one with the Steelers vs. the Rams. As wicked cool as that would be, it still paled in comparison to the orange-and-black Ross with its three-geared stick shift and hand brakes.

Chris was all of seven, so time and space worked differently for him than they did for adults. What they would think was half an hour was actually several days for Chris, especially with his bike just sitting there waiting to go on its maiden voyage.

He clasped his hands in prayer and made a silent invocation toward his father. His dad scrubbed the stubble on his chin and shook his head. "How about ten minutes? You think you can hold out?"

"That's too soon," his mother said, her voice low and husky.

"I'll take him," Chris's brother, Dylan, said. He'd been sitting in the chair farthest from all of them, quietly opening presents with little or no fanfare.

"What kind of Christmas is this when everyone wants to leave?" his mother asked, clearly exasperated.

"The kind that comes at the end of a total shit year," Dylan said, getting up and heading for the closet.

"You sit back down."

"What's the big deal? I'll take him out for a quick spin and we'll come back and finish. You can take an aspirin or something and relax." He shrugged his jean jacket on, the one with the cover of Led Zeppelin's *Houses of the Holy* album painted on back.

"Don't you dare talk to me like that," his mother shouted.

"She's right. Can we not have any drama today?" his father said, settling back into the couch, his voice and body language spelling defeat.

Dylan muttered, "That ship sailed long ago." Then to Chris, "Come on, before I change my mind."

Chris's eyes darted between his parents and brother. Dylan never, ever did anything with him. This was kind of like a Christmas gift all its own. But it came with a price. Chris was too young to know that anything good had a catch.

His father rose from the couch and clapped his hands. "You know what, that might be a good idea. We're all tired because someone was a little anxious and couldn't wait to get started." He winked at Chris. "You guys get some fresh air while I make bacon. Honey, you can just sit back and relax. How's that sound?"

Through a clenched jaw, Chris's mother hissed, "Fine. You're all against me anyway."

All Chris cared about was the one word – *fine*. That was all the permission he needed. He grabbed the bike by the handlebars, weaving through ripped wrapping paper, boxes and bags. Flipping his coat over his shoulder, he followed Dylan out the front door. His brother's scratched-up ten-speed was on its side next to the lilac bushes.

Chris slipped one leg over the bike and settled into the soft motorcycle seat. It was comfier than any chair in the house. He put one foot on the pedal, hands squeezing the brakes, testing to make sure the rubber stoppers made contact with the rims.

Dylan flipped his long hair from his face and said, "You gonna sit there with that doofy grin all day or do you want to ride?"

Chris didn't need any further prodding. Shifting the bike into gear, he started pedaling. The front tire wobbled on the first few pumps of the pedals and for a second, he thought he was going to crash. But he managed to steady himself, riding in Dylan's slim wake.

The crisp morning air burned his cheeks as they picked up speed, zipping down Logan Hill and easing onto Zander Avenue. This time of the morning, the neighborhood was usually shuttered. But this was Christmas morning, so Chris spied a lot of open windows and lights on, families gathered under their trees and ripping through multi-colored paper, searching for treasure.

The Ross rode like a dream, just like he knew it would when he first saw it in McCann's bicycle shop. The tires were thicker than the ones on Dylan's sleek Schwinn and the frame was bulky and built to withstand some serious punishment. The whole thing resembled the structure of a motorcycle on a smaller and more manageable scale. It was beyond awesome.

Dylan rode ahead of him, not bothering to look back to see if Chris was keeping up. Dylan had never been talkative or prone to spontaneous bouts of joy. Things had hit a new dour low over the past four months, though. Something had happened to Dylan, or was happening, and no one told Chris what it could be. He was left with unanswered questions and having to live in a house mired in a thick sludge of tension. It wasn't cool to leave him out like that. He was old enough to be clued into why his family was in such a sorry state.

Maybe now was the perfect time to ask his brother. Time spent with just Dylan was rare. He pumped his legs harder to catch up. He heard the gears click in Dylan's bike. He must have sensed Chris was getting closer and wanted to put some distance between them. Typical.

They cruised onto Palmer Street, houses giving way to vacant lots and the old baseball field that had been left to the weeds when the city council had built Nugent Park on the other side of town. The weeds had withered and fallen flat. As Chris sped past, he saw the top of the home-plate cage sagging under the weight of dozens of heavy rocks. It wasn't a stretch to imagine Dylan and his friends heaving them up there, waiting to see how much weight it could hold until the whole thing collapsed.

Teenagers never failed to perplex Chris. The things they found funny, the way they seemed to distance themselves from everything around them, and the sleeping, oh how Dylan could sleep. It just didn't make any sense.

Beyond the old field was a lot of nothing and then....

And then....

"Hey, Dyl, wait up," Chris cried against the wind.

Surprisingly, his brother slowed down. He sat straight and rode with no hands. "How's the bike ride?"

"Amazing. You can try it if you want."

"Nah. I'd be eating my knees when I pedaled. That bike is all yours, short stuff."

Chris bristled at his least favorite nickname. But it was Christmas, a time to forgive and forget. Though no one seemed to be doing either with Dylan, or vice versa.

They pulled to a stop. The paved street was a few feet from giving way to a dirt road that meandered into the dead tree line.

"Maybe we should go back before Mom gets really upset," Chris said.

Dylan chuckled. "All the more reason to stay out longer."

Chris played along as if upsetting the hornet's nest that was their mother was the best idea in the world. "Yeah, but I bet the bacon will be nice and hot by the time we get home."

Dylan stared at him with his patented dead glare. It made Chris feel stupid.

"Just admit you're scared," Dylan said.

"Scared? Of what?"

A bird cawed in the expanse ahead of them. It sounded hungry. It sounded mean.

Dylan backhanded him on the arm, but not too rough for a change. "We go there all the time. There's nothing to be afraid of."

Chris swallowed hard and wished he'd listened to his mother and waited until all of the presents had been opened before going out and giving his new bike a test ride. Because then he could have done it alone. Because Dylan had that look that said they were going to do something Chris didn't want to do no matter how much he hemmed, hawed, pleaded or cried.

His throat clicking, Chris softly muttered, "I don't wanna go down Dracula Drive."

"You know it's not actually called Dracula Drive, right?"

The wind lifted the hair from Dylan's forehead, giving full view to the cluster of red, angry pimples that cowered under his locks. He was supposed to use this special cream the doctor prescribed, but hygiene was not one of Dylan's greatest traits. In fact, all of his friends looked like they needed a long, hot shower. And they smelled funny a lot of the times, too. Not just like teenage BO. There was something else riding herd over their denim-clad bodies that Chris could never place.

"I know that," Chris said defiantly, though in actuality, he had assumed that was the god-given name of the road that should not be spoken about, much less driven down.

"Well, come on." Dylan rolled a few yards, stopped and turned around. "There's nothing to be scared of."

Chris fiddled with his gear shift. "I just don't wanna."

"Suit yourself," his brother said. He shrugged his shoulders and resumed pedaling. "I'll see you back home. And don't eat all the bacon."

He watched Dylan go, the skinny tires having a hard time navigating the rough road. Bare tree limbs rattled like old bones overhead. Chris shivered, and it wasn't from the cold. He cast a quick look behind him where the road home lay waiting. It was going to be a bit of a ride before he got to what passed for civilization in the burbs.

Then he looked ahead, Dylan still visible but growing smaller with each push of his legs.

Home was where Dad and bacon and presents were waiting for him. And Rude Mom, though there was hope a little nap might have lifted her spirits.

To get there meant several long stretches of isolated riding.

He wanted to call out to Dylan, to ask him to come back. It was Christmas after all. He couldn't just leave Chris like this.

You don't go down Dracula Drive.

It was a fact, plain and simple.

Besides, why would anyone bother? There was nothing down there anyway but a few abandoned houses. Dracula Drive marked the part where Milbury had started, and then failed, waiting for a better time, a more lucrative time, to spark the sprawl. When Milbury proper inevitably began to unfold, Dracula Drive was left to be willfully forgotten.

There were no vampires on Dracula Drive.

No, something far worse.

Dare to walk,
Down Dracula Drive,
In day or night,
You won't survive.
They wait in trees,
And hide below,
Hungry for people,
Too blind to know.

Chris and his friends chanted the Dracula Drive rhyme sometimes to scare one another during sleepovers. Truth was, it wasn't so creepy when you were safe in a locked house with your friends and parents in the next room.

Just thinking about it now birthed an icy tingle of fear that inched up Chris's spine.

Something skittered in the brush to his left.

"Dylan, hold up!"

He pedaled faster than he'd ever done before, even counting the day he had to outrun Mrs. Dodson's butthole rottweiler on his old, rickety bike that had been Dylan's much abused hand-me-down. He'd been scared to the point of filling his pants with the previous night's meatloaf that day. Max the rottweiler had almost gotten the back of Chris's leg. Chris had thrown a backward kick mid-pedal, catching Max on the snout. The devil dog snapped away and got a mouthful of spokes for his trouble. Chris would have whooped with victory if not for the tears of terror blurring his vision.

The Ross hit the bumpy road, the wide tires chewing up the uneven grit and potholes. Chris rose from his seat, giving his legs everything he could, desperate to catch up to his brother. The back of his neck tingled the way it would when he pretended he was asleep and knew his mother was hovering over him, his flesh anticipating the moment when she would brush a kiss against his cheek or finger his hair, the smell of that brown stuff she drank sharp enough to make his toes curl.

"Dylan, please! I'm coming, I'm coming."

His brother didn't hear him. Or was ignoring him. But Dylan wasn't a small, wavering figure in the distance anymore. Chris was gaining on him. Yes! This beat-up road was no match for the Ross. Chris downshifted into third gear, the final gear, each pump of the pedals propelling him faster and closer to Dylan. He was cruising now, skirting potholes and ruts with ease, his body and the bicycle merging into one gliding machine. The cold air stung his eyes as he picked up speed. He looked away from Dylan's back for a moment to blink a tear away. For the first time, he noticed the density of the woods on either side of the road, how the early morning light struggled to penetrate the black, gnarled trees even though the leaves had fallen months ago. It was as if the sun, like all of Chris's friends, was afraid to come here.

Close enough now for Dylan to hear him, he said the one thing he knew would snag his big brother's attention. It usually meant getting a pink belly or being thrown in a headlock, but he was willing to risk it.

"Hey, ass face, slow down!"

Dylan came to a screeching halt. He turned the bike around to face him. Chris caught up to him seconds later, kicking up dirt as he squeezed the hand brakes. The bones in his hands crackled.

To Chris's surprise, Dylan was smiling. He spread his arms wide, scanning the empty woods. "See, I told you there was nothing to be afraid of." As if he were in league with Mother Nature, a chirping, harmless sparrow flitted on a branch to their left, cocking its head toward them.

Chris was about to protest, about to once again implore Dylan to go home now that he'd made his point so they could resume Christmas. It was at that moment when the reluctant sun kissed the strip of road, the shinier rocks sparkling like found treasure.

"I...I guess you're right."

Dylan twisted his front wheel so it bumped the Ross's front wheel.

"Of course I am, hammer. Now you can tell your fag little friends that you've been on Dracula Drive. They'll look up to you, at least for a little while. Merry Christmas."

The sparrow lit off the branch, heading up and away. Its absence gave the ensuing silence the weight of lead. Chris's fear would have returned, but Dylan was smiling, a thing as rare as a seven-year-old riding his bike down Dracula Drive.

"Why do you and your friends come here?"

"Why not?" Dylan turned and spit. He loved to spit, another thing that angered their mother. "There's cool places to hang out. You just have to find them."

Chris thumbed the hand brakes. "Weren't you ever scared? Like even the first time you came?"

Dylan rolled his eyes and shook his head, but Chris would swear he saw something else flicker across his brother's face before his question was dismissed.

I'll bet they were all scared, even if Dylan and his stinky friends all came together. Everyone knows what they say about this road. They're not as tough as they pretend to be.

That was something he could prove. Chris had heard Dylan crying in his bedroom one night after getting off the phone. And another time after a fight with their parents.

And hadn't he seen Hader, the one who liked to flick Chris's ears hard whenever he came to the house, running scared from Mr. Everson when he'd tried to snatch a pumpkin from their neighbor's porch? Everson had given chase and was remarkably fast for an old man (old in young Chris's eyes at least). And he remembered Steven, who wore black rock T-shirts all the time and kept a feathered roach clip in his hair, when he'd accidentally peed himself at the playground and took off running for his house seven blocks away, Dylan and his friends waving their hands across their noses and cackling.

No, they weren't the big shots they wanted the world to think they were.

"What do you do when you hang out here? It seems pretty boring." Now Chris was playing the big shot, belittling Dylan's tough-guy secret. It felt good to turn the tables for once. He'd earned it.

Dylan fished a pack of cigarettes from his inner vest pocket and lit up. Chris knew he smoked, he'd spotted him flicking his butts into the street before walking in the door at home a few times, but he'd never been face to face when his brother dragged on a coffin nail, as his father called them.

"What do you know?" Dylan said, exhaling a thick plume of smoke. "We're not like your friends playing with Barbie dolls."

"They're action figures, not Barbies."

"They're still dolls. You wouldn't understand what we do. You're too young."

"But not too young to follow you here."

He blew smoke in Chris's face and laughed. "You got me there. You wanna go to one of the houses?"

"No. I want to open my electronic football game. And I'm getting hungry."

Dylan dropped the half-smoked coffin nail and ground it with his sneaker. "Maybe you're right." His eyes darted to the woods, as if he were expecting someone…or something. Chris turned his head, wondering what his brother was looking at, expecting to hear something crunching in the deadfall. It wasn't a stretch to imagine Hader waiting to pop out and scare Chris, even though he was expecting it. Hader had what his mother called a face made for radio and could be the cruelest of Dylan's gang.

Please don't be Hader. Please don't be Hader.

Dylan started to pedal in the direction of home and people and Christmas. Chris was quick to follow. They slowly rolled along until Dylan stopped. He looked back at Chris, something worrying his close-set eyes.

"You know what they say isn't all made up," Dylan said, sounding more like a scared little kid telling stories at a campfire than the big brother who would use the f-word in front of their parents with reckless abandon.

Chris squirmed in his seat. It felt like a sharp-clawed finger was poking at his lower back. "Wh-what do you mean?"

"*They* do live out here." The beginning of a grin stopped and died at the corners of his mouth.

The silence between them stretched on for infinity. Chris expected

Dylan to break out in pubescent guffaws any second. When he didn't, Chris suddenly felt like he needed to go to the bathroom, real bad.

"You don't mean that."

"Seriously, they do."

Chris's heart skipped a beat. "But you guys wouldn't come out here if they did. They wouldn't let you."

A cold wind whispered down the empty road.

"They would, and they do, but there are rules."

"Rules? How can they have rules?" A realization bashed Chris in the center of his chest. "Do you talk to them?"

Dylan shook his head. "Nah, they can't talk. At least not in any language we'd understand."

"Then...then how do you know the rules?" Chris was beginning to feel like the butt of a creepy but well-played joke. Dylan could be flat as the surface of a lake when he wanted to be. It made him a damn good liar and faker. Was Hader listening in right now, waiting for the right moment to pounce on him?

Dylan shrugged. "People, the right people, pass them down."

Leaves crunched behind them and Chris twisted around. There was nothing he could see, but he would bet his entire *Star Wars* action-figure collection that there was something in the woods.

Them.

No. They didn't exist. His father had told him so two years ago at a Memorial Day barbecue when the dads were buzzed on Schlitz and overheard Chris and his friends talking about them.

"Stop scaring yourselves with nonsense," Dad had said, slurring the end of 'nonsense'. "One day you're going to grow up and laugh that you scared yourselves silly over a fairy tale."

The things in the woods were no fairy tale. Of that, Chris was certain. If they were, where were the good guys? There were good guys in every fairy tale.

But the way the dads had laughed it all off, patting the skinny backs of their sons, felt like a passage into a special club, a club where you left baby fears behind.

Chris tried his best to put on a brave face. "You're just trying to scare me."

Dylan toed his kickstand. "I wish I was."

That was it. Those four words, conjoined with the look of fear and sadness on Dylan's face, made Chris want to cry out for his parents while motoring the Ross as fast as it would go on the uneven terrain. His brother wasn't kidding. Not by a long shot.

"I'm going," Chris said. He didn't need Dylan to lead the way. If his brother wanted to stay there with them, let him. He knew the rules, or so he said, so he'd be fine.

"Just wait up," Dylan said, angling his ten-speed so it was in his way.

Chris pushed his front tire against Dylan's leg. "No. I want to go home now."

Crunch, crunch, crunch. Those were definite footsteps in the dead leaves.

Chris's eyesight blurred with tears. His head flicked from side to side. He couldn't see anything within the gnarled, dead trees. "*Please*, Dylan. Let me go."

"Fennerman says if I help them, they'll help me."

Wiping the tears from his cheeks with his hand, Chris asked, "Who's Fennerman?"

His brother ignored him. "I'm in a lot of trouble, bro. Like the kind that will change your life forever."

"Just get out of my way," Chris said feebly. He'd tried to extricate himself from Dylan's little traps in the past to no avail. His brother was more than twice his age, three times as strong and could be five times more determined.

Dylan reached into his pocket and extracted the butterfly knife their parents had confiscated more than once. They worried more about him stabbing himself than someone else.

"Are they coming?" Chris asked, eyes wide and muscles flooded with adrenaline.

Instead of using the knife to defend them, Dylan sank the sharp tip into the rubber of Chris's front tire. The air exploded in a screeching hiss.

Chris watched it happen in mute confusion.

The Ross had only been his for less than an hour and it was already screwed.

Worse still, with only one tire, *Chris* was screwed.

Now the tears flowed freely. "Why did you do that? You ruined my bike! I'm telling Mom and Dad!"

Dylan sounded like he was choking back tears of his own. "I'm sorry. I'm really sorry. But this is the only way."

With that, he stood high over his seat and spun away, leaving Chris weeping on his disabled bike, Christmas ruined, everything ruined.

Sniffling back a wad of snot that would choke a dog, Chris wailed, "Don't leave me here! Dylan, come back!"

His brother seemed to slow down for a moment, but then he pushed on even faster.

Now the woods came alive with the cacophony of rushing feet. Chris cried out, his voice hitting an octave that would have landed him a soprano spot on the Mormon Tabernacle Choir. That wasn't Hader. He willed his right leg to pedal, flat tire and all, but the bulky Ross wouldn't respond. The front rim jittered on the loose ground, the handlebars almost slipping out of his grip. Chris accidentally pressed the hand brake and nearly flipped over the handlebars. His tongue stung with the salt from his tears and his body quaked with racking sobs.

"D...D...Dylan," he whimpered into the still December air.

They were coming for him.

Chris jumped off the Ross, cringing at the sound of metal clanging against the hard, uneven road.

He would run home. It wouldn't be as fast as riding his bike, but he was plenty scared and was the fastest of his friends. Dylan's ten-speed, with its skinny tires, was barely a match for beat-up Dracula Drive. Chris bet if he tried real hard, he'd leave his brother, his cold-hearted kin, in the dust.

In fact, he was gaining on Dylan. The ten-speed tottered from side to side. It gave Chris hope. Was Dylan having second thoughts? He had to regret being such an asshole. Maybe he would turn back and apologize, let Chris ride on the back of the bike. Their dad could come back in the car with them to collect the Ross. It wasn't as if anyone was going to be around to steal it. Not on Dracula Drive.

On either side of Chris, something, someone, *they*, were matching him step for step. Chris ran as fast as he could, possibly faster than he'd ever run, fighting to maintain control and not collapse in a big, weeping, defenseless heap. Arms and legs pumping, he caught up to an astonished Dylan. Chris's chest burned and his lungs felt like they were going to plop out of his mouth like a cartoon. He looked down and saw that the rim of Dylan's front tire was dented. It looked like the edge of the tire was rubbing against the frame's fork. It hadn't been regret that had slowed him down. A hot ball of anger surged into Chris's chest.

"What the fuck?" his brother shouted.

Chris wanted to say something nasty, maybe give him the finger, but he couldn't spare the energy. He had to keep running now to outpace them.

He'd gotten a good twenty feet in front of Dylan when he heard his brother shout in pain.

Slowing down just a bit, Chris shot a quick look behind him.

Shadows burst from the woods, descending on Dylan. His brother jumped off the ten-speed…and into the arms of someone shorter than him but wide, with arms that could wrap around a bear. Dylan shrieked, "No! Not me! Not me!"

Dylan called out for Chris, pleaded for Chris not to leave him.

In time, Chris would learn about selflessness and bravery.

But at this moment, he was seven and batshit terrified.

Chris ran all the way home. His legs gave way the moment his feet touched upon the dead front lawn, too exhausted to cry out for help, his brain a buzzing hive of bees, unable to comprehend the horror that he'd narrowly escaped but would haunt him for the rest of his life.

CHAPTER TWO
Millbury, CT – 1993

"Come on, you little ball sack. I know you're up there." Mark McNeil, Mick to everyone but his mother, and he hadn't seen her in months, sat on top of the dented Airstream trailer, the BB gun held in both hands pointed at the trees. The Airstream looked to have rolled off the production line right around the time Hank Williams had last sung he was so lonesome he could cry. Mick's long vermilion hair was tied back with the rubber band that had held yesterday's mail together. (The same mail Mick hadn't bothered to open, merely using it to start a fire.) He squinted down the sightline, waiting for the woodpecker to poke its head out from behind the branch full of leaves it had been hiding behind.

The end-of-summer air smelled of onion grass and mud, two days of storms having found new holes in the Airstream's rusted roof within which to deposit steady drips of water. Mick had pots all around the trailer, the steady plop-plop of water enough to qualify as torture under the guidelines of the Geneva Convention.

No matter how many leaks the Airstream sprung, nothing grated on Mick's nerves more than that goddamn woodpecker. The bird had made his mornings and days a living hell. Mick was sure the woodpecker knew exactly what it was doing and took great pleasure in screwing with him. This was the start of week three since the peckerhead had made Mick's part of the woods his home and there would not be a fourth.

In place of the usual round BBs, Mick had swiped a box of the pointed-tip ammo from Baterman's the other day during his weekly run for pilfered comics and purchased smokes and Slim Jims. If you are what you eat, Mick was a thin stick of overly salted beef jerky.

He didn't want to just hurt ol' Woody. No, this head-banging son of a biscuit eater had pecked his last tree.

I wonder how many in a bush a dead bird in hand will get you.

He shouldn't count his woodpeckers before they'd death-spiraled into the forest carpet.

Mick's nose twitched from an incoming sneeze. He pinched his eyes shut, willing the sneeze to go away. He couldn't make a noise and spook Woody now. If he was woken up one more morning just before sunrise, he was going to lose his mind.

Or whatever was left of it, if you asked every teacher and administrator in his school. He'd heard there was a big math test today and a social studies project was due. Not that he gave a frog's fat ass.

Wings flapped above. The branches shifted under a gusting wind. Daylight sparkled through the gaps in the leaves. Mick winced as he came eye-to-supernova with the sun.

"Dammit."

The second he regained his vision, the woodpecker sprang into view, settling on a dead branch as if daring him to shoot it.

Mick took aim, squaring his ass on the Airstream's roof.

"Whatcha shooting at?"

The woodpecker took off in a mad flurry. Mick squeezed the trigger but was too late. The deadly BB embedded itself in the old bark.

He turned to face the intruder who had just ruined his tomorrow, his eyes radiating nuclear anger. Without hesitation, he swung his arm down and around and pulled the trigger.

"Shit! Oh shit! That hurts. Holy shit that hurts!"

Anthony Ventarola, Vent not only to his friends but his teachers and even his mother, writhed on the ground clutching his right thigh. There was a hole in his dirty, faded jeans. Underneath that hole was another hole in the meat of his leg. The back end of the BB could be felt if he dared stick his finger in the hole. At the moment, he settled for rocking back and forth and howling at Mick.

"You're an asshole, man! You fucking shot me!"

"Calm down. It's not like I took you down with a .44." Mick jumped off the trailer and tucked the gun into his waistband.

"You think it's nothing? Give me the gun and I'll return the favor."

Mick's initial anger easily gave way to amusement. Pissing Vent off wasn't just a fun pastime. It was a vocation. He offered his hand to help his friend up. Vent smacked it away.

"Kiss my ass, psycho," Vent seethed. Now he had his hand over the wound as if to stanch a heavy flow of blood. So far, there'd barely been a trickle.

"You messed up my shot."

"And for that you shoot me instead?"

"I've had a really bad morning." Mick pinched the bridge of his nose. Aside from not getting enough sleep, he hadn't eaten in two days. He really needed food. Maybe they could swing on down to 7-Eleven and while Vent bought a Big Gulp, Mick could stick a few Slim Jims in his pockets.

Vent got up, unbuckled his belt and let his jeans drop. It was easy to find the BB entrance wound. The skin around the hole was red and puckered with a penumbra of blood. "I can't afford to go to the hospital, man."

Mick picked up a folding lawn chair from the side of the trailer and set it behind his friend. "Pop a squat. You don't need a hospital."

Vent's face was red as an apple. "Oh, so you're a doctor now?"

"Even better. My dad used to take potshots at me when I was ten to, in his words, knock the pussy out of me. Those BBs hurt like a motherfucker, but they don't go in deep. It's like taking out a splinter." Mick took a switchblade out of one pocket and a Zippo lighter from the other. He sparked the Zippo to life and flicked the tip of the knife over the flame until it glowed.

Vent covered the wound with both hands. "You don't remove splinters with knives, dude."

"I said it's *like* removing a splinter. Same concept, bigger needle. Now hold still."

Before Vent could protest, Mick straddled his knees, locking him into the chair. He pushed Vent's hands away and plunged the knife right in, the metal-on-metal sound the proof he needed that he'd hit home. His hand and the switchblade were one. He could feel the blade scrape down the side of the BB and knew the instant he struck the meat beneath it. With a flick of his wrist, the BB slipped out of the now bloody hole and thumped on the pine-needle-strewn ground.

It was all over in seconds. Vent waited for Mick to get off of him before letting out a sharp cry of pain, followed by a choice selection of particularly blue phrases.

"You want a bandage and a kiss to make it all better?" Mick asked, a devilish grin on his face.

Vent tugged up his pants. "What I want is to punch you in the face. It's not funny."

"I never said it was."

"So why do you have that retard smile on your face?"

"Retard?" Mick placed his hand over his heart. "I guess it takes one to know one."

Vent reared back to punch him. Mick became instantly serious. "I wouldn't do that if I were you."

There was a brief moment of consideration on Vent's part, and then logic won the moment. He dropped his fist. Mick hated to be touched, everyone knew that. That would get you a stiff punch in the chest or worse. And if Vent punched him back....

Hitting Mick would set him in a blackout rage. When those came over him, there was no rationalizing with him, no telling him when to stop, unless several people made a concerted effort to bring him to the ground. No one wanted to mess with Mick when he was in a blackout.

"You can at least say you're sorry." The pain and anger bled from Vent like draining an old radiator.

"I thought that goes without saying."

"Actually, it doesn't."

Mick kicked a pine cone and watched it bang against the Airstream. "I fixed you up, didn't I?"

Vent paused, and then shook his head, realizing defeat. "I came to give you something, but maybe I shouldn't."

Mick arched an eyebrow. "Is it weed?"

"Yeah, I came to drop off a dime bag." The sound of the woodpecker hammering at a distant tree echoed over them. Mick felt like shooting Vent again. "Dummy. Here, take this." He handed Mick an envelope. Inside was a small stack of dollar bills.

"What is this?"

"I found it in the lost and found at school. I was waiting to see Mr. Templeton when that fat secretary with the mole on her nose dropped the box next to me and just walked off. I thought you could use it. Last time I saw, you were low on beer."

Truth was, Mick was low on everything. That's what happened when your mom and stepfather were MIA and you were a seventeen-year-old stoner who everyone assumed would end up in prison or dead by nineteen, so what was the sense of trying to help?

If anyone else had given him charity money, he would have told them exactly where to stick it. But he'd been friends with Vent since they were just out of diapers. No one knew the real story of what went on in Mick's family but Vent, and he was going to keep it that way.

Mick took the envelope and shoved it in his back pocket. "Thanks, man. I owe you."

Vent looked at his leg. "Yeah, you do."

"Did you take that math test?"

"I cut right after. It was easy."

"Easy for you. You're a math egghead."

"Hey, I saw the video store just got a copy of *The Hills Have Eyes*. I asked them to put it on hold for me for Saturday. Wanna come over and watch it?"

"That sounds cool."

"Bring a bar of soap and some clothes while you're at it," Vent said.

"You saying I smell?" Mick puffed up his chest.

Vent took a loud sniff in his direction. "Yeah. You stink, bro. I'd stink too if I was living in a trailer without running water."

"That's still fucked up, man."

"I want my mother to leave us alone, not bug me to get you to leave so we can air the place out." Vent smirked and wiggled his eyebrows. Mick was self-conscious about his hygiene lately and would have felt hurt, then exceedingly angry, with most people. Vent had a point and he was only trying to help, which earned him a pass.

"Look what else I got." Vent pulled a CD of the Stone Temple Pilots album, *Core*, out of his well-worn jacket pocket. The jacket had been a thrift store find, like most of his clothes, and looked like it had been worn by someone who had subsequently been blown up wearing said jacket. Then he waved a dime bag in Mick's face.

"I knew it," Mick said.

"So, you wanna get high and listen to STP?"

Who was Mick to say no?

CHAPTER THREE

Heidi Jennings frowned at her image in the mirror. She'd cheaped out and gone for a store-bought dye kit, hoping to add some green highlights to her auburn hair. It came out more like a light blue. "Well, that was a disaster."

Nirvana's 'Lithium' warbled from her bedroom.

"I think it looks cool," Marnie said. She sat on the sink counter painting her toenails black.

"Blue is so boring. I wanted the green to match my eyes."

"If you want to match, why not go retro metal and go all black?"

Heidi twirled the blue lock of hair in her fingers. She wished she'd started on dreads a few months back when she swore to Marnie and everyone that she would get them. Her father had promised that if he saw dreads in her hair, she was out of the house, good luck living on your own. Now she looked like a Smurf fairy. She hoped it pissed him off royally.

"Metal? Been there, done that. Remember when we went to that Firehouse concert and you puked on the guy in front of us?"

Marnie blanched. "He deserved it. What was he, like forty? Why the hell was he even there?"

They laughed, remembering how Marnie had then tried to apologize and burped in his face, the foul smell of beer, burritos and cigarettes making the old man gag.

"Hey, I'm sure we'll be rocking the fuck out in our forties, too," Heidi said.

"Damn right we will, sister," Marnie said, tapping Heidi with her leg.

"You think Dustin will be at Benny's tonight?"

"It's dollar beer night. He'll be there."

Heidi considered the rack of clothes she'd hung on the shower rod. Almost everything had been purchased from thrift stores. It was the polar opposite of glamorous, but Dustin, like most of the guys in their town, was totally into grunge. Her mother had loved to tell her that if she wanted to succeed in life, she had to dress for success. Well, success at this time in her life meant getting Dustin to not only notice her, but want to take her in his remodeled Charger and fool around. Needless to say, her wardrobe was a source of constant bickering with her mother, with her old-fashioned beliefs about how ladies should dress and present themselves. What the hell did she know about being a teen now?

"So, should I go with the blue?" she asked Marnie, who was wearing baggy jeans with holes in the knees and a white T-shirt with a rip on one shoulder.

Marnie flicked a glance at the blue and black flannel shirt that was two sizes too big for Heidi's slight frame, and shook her head. Heidi wished she had Marnie's chest, but she made up for any shortcomings with long legs that she knew made boys stop in their tracks when they were at the public pool. It would be a long time until her legs saw the light of day again, though. "No, that one." She pointed the end of her nail polish brush at a yellow and black flannel. "It'll make you stand out."

Benny's Tavern was dark and smoky. The owner was a cheap bastard. Heidi doubted he bought any light bulbs over forty watts. It was a haven for underage drinking without the need for fake IDs, quickies in the unisex bathroom and rock music from local bands who hated the place but loved the insane sound system that Heidi had heard had been stolen from a much nicer club in New Haven. It was easy to get lost in the sea of muted colors there. Yellow would definitely catch Dustin's eye...and hopefully more.

She tugged the shirt off the hanger and slipped it on, leaving the top three buttons undone so the upper crest of her black bra could be seen. She adjusted her bra straps, plumping her small chest. "How's this?"

Marnie fanned her hands so the polish could dry. "I'd do you."

"You'd do anyone."

"Not true. If you ever see me making out with Ralpie Viger, shoot me."

Heidi went into her bedroom to find her good jeans, which would be most people's bad jeans considering their beaten-down condition.

"I won't have to shoot you. The cooties will take care of everything."

Marnie popped her head out of the bathroom, waggling her eyebrows. "Cooties? Really? Maybe you can teach me how to give myself a cootie shot."

Heidi grabbed Marnie's wrist and twirled her finger on the inside of her wrist. "Circle, circle, dot, dot, now you've got the cootie shot."

"You're such a dork."

"I am. It's part of what makes me adorable." Heidi then felt the need to add, "Now, what if I caught you making out with Mick?"

She instantly worried she'd taken it too far. Marnie and Mick hung out a lot, especially lately. Of their group of friends, they were the most similar to one another, which used to be the reason behind their squabbles. Heidi suspected something was brewing between the two, but she didn't want to bring it up. Marnie would only deny it.

"I'd probably puke," Marnie curtly replied.

"Mmm-hmmm."

"What? I would. He's my friend, not someone I want to stick their tongue down my throat."

"Gotcha," Heidi said, grinning. Marnie started to smile and quickly turned away. She closed the bathroom door. "You think you can get your adorable ass downstairs and steal me a beer?" The sound of her pee hitting the water echoed in the tiny bathroom. Heidi turned up the music, which had shifted to Soundgarden, to block the noise.

Heidi went to the kitchen, opened the refrigerator and stared at the sea of green Heineken bottles on the bottom shelf. Her father loved his Heineken, more so now that he'd been out of work this past year. He and her mom were at the Post right now, probably drinking their stress away on the cheap. Vietnam vets and their wives could get totally blitzed at the Post for under ten bucks. He wouldn't notice if she took one beer from the back.

She popped the top off, and, not wanting to leave any evidence behind, stepped into the yard and flicked the cap over the fence into their neighbor's yard. Sipping from the cold bottle as she made her way back to the bedroom, she couldn't stop thinking about Dustin. He'd changed dramatically over the summer, his muscles filling out, hair growing past his shoulders, mustache and goatee making him look five years older. She'd been obsessing over him since he came back from the summer break at his father's place in Kentucky. That's what she did with boys. She'd moon over them for weeks, if not months, until the next one entered her orbit. Of all her crushes, she'd only made it to first base with Bobby Trainer.

Other girls in school assumed she had screwed a ton of guys because of the way she looked and the people she hung out with. It didn't bother her, most times. They didn't need to know she was a virgin. It wasn't as if she was waiting for the perfect guy. The opportunity had just never presented itself, which bludgeoned her ego way more than some preppie bitches calling her slut when she walked down the halls in school.

"Hey, don't drink all of it," Marnie said.

"I should chug it just to spite you," Heidi said, smiling. "It's all yours."

"Can you hold it for me? I don't want to mess up my nails."

Heidi rolled her eyes, put the bottle to Marnie's lips and tilted it back so she could draw from it. When Marnie waved her hands, she angled it down. Marnie burped, sending them into a fit of giggles. It took three more assists for Marnie to drink it all. Heidi jammed the empty in her purse so her father wouldn't find it in the garbage. They locked up the house and jumped into Heidi's dented but serviceable Cougar.

★　　★　　★

Benny's was packed, which was not unusual for a Thursday night. Marnie scanned the room, seeing mostly familiar faces, some she'd rather forget, others she'd endeavor to avoid. That went especially for Joe McMurray, who bragged to everyone that he'd banged her when all she'd ever given him was a two-minute make-out session down by Strathmore Beach. Total asshole.

Heidi clutched her arm as they wove their way through the crowd, everyone drinking brightly colored, sugary-sweet booze from cheap plastic cups. Marnie looked for any signs of the stuck-up bitches from school. They mostly stayed away from Benny's because it catered to what was considered a lower class of teens. Even though none were around and the music was ear-blasting, she could still hear their hurled insults of 'double dyke' and 'the lezzie twins' in her head. Marnie and Heidi had grappled with rumors that they were lesbians since last year. It made them oddly more attractive to the boys and pariahs to the girls (who had started the rumor to destroy them in the first place). To combat their nonsense, neither Heidi nor Marnie had said anything to dispel the notion, going so far as to hold hands every now and then when they walked the halls. If calling them lesbians was the worst those bitches could do, they were a sad gaggle of pukes. Sometimes Marnie wished they'd come to Benny's and say something. This would be the perfect place to give one of them a hair ride without the threat of being suspended.

The floor was littered with sawdust to sop up the puke and spilled drinks. Marnie figured maybe seven out of the sixty people in the place were actually of legal drinking age.

She pushed her way to the bar. Lance was tending bar tonight. He had a face like a bloodhound and a sagging belly to match. He didn't give a shit about anything and was always happy to reiterate that point to anyone who asked him to do something.

"The toilet is overflowing!"

"Ask someone who gives a shit."

"Lance, there's a fight outside and someone needs to call the cops."

"Not my fucking problem."

He didn't say much, and when he spoke, it was usually a choice between either of those phrases.

Marnie caught his rheumy eye. "Two Woo-Woos."

He turned away as if he hadn't heard her. She was about to yell to get his attention again when she saw him amble over to the well and extract the makings for a Woo-Woo.

"You see Dustin?" she shouted at Heidi to be heard over the music. Screaming Trees blared from the suspended speakers affixed to every corner of the room.

Heidi chewed her pinky nail and looked around, going on tiptoe to see over everyone's heads.

"I don't think he's here, unless he's in the bathroom."

Lance pushed the half-filled cups to Marnie and she slid a ten-dollar bill his way. He looked through her, plucking the bill with his thumb and forefinger and opening the register.

"He'll be here," Marnie said, handing Heidi her drink. They sipped at the same time. The Woo-Woo was sweeter than candy but had enough alcohol to pack a punch. Neither of them had much money to spend tonight, so they would have to nurse their drinks. She pocketed the change Lance had dropped on the bar, leaving a dollar for his efforts.

Heidi tugged at her sleeve. "Look over there."

Marnie followed her friend's head nod. "What the heck is he doing here?"

"Weird, right?"

"You think he's stalking you for Chad?"

"Stop. You're gonna freak me out."

Marnie had broken up with Chad Dunwoody a few months back after an ill-conceived and short-lived run as a kinda couple. Chad was broke as a joke, didn't have a driver's license, had dropped out sophomore year and used her like his personal piggy bank. He was also an abusive alcoholic in the making who slapped her one night during a drunken rage. That had done it. Marnie told him to take a hike and promised she would have Mick cut his balls off if he ever so much as looked at her again. He'd steered clear of her since then. She heard he had conned a girl from another town to be his newest enabler. Marnie wished she knew the girl so she could warn her to get the hell out now.

Chad's father, Harold Dunwoody, sat by a raised bar top on the other side of the room. He was drinking alone, a pitcher of beer and a sweaty mug before him. Everyone else in Benny's was in full grunge mode, whereas Harold was wearing a suit, the jacket slung over the back of his chair, his collar open and tie pulled down to half-mast. There were plenty of older-guy bars in town. Why was he even here?

"You should go say hi to him," Heidi said playfully.

"Yeah, right. I should kick him in the nuts for raising such a piece of garbage son."

Heidi pulled Marnie down so they were hidden by the people crowding the bar. "I think he saw us." She couldn't stop laughing.

"Oh god, the last thing I need is him asking me why Chad and I aren't dating anymore."

Marnie had only seen Harold a few times when she'd been by Chad's house, a two-bedroom ranch over on Vladmere Street. Harold had always been nice enough to say hi and just move on with whatever he was doing instead of leering at her like other fathers. He seemed like the quiet, sensitive type, the kind of dad who would ask his son's ex what went wrong.

"I'm going out for a smoke," Marnie said.

Heidi was looking over her shoulder and her eyes lit up. Marnie didn't have to turn around to know that Dustin had just walked into the bar.

"I'll come with you," Heidi said, not taking her eyes off Dustin.

"No you don't. You're going to do whatever you can to get his attention when he comes here for a drink."

"Stay with me."

Marnie grinned. "There are some things you need to do alone. Getting the guy is top of the list."

"You don't want to be my wingman?"

"Guys need wingmen. We just need to be our dead-sexy selves." She saw Dustin heading their way. She gave Heidi a quick peck on the cheek. "Good luck. I'll be back in a few." Heidi tried to stop her, but Marnie was too quick, slipping between two beefy guys wearing brown leather jackets. A bit of her Woo-Woo sloshed onto her wrist.

As she passed by Dustin, she intentionally bumped hips. "Hey, Dustin."

"Oh, hey. What's up?"

"A lot if you go buy Heidi a drink."

He looked over her shoulder. "I think she ditched you."

Marnie rolled her eyes. "No, she's at the bar. Now, go be a big boy."

He fingered his long hair, his eyes latching onto Heidi's bright yellow shirt. "You think she'd be cool with that?"

"You have to try it to find out."

The little bit of mystery was enough to send him Heidi's way. Marnie watched him roll up beside her, Heidi taking some visible deep breaths and doing her version of playing it cool.

"Nobody beats this wing chick," Marnie said to herself before heading outside. She caught the attention of a few guys she knew but kept her head down. She wasn't in the mood to be pawed at tonight.

The cooler, fresh air felt like a slice of heaven. The only way to make it better was by filling it with smoke from her freshly lit Newport. She took a long and hard first drag, savoring the slight burn in her throat and lungs. Marnie leaned against the wall, one foot raised and flat against it. She stared at the flickering streetlight across the way.

I wonder if I can get hypnotized if I just keep looking at it.

Regardless, it was oddly relaxing. The past week had been stressful at home, what with her mother losing her job and her stepfather about to run out of unemployment checks. She fell asleep each night listening to them argue about how they were going to pay the bills. Bickering was a way of life for them, but this time around they had sounded not just angry, but desperate. She didn't have the heart to tell them she'd lost her job as a cashier at Caldor. Not that her crappy paycheck paid the bills, but she just knew they'd blow their stack, especially if they found out she'd been canned for being late.

School sucked even harder than home. All she wanted to do was graduate next year and get the hell out. She'd need to find some other low-paying job between now and then so she had enough cash to leave Milbury behind for good.

She flicked the butt of her Newport into the street, just missing a guy and girl she'd never seen before. It was too early to check on Heidi. She wanted to give them time to talk. Plenty of time for another cigarette.

"Need a light?"

"Oh, hey, Mr. Dunwoody. Sure."

He lit her cigarette with a dime store Bic. Up close, he looked tired and smelled like he'd been swimming in a vat of beer. Harold Dunwoody lit his own cigarette and craned his head back to look at the half moon.

"Funny seeing you here," he said, a plume of smoke hovering over their heads.

More like it was funny seeing a grown-ass man in a teen bar.

"I come here all the time," she replied, studying the black band on her wrist for no particular reason. No, there was a reason. It was better than looking into the face of defeated middle age.

"You and Chad come here?"

And there it was. She didn't want to talk about Chad, so she chose to pretend he hadn't asked the question.

After a while, he snickered and said, "Sorry, sore subject. Just a dad grasping for something to say."

Marnie checked her watch. "It's okay."

She pinched her cigarette butt between her thumb and middle finger, ready to send it sailing, when Harold Dunwoody punched her in the side of the head. It rocked her and sent her vision spinning.

"Whuh?" she muttered, trying hard to keep to her feet.

He punched her again, this time an uppercut that clacked her teeth together. It felt like her brain bounced off the inside of her skull. He slipped an arm around her waist before she fell, whisking her into the alley between Benny's and the abandoned house next door. After practically dragging her midway down the alley, he deposited her on a haphazard stack of dirty milk crates. Something skittered away, alarmed by the sudden intrusion on its hiding place.

Marnie thrust her hands out to push him away. He smacked them off his chest and grabbed her by the throat.

"P-p-p-p-p-please," she whimpered, going rigid when she realized she could barely draw a breath.

He let her go, but not without a punch to the gut. She bent forward, desperate to breathe, her face touching the filthy ground. She heard his feet shuffling around her. She wanted to get up and scramble away, but it was hard to do when she was running out of oxygen and couldn't see straight.

Rough fingers grabbed her hair and lifted her roughly back onto the milk crates.

Harold Dunwoody didn't say a single word as he ripped her shirt off, then her bra, the straps digging harshly into her flesh. She could breathe again, but everything was going hazy real fast. For a moment, she lost consciousness, then came to seconds later (even though it felt like a day) when he yanked off her jeans and panties. His belt buckle clinked as it, along with his pants, dropped to the ground. He spit on her vagina and clamped his hand over her mouth. The back of her head banged against brick and this time she couldn't stop from going bye-bye, no matter how much she wanted to stay alert and find a way to escape, but not before killing him.

His angry cock split her in a savage thrust.

And then she was out.

CHAPTER FOUR

The newspaper was useless. How could Chuck find a part-time job if there were barely any listings? He balled the paper up and tossed it in the trash can beside his desk. Smoke curled from the Marlboro he'd been neglecting. It tilted into the ceramic ashtray like a teeter-totter. Looking into the glazed eyes of Courtney Love, the poster dominating the wall in front of him, Chuck said, "I know what you'd do. You'd say fuck it and go out and party. I bet you always knew you were going to be a rock star."

He considered doing his AP calculus homework but decided he wasn't in the mood. He could do it tomorrow morning on the bus. Math always came easy to him. He was the only student who not only had passing grades in Mr. Peterson's class, but had yet to score less than a ninety on any of his tests or pop quizzes. In another school, he could have made some good dough as a math tutor, but his fellow students didn't give a crap enough to ask for his help, unless it was Donna and her friend Joanna. They were both hot and way out of his league. No way was he going to ask them for money. He would *pay them* to be their tutor.

Just because the kids in Polk High didn't care about their grades, didn't mean the ones in the surrounding schools didn't. Chuck made a note to himself to create a flyer for his tutoring services. He'd post them in the library and on the community board in the Gristedes supermarket on the edge of town.

He stubbed the cigarette out, opened his bedroom door and called out for his mother. When there was no reply, he shouted, "Dad?"

They weren't home yet. Maybe they'd stopped for a drink after the movie.

Good. He opened his drawer, lifted the false bottom he'd built and selected the fattest of the joints he'd stashed there. With the window wide open, Chuck sat on the sill and sparked up. He needed to relax.

The pressure was on this year to finish high school with straight As so he could get a full scholarship to fucking anywhere. Math and science were no problem, but he had to work his ass off in social studies and English. The 78 he'd gotten on his last social studies test had scared the hell out of him. He'd been obsessing over it for a week now. And then there was the pressure of scrounging up money. Sure, he would probably get a scholarship, but he'd need a better car (his beater was on its last legs), gas and spending money if he wanted to eat and have any kind of a social life.

"Fuck me," he said, exhaling a lungful of sweet smoke.

His shelf of VHS tapes was filled to the max with horror and action movies. It could be fun to watch *From Beyond* high, especially when those big-ass worms wriggled through the air, or when the guy from *Re-Animator* went to the lab and ate those brains. That would definitely relax him, at least for an hour and a half. Then it would be back to obsessing about school again.

He should be more like his friend Vent, who barely passed and didn't seem to have a care in the world. Or he could go to the extreme and emulate Mick. No, that was too far. Mick was destined to rot in Milbury. The only way he'd escape the run-down town was if he was sent to an out-of-state prison, which was a real possibility.

High, dark clouds obscured the stars, the moon just poking out from behind their puffy veil. Chuck turned his face into the breeze, feeling the tension bleed from his muscles. Mick had scored this weed from some new guy. It was strong stuff. If Chuck had money, he'd buy more, because as close as he and Mick were, his wayward friend wasn't into charity.

Twin beams of light swept across a swath of the back lawn. Chuck jumped off the sill, pinching the end of the joint out and fumbling for his can of Lysol. He sprayed the room down as quickly as he could.

A rock pinged off his window. In his panic, Chuck barely registered it. When a larger one hit hard enough to crack the glass, he dropped the Lysol.

Mick.

He stormed to the window. "You asshole—"

Heidi stood under the window. It looked like she was holding up a very drunk Marnie.

"Are you alone?" Heidi said. It sounded like she was crying. Chuck's mouth went dry. Had Marnie taken something and OD'd? She was a smart girl with a wild streak, but not half as wild as her reputation. Still, he could see her taking a hit off of a joint that was laced with something.

"Yeah."

"Come down and help me."

Marnie started to slip out of Heidi's grasp, her arms hanging limply, head facing the ground. Heidi let out a sharp yip and caught her before she dropped.

"I'll be right there."

Chuck flew down the stairs in his bare feet and threw the front door open. It slammed against the frame with a heavy thunk. He got to them just in time. Heidi was bent over, trying to maintain her hold on Marnie's waist. Chuck scooped Marnie into his arms and almost lost her, too. She was complete deadweight.

"We need to get her inside," Heidi said. Her eyeliner streaked her cheeks. She trembled uncontrollably with her arms crossed over her chest.

Chuck carried Marnie like a groom whisking his bride over the threshold. In the light of the living room, he saw that she wasn't drunk or tripping. Her lips were split and twice their size, a pair of pink hotdog buns. Blood stained her teeth, with more dried blood in her nostrils. Her left cheek was a light shade of purple and swollen, and her right eye was sealed shut, turning all sorts of horrible colors. What the hell had happened to her?

He gently laid her down on the couch.

"Do you have a first aid kit?" Heidi asked, pacing.

"Upstairs. I'll get it." He stopped, took hold of Heidi's arm. "Was she in a car crash?"

Heidi shook her head and her lips quivered when she tried to speak. He cupped her cheek. "It's okay. Let's take care of Marnie first."

Chuck ran upstairs to the bathroom, ripped the cabinet under the sink open and wildly pushed everything aside, grabbing the plastic first aid box in the back. His heart thundered. He was no doctor. Marnie was in bad shape. What could he possibly do? Heidi looked ready to break down. It was up to him to take care of the situation, whether he wanted to or not.

Thundering back down to the living room, Chuck saw Heidi was now on the plastic-covered couch, Marnie's head resting in her lap. Chuck dropped to his knees and opened the kit. A slew of bandages flew out like doves springing from a magician's hat. Marnie was unconscious. He found a cotton ball and dabbed at the blood.

"I...I don't know where to start."

"I don't know either," Heidi said, nearly screeching, clearly riding the edge of hysteria.

He fumbled through the first aid kit, hoping there were some smelling salts. Marnie's lack of response to all the jostling around and their voices was his overriding concern. She could have brain damage. It looked like she'd taken a hell of a blow – or blows – to the head.

"Marnie, can you hear me?" His brief mellow was long gone, replaced by panic and confusion. She didn't so much as groan.

Upending the little box, he scanned the contents lying about the rug. No smelling salts.

He dripped some alcohol on a ball of gauze and dabbed at the split in her lip. If anything, the burning pain of alcohol in her wound should wake her up. When her lips parted, he saw that one of her top front teeth had been chipped. Jesus Christ.

Heidi's tears dropped onto Marnie's forehead. She wiped them away as quickly as they fell.

"Where were you guys?" Chuck asked. He needed to know what had happened if he was going to do any good.

"B-B-Benny's." Heidi's shoulders jittered as she sobbed.

"Did Marnie get into a fight?" He cleared her nostrils of the dried blood with a Q-tip.

Heidi shook her head. "She, she went outside to smoke. When she didn't come back, I-I-I went out to look for her. I thought she'd left me there, or maybe, or maybe went to make out with someone. I was about to go back inside when...when...."

Chuck took Marnie's wrist and checked her pulse. He had no idea what a good pulse should feel like, but there was a beat and he guessed that was good. "When what? Help me out here, Heidi."

"That's when I saw her." A river of tears spilled from Heidi's tightly shut eyes. "She-she was crawling out of the alley. I said something and she looked at me, and then, and then she collapsed. Tito Hernandez was just walking into the bar and helped me get her in the car."

The alley? What was Marnie doing in the alley to end up like this? Chuck had just noticed how filthy her clothes were. She must have dragged herself down that nasty, narrow passage.

And now he also saw that most of the buttons on her shirt had been ripped off. It didn't look like she was wearing a bra, which was unusual for her. Marnie needed the support.

"Did she ever wake up to tell you what happened?"

"No."

"We need to take her to the hospital."

Heidi shook her head defiantly. "We can't. Her parents don't have insurance."

Chuck rubbed Marnie's right hand between his own. It was frighteningly cold. "So? It's not like they'd dump her in the street. Hospitals help people who are sick and hurt. It's their job."

Heidi's eyes glazed over. He figured in her panic, she'd never considered it.

He was about to tell her they were going to the hospital when he saw the bloom of blood in the crotch of Marnie's jeans.

The realization of what had happened hit him like a mule kick.

"Did you see her go outside with anybody?"

Heidi wiped her eyes. "No. She, she left so I could talk to Dustin. I was too busy…too busy…."

He refrained from asking her why she'd want to talk to a tool bag like Dustin. The guy was a pretentious prick who thought his shit smelled like ambrosia.

Chuck sat back on his heels and dabbed at the sweat on his face with his shirt. "I think Marnie's been raped. We absolutely need to get her to the hospital. And we need to call the cops."

She followed his gaze to Marnie's bloody jeans. Chuck shifted Marnie's legs. Spots of fresh blood dotted the plastic on the couch.

"Oh, god," Heidi yelped, covering her mouth with a shaky hand.

"Maybe I should just call 9-1-1. It might not be a smart idea to move her ourselves. We could end up doing more damage."

Heidi simply stared into Marnie's battered face. Chuck got the new push-button phone his father had bought from its cradle on the end table. He pushed the green phone button to get a dial tone.

Marnie suddenly came to and said, "Don't call the police." Her voice was weak and thready, but forceful.

She opened her one good eye, pleading with Chuck.

"Marnie," Chuck said, standing over her, "you need real help." He staggered with relief that she was awake and talking.

"No. No police. No hospital."

She wasn't thinking straight. She probably had a concussion. She was in no frame of mind to make big decisions, or even small ones.

Before he could finish dialing, Heidi ripped the phone from his hand.

"Are you crazy?"

"You don't understand," Heidi said. "If the police find out, everyone will know."

Chuck could barely stifle his anger and bewilderment. "Good. That means more people will be out looking for the douchebag that did this to her."

Marnie coughed and shook her head, either too weak or unable to speak again.

She exchanged a knowing glance with Heidi.

"She doesn't want to be the girl who got raped. It'll destroy her life."

"It'll bring a man to justice."

"You don't know that. Do you see much justice in the world?"

She had a point about there being a lack of justice all around, but this was still ridiculous.

"Well, we can't just leave her here. My parents will be home soon and they'll call the cops whether you like it or not."

Marnie moaned as she turned herself onto her side with Heidi's help. "Take me home. Please."

"You need an X-ray, maybe one of those CAT scans, too," Chuck said.

She touched her swollen eye and winced. "I'll be fine."

He wanted to tell her she was as far from fine as Milbury was from Pluto.

Chuck sagged. He was not going to win and Marnie had already been through hell. He was her friend and he was not going to subject her to anything else she didn't want to do, even if it was in her best interest.

He covered her with a blanket they always kept thrown over the couch. "Don't you at least want the guy to pay for what he did?" The guy. What if she couldn't remember who the man was or what he looked like?

She rested her head back onto Heidi's lap. "He will." Heidi pulled the blanket up to Marnie's shoulder. "I know he will."

CHAPTER FIVE

Vent used his finger to scan down the list of names posted outside the science lab's door. Because Mr. Manton reveled in humiliating his students, he liked to post their grades for each test for the world to see. Vent had skipped the last couple of days of school, so there wasn't a crowd to shuffle through.

"Sixty-eight. Huh, I passed."

He thought for sure he'd failed. It was enough to make a boy believe in miracles. Someone called his name and when he turned around, he was hit in the face with a ball of tinfoil, the sharp edges lancing a burning cut in his cheek. Momentarily stunned, he watched three of the dudes on the basketball team, all of them black and twice his size, laughing and pointing. He wiped his cheek with the back of his hand, saw the smear of blood, and turned away. Now others were joining in tittering over his humiliation, including some hot girls. Jamming his hands deep in his pockets, he picked up his stride.

"You might want to hit the showers, since you're going in that direction. You stink like shit!" one of the basketball players shouted after him. Jesus. Vent didn't even know their names, but somehow they knew him and loved to pull crap like this. To make matters worse, they were underclassmen.

"Fucking stoner loser."

"Nice hair, faggot."

He slammed his hip into the door's exit bar and stepped out into the harsh light. Indian summer was in full bloom. The return of the heat and humidity sucked, especially under two layers of flannel, a leather jacket and jeans, but anything was better than being inside. He swore he could still hear everyone cackling, even though there was no way the sound would travel this far.

Tromping across the field, he jumped the small fence lining the outfield and ducked into the trees.

"Fucking assholes. Goddamn fucking assholes."

His eyes stung. He refused to admit even to himself that he was crying.

Leaning his back against a trunk, he found the half joint in his jeans pocket and lit it. It was down to the barest nub by the time he settled down.

"You got any left?"

He jumped at the sound of someone else's voice. Panic gave way to relief when he saw it was Heidi.

"This is all she wrote," he said, passing over the smoldering stub. Heidi inhaled until it was gone.

"What are you doing out here so early?" he asked. This little patch of trees and darkness had belonged to the stoners for as long as anyone could remember. Kids from other social cliques steered clear, as did the teachers for the most part. It was known as the 'Losers' Lair' which was fine by Vent and his friends. It seemed a small price to pay to be left in peace from the jocks, guidos, eggheads and stone-cold bitches.

"I think I'm just gonna cut," Heidi said.

Vent had known Heidi since they were in Miss Macia's homeroom in fifth grade. She could easily have gone the way of the bubbly cheerleader who dotted her 'I's with hearts and spent her days cutting down any girl who she didn't deem as smart, pretty or ambitious as her or her friends. At least that was a simple surface evaluation, considering her bright blue eyes, wavy chestnut hair and perfect teeth when every other girl was wearing braces.

Perhaps the best trait of Heidi's was that she didn't know or care about how beautiful she was. She was the most down-to-earth person he'd ever met, just happy to chill and not get excited about all the crap that drove other teens into fits.

They made the transition from hair metal to grunge together and even smoked their first joint at the same time at Mick's place two years back when he threw a rager, complete with firing off rifles into the air when everyone was thoroughly baked. They were lucky no one got killed that night.

Everyone in school, including the parents and teachers, assumed Vent, Heidi, Chuck, Marnie and Mick hung out because they had one thing in common – weed. That wasn't the case at all. For whatever reason, despite their sometimes wild differences, they just clicked. Weed was simply a common interest. They were all just a little bit different, whether it was their looks or way of thinking, five salmon who preferred to swim downstream.

Heidi could run with the bad boys (and Marnie) but one thing she never did was cut class.

"Yeah, right," he said. "And miss all the homework assignments?"

"I'm serious."

He looked into her deadpan eyes and knew she was telling the truth. That got him worried.

"What's wrong?"

She looked away, either searching for something or avoiding his gaze. "Nothing. I just don't feel like going."

"What did your mother do now?"

Heidi's mom was, in Vent's opinion, an undiagnosed bipolar nutjob who vacillated between being a Kool-Aid mom and Joan Crawford on her worst day. When he'd discovered Blue Oyster Cult's song, 'Joan Crawford Has Risen From The Grave', he ran to Heidi's house so they could listen to it together, laughing at some points and getting quiet at others, knowing Heidi was a modern-day Christina Crawford. Her mother could say vicious things, loudly for the neighbors to hear; everything from, "I wish I had taken a coat hanger to you when you were inside me!" to, "You're nothing but a worthless slut that will end up dead by twenty!"

And when the words didn't do the trick, she'd use her hands on Heidi, or any object that was nearby.

The next day, she'd serve Heidi breakfast in bed and dote on her, telling her how much she loved her and how sorry she was for lashing out the day before. Heidi knew her mother needed help and wasn't able to control herself. It kept her from hating the woman who gave birth to her. No, most times, she simply felt sorry for her.

Heidi shook her head. "It's not my mother. Surprising, right?" She lit a cigarette with a trembling hand.

"Well, something happened. You know you have to tell me."

Heidi pursed her lips. She looked like she was about to say something, and took another drag instead.

"I'm going to keep bugging you until you spill it, dude," Vent said, extracting a cigarette from her pack and using her cigarette to light his own.

"Nothing happened to *me*."

"Okay, so then why are you so upset? You need me to kick someone's ass?"

There was a long pause, and then Heidi crumbled. Tears snaked down her face. "It's Marnie. We went to Benny's on Thursday and she was...she was raped."

Vent reeled. Marnie was raped? Come to think of it, he hadn't heard from her since last week. It wasn't like Marnie to disappear. He should have known something was up.

"Raped? Are you shitting me?"

Heidi looked down at the ground and shook her head, sniffling.

"Who the fuck did it?"

When she looked up, the rims of her eyes were red. "She won't tell me."

"Do the cops have any ideas who it could've been?"

"She wouldn't let us call the police."

Vent opened his mouth but then closed it. The Milbury PD was comprised of world-class assholes who looked at Vent and his friends as if they were nothing but cockroaches. No one gave a turd about the kids with families just barely scraping by. Their parents were losers and their children were doomed to be even worse losers. Why treat them like regular people, people who mattered? He could see the cops snickering behind Marnie's back, figuring she'd brought it on herself.

"Jesus, Heidi, is she all right?"

"She's all messed up." Heidi ground the remains of her cigarette into the trunk of the nearest tree. 'Jenny Fowler sucks ball sack' had been carved into the tree so long ago, the words appeared to be sinking into the trunk. They often wondered what had become of Jenny Fowler. Was she a mom now? A grandma? Did she still suck ball sack? "Her face is all busted up and I think he hurt her real bad in...you know."

Vent balled his fists. He wanted to lash out and hit something, anything. "And she doesn't know who did it? Was it some dude from another town?"

"She knows who did it. She's just not saying." Heidi gasped. "Wait. She said she was going to hang out with Mick today."

"So?"

"So, I'll bet she'll tell him who raped her, because she knows he'll do something about it."

"We all would."

"No, not like Mick and you know it."

As much as he hated to admit it, she was right. Vent could talk the talk, walk some of the walk, but Mick, he could be a force of nature if he was set loose. "Is she there now?"

"I don't know. Maybe I should call her."

They ran out of the woods and across the field, then made a left out of the field and headed to Neried Street instead of back toward the school. Heidi picked up the payphone's receiver and held out her hand. "You got a quarter?"

He fished around his pocket and handed one over. She dialed Marnie's number and waited. After seven rings, she hung up. "She's not home."

"We gotta go to Mick's."

"Come on, we'll take my car." They jogged to the school parking lot, the section for student cars way in the back.

The Cougar belched to life. Back tires screeched as Heidi made a tight U-turn, heading to the very worst part of town and beyond to Mick's Airstream trailer.

★   ★   ★

Mick looked up from his *Mad* magazine when he heard Heidi's junker Cougar rumble down the unpaved path. *I guess* Spy vs. Spy *will have to wait.*

Was it still the weekend? He thought for sure it was Monday, but without a place to go or a thing to do, it was easy to lose track of time. It couldn't be Monday because if it was, Heidi would be in school and not driving toward him.

Vent was the first to jump out of the car, slamming the heavy door hard enough to send every bird in the trees overhead to less disturbing branches.

"What's up, bro?" Mick said. He was sitting in an aluminum folding chair with an open cooler between his feet. Two warm cans floated in dirt-specked water in the cooler.

"Is Marnie here?" Heidi asked, still half in the car.

Oh, now this was all making sense. "Yeah. She's sleeping inside. Someone busted her up pretty bad. She said she walked all the way over here. I thought she was gonna puke or pass out, so I told her to lie down. She just kinda passed out. Were you with her when she got in that fight?"

"There wasn't a fight," Vent said.

"What, did she get mugged? I know her stepfather didn't do that. He has girl hands and couldn't punch out a cat."

Heidi said, "She didn't tell you?"

"Tell me what?"

Heidi and Vent exchanged a secret glance. Mick didn't like secrets. Especially ones going on right under his nose.

"Why the fuck is everyone coming to me but doesn't want to tell me nothing?"

Heidi chewed on her lower lip. Vent kicked at a pine cone.

Mick said, louder, "Well? What the hell is going on?"

"Somebody raped me."

Marnie clutched the trailer's open doorway. Her face was a mass of deep purple bruises. Her busted eye looked like bloody wet tissue, at least the little of it they could see.

Mick's blood went into an instant boil. "Who's the fucker who did that to you, Marnie?"

"Since almost everybody's here, I think maybe I should wait until Chuck comes. No sense leaving him out, especially since he took care of me that night."

Vent and Mick looked confused. Chuck knew about this and didn't tell them?

"I don't want to wait for Einstein to get out of school," Mick said.

"I can call the school and pretend to be his mother, tell them there's a family emergency and he needs to get early dismissal," Heidi said. "I'll pick him up when he gets out."

"My phone's toast," Mick said. He could count on one hand with missing fingers the number of things not broken in the trailer. The generator went out on Saturday. The place was falling apart with the same steady decay as his family. His mother and stepfather had been gone now going on four months, to where, he had no clue. His real father had been MIA for years. Mick may have long ago given up looking for love from the people who brought him into this world, but he could sure use their money to keep from ending up in a tent eating squirrels he hunted and drinking puddle water. "You can use the one at Hale's Dairy Mart."

Marnie winced and clutched her stomach. "Get him." She disappeared back into the Airstream, walking like a hunched-over old lady. Heidi and Vent hopped back in the Cougar.

Mick took the Bowie knife from the sheath strapped to his leg and took out his anger on a tree.

It only made him angrier.

★   ★   ★

Chuck didn't like this one bit.

He sat in the back of Heidi's car, choking on exhaust fumes, and mulling over the hundred ways this could go wrong.

He knew exactly why Marnie wanted to reveal the name of her rapist to Mick. Because Mick would do what the police and courts couldn't. Even though his mother and stepdad, Dwight, were the farthest from parents of the year, they kept him from going completely off the tracks. Now that they'd been gone so long (and who knew if they were ever coming back or even alive at this point), Mick's attitude was getting darker, his actions more reckless. He'd basically dropped out of school and Chuck had to stop him from taking random shots with his BB gun at passing buses one day.

Vent slid a Pearl Jam cassette into the radio and cranked up the volume. None of them wanted to talk about what was going to happen. Emotions were high and Chuck was sure each of them was partly hoping Mick would do something bad, real bad, to the son of a bitch. Maybe not all of them were thinking ahead to the potential fallout. Maybe Chuck was the only one.

Milbury's suburban streets gave way to empty lots and trees, asphalt to rocks and dirt. The Cougar's rusted shocks wailed. Each pothole felt like dropping into a sinkhole. The only person living out here was Mick. Once upon a time, there had been Victorian houses, attempts at taming the wild, but they had been long abandoned. Mick's waste of a stepfather had moved them out here so he could grow weed. The problem was, he had a black thumb and all the get-up-and-go of a corpse. Then there were illegal fireworks, but that was a short-term business at best. He next tried selling knock-off handbags at the Sunday flea market, but they were cheap looking and fell apart before women made it home with their purchases. Word got around to steer clear of his table. When that failed, he took Mick's mom and bailed. Neither had bothered to tell Mick they were leaving or when they'd be back, if ever. Chuck brought care packages of food to his friend every week, but his parents were getting suspicious about the strange disappearance of their food stores. They hated that he hung around Mick. If they found out he was feeding him too, that would be a problem Chuck didn't need.

Like this one.

When they pulled up to the Airstream, Mick was carving curlicues of wood from a gnarled branch. He looked crazed. Not good.

"Marnie still inside?" Vent asked. One of his work boots was untied.

"Yeah."

"I'll get her," Heidi said, hurrying into the trailer.

Mick gave a quick head tilt. "S'up, Chuck."

"Hey."

The three boys stood apart from one another, avoiding eye contact, waiting in an uncomfortable silence. Chuck heard Heidi and Marnie talking in hushed voices. Marnie must still be in bad shape if she willfully slept in there. The funk in that Airstream could only be banished by the workings of a match and some kerosene. Normally, Heidi and Marnie kept outside, their noses crinkling every time they walked past the screen door.

When Marnie stepped out, Heidi crooking a finger in her friend's belt loop, Chuck felt both queasy and madder than hell. Her bruises had gotten worse, the purpling spreading from ear to ear and chin to forehead. She moved like every cell in her body was in rippling agony.

Heidi helped her into the best of the folding chairs, the one usually reserved for Chuck since he was the biggest of them all and would bend the frames of the other castaways littered about the trailer. He may have been seventeen, but he was physically a full-grown man, looking much older than his years thanks to his full brown beard. When all 3the boys had bragged about getting their first baby hairs on their upper lips, Chuck had a full five o'clock shadow by late morning.

Heidi whispered something in Marnie's ear and she nodded, letting her stringy hair cascade over her damaged face.

Mick fished a joint out of his shirt pocket, lit it and handed it to Marnie. "It'll help the pain."

She took a couple of drags. Her shoulders drooped a bit and she sat a little straighter.

Chuck wished he'd brought beer. He needed a drink in the worst way. A tiny throb blossomed at his temples.

Mick, who was as subtle as a fart at a funeral, dove right in. "So, who did it, Marnie? Who's the piece of shit?"

Marnie pushed the hair from her good eye. There were no tears, just the glaze of pain. She looked to Mick and only Mick. "It was Harold Dunwoody."

Heidi jumped from her chair. "What? He followed you out of the bar?"

Marnie nodded, keeping her eyes on Mick.

A darkness seeped over Mick. "I know that guy." He looked to Chuck. "Remember when he coached RS Auto's team in Little League?"

Chuck, who had been staring at Marnie, snapped out of his fog. "Oh yeah, that was him. The guy who always carried the clipboard and wore those green visors."

"That's him," Mick said. "I don't care what anyone says, he told his pitchers to throw at me after I slid hard into his fag son at third that day we crushed them. Looks like he's still sticking up for the loser he should have shot into the sheets. He's gonna wish they'd knocked my brains out."

"He didn't just beat me," Marnie said softly.

No one spoke for a while. Chuck and Heidi already knew about her being raped, but it still felt like hearing about it for the first time. The shock was as raw as sunburned skin.

Mick got up quietly and went inside the trailer. He used to tell everyone that Marnie was his sister by another mister, what with the both of them growing up in similarly fucked-up families and being more marginalized by the town than most. He closed the door behind him; the absence of any sounds of him moving about was unsettling. Minutes later, he kicked the door open, a heavily scuffed Louisville Slugger resting on his shoulder.

Vent had been pacing around the circle of friends. He tossed a stick in the bushes. "What are you gonna do with that?" There was genuine trepidation in his voice.

"Just a little batting practice."

Chuck stood up. Mick was holding Mr. B, his old bat that got him through three years of Little League. He'd been damn good at the plate, him and Mr. B swatting quite a few game-winning hits. But by the time he was twelve, Mick had no tolerance for coaches telling him what to do and Chuck assumed Mr. B had been thrown in the woods somewhere or cut down or set on fire.

The tiniest bit of a smile bloomed on Marnie's face. Heidi held her close, giving Mick an approving nod.

Chuck knew he had to step in before things got out of hand. Mick plus unbridled anger and a bat would equal twenty years' hard time if he got off easy. "Hold on. You're not going to smash Dunwoody's head in."

"Never said I was."

A cyclone of leaves whispered past him.

"Or any other part of him," Chuck was quick to add. "You'll kill him for sure and then what? You go to prison until you're an old man."

Vent massaged the back of his neck as if he'd been stung by a bee. "Chuck is right, dude. Even if you just threaten the guy, he'll call the cops and that'll be a whole other mess."

Mick sauntered over to Marnie and stood behind her chair. Chuck noticed the tiny flinch of her shoulders when Mick touched her. "First of all, I'm not going to just sit around and do nothing. Second, I'm not going to kill him. Hell, I might not even hurt him."

"So, then what do you need the bat for?" Chuck asked.

"To get him to do what I say."

"And what are you gonna tell him to do?"

"Simple. I'll inform he has to get in his car and we're gonna go for a little drive. You all can come if you want, if his car can fit everyone."

A cold knot of dread twisted Chuck's gut. "Where do you want him to drive to?"

Now Mick grinned. It was an evil villain grin that made dogs dash under the bed and grown men make the sign of the cross. It was the very same grin that made his teachers reluctant to deal with him and quite possibly made it easier for his mother to leave him. "I'm taking him to the people who will do what the cops can't." Tapping the barrel of the bat in his hand, he said, "I'm gonna feed him to the motherfucking Melon Heads."

CHAPTER SIX

Despite Heidi's high, whining protests, Chuck made her drive them all to his house so they could pick up his car. He told Vent to stay with her at Hanson's arcade where they could be seen. When Vent asked him why that was important, Chuck said, "Let's hope we don't have to find out."

When Marnie said she was coming there was no denying her.

Mick sat in the passenger seat as they rumbled down Fletcher Street in Chuck's Buick Skylark. It was a hand-me-down from his grandfather and looked the part of an old-man car. It even still smelled like him.

They rode in silence, each lost in their thoughts, Marnie lying down in the back seat with her eyes closed but her legs crossed, the right bouncing off the left in a steady rhythm that had nothing to do with the music playing on the radio. One of the speakers had blown out last fall, so the stereo had been reduced to old-time mono.

The only reason Chuck had agreed to drive them was because he was sure he'd be the only one to stop Mick. Not from taking Dunwoody to the Melon Heads. There was no such thing as Melon Heads, no matter how many times the story had been told from generation to generation. Yes, there was a time he had wholeheartedly believed the urban legend and had even ridden his bike out to Dracula Drive – which was actually Wainscott Road – along with Vent, Mick and Nelson Santos, the only twelve-year-old boy in their class with an ear piercing. They dared to go where older kids said they would have been snatched up by the deformed band of Melon Heads living in the woods for generations. They had just watched *Escape from New York* and were high on what seemed like gallons of Hawaiian Punch and Snake Plisskin. The VHS, Nelson's prized possession, had been played over and over until the magnetic tape was ready to give up the ghost. One of them had to sit inches from the television to keep adjusting the tracking. For that moment after the movie had ended, they felt like they could conquer anything. What better way to test their mettle than by taking a cruise down Dracula Drive? Granted, it had been mid-afternoon and without a cloud in the sky, but still, that was a place where deformed Melon Heads lay in wait for anyone stupid enough to traipse into their deep, dark and wooded territory.

The boys sang the Melon Head song as they rode.

Dare to walk,
Down Dracula Drive,
In day or night,
You won't survive.
They wait in trees,
And hide below,
Hungry for people,
Too blind to know.

It was said the Melon Heads had lived there since the 1700s, the continuing offspring of a line of encephalitic, feral settlers who had been cast out by the founders of Milbury because they were deemed unfit, both mentally and physically. Best to let nature correct its mistake and leave them in the woods to their fates. Or there was the second theory that there had once been a sanitarium out here where the town line died in the late 1800s. Of course, there was the ubiquitous doctor who performed brutal experiments on the insane left in his care. What his goals were was anyone's guess. Perhaps he had tried his hand at building the ideal man like others had attempted, some in esteemed institutions, during that time period. Eugenics back in the day was more than just an immoral pipe dream. No matter his intentions, things had gone terribly wrong. Each manipulation of his subject's genetic makeup resulted in gross and horrible failure. His botched experiments, each one more disfigured and mentally incapacitated than the next, were kept in a locked wing of the sanitarium. That is until the night of the fire – because isn't there always a fire? – when his bastard creations escaped, killing the doctor and everyone around him, fleeing into the forest and forgotten by society.

No matter their origin, they were still out there, hungry, angry, incapable of pity, defiant of fear, waiting. If you were lucky, a trip down Dracula Drive ended in the rustling of bushes and a Melon Head simply scaring you off with a growl. The unlucky might be chased, perhaps suffering a small injury as they swiped at you or threw things at you.

For the tragically unfortunate, there was no coming back from Dracula Drive. Your screams as the Melon Heads captured you with gnarled hands as unyielding as steel, fingernails sharp and deadly, would be heard by no one. Not a soul lived close enough to the Melon Heads to hear you. The only saving grace is that your terror would not last long. They would see to that.

Needless to say, Chuck, Mick, Vent and Nelson didn't encounter a single Melon Head. Not even a growl from an animal skulking in the brush. They returned home victors, just as Snake had made it out of New York. They told their friends about their daring adventure and almost no one believed them. It wasn't until Nelson had started embellishing on the story, talking about a feeling of being watched and seeing something tracking them in the woods, that ears started to prick up. Mick was only too happy to jump on the bandwagon, adding that a stick had sailed over his head and would have knocked him off his bike if he hadn't seen it at the last second and ducked. Strange voices were heard muttering in a language that defied translation. Mick boasted he would have faced them if he'd had his BB gun. Maybe he'd go back someday and finish what he started.

Most kids thought Mick's story was bullshit, but there was just enough in Nelson's to pique their interest and believe the boys had bravely or stupidly plunged into Melon Head land. That's when Chuck learned people were generally gullible and stupid.

Now, Mick generally wasn't stupid, just prone to say and do dumb things. What made him think he would feed Dunwoody to Melon Heads? Had he been smoking weed laced with something? All that time out there in the trailer alone, on the verge of starving, was screwing with his head.

"Take a right there," Marnie said from the back seat. She had propped herself up on her elbow and was looking out the front windshield with her one good eye.

"You sure?" Mick asked.

"I dated Chad long enough to know where he lives."

Mick tapped his fingers on the dash. "Oh yeah. Right."

Chuck slowed down to make the turn.

"It's just three blocks down and then make a left on Rossiter."

Not much further to go. Chuck pulled the car over and put it in park, but left the engine running. "Seriously, Mick, what do you plan on doing?"

He'd convinced his friend to leave the bat behind. Mick creeped most adults out, and at six-foot-four and two-hundred-fifty pounds, Chuck was a walking brick wall. It was why people called him Pink Floyd in middle school, when he was taller than every teacher thanks to an insane growth spurt between fifth and sixth grades. Neither of them needed a weapon to intimidate a flabby popcorn fart like Harold Dunwoody. Chuck didn't want to hurt him, but he did want to put the fear of god and prison time into him. At least if he was with Mick, he could prevent him from doing something terrible that couldn't be undone.

The cracked leather seat crumpled as Mick shifted. "Exactly what I said, man. You think I'm joking?"

"Uh, yeah, I do. I was with you when we went down Dracula Drive, remember? There was nothing there. Plus, we're not kids anymore."

"Exactly, there was nothing."

Marnie rested her chin on Chuck's seat back. "Tell him, Mick."

"Tell me what?"

"That day we went there, did you hear or see anything?"

Sighing, Chuck replied, "Not a Melon Head in sight. Like any rational person would expect."

Mick shook his head. "No, you're not getting it. I noticed because I live in the fucking woods. There wasn't a single bird, not a squirrel, shit, not even an ant, on that road. Which tells me there was something out there. Something that everything else was afraid of."

"And the natural assumption is that it was Melon Heads?"

"It's more than that, but that's what clued me in to it all at first."

"Tell him the rest," Marnie said with the most animation he'd heard in her voice all day.

Mick squinted at Chuck, opened his mouth, and then wiped at his nose with a fist. "Nah, he's not going to believe me."

Chuck knew there was no sense trying to lie to Mick. "You're right there."

"But you will," Mick said, wagging a dirty finger at him. "If you can give me just a little trust, you will."

"I think we should go back and think of a better way, a *realistic* way, to get even with Dunwoody."

Mick got in Chuck's face. His breath smelled like stale weed and yesterday's bologna sandwiches. "We're doing this for Marnie and we're doing this now! Why do you think she came to me? Because she knew exactly what would happen."

Chuck looked at Marnie. "He's right," she said.

Both of them were out of their minds. Mick pointed at Marnie's swollen cheek, the skin tight and shining like a black-and-purple-swirled marble. "You see this? Dunwoody did this. And that's not even close to the worst of it. He doesn't deserve a beating until he's nothing but a grease stain. He deserves to be nothing. Disappeared. Forgotten. A fucking zero from here on, man. I'm doing it with or without you. I don't know see how you can look at Marnie ever again knowing you ditched when you had a chance to do something right."

Marnie's fingertips brushed Chuck's shoulder. She said, "I'm still bleeding."

Chuck turned to look at her. Her eyes swam in tears. He barely recognized the girl he'd known the past seven years. When he was ten, he had a huge crush on Marnie, the girl who could seemingly do whatever she wanted, coming and going as she pleased. How many times had Chuck's parents had her over for dinner? He couldn't count the hours they'd spent watching *Voltron* and *Battle of the Planets* after school. She was like a member of the family, she'd been with them so much. Back then, Chuck was too young to understand that she was adrift, a latchkey kid and beyond, her parents too self-indulgent in their own issues to cook her meals or care if she was out well after dark. All he knew then, was for sure positive of, was that one day they would be married.

All that puppy love resulted in one quick peck on the lips when they'd played spin the bottle in Heidi's basement the summer he'd turned eleven. Marnie developed early, grew up too fast, and soon he was watching *Voltron* alone.

But he still cared for her, maybe even loved her on a platonic level. *I'm still bleeding.*

There weren't going to be any Melon Head feedings, but he sure as hell needed to have a heart-to-heart with Harold Dunwoody.

Chuck put the car in drive.

★   ★   ★

"Marnie, you stay in the car," Mick said. He told Chuck to keep the car running.

"I'm coming with you," she said.

The rage he'd been feeling over what had happened to Marnie had kept him humming. It was as if his nerves were plugged into an outlet, the current buzzing in his brain. He wanted – no, needed – to get revenge. Only when that hum was silenced could he go about doing whatever he could to take care of her and help her recover. No one messed with Marnie. No one. He wished Dunwoody knew what was coming and he was inside right now crapping himself.

Mick saw some of that rage in Marnie's eyes, whatever anger could penetrate the wall of hurt that kept threatening to sweep her under.

Mick shrugged in quick and rare defeat. "At least stay behind us." He looked over at the ranch house, paint fading, one of the gutters broken and dangling, the front yard about three weeks past its mowing due date. It was not the home of someone who gave a crap.

Son of a bitch has a house and lets it waste away, Mick thought. *Maybe I should set it on fire and make him watch it burn. I bet he'd find a real quick appreciation for what he had after it's a pile of ashes.*

It was a great idea, but it had two flaws. The houses here were spaced too close together. Torch one and the rest would go up like tinder.

Second, nothing was cooler than handing the rapist fuck over to the Melon Heads. Nothing. He couldn't wait to see Chuck's face when it happened.

If it happens.

No, it will happen!

With towering Chuck beside him, he rang the bell. He could hear a TV on inside. It sounded like a game show. There was a lot of applause and bad music.

When no one answered, he banged on the door, pounding it as hard as he could.

"I think he hears you," Chuck said.

"I want him worried."

He was about to start kicking it with the business end of his Doc Martens when the door flew open.

Harold Dunwoody looked like he was at the tail end of one hell of a bender. His eyes were red and glassy, what looked like dried vomit caught in his week-old beard, and he stank something fierce. All he wore was a dirty white T-shirt with holes on the shoulder and blue-and-white-striped boxers.

"What the hell do you think you're doing?" he shouted, slurring and weaving in the open doorway.

"Is Chad home?" Mick said, careful to keep Marnie out of Dunwoody's sight.

"Are you crazy banging on my door like that? I should call the cops."

"I don't think you'd want to do that," Chuck said. "Though I'd love it if you did."

Dunwoody lifted his head to take all of Chuck in.

Mick snapped his fingers in his face. "Yo, is Chad home?"

Running a hand over his face, Dunwoody said, "No, and who the hell are you?"

That's when Marnie pushed her way between Mick and Chuck. Dunwoody leaned forward, narrowing his eyes. "You look like you need a hospital, young lady. Don't tell me. You walked into a door."

He did the worst thing he could have possibly done at that moment.

Dunwoody started to laugh.

Chuck beat Mick to the punch, literally. Bad breath and a torrent of booze, bile and chunks rocketed from Dunwoody's mouth the instant Chuck's fist connected with his belly. Dunwoody folded over, alternating between puking and gasping. Some of his filth got on Mick's boots. Mick wiped it off by kicking the man in the ribs, leaving a yellow smear on his T-shirt.

"Jesus Christ," Chuck bellowed. Mick couldn't tell if he was alarmed by the fact he'd just walloped an adult or by the volume of vomit coming out of the man. Marnie had backed away, staring daggers of hate at the man.

"Help me get him in the car," Mick said.

Dunwoody looked up, tiny red dots peppering under his eyes, with more burst capillaries to come if he kept heaving like that. "Whuh car?"

When Chuck didn't move, Mick shoved his shoulder. "Come on, before anyone sees us."

"Maybe that's enough," Chuck said.

The rapist pig was on his hands and knees. He clutched his belly, going stiff when the next wave of vomit exploded. This one hit hard enough to make him shit himself.

Mick was repulsed. There was no way he was letting all that stink and nastiness in the car. "Take him to the backyard."

Chuck brightened, lifting Dunwoody under his armpits and keeping him as far away from his body as his arms would allow. Dunwoody muttered something and burped.

"What about the Melon Heads?" Marnie said.

"Don't worry about it," Mick said, checking to see if any of the neighbors were peeking out their windows. This was a pretty apathetic part of town, but the down and out loved the spectacle of another man's misery.

Chuck hustled down the side of the house and deposited Dunwoody on a picnic bench. The yard was way overgrown. Bags of garbage, birds and animals having poked dozens of holes in the plastic, lay strewn about.

"Now what?" Chuck asked.

Mick looked around and found the hose. "Turn that on," he said to Marnie. He pulled the nozzle handle so it was on full blast, hammering Dunwoody with water. Dunwoody sputtered and almost fell on his back. "Now get up and turn around."

He had his hands in front of him, trying in vain to keep the water from hitting him. "Please, leave me alone."

"I said get up and turn around." He aimed the nozzle lower, the jet stream pounding Dunwoody's balls. It elicited a girlish yip. Dunwoody jumped from the bench, both hands protecting his crotch. Chuck grabbed him by the shoulders and spun him around the way a parent twirled a blindfolded child before they took a whack at a piñata. When Mick saw the brown stain and sludge on the back of his legs, he almost puked. Pinching his nose, he hosed the feces away. Harold

Dunwoody kept still, starting to shiver. It wasn't exactly swimming weather at the moment.

Once he was sure most of Dunwoody's shit was settling into the lawn, Mick tossed the hose. "Now let's get him in the car."

Chuck looked like the air had gone out of his sails. "Look, kick him around a little more if you want. That'll be enough."

Marnie said, "No, it's not." Whether she was faking it to make a point or really in pain, she winced, one hand on her lower abdomen. If she'd gone pale it would be impossible to tell through all the bruising.

Mick looked at Chuck and shrugged, as if to say, *well, you heard what the lady said.* He could see Chuck's big brain going into overdrive, calculating all of the potential outcomes to their misadventure. That was the problem with Chuck. He always thought with his brain, never his heart. This was a big heart moment.

One thing that surprised Mick was the fact that all that puking and cold water hadn't sobered up Dunwoody. He stormed over and clutched the back of Dunwoody's neck. "Let's go, asshole." Dunwoody stumbled while Mick pushed him along. Marnie opened the back door of the car and Mick shoved him inside. Dunwoody started to yell. Mick punched him in the nose and wagged a finger in his face. "Not a word outta you." Then he looked back at Chuck. "I'll stay in the back with him. You know where to go."

The key ring dangled over Chuck's index finger. He sighed and got behind the wheel. "Promise me we'll just take him back when you're done with...whatever you think is going to happen."

Mick smiled. "You have my word."

Marnie got into the car slowly, pain etched all over her face.

"You okay?" Chuck asked, cranking the ignition.

She pushed her hair over her ear. There was a tear in her eye. "Yeah. Let's go."

All along the trek to Dracula Drive, Dunwoody moaned and complained that his nose was broken. He still smelled like shit. Mick kicked his legs whenever he got too close to him and had to roll down the windows in back. They couldn't get to Dracula Drive fast enough.

CHAPTER SEVEN

A bitter burp almost had Marnie asking Chuck to pull over. Her insides still felt as raw as they had the night Dunwoody raped her. For once, the pain was welcome. It reminded her why she had agreed to Mick's plan and it also kept any sympathy for the sniveling bastard at bay. She worried that if she didn't feel so broken, she might have called the whole thing off, especially once he'd crapped his pants.

He'd stopped carping about his broken nose, though each wet, ragged, whistling inhalation was proof that Mick had busted it good.

Don't look back there.

Marnie had never seen a dead person. Her extended family was just as poor as her own. When someone kicked the bucket, usually an old aunt or uncle she'd rarely seen, there was just enough money to plant them. A wake with a viewing of the body was outside the budget. Harold Dunwoody might still be breathing (rather crudely at the moment), but he was as good as dead.

She bet he wouldn't laugh at her now.

Chuck's knuckles were white little mushroom caps. He hadn't said a word. Just kept driving, not even bothering to look in the rearview mirror. She touched his arm and he looked at her, some of the anger and trepidation melting from his gaze.

When she gave his arm a squeeze, she hoped it wordlessly conveyed *we're doing the right thing*. It didn't look as if he was getting the message. His eyes swiveled back to the road, his jaw flexing.

He didn't believe in the Melon Heads and she couldn't blame him. She didn't either, at least until last year.

"Go up there," Mick said.

"I know where to go," Chuck replied sharply.

The bent sign for Wainscott Road loomed ahead of them. Holes had been poked out of the metal by people taking potshots with their rifles during hunting season. It was as far as they would dare travel

on Dracula Drive, taking their frustrations out on the puny sign. It
was funny how all the adults in Milbury laughed at the Melon Heads
legend, yet none of them dared go into these woods to hunt.

The old shocks creaked and groaned as the Skylark took to the road
left to rot and ruin. Each shimmy and shake birthed a fresh hell of pain
in Marnie's abdomen. She bit back her tears, telling herself to keep it
together. The pain was a necessary thing now. Just a little bit more
suffering until things could be set right. For once, Chuck was wrong
and Mick was right.

Her grandfather was the only one she knew who took the Melon
Heads seriously. At the time, he was, as her mother would say,
starting to slip. Marnie was nine and had no idea what that meant.
He walked just fine. But he did forget a lot of things, like where
he'd put his glasses or even her name, calling her Maggie, which
was her aunt's name. She once watched him pour a glass of juice,
start to walk out to the porch, stop and put the glass in the oven.
Seconds later he noticed her standing by the pantry and said he sure
was thirsty. Slipping wasn't his problem. Thinking was his real issue,
as far as Marnie was concerned.

During hunting season that year, there had been a lot of fighting
between Marnie's mother and grandfather. He wanted to 'pop a son
of a buck' but she'd hidden his guns. It was a standoff that lasted
for weeks. When there was a lull in the fighting, Marnie asked her
grandfather why no one ever hunted in the woods along Dracula
Drive. Were they afraid of the Melon Heads?

With his wiry white hair and pale blue eyes getting paler by the
day, he'd pulled her onto his lap and said, "Nah, ain't nobody scared
of them Melon Heads when they got a gun on 'em. The Melon Heads
may be dumb, but they ain't stupid. They know what a gun can do.
It's a good thing they don't have any of their own, though."

"So how come nobody goes there?"

He looked around to make sure her mother wasn't around to
overhear him. She knew he was going to share a secret with her.
There were no greater secrets than the ones shared between Marnie
and her grandpa.

"I'll tell ya, there's no sense hunting there because there's no deer."

"Where did they all go?"

"In the bellies of them Melon Heads. They gotta eat, too, and they don't have a Shopwell to bring their list and coupons."

"If they don't have guns, how do they kill the deer?"

He hugged her and she rested her head against his chest. He smelled like Old Spice and root beer. He always had one of those root beer barrel candies in his mouth.

"They're expert hunters who don't need a gun. And that's why I don't ever want you to go out there, even if your friends try to bully you to do something stupid. You got that?"

"Got it."

"There's an old man out there who watches out for them. You stay away from him, too. He's not right in the head. What kind of a person would help those freaks? You ever hear somebody say they want to go see a fella named Fennerman, you run the other way."

"I will."

"Promise?"

"Promise."

She was going to ask him more about this Fennerman, the guardian of the freaks, when he suddenly got up and went into the living room. She heard him ask her mom, "Where's that little Marnie?"

He died the next year. Marnie stayed true to her word for the next six years. Mick hadn't bullied her into going down Dracula Drive. He said the guy he bought weed from actually lived out there and she was curious. As far as she knew, no one lived in those woods. Word had it that even Fennerman, if there ever was a Fennerman, was long gone.

So she went with him, and everything changed in a matter of hours. Everything.

The *thup* of a lock being undone made her whip around to look at the back seat. Dunwoody was trying to open the car door. Mick pounced on him. The door flew open. Chuck yelled, "What the hell is going on back there?" He hit the brakes just as Mick slammed the door. It thumped against the top of Dunwoody's head. The man howled in pain.

"That's what you get for trying to escape," Mick said, breathing heavily. He straddled Dunwoody, his fists at his sides, waiting for him to make another attempt to get out.

Marnie had seen enough. She turned back around, keeping her gaze fixed on what passed for a road.

"We okay now?" Chuck asked.

"Yeah. We're good." Mick flicked Harold Dunwoody's ear. "Right?"

Dunwoody said something that was hard to understand thanks to his broken nose. It sounded like, "I'll fucking kill you," but there was no menace behind it.

Chuck took the road cautiously, the frame of his old car practically shouting that it wanted to be anywhere else but here. Marnie had to grab the dashboard a couple of times when one of the front tires dipped into a deep rut. They'd gone a quarter of a mile in when Mick popped his head between them and pointed to the right. "You see that path over there?"

Chuck grumbled. "Yeah. So?"

It wasn't much of a path. It looked just wide enough to accommodate a motorcycle. Heavy brush was on either side of the entrance. The trees were thick and ancient here and blotted out the sun entirely.

"Go down there."

"I'm not getting my car stuck out here."

"Just trust me," Mick said.

"You keep saying that," Chuck said.

"Because you keep doubting me."

"Fine."

Chuck turned into the path like an old lady pulling into a parking space. The brush moved aside as soon as the fender nudged it. It had been put there to make it look like you couldn't go down the path. In fact, the little off-road was smooth sailing. There were well-worn tire tracks in the ground.

Seconds later, the path, which was actually a driveway, stopped before a cabin. The front porch had an Adirondack chair and small table with a can of Budweiser atop it. Firewood was stacked seven feet high in one corner of the porch.

"What the hell is this place?" Chuck asked. "And please don't tell me it's a Melon Head clubhouse."

Mick slapped the back of the seat twice. "That's Dredd's house. Sweet, huh?"

A thin wisp of smoke trailed from the chimney. The cabin looked old but well cared for.

"Who's Dredd?"

"He's cool," Marnie assured him. She'd only met Dredd the one time. He was out there, like way out there, but that one meeting had blown her mind. Or maybe not. She still wasn't sure. Dredd and Mick had sworn her to secrecy, which wasn't easy, especially whenever she and Heidi had had a couple of beers. Dredd sold very powerful weed, but as far as Marnie knew, it was only to Mick. Who else would venture out this way, even to get high? Only Mick. And Marnie, on that one day. Without that day, they wouldn't have this moment. The jury was out on whether or not that was one for the pro or con column.

A niggle of doubt wormed into her brain. How would Dredd react when he saw that they had broken his trust?

"You know him?" Chuck asked incredulously.

"I've been here before. I wouldn't say I know Dredd, but—"

The cabin's front door opened. A man sheathed in darkness emerged, pointing a very big rifle at Chuck's car.

★   ★   ★

Mick stopped Chuck from putting the car in reverse and motoring out of the driveway. He pulled the keys out of the ignition and stuffed them in his pocket.

"Chill out, man. I got this." He grabbed Dunwoody by the collar and said, "Try to run for it and my friend out there will blow your balls off. You got me?"

Dunwoody looked over the seat, saw the gun, and nodded vigorously.

"Marnie, come out with me."

As soon as Mick stepped out of the car, he was met with, "Who the fuck are you?"

"Yo, Dredd, it's me, Mick."

"Who?"

The normal first instinct when a gun was pointed directly at you was to put your hands in the air to show you surrendered and meant no harm. Mick wasn't going to look like a pussy, so he jammed his hands in his pockets and approached the porch slowly but steadily. There was a good chance Dredd was riding a weird high and wouldn't know Mick from Ronald Reagan. With only ten feet separating them, it was too late to turn back now. "Dude, it's Mick. You sell me weed from time to time. Remember me?"

Dredd racked the shotgun. "Get on the ground now!"

Mick's heart fluttered. Dredd was wearing sunglasses, his lip curled, showing a yellow eyetooth.

"You in the car. Get the fuck out and hit the ground!"

Mick looked over his shoulder. Chuck was out of the car with his hands up, getting to his knees. Marnie was already on her stomach, her arms crossed and her head resting on them, not daring to look up. Dunwoody stumbled from the car and said, "Call the police. You have to help me. They beat and kidnapped me."

The gun swung toward Dunwoody's direction. "Shut up and eat dirt."

"You don't understand...."

Dunwoody started running toward the porch. A shotgun blast roared. Mick swore he felt the displaced wind by his face as buckshot just missed him. Dunwoody and Marnie screamed. The man dropped as if he'd been hit, which was a real possibility.

"Now you," Dredd said flatly.

Mick realized he was the only one still standing. He took a knee. "Remember the time I brought you that dirt bike some kid had left by my place? We fixed it and tore the hell out of the trail over in Kittsfield. I tried to jump it and the damn thing lost its front tire the second I hit the air."

Dredd came up on him fast as a cheetah. Mick jumped back, falling flat on his ass. The hot muzzle of the shotgun touched Mick's chest. Even through his two layers of shirts, it felt like it was going to brand him if Dredd didn't pull it away immediately. Mick couldn't control his breathing. He got lightheaded, which made it even harder to come up with a clear way to cut through whatever shit Dredd was on and convince him they knew each other.

"This is my property. I don't like people trespassing on my property. Best part is, there's no one around for miles to see how I handle trespassers." He gave a low chuckle and Mick felt the alien sting of tears in his eyes.

"Please, we didn't mean to come onto your property," Chuck pleaded. "We're lost and just need some directions."

"Bullshit you're lost," Dredd spat. "This pile of shit knows my name, so you're not here because you took a wrong goddamn turn."

Mick shrank away from the shotgun, affording him a couple more inches of space before the ground stopped him cold. "Come on, Dredd, you know me. Don't do anything stupid."

The muzzle jerked up to his face. "You calling me stupid?"

"No! No! I'm not. Please don't shoot us!"

"You should have thought of that before you waltzed on up here. Hope it was worth it."

Mick shielded his face with trembling hands. He shouted an incoherent string of entreaties.

"Bang!"

Mick's entire body flinched.

Dredd started laughing. The shotgun was mercifully pointed at the ground. He took off his sunglasses, sliding an arm between the buttons of his shirt. The corners of his eyes crinkled as he smiled. "You all might want to check your underpants, because I'm pretty sure there might be a little pee...or worse." He looked over at Dunwoody, who had propped himself onto his hands and knees, appearing dazed and on the verge of passing out. "Especially you, big guy."

Mick thought his heart was going to break free from his chest and fly away. He wanted to tell Dredd he was a fucking asshole for his little stunt, but he didn't have the capacity to speak.

He did hear Chuck say, "Oh yeah, he's real cool."

"So, Mickster, who are your friends?" Dredd saw Marnie as she stood up and pointed. "I know you! You're Marie, right?"

"Marnie," she said, dusting herself off. Dredd's smile faded when he really took notice of her face.

"What happened to you?"

Now Mick found his voice. "*He* happened." He gestured with his head toward Dunwoody.

"No shit?"

Dunwoody was on his feet, eyes flitting around, searching for a way out.

"No shit," Mick said.

The shotgun came up again. "You take one step and it'll be your last," Dredd said to Dunwoody. "And I'm not fooling around this time."

Chuck and Marnie sidled up next to Mick, leaving Dunwoody by the car with his hands up, begging Dredd to call the cops, snot and blood running from his squashed nose. Dredd wasn't taking his eyes off the man. His long hair was tied back in a ponytail and it looked like he hadn't shaved in a week of Sundays. He wore a full camouflage outfit, complete with black combat boots. Mick never saw him in anything else. Dredd once explained that clothes at the military surplus store were cheap and durable. Why bother going to J.C. Penney or Caldor to pay double for duds that would make him look like some Little League coaching douche of a dad?

"We need your help," Mick said.

Dredd chuckled. "Looks like you've done pretty good on your own." The aroma of weed clung to Dredd like a second skin. His eyes were twin pools of glass. The guy was high as the clouds. Mick realized how lucky they were that he still had enough coherence to joke with them and not blow them away for traipsing on his hideout.

"Kicking him around won't be enough," Mick said. "We wanna take him to the Melon Heads."

Dredd looked them each in the eye while keeping the gun trained on Dunwoody. His expression had gone flat, his tone measured. He looked at Chuck when he said to Mick, "There's no such thing as Melon Heads."

"Come on, man," Mick said.

"I don't know what the hell you're talking about, brother."

Chuck groaned. "See? Let's take this asshole back."

Mick shook his head vigorously. "No going back, dude. You and I both know that." To Dredd he said, "Tell him."

"That you think a fairy tale is real?" Dredd replied, one eyebrow riding high. "Even I'm not that stoned."

"Jesus," Marnie mumbled. She looked like she was about to collapse. Mick couldn't tell if it was from disappointment, fear, the pain, or all three.

"Now, if you came with some cash, I might have something that'll chill you all right out," Dredd said. He pointed at Dunwoody. "Even him."

Was he still fucking with them? Mick started to get angry.

"Quit messing around," he said. "This is serious shit."

"Oh, it looks pretty serious, believe you me." Dredd grinned.

"I told you this was a waste of time," Chuck said. He leaned against the car and ran his hands through his hair, looking like he wanted to tear it out.

That's when the first tears fell from Marnie's bruised eyes.

Mick lowered his voice and said, "Look at her. See what that dirtbag did to her?"

To his surprise, Dredd did just that. All was silent for a moment that felt like weeks.

"You sure you want to do this?"

"Totally," Mick replied.

Marnie nodded.

Chuck stared back at Dredd, uncommitted. "You're still joking around, right?"

Dredd sucked on his teeth. "Afraid not, big man. I'm not too keen on Mickster opening his big mouth about it, but from what I can see, this can be considered a special exception. Plus, times have been tough lately. Summer was lean and things are getting restless. It's hard to keep the natives calm when they're starving." His gaze danced again toward Marnie and he winced. "This isn't going to be pretty, but it looks to me like your man over there earned it. I may look like a scumbag and, hell, I may be a scumbag, but you don't hit women. Ever." To Mick, he said, "Go inside and under the bench by the door you'll find some rope. Bring it out here and let's get to work."

CHAPTER EIGHT

The business of tying Dunwoody up had made Chuck nauseous. What with all the struggling and crying and screaming, which brought swift kicks and punches from Dredd and Mick, it was all getting to be too much. Each time Chuck was about to intervene and call for cooler heads, Marnie, who must have been able to sense his distress, would do something as simple as touch him, forcing him to look at her, and he would sigh and shut his mouth.

The question of whether Dunwoody would tell the cops if and when they released him sent icy bolts of panic down his spine. Chuck's entire life was now going to be decided by this moment, a moment that had spiraled out of his control by their collective emotions over what had been done to Marnie. He finally understood the true nature of a crime of passion, and while he couldn't use it to excuse some of the more heinous atrocities committed in the name of love or betrayal or hate, he did feel a measure of sympathy for those who had simply been caught in the throes of letting their hearts overtake their brains.

Dunwoody had been gagged and tossed in the back of Dredd's Ford pickup, which he kept under a green-and-brown-painted tarp behind the cabin. He'd been tied up good, so there was no worry about him leaping out of the back and running for help. It was small comfort.

Dredd, who had to be in his mid-twenties, but at some angles looked to be far older, had given them each a cold can of Piels. Some of the suds remained in his wild mustache. They sat on stumps of wood he'd cut from a fallen tree. Mick had been growing more and more restless, his hands and legs fidgeting. Chuck felt like he could sleep for days, while Marnie probably needed a hospital bed. She sipped at her beer, each swallow looking as if it hurt going down.

"So, how long do we have to wait?" Mick asked, crumpling his can.

Dredd checked the sky, which was barely visible through the trees.

The small patch of sunlight was starting to turn a darker shade of blue. "Give it another thirty minutes or so. If it's still light, they'll stay away."

"Why?"

Dredd scratched the back of his neck, snorted and spit out a wad of phlegm. "Because they live in the shadows. They know it's what keeps them alive."

Snickering, Mick said, "They tell you that?"

Dredd shot him a withering glance. "I don't need to talk to them to understand. And vice versa."

Silence settled over them. Mick turned away like a scolded child. Chuck had never seen his friend defer to an adult like this before, not even to his own mother. That meant he either looked up to Dredd, which seemed a stretch, or, more likely, he was scared of him. The alarm bells in Chuck's head had been ringing like it was New Year's ever since Dredd came out of the cabin wielding his shotgun. And what kind of a name was Dredd? The kind of nickname a person earns when they instill actual dread in people.

Taking his chances, Chuck broke the uneasy hush with, "I'm still finding it hard to believe that the Melon Heads exist. No offense, Dredd. We're just going to dump Dunwoody in the woods, right? And when he gets out, then what?"

Instead of getting the ire he expected from Dredd, the older man nodded, looking at the ground between his own feet but seeing something far, far away. "I hear you, man. I hear you. I was the same way, or at least I'd talked myself into thinking they didn't exist when I was a kid. I could have stayed that way for the rest of my life if it wasn't for that Christmas morning."

He paused, finished his beer, and tossed it into the trees.

"What happened on Christmas?" Marnie asked, her voice weak and broken and a tinge scared.

Dredd took a deep breath and said, "That's when I lost my brother. I had just gotten this new bike, a sweet three-speed that all us kids wanted at the time. I was being a pain in the ass because I wanted to ride it and my older brother, Dylan, he convinced my parents to let me go with him for a quick spin. I was shocked because he was a lot older than me and never wanted me around."

A bird flapped its wings above them. Pine needles rained down on Mick, who flicked them away.

"He insisted we ride down Dracula Drive. Said him and his friends hung out here all the time. I thought he was trying to make it so I wasn't scared of the Melon Heads anymore. So I followed him. But I was wrong. He'd set me up. He wanted to leave me out here for them. I found out later he'd gotten this girl pregnant. He was in real trouble and didn't know what to do. He said to me, 'This is the only way.' I didn't know what the hell that meant. I was so damn scared. Dylan took off, leaving me there. And then they took him instead."

He took a crumpled pack of Backwoods cigars from his pocket and shook out a slightly bent, narrow cigar. It had been intentionally made to look roughly hand-rolled and smelled sweet as candy for the first few puffs. Only after he'd smoked it down to the halfway point did he continue. Chuck heard Dunwoody's muffled pleas in the distance, each mumble or shout putting him closer to thinking he'd just thrown his life away. There had to be a way to get out of this with minimal repercussions. Unfortunately, anything close to a solution was evading him.

"I learned later when I tracked down Dylan's friends what my brother was talking about and why he did it. I've just never been certain why they turned on him. Maybe because I was faster. Maybe not. I expect I'll never know."

Mick batted a rock into the trees with a random stick he'd picked up. "Tell him why." He pointed the stick at Chuck.

Dredd's eyes slid over to Chuck, veiled behind a cloud of smoke. "If you take care of the Melon Heads, they'll take care of you. Life isn't easy out here, especially for them. Lean times happen more often than you think. Now don't get me wrong, they don't like people coming out here. I don't know whether it's fear or hate, probably both. But sometimes, they let someone in, and as long as that someone figures out the rules, well, they'll do things for you."

Chuck thought Dredd was full of shit, but he needed to play along, if only to allow him time to figure out a safer endgame. "What would they have done for your brother?"

He took a very long drag on the cigar. "I think he was going to have them kill that girl and the baby inside her. Problem was, her parents wouldn't let her go near Dylan. So he had to get the Melon Heads to go to her. They don't do that for nothing. Part of the rules."

"Jesus," Marnie whispered, wrapping her arms around herself as if she'd caught a sudden chill.

"You really think your brother would have done that?" Chuck asked.

"I once saw him push a shopping cart into I-95 during rush hour. He said it would be cool to watch a car crash. Luckily, the drivers were quick enough to swerve around it and not hit each other in the process. The cart rolled over three lanes and hit the guardrail on the opposite shoulder. He told me he would stomp my head in while I slept if I ever squealed to my parents. I didn't think he would, but I was never a hundred percent sure. So yeah, I think he was capable of it. Just like I'm capable of helping you all out now because Mick is a friend and no woman deserves what happened to Margie. Plus, this is one of those lean times. The Melon Heads'll appreciate the help."

"Marnie," Chuck said.

"Yeah, Marnie."

Marnie didn't bother looking up. She was either lost in pain or thoughts, with neither being a happy place.

Dredd ground the cigar out with his boot, slapped his knees and stood up. "Time's about right. Let's get this over with."

★   ★   ★

They all piled into Dredd's truck and headed for some serious off-roading. Dunwoody thumped his feet against the tailgate. Twice, Dredd stopped the truck to threaten him. "He better not dent my truck." The truck was riddled with dents and dings and rust. His promises to beat Dunwoody senseless only quieted the captive man for a minute or so before he started up again. Marnie figured Dunwoody knew he was in for worse than a beating, so why not make a scene? It wasn't as if anyone was going to hear him way out here. She remembered what Mick had said about even the bugs and animals being scared off by the Melon Heads. If Dredd stopped his truck and they sat still for a moment, would there be birdsong in the air? Or crickets chirping? Or even the crunch of deadfall from skittering chipmunks?

They wove around thick-trunked trees bathed in almost total darkness. The thick canopy above was like a dome, keeping the real world out.

And the Melon Heads in.

She curled into herself, the icy touch of a finger slowly running up and down her spine. This was a bad place. You didn't need to know the legend of the Melon Heads to sense that something was very wrong here. If they thought she was going to get out of the truck, they were sadly mistaken.

With his head out of the window, Dredd said, "All that banging around is only sounding the dinner bell, moron. But hey, it's your funeral."

Mick had another beer in his lap, holding on to Dredd's because the wheel kept jumping out of his hands when the truck dipped and swayed. Marnie felt Chuck's body heat. At one point, when Dredd was outside yelling at Dunwoody, Chuck touched the back of her hand as if to say, *We can just get out of here and run.*

She understood he was scared. She was terrified.

But he hadn't been raped. He hadn't had his insides pounded and scrambled by a sloppy, violent drunk. He hadn't had something vital carved out of him, a whittling of his personality and soul and maybe even his future. Maybe he could empathize – he was here, after all, part of their foolhardy, quite possibly dangerous plan – but he could never, would never, fully understand.

The truck's headlights lit upon a wooden structure smack dab in the middle of a clearing that could be no more than fifteen feet around. The decaying trunks of fallen trees draped in thick carpets of moss lay at the circumference of the clearing, almost as if they had been put there intentionally as a kind of wraparound bench. In the center of the rough circle stood the gutted remains of a tree. It was no taller than Chuck. All of its bark had been stripped away. Thick, arthritic-looking branches were tied around the tattered trunk by frayed cord so it looked like it was thrusting out of a crude teepee. There was even a triangular entrance, the threshold jammed by a jumble of something that Marnie couldn't make out.

Dredd hit the brakes and the truck rocked for a moment. "This is it."

Mick, Chuck and Marnie stared at the wooden teepee. It was not a random creation of nature, that was for sure. This time, it was Marnie who took Chuck's hand.

"What the hell is that?" Chuck said.

Even Dredd had taken on a kind of quiet reverence. "That's where they come."

A voice inside Marnie's head began to scream. *"I don't want to do this anymore! Please get out of here! Please, dear god, take me home!"*

Her burst of internal panic made her cringe. The act of cringing elicited a bolt of pain from her core that drowned out that frantic voice.

For a long moment, no one moved or spoke. Even Dunwoody had fallen silent. Looking out the back window, she saw him trying to lift his head up to see where they had stopped, but the ropes binding his legs and arms made it difficult. When his watery eyes lit upon the teepee, he sagged into the bed of the truck.

She listened hard. There was nothing out there. Even the wind refused to wend its way this deep into the forbidden woods.

"They're watching us, aren't they?" she whispered.

Dredd gnawed on the corner of his lower lip. His eyes roamed the surrounding trees. "They've been watching us since the moment we got in the truck."

Mick leaned forward until his forehead touched the windshield. "I don't see them." Marnie could tell he was scared, but he was also curious.

"That's a good thing," Dredd said. He opened his door, hesitating before setting one foot out. He looked all around, took a deep breath, and swung completely out. Mick slid over to Dredd's vacated seat.

"You're not really going out there," Chuck said.

"Like hell I'm not."

Chuck tried to grab his shirt sleeve, but Mick was too quick.

"Just take it slow and stick close to me," Dredd said to him. "They don't know you. They don't like strangers, especially out here."

"I gotcha," Mick said, standing just beside the open door, his eyes as wide as ping-pong balls.

"I'm serious. You do anything stupid and there's nothing I can do to help you." Dredd walked slowly to the back of the truck and opened the tailgate.

"You okay?" Chuck asked.

"Yeah, I guess," Marnie said.

They both knew it was too late to turn back. Part of Marnie wanted this to all be a big joke, like Dredd's pretending he didn't know Mick and threatening to kill them. But the ghost of the parts of her that Dunwoody had forever ruined or taken away hoped to hell everything everyone had ever said about the Melon Heads was true.

"Hey, big guy, help me get this asshole out of the truck. But do it slow as molasses in winter."

Chuck didn't move, his gaze locked on the foreboding teepee. Marnie squeezed his hand. "You don't have to do it. I'll do it. All of this is because of me, anyway."

He shook his head. "No way." He looked at her and she almost didn't recognize him. Chuck had always stood head and shoulders above everyone and carried himself like a benevolent giant, unafraid because there was no one to be afraid of. What she saw now was unadulterated fear. It twisted his features and made him look like a little boy scared of the dark corners inside his closet.

He opened the door, the squeak of the hinge sounding like feedback at a Nirvana concert.

"You stay in here. And don't you ever think you're the cause of this. Whatever happens today, you're never able to blame yourself. Promise me that."

Marnie wanted to cry for more reasons than she could count. "I promise."

Chuck got his wind and stood tall. "Let's get this over with."

He'd only taken three steps out of the car when Dredd hissed, "Slow the fuck down, man."

"I am going slow."

There was real fear in Dredd's eyes. "Then go slower."

Dunwoody thumped his feet against the side of the truck bed. Dredd raised a fist high. "Do that one more time and it'll be the last."

Marnie was on her knees looking out the back window. She caught Dunwoody's tear-filled gaze and felt nothing. Mick swayed from side to side, anxious, she was sure, to see what would come next. He saw her and settled down, giving a simple nod. Chuck walked like he was on the moon, but his large strides had him behind the truck quickly.

"Mick, you take that cord of rope," Dredd said. Mick looped the rope over his shoulder. "All right, you rapist pig, time to meet my friends."

If Dunwoody hadn't been gagged, his scream would have echoed for miles. Marnie saw a fresh wave of sweat break out on his exposed flesh. He squirmed mightily as Dredd, Mick and Chuck reached in to grab hold of him. Chuck wrapped his arms around Dunwoody's legs while Dredd and Mick each took an arm. They carried him over to the eerie trunk and branch-woven teepee. He flailed in their arms like a giant catfish brought to land. This time, Dredd didn't say anything. He just kept looking around worriedly, his jaw set, straining against Dunwoody's protestations. Marnie swiveled in her seat, watching the slow, grim procession. A knifing ripple of pain went from between her legs to her chest. She really did need to see a doctor. Maybe Heidi could take her to one in another town, miles away. How much had Dunwoody ruined her? Would she ever be able to have kids? Did she need surgery? There sure had been plenty of bleeding the past few days. Just thinking that she might never be a mother restarted her rage.. She knew they were here. A couple of times, she thought she caught shadows shifting behind the trees. She'd seen the one before when she was with Mick and Dredd last year. It – she hated thinking of the Melon Head as an it, but she really couldn't tell if it was a man or woman – had been behind Dredd's cabin, collecting a sack of turtledoves he'd shot for them. It had been going on dusk so she couldn't make out any features, but even the meager light was enough for her to notice the outline of a large, bulbous head as it dipped low and then, upon sensing them, darted into the forest clutching its bag of birds.

When she got back home that night, she'd convinced herself that the Melon Head had actually been one of Dredd's friends who'd dressed up to scare them. But the more she thought about it, the more she came to realize Dredd had no friends. That's why he'd stuck himself way out where no one else would dare to go. Well, no one but Mick, who wasn't afraid to take a beating from his stepfather when he was six.

Mick and Chuck were using their body weight to peg Dunwoody against the severed tree in the center of the teepee while Dredd tied him up. Dredd had broken his rule about moving slowly. Sweat dripped from his nose as he worked the ropes. Once Dunwoody was secured, Dredd leaned into Mick and then Chuck, whispering something in their ears. Her friends started to walk backward very slowly, their heads swiveling in every direction. Dredd stood before Dunwoody with his hands on his hips as if admiring his handiwork. He stayed there until Mick and Chuck were back in the truck. They both stunk to high heaven.

"I think he shit himself again," Mick said. He couldn't take his eyes off the teepee.

Chuck's shirt and pants were wet. "And pissed himself. Be glad you had his top half." His eyes were glazed, as if he had a fever.

Dredd shot a look back at the truck. "You ready, Marina?"

Marnie wasn't amused. Was he fucking with her? Was all of this a big joke? The urge to flip him the bird almost overcame her.

Even if this was Dredd's way of amusing himself, the whole experience had literally scared the crap out of Dunwoody. She hoped it left him with some Vietnam-grade PTSD.

Instead of giving Dredd the finger, she raised her thumb like a Roman royal in the Coliseum.

"Feel free to scream your heart out," Dredd said, plucking the gag from Dunwoody's mouth. Dunwoody didn't fail to comply. He let out a pained wail that made Marnie's ears hurt. Dredd ran back to the truck, slammed the door and locked it. "Roll up your window," he said breathlessly to Chuck.

Dunwoody's soiled boxers sagged until they were at his knees. His pathetic, flaccid penis was nearly lost in a nest of graying pubic hair. He screamed for help. He cried for god to save him. At one point, he even said he wanted his mother.

"Pathetic," Marnie mumbled.

The truck roared to life. Dredd had one hand on the gear shift, the other on the wheel. Dunwoody squinted against the harsh glare of the headlights.

"You can't leave now," Mick said, sounding like a little kid that was told he had to come in for dinner while all his friends were still outside playing.

"I'm not," Dredd said irritably. He turned to Mick. "This isn't fun and games, bro. There are rules. If I break 'em, we're as dead as

Dunwoody will be. So shut the fuck up."

"Don't tell me to shut up," Mick retorted.

"I just did. And if you think you're such a hardass, why don't you get out and watch the show up close?"

"Maybe I will."

Dredd unlocked the door. "Well then, get out."

Marnie barely paid attention to their stupidity. Her eyes danced from tree to tree and back to Dunwoody. Despite all his screaming and rocking, the only response was the all-encompassing silent darkness. He was blubbering now, a wilted sack of wasted humanity, the ropes the only thing keeping him up.

"Can you guys just stop it?" Marnie said. She couldn't hear if anything was coming.

Dredd punched Mick in his upper arm just hard enough to make him wince. "You need to fucking chill."

Mick rubbed his arm, but he'd stopped arguing his pointless point.

"You both need to chill," Chuck said. Dredd gave him a dirty look but didn't hold it for long. He was too busy twisting around in his seat so he could look out of all the windows.

"Do you see any?" Marnie asked. Before Dunwoody had been tied up, she swore the Melon Heads were everywhere. If any loud noises or fast movements could draw their ire, Dunwoody should be surrounded by now.

Dredd gripped the wheel. "Nah. Don't you worry, they'll come."

They waited for several interminable minutes. Chuck started to get antsy, rocking in his seat, his thumb lightly tapping on the door lock. Marnie's nerves rode on a knife's edge. Where were the Melon Heads?

Mick said, "See, even the Melon Heads don't want anything to do with a sack of shit like that."

"Be careful what you wish for," Dredd said. "When they come, you'll wish you'd never rolled up to my place. Normally, I just leave game here for them and take off. Considering your situation," he cast a quick glance at Marnie, "I figure it'll give you some measure of satisfaction in seeing this all the way through."

"If they come," Chuck muttered.

Dredd flashed a wicked wolf's grin. "Oh, they'll come."

More time passed. The interior of the truck was bordering on stifling with the windows rolled up. It stunk like bad breath, sweat and Dunwoody's piss and shit. Marnie's stomach rolled.

Dunwoody had gotten quiet. If not for the visible rise and fall of his chest, she would have sworn he'd died. His head hung low, his hair like a curtain of wet spaghetti hiding his face.

A thought occurred to Marnie that had somehow evaded her consideration. Or was it that she had intentionally avoided it in case it made her change her mind?

What would become of Chad if his father never returned? Chad's mother had passed away from breast cancer years ago. Did they put seventeen-year-olds in foster homes? Would there be any kind of inheritance he could use to restart his life? It was doubtful, considering the state of their house. Chad wasn't high on her list of favorite people, but no one deserved to be robbed of their family, even if said family was a shitheel like Harold Dunwoody.

Everything was wrong.

The shadowy Melon Head she'd seen that first time was a trick of the light and part of a dumb prank.

There were, in fact, no Melon Heads out here. That stick teepee was creepy as hell, but that's why it was there. To freak them out.

And finally, they would have to bring Dunwoody back. They'd busted his nose, scared him half to death and made him crap himself. It might not balance the scales, but it would have to do.

"This is ridiculous," she said. Marnie climbed over Chuck's lap and opened the door.

"Don't go out there," Dredd spat. He reached over to grab her arm, but she yanked it away.

"Chuck, help me untie him."

His hesitation to get out of the truck stopped her from running to Dunwoody. A lone leaf twirled down from its lofty perch and stuck in her hair. "Chuck!"

"Yeah, yeah."

Chuck unfolded himself out of the truck. Mick was right behind him. "Don't untie him, man."

"Enough of this shit," Chuck said. "We're probably going to jail for this, Mick. Enough already. Maybe if we let him go now, they'll take it easier on us."

Mick tried to spin him around, but his fingers weren't up to the task of changing Chuck's course. "That's why we need to leave him. Let the Melon Heads finish him off. We can't go to jail if he's never found."

Now Chuck turned around, lowering his head so they were eye to eye. "You see any Melon Heads?" His beefy arm swept around the clearing.

Mick folded his arms across his chest. "No. We need to give them more time."

The truck door slammed shut behind them. They watched Dredd palm the lock shut. He smiled at them and waved bye-bye.

"Dude, what the hell?" Mick said.

Another stabbing pain hit Marnie's lower abdomen. "Guys, please."

Chuck rushed ahead of her. "I got it. Mick, toss me your knife."

"No way."

With a grunt of disgust, Chuck got behind an unconscious Dunwoody and began grappling with the knots.

The pain rocketed from a mild hurt to unbearable with breakneck speed. Marnie's head spun. She felt warmth between her legs and knew it wasn't pee. Chuck and Dunwoody's images slid sideways for a moment and she was sure she was going to pass out.

She reached out for something to hold on to, her fingers grasping air. She heard Mick pulling on the door handle and cursing at Dredd, but he sounded very far off. Had Dredd pulled away, heading back for his cabin? Or was her consciousness dragging her away?

She thought she said, "Help," but couldn't be sure.

She looked to Chuck. He would help her.

A ball of white light emerged from the forest to Chuck's right. What was that doing there? Was it a flashlight? Had someone else heard Dunwoody's screaming? Was it the cops?

Another white orb formed to Chuck's left.

Marnie dropped to one knee, peering at the lights. Chuck still worked at the knots. He hadn't seen them, if they were even there. They may have just been neural explosions signaling an imminent shutdown.

More and more lights appeared.

But no.

They weren't lights.

They were shapes illuminated by Dredd's headlights.

The closer they came, the bigger they got, some much larger than the others, the shapes not quite round or even oval.

Those shapes were heads. Large, misshapen heads.

And they were heading straight for Chuck.

CHAPTER NINE

Jesus Christ, what were we thinking? We are so fucked. Is this guy even alive?

Dunwoody's sagging weight made untying the knots nearly impossible. Chuck was all sausage fingers, tugging uselessly at the top knot that secured Dunwoody's torso to the tall stump. One of the branches kept stabbing Chuck's back whenever he moved. He was pretty sure it had broken the skin, judging by the faint wetness he felt sliding down his back. It didn't matter. Nothing mattered at this point except untying Dunwoody. Chuck could then spend his time waiting for his future to collapse before his eyes.

What he needed was a knife. Mick always had some kind of knife on him. Where was he?

Chuck leaned around Dunwoody and saw Mick trying to get back in the truck, arguing once again with Dredd.

"Mick! Get the hell over here and stop fucking around. I need your knife. Now!"

A tired groan escaped Dunwoody's lips. At least he was still alive. Maybe the trauma would cause some kind of amnesia. Once they got him back home, they'd plop him on his couch and the rapist would wake up in the morning none the wiser about why his nose was broken and how he had come to be covered in his own waste.

No, they were not going to be that lucky. That was the kind of crap that only happened in soap operas like *The Young and the Restless* that his mother watched religiously every day at twelve thirty. Amnesia was as common as a cold or barking your shin against the furniture on soap operas.

What had happened today was a total shit show, and amnesia would not be on the menu for the final act.

"Mick!"

That's when his gaze lit upon Marnie. She was pointing at something behind him, her eyes practically bulging out of their sockets. Her mouth was covered by one quivering hand.

"What is it? Marnie, what's wrong?"

She wouldn't answer him. Dredd put the truck in drive and was starting to make a three-point turn.

Chuck stopped worrying at the knot. He turned around.

The scream couldn't pass the lump in his throat.

People were coming out of the woods, slowly making their way to the makeshift teepee. As the truck turned, the headlights swept over at least a dozen of them.

They were hideous.

In that brief glimpse, Chuck saw deathly pale faces, some with eyes spaced too far apart, others pinched close together, slack-jawed mouths with more gums than teeth, the bone structure of the faces and heads looking as if they'd suffered some kind of tectonic upheaval. Sprigs of ratty hair hung limply from their heads. They wore patchwork clothes that looked like they had come fresh off the assembly line in Mexico around the time Nixon was resigning. Their arms were stretched out, hands grasping, making them look like a swarm of hungry sleepwalkers. Eeriest of all was how little sound they made. If he hadn't seen Marnie pointing, he never would have known they were coming.

Goddammit, they were real! The Melon Heads were real!

But what people had neglected to mention in their tales of the offshoot of humanity living in the woods was their sheer numbers. An entire village was descending on the teepee.

Chuck spun around to see if any were close enough to grab him. The nearest was maybe fifteen feet away, though with the truck now facing away from him, he'd lost most of the light to see them. He tried frantically to loosen the knot again. "Mick! Your knife!"

Mick was now pounding on the side of the truck with his fist. Chuck wasn't sure he noticed the Melon Heads.

Even if this knot somehow miraculously came loose, there were still four others to untie. Chuck flicked a glance to either side. They were coming closer. Now he could hear them; the shuffling of their feet through the crackly foliage and worst of all, the smacking of their lips. It made his skin crawl. They really were coming to eat Dunwoody. And if Chuck didn't haul ass, he was next.

Marnie finally broke her silence, shouting, "Run!"

Something hard as steel dug into Chuck's shoulder. He was spun around as if he were made of cotton candy.

When Chuck stopped, he was looking down at a woefully deformed person. Their sex was unfathomable because the face was unlike anything he'd ever seen before, the loose clothes revealing no clues. It opened its mouth wide and the stench that emanated from that maw made Chuck's eyes water. It grasped his arms to hold him in place, reared its head back and slammed its face into his chest. His flesh was pinched hard enough to elicit a sharp and terrified yelp.. His only saving grace was that this Melon Head had no teeth. That didn't stop it from suckling at him through his shirt, its hard jaws locked on him like a vise.

The teepee sticks crackled as Melon Head bodies pressed against it. Dear god, they were surrounding him.

Chuck flexed his arms, loosening the Melon Head's grip. He took two big strides, the Melon Head still latched onto his chest like an enormous sucker fish. More hands shot out and tried to grab hold of his arms, his hair, his legs. He looked down for a moment and saw a child Melon Head with bulbous protrusions on each side of its skull lying flat on the ground, grasping for his ankle while moving like an inchworm, its back rising and falling, gaining ground on him. Even though it was small and young, he kicked at it, connecting with its lower jaw. The Melon Head didn't make a sound. It rolled away, clutching the lower half of its face. Chuck grabbed the Melon Head stuck to his chest by the sides of its head. It gave out a tiny shriek and mercifully released its mouth hold on him. He tossed the Melon Head aside. It landed on its back and was up on its feet quicker than a cat. It even made a kind of hissing noise at him, its lips and gums red and raw and just plain horrid.

A branch cracked overhead. Chuck jerked his head up and saw they were scaling their way down the trees. They'd been above them the entire time, watching, waiting for their moment to attack.

The gap between him and Marnie quickly filled in with slobbering Melon Heads. So many of them had twisted bodies, hunchbacks, one shoulder dipping low enough to make their frames resemble the Leaning Tower of Pisa. Chuck had a considerable height advantage over even the tallest Melon Head. He saw over them easily. Marnie looked as if she didn't know whether to help him or run.

"Get to the truck!" he shouted.

With fat tears running down her cheeks, she took one last look at him and ran. The truck was pointed at the path leading far away from this terrible place. Mick had darted in front of the truck, preventing Dredd from leaving...at least for the moment.

A Melon Head tried to take Chuck down from behind. It impotently rolled off him and was swiftly replaced by another. The ones in front went for his arms again. Chuck side-stepped their advance, hip checking a Melon Head in his way, sending it sprawling in the moldy leaves. Another lashed out at him, connecting with his side. It felt like getting hit by a brick. They may have looked weak and broken, but they were strong as hell.

Marnie dashed toward the truck. Dredd revved the engine. Was he going to run Mick over? Chuck ran through the Melon Heads the way Mark Bavaro on the Giants plowed through defensemen. Fingers hooked into the back of Chuck's belt. He kept his legs moving; the added weight slowed him down but did not stop him. Marnie had made it to Dredd's door and was slapping her hand on the window, screaming at him to stop and let them in.

A Melon Head dropped from the sky and landed in front of Chuck. This was most certainly a male, as he was completely naked, his flaccid penis stuck to his inner thigh by grime and who knew what other dried fluids. Chuck punched the Melon Head in the throat, staggering it. The Melon Head kept on his feet, one hand on his throat, the other lashing out for Chuck. It got him by the collar, pulled its legs up and started swinging like a pendulum. Having one in front and one in back was more than Chuck could carry. He began to waver, weaving from side to side and front to back. He wasn't going to make it to the truck. The others were right behind him.

"Mick!"

Mick spun to face him. "Marnie, come here!" Marnie took his place in front of the truck. He'd gone paler than milk. He ran to Chuck, extracting his switchblade from the back pocket of his jeans.

It was like running through wet cement. The Melon Heads knew enough to go slack, hoping to drag him completely down so the others could pile onto him. Chuck had thought it sad and ridiculous earlier when Dunwoody had cried out for his mother. He didn't think that anymore. He and his mother hadn't been on the best of terms lately, but he would give anything in the world to have her here at this moment. She would save him. She always had.

"Fucking freak," Mick blurted, awkwardly ramming into the Melon Head that had Chuck's collar. When he pulled away, there was a fresh, red crater in the Melon Head's back. A steady stream of blood poured out of the hole. The Melon Head released its grip, trying in vain to touch the wound near the center of its back. When the one stuck to Chuck's belt saw what had happened, it let go too, scampering to its wounded comrade.

Mick looked down at them, admiring his work. "I just stabbed a real live Melon Head."

"Let's go," Chuck said, feeling hundreds of pounds lighter. He hooked his arm through Mick's and practically dragged him to the truck. The other Melon Heads stopped once they reached their fallen brother.

Mick scrambled into the truck bed. Chuck called over to Marnie, "Back here!"

She skirted around the truck. For some reason, Dredd didn't lay down rubber and peel away. Chuck helped her into the truck. A wincing pain in his chest made him hiss. It felt like he had the world's worst hickey. He dreaded seeing the damage the sucker-Melon Head had wrought upon his skin. He got into the truck and pounded on the roof. "Get us the hell out of here."

Only Dredd didn't move so much as an inch.

The Melon Heads gathered around the wounded one. In the dark, Chuck couldn't see their eyes, but he could feel the hate and hurt just the same. Several more dropped from their hidden branches.

"What are you waiting for?" Mick shouted, hitting the back window with the end of his switchblade.

Leaning over the side of the truck, Chuck was able to see Dredd staring out the window at the cluster of Melon Heads. He looked like death warmed over twice. His mouth hung open in stunned silence.

An instant later, the Melon Heads belted a chorus of wailing that set his teeth on edge. It sounded like every instrument in an orchestra being played out of tune. Marnie grabbed his arm and dug her fingers in deep. A faction of the Melon Heads tore away from the group, loping toward Dunwoody, who had remained out of it the entire time. The moment they bit into his flesh, he came instantly awake with his own matching shriek. As one, the Melon Heads changed their caterwauling to match Dunwoody's tone.

Chuck felt as if he were going to be sick. Even through the shadows, he was able to watch them pull Dunwoody's arms off. Wet ropes of gore hung from the stumps. Still Dunwoody cried, and still the Melon Heads matched his lamentations.

"I think you killed him," Dredd said. He'd rolled the window down halfway and pointed at the Melon Head Mick had stabbed. The truck pulled away from the gruesome scene. "Now we're all gonna die."

CHAPTER TEN

Heidi heard the chugging of Chuck's car roll up her driveway. She was sitting in the backyard with Vent, sharing a warm bottle of Miller beer. Earlier, the two of them had watched *Witchboard*. Vent drooled over Tawny Kitaen while Heidi did a little bit of ogling of Stephen Nichols, the guy who played Patch on *Days of Our Lives*. Her mother was in one of her good moods today, going so far as to pop them popcorn before the movie had started. Normally, Heidi would have loved a movie about Ouija boards, but she couldn't get into it. Not when she was filled with so much worry. At eight o'clock, her parents gave them the boot so they could watch their shows. Soon canned laughter emanated from the living room. It was now well past dusk, and each passing moment had been cranking her anxiety up another intolerable notch. The beer bottle slipped from her hand when she tried to hand it to Vent. "They're back!"

Both lawn chairs tipped over as they scooted to the front of the house. She was glad that Vent had stayed with her. He was one of the few people she could just be quiet around and not feel weird. Even with Marnie she felt she had to fill any pauses with conversation, no matter how inane. He'd eaten dinner with her family and did most of the talking so her parents wouldn't keep asking her if anything was wrong. To her, Vent had always been the living equivalent of a warm blanket. He was always there when you needed him, was comforting in his stillness, and didn't cause a ruckus.

Chuck was already out of the car, reaching inside to help Marnie. Mick sat in the front passenger seat tugging at his hair, lost in thought. He didn't even look up when Heidi and Vent came to the front of the car.

"What happened?" she asked.

Chuck's lips were drawn in a grim line. He looked frazzled and upset. As Heidi got closer to Marnie, she nearly gasped. Her friend looked like she was terminally ill, her skin paler than the moon, her eyes bloodshot with dark circles under them. Even her hair looked sick, every end suddenly split and limp.

Vent put a hand on Chuck's shoulder. "Dude, did you get Dunwoody?"

Chuck nodded, his eyes downcast. "Yeah, we picked him up at his house."

Heidi slipped her arm around Marnie's waist and held her close. Marnie hissed when Heidi squeezed too hard. She felt so fragile, like an old Christmas ornament. She had a million questions she wanted to ask, but Marnie's body language screamed that she wasn't well enough to handle an interrogation.

"Where is he now?" Vent pressed, casting a wary eye at a sullen Mick. "Did you scare the crap out of him? Do you think he'll keep his mouth shut?"

Chuck closed the car door and leaned against it, taking a moment to stare at the night sky. "He's dead."

Heidi's heart fluttered. "Wait. What? Did he have like a heart attack or something?" She never believed that Mick had the inside scoop to the Melon Head feeding ground. But she was all in for Mick and Chuck putting the fear of god in Harold Dunwoody. Sure, Mick and more than likely Marnie wanted to see him dead, but Heidi never thought it would go that far.

"They ripped him apart," Marnie said, the words tumbling from her lips and down her body.

"Who ripped him apart?"

The other car door opened, the hinges protesting so loud they echoed down the deserted street. "Who do you think?" Mick said.

Heidi and Vent looked at one another. Vent said, "I don't know. Was it you? What did you do?"

Of course it was Mick. Heidi would never categorize him as a killer, but he had been known to take things too far. And ever since his mother and stepfather had abandoned him, leaving him out in the woods in that rotting trailer, he'd been acting stranger than usual, as if any controls and filters were off for good.

"It wasn't Mick," Chuck said. "It was *them*."

Vent laughed and cut it short. "What, the Melon Heads? Yeah, right."

"It's true," Marnie said. "We...we tied him to this kind of stake. It looked like a teepee or part of some sacrificial altar. They came for him. There were...so many of them. They almost got Chuck, and then they turned to Dunwoody and, and...." She broke into heaving sobs. Heidi pulled her head onto her chest and stroked her hair.

This couldn't be right. The Melon Heads were just a scary story to tell little kids.

Chuck and Mick gazed at Marnie. They looked like they'd seen something far worse than a ghost. They liked to kid around, but this was no joke.

"No way, man," Vent said. "That can't be true."

"I don't give a shit if you believe me," Mick said.

"I wish it wasn't," Chuck said. "I wish we'd never gone to Dunwoody's house."

Did Heidi see a tear in the corner of his eye? Marnie's crying started to subside. They really had seen the Melon Heads. And the Melon Heads really had murdered Harold Dunwoody. Heidi swooned from the information overload. She shuffled closer to the car, Marnie sluggishly moving with her, so it could hold them both up.

"What were they like?" she asked.

"Exactly like they say," Mick replied. "Only there was a lot of them. And they're vicious. Like animals."

"And strong," Chuck said. "One of them tried to bite me, but he had no teeth. This is what his gums did to me." He lifted his shirt to show them the angry red-and-purple circle on his chest. It looked like he'd gotten stuck on an industrial vacuum. His arms were covered in bruises the shape and size of fingerprints. "Or maybe it was a she. It was hard to tell." He took a deep, tremulous breath, pulled his shirt back down and wandered off, heading toward the street.

"Chuck," Vent called after him.

Mick said, "Let him go. He needs some time. Shit, we all do."

Heidi pushed the hair out of Marnie's face, a face that no longer resembled her shining, pretty friend. "Are you all right? Did they try to hurt you?"

Marnie sniffled. "They didn't get close enough to me. Dredd wanted to leave us there. If he had, we'd be just like Dunwoody."

"Dredd. Who's Dredd?" Vent asked. He scratched behind his right ear. It was a nervous tic he'd had ever since grade school.

"Don't worry about it," Mick said. "We can talk about it all later. Right now, I'm just fucking tired."

"You can stay at my house tonight," Heidi said to Marnie. She didn't need to add that she would have to sneak her up later after her parents went to bed at ten. They weren't fans of Marnie to begin with. Seeing her in such a physical and mental state would send them over the edge.

Marnie nodded against her chest.

"If you want, you can crash at my place," Vent said to Mick.

"I'll be fine back at mine," Mick said.

"No, you won't," Marnie said.

Heidi's confusion grew. "Why wouldn't he?"

"Because he killed one of them. At least we think he did. He was trying to save Chuck. Dredd kept talking about the rules, how we'd broken the worst of them all. He said the Melon Heads would find us."

"You freaking killed a Melon Head?" Vent said breathlessly.

"I stabbed him. I don't think I killed him, though." Mick's bravado faded for a moment, the realization that he'd driven a knife into another living being, even if it was a Melon Head, unmooring him.

"You live in the woods, man," Vent said. "You don't think it'll be easy for them to get at you?"

"I don't live in *their* woods."

"Big deal. Woods are woods. They could come up on you and wipe you out with no one being close enough to hear. Stop being stupid. You're staying with me."

"I said I'll be fine."

Only he didn't sound fine.

"Just stay with Vent," Heidi said. "Please. Even if only to make us feel better."

Mick toed the sidewall of Chuck's tire. "Fine, if you're all going to be little bitches about it."

"Yes, we're going to be little bitches about it," Marnie said. She pressed herself into Heidi. "I need about ten aspirin, a beer and two days of sleep."

"I can get your aspirin. Don't think I can swipe another beer out of the fridge, though," Heidi said. She watched Chuck make his way back to them. He walked and looked like someone who had just had a brush with death. It reminded her of this new report where a plane had crashed in Nigeria. Some had made it out of the plane before it was engulfed in flames. They did the same kind of zombie walk as Chuck when they were filmed shuffling into the terminal surrounded by police and medics.

"I'm going home," Chuck said.

"Can you drop us off at my place?" Vent asked.

Chuck nodded. He flicked the car antenna over and over, the dull twang grating on Heidi's nerves. She didn't tell him that, though. After what he'd been through, he could do anything he wanted.

"What are we gonna do?" Heidi asked before their group drifted apart.

The boys looked to one another, but no one had an answer.

"We're going to hope that Dredd is full of shit," Marnie said. There was a dry click in her throat when she swallowed. "Though from everything he's said and shown us so far, we shouldn't bet our lives on it."

CHAPTER ELEVEN

Chuck woke to birdsong outside his window. It was an hour before his alarm was set to go off. He rolled onto his side, and the motion made it feel like sludge water was rolling in his skull. The headache hit him hard and he closed his eyes against the slats of light stabbing through his blinds.

Images of what had happened the day before flooded his brain, only making the pain worse. Dammit. For a moment there, he'd held on to the hope that it was all just a terrible nightmare, a twisted dream brought on by Mick's dope that never gave a consistent high.

It had happened, all right. None of it made any sense, but there was no denying he had seen what he had seen, had felt the iron grip of the Melon Heads, had heard their awful cries and Dunwoody's soul-shattering shrieks of agony.

Dredd hadn't spoken much on the ride back to his cabin. He just kept repeating that they were up shit creek. Rules were in place for a reason and by keeping to those rules, there had been peace for as long as anyone could remember. Mick had fucked it all up. They all had. Dredd wished he'd shot them when they'd showed up at his place.

Chuck had wanted to tell him that they had not put a gun to his head, that he had willfully taken them to the Melon Heads. If there was anyone to blame, it was Dunwoody, and he was beyond caring now.

An even bigger question was bothering him. Why, if the Melon Heads had killed Dredd's brother, had he willfully been the one to be the caretaker of their rules and secrets? If anything, he should be the one exposing them, getting revenge for what they did to his family.

Now there was Dredd's threat that the Melon Heads would find them.

Had there ever been stories about the Melon Heads venturing past Dracula Drive? There was no point in going to the library. He highly doubted there would be credible reference books dedicated to the subject. Hell, there wouldn't even be trashy reads about the Melon Heads. He could ask around, but he doubted he'd get much more than eye rolls, laughter or, if he was lucky, a tall tale or two.

If the rules had been kept (and who the hell created the rules?) there would not have been a reason for the Melon Heads to leave their sanctum. If there were rules, there had to be an origin story, like in comic books. Were any of the legends true, or were they the product of something else? Maybe knowing how they had come to be would help him figure out how to deal with them now.

He tossed the covers aside, still tired and feeling like a dog's chew toy, yet unable to stop the buzzing in his brain. Not the least of his concerns was what if someone had seen them take Dunwoody from his home? Milbury wasn't a sprawling metropolis. Most people knew who he was, especially considering his size. He remembered adults calling him Baby Huey, the overgrown duckling from the cartoons, when he'd been younger. The police could come knocking on his door any minute. What would he say to them? The truth? They would just think he was a liar. Who wouldn't? "Where did you take Harold Dunwoody?" they would ask over and over, trying to break him. Mick would tell them nothing. If anything, a prison cell was a step up from his current living conditions. At least it was a warm place to stay with steady meals and people looking out for him. His distrust of authority would only lead to an improvement in his situation.

If they picked up Marnie, it would all be over. One look at her and they would know something bad had gone down. She'd be taken to the hospital, where she rightly belonged, and the telltale signs of sexual assault would be written large on and inside her body. Chuck and Mick had helped her get revenge on Dunwoody, clear and simple. Heidi and Vent would be called in for questioning, because why stop at three of the five stoners?

Chuck pulled on a Smashing Pumpkins T-shirt, the smiling young girls from their *Siamese Dreams* album in direct contrast to the darkness in his turbulent soul. The Melon Head bite – more like a nuclear gum pinch – hurt like a mother. Chuck patted the hickey-like wound and winced. He needed a smoke to calm down, but he was tapped. It was too early to go to Vent's house. It was too early to do just about anything but worry.

No, he could get in his car and visit Dredd. Only he could answer Chuck's questions. Maybe after a night of sleep, he'd be more forthcoming. He looked just as frightened as they had felt. They all needed some time for their nerves to calm down.

It was no easy feat sneaking down the creaky stairs and out the squeaky front door. Chuck was anything but light on his feet, and the old house had the bones of an octogenarian. He put his car in neutral, rolled down the drive, and turned left into the natural decline of the street. Only when he was two houses away did he fire up the jalopy.

The interior of the car still smelled like all of the bad things that had poured out of Dunwoody. Chuck had to roll the windows down, and pulled to the curb so he could get at the back windows. The ride to Dredd's was very different this time around. He remembered how to get there, crossing onto Dracula Drive and easily finding the hidden drive, which wasn't as hidden as it had been a day ago. The brush had been kept aside, allowing easier access. This was not a good sign.

The cabin was dark, the shade pulled down over the lone window facing him.

Chuck stepped out of the car and felt a chill. It was so much colder under the thick canopy. And damp. He was reluctant to step onto the porch. Dredd was slightly, if not entirely, mad. What other way could a man who guarded the Melon Heads possibly be? *Shithouse nuts*, is what his grandfather would have called him. He had weapons. Odds were at fifty-fifty whether he'd shoot Chuck the second he knocked on his door.

It might be a mercy kill.

The thought made Chuck sick to his stomach. That this might be his last quiet moment before his life turned to shit…or was taken from him.

He stood to the side of the door, heart racing, reached over and knocked three times, waiting for buckshot to come flying through the wood. When there was no answer, he knocked again, only harder. His body was beyond tense. He felt as if his bones had been dipped in adamantium, like Wolverine. His lungs hurt and he realized he'd been holding his breath.

"Hey, Dredd, it's Chuck," he said, rapping his knuckles on the door.

Silence.

He couldn't see through the window. The shade didn't have so much as a centimeter gap. Dredd could be there right now, inches away, waiting for Chuck to give up and go home.

There was no chance of that.

Chuck walked to the back of the cabin, eyeing the stumps they'd sat on a little over twelve hours ago, hatching their plan to take Dunwoody to the Melon Heads. Chuck never wished harder that he'd had a time machine. If only....

The first thing he noticed was that Dredd's truck was gone.

And the back door was wide open.

His mouth went dry. He became aware of the utter stillness of the forest. Not so much as a crunchy leaf skittered along the ground.

He peered into the dark interior of the cabin.

"Hello. Dredd, are you in there?"

Of course he wasn't. He'd gotten in his truck and headed for safer ground, wherever that was. But why had he left the cabin wide open like this?

Reaching inside, he fumbled for a light switch. No, there wouldn't be one because electrical lines didn't run out this way. What he did find was a hurricane lamp hanging from a nail beside the doorway. A box of matches was on a small plastic table outside. Chuck had a hard time getting a match to light, the wooden sticks breaking in half in his thick, clumsy fingers, the damp heads reluctant to spark. He almost whooped for joy when one finally lit. He lifted the glass and touched the flame to the wick. The smell of burning kerosene was instantly nauseating.

The floorboards cracked under his foot as he stepped inside.

"Hello?"

He brought the lamp forward. The dim light couldn't reach the distant corners of the room, but it illuminated enough to send a shock down his spine.

The cabin was in complete shambles. This wasn't the kind of mess a person makes when they're in a rush to pack and leave. Everything had been turned over and broken. Stuffing spilled from Dredd's mattress. It had been thrown off the bed frame, landing upright in the makeshift kitchen, leaning against the leg of a table that had been flipped over as well. Clothes had been ripped to shreds, firewood scattered about, cans of food dented and pried open, their contents drying on the floor. A bag of flour had been used to paint the ceiling white. Shards of glass glittered under the lamplight. Newspapers and magazines were everywhere, like confetti. Chuck saw several torn covers of Judge Dredd comic books, imports from Ireland that sold for twenty-five pence.

That makes sense now, he thought.

What shook Chuck even more, once he got over what he was seeing, was the redolent stench of shit. Piles of excrement were everywhere, some of them watery and peppered with what looked like lumps of berries. He had to back out of the cabin and tuck his nose under his shirt to keep from gagging. His own unwashed body was nothing to write home about, but it was akin to the fresh scent of a summer breeze compared to the compounded waste in Dredd's cabin.

Had Dredd gotten out before his place was trashed? Yes, his truck was gone, but could the Melon Heads figure out how to drive, if only for a short distance?

He stumbled into the yard. There was Mick's crushed beer can from yesterday.

"Dredd!"

Nothing answered him back, not even the chirp of a cricket.

He was suddenly very aware of being utterly alone.

Or was he?

Hadn't Mick said that the silence of the woods was a sure sign that the Melon Heads were near? They had certainly been here. Dredd wouldn't do this to his own cabin.

He had to get the hell out of here. The feeling that he was being watched bowled him over. Something moved in the bushes behind him. He dropped the hurricane lamp. The flame sputtered out. No matter. He didn't need it anymore.

Chuck hurried away from the yard, his hand running along the side of the cabin as he headed for his car. He kept taking worried glances behind him, waiting for the Melon Heads to attack as they had by the teepee. Once he saw his car, he started running.

The sound of breaking glass stopped him.

He spun around, his heart inching up his throat.

"Who's there?"

It was the stupidest thing he could say, but his brain was wrapped in a panicked fog.

He heard crackling, like someone was breaking twigs.

Chuck slowly walked backward to his car. Something told him not to take his eyes off the cabin, not to turn his back on where the Melon Heads' attack would originate.

A curl of black smoke licked over the roof. More smoke billowed upward.

They'd set the cabin on fire.

His feet grew three sizes and went numb. They crossed over each other and he fell.

I have to get out of here! I have to get out of here!

With an agility he rarely displayed, Chuck turned over, got on his hands and knees, jumped up and sprinted the final ten feet to the car. He slammed the door shut and keyed the ignition, pumping the gas pedal. The engine coughed but wouldn't turn over.

He slammed his elbow on the lock, and then realized all of the windows were open. With one hand cranking the starter, he rolled up the window on his side. It was a very small measure of the illusion of safety, but it was all he had at the moment.

A rock the size of a man's head dropped from the trees, slamming the hood of his car. It made a big dent, settling into it like a meteorite.

"What the hell?" He cast his eyes onto the fabric-covered roof of the car as what sounded like hail pounded from above. A rock pinged against the back window. A spiderweb of cracks spread out from the epicenter of the impact.

Chuck forced himself to stop hitting the gas. If he flooded the engine, he was as good as dead. A stick came whooshing out of the shadows, spinning end over end until it clanged against the car's front grille. He thought he heard the crack of plastic. More sticks and stones rained down on his car. He couldn't see who was throwing them, but his memory of their attack last night filled in the gaps.

Letting out a roar of both fear and agitation, Chuck twisted the key one more time. The engine belched and roared. He shifted into reverse, hit the gas, and barreled down the narrow drive. The rocks followed his exit. One of them sailed through the open passenger window and hit him in the temple. The pain didn't register. He was only fixated on one thing: getting back to Dracula Drive.

The car bounced as it hit the lip of the decrepit road. Chuck jerked the wheel. The front of the car swung in a hard forty-five-degree turn, the frame rocking on its old shocks. His window shattered. Chuck slammed into drive and pinned the gas pedal to the floor. The back tires kicked up a whirlwind of dust and pebbles. The trees on either side of Dracula Drive whizzed by. Chuck kept his eyes forward, his chest almost touching the wheel, as he raced home.

Rocks and sticks quickly stopped coming his way, but in his head, he could still hear them bashing the steel and glass. Before he turned off Dracula Drive, he cast a quick glance in his rearview mirror.

Were they following him, sticking to the shadows?

How long would it be before they found him and burned down *his* house?

He had to warn the others.

CHAPTER TWELVE

On a normal night, Mick wouldn't have been able to sleep. He could forget about even trying now. The thick blanket draped over a sliver of the floor in Vent's room provided little comfort. Dawn was just beginning to touch down. Mick lay on his back with his hands behind his head, replaying over and over what had happened out in the woods. He tried to carefully reconstruct every single moment from when they'd pulled up by the stick teepee.

A shiver ran through him every time he conjured up the images of the wild Melon Heads. Sure, he'd kind of seen one before with Dredd, but this was something out of a horror movie. It was like *The Hills Have Eyes* with those crazy post-nuke oddballs, but way, way worse. In the movie, some of the cannibals were scarier than the others, but you could still get a sense of their humanity. Not so with the Melon Heads.

Was that what happened when you were cut adrift from people? Or had they always been that way, only made worse by generations of inbreeding?

They scared the living daylights out of him. And they also held his fascination in an iron grip. He couldn't stop thinking about them, no matter how repulsed he was by even the recollection of their faces.

"Fucking zombies on speed," he whispered. Vent snored in the bed. They'd spent a couple of hours talking before Vent went all lights out. For a dude who only had to sit around with Heidi all night, he was weirdly worn out.

Mick, on the other hand, was amped. The adrenaline jolt had yet to wear off. He desperately wanted to go back to his shit-heap trailer, yet he was also terrified of what he'd find there. Or that they'd find him. Part of him thought, or maybe it was just a bit of lunatic fantasy, that the Melon Heads would leave him alone. That he could somehow communicate with them, much like Dredd must have, that he was on their side. Maybe he could even take Dredd's place. Dredd's cabin was no prize, but it was a hell of a lot better than Mick's Airstream.

He had to talk to Dredd. The guy was pretty pissed last night – or maybe he was just wigged out. Either way, Mick could talk him down. *There goes my supply of killer weed*, he thought at the exact same moment Vent let out a room-quaking fart in his sleep.

Man, what the Melon Heads did to Dunwoody was insane. He'd caught glimpses of them going at the piece of garbage. It was hard to see with all their bodies crowded around him and the low light, but the sounds of his limbs being ripped free, and his screams would live with Mick forever.

Mick looked deep within himself for any sign of regret. So far, he couldn't find a single shred. Any time it might have taken hold, he thought of Marnie's face and the way she kept clutching her stomach and it simply fell away. Harold Dunwoody got what was coming to him. It saved the police and the courts a whole lot of trouble and money. Most of all, it saved Marnie from public embarrassment. It was like feeding criminals to the lions. The Romans were looked at as this incredible, advanced civilization, and they did shit like this all the time. It was a sport that people brought their kids to, for crying out loud. So no, Mick wasn't going to feel sorry for what they did.

Okay, maybe stabbing that Melon Head crossed a line. If he hadn't, Chuck might be right alongside Dunwoody, and that wasn't an option. Dredd said he'd broken a rule. On the other hand, the Melon Heads needed someone to help them, especially in times of trouble. How many of them had feasted, or were still feasting, on Dunwoody? There was a chance Mick could redeem his trespass. He could show them that he was there to help. There were plenty of other wastes of space living in Milbury; wife beaters, child abusers, crooks who lived large by taking advantage of those less fortunate. Maybe he could scoop one of them up and bring them out to the woods. Let the Melon Heads see he was their new benefactor.

Brian Goodman was a prime candidate. Everyone knew he beat his wife and his kids. He cheated on his wife on a regular basis, mostly sticking it into bar whores for barely enough money to buy a pitcher of beer. Mick had even seen him take a piss on a stray dog outside of Kieran's Pub, laughing like a hyena with his needle dick pinched between his fingers.

Yeah, no one would miss Goodman, except maybe the people he owed money to. And the bartenders. Mick would bet good money his own mother wouldn't give a frog's fat ass if he dropped off the face of the earth.

Too excited to lie around, Mick got up and slipped out of Vent's window.

There was too much work to do. He couldn't wait to get started.

* * *

Marnie woke up to Heidi nudging her shoulder. For a brief, blessed moment, she was pain free. Once she opened her eyes and became aware of her surroundings, it all ended. Her stomach felt like it was on fire.

"You want something to eat?" Heidi whispered. Marnie had slept next to Heidi, clinging to the edge of the bed, both to give her friend space and because she needed to crush the edge of the mattress with her hands every time a fresh wave of agony hit. She tried to roll over to face Heidi. The effort wasn't worth the pain.

"I don't think I'll ever eat again," she said into the pillow.

"When's the last time you ate anything?"

"I don't know."

"You need to get your strength back. At least let me bring you up some toast."

Marnie's hand found its way down to her lower abdomen where the worst of it all blossomed like a mushroom cloud. "You don't understand. I couldn't eat if I wanted to. Everything feels full...and strange. I don't know how to describe it."

The echo of Harold Dunwoody's pained screams had haunted her all night. She thought it wouldn't bother her, but it did. Sleep came in fits and starts and was filled with nightmares she thankfully couldn't remember.

Heidi pressed the back of her hand to Marnie's forehead. "I thought so. You have a fever. Sleeping next to you was like falling asleep by a fire. I'll get you some aspirin."

Marnie had to pee. She slipped out from under the covers, pulling the sheet back. Standing on wobbly legs, she glanced down at the bed, saw a circle of blood on the bottom sheet. It surely had soaked right through to the mattress.

Heidi came back with a glass of water and two aspirin. "Oh my god."

"I'm sorry," Marnie said, her eyes filling with tears.

Heidi put the water and pills down and covered up the stain. "I don't care about that. I'm worried about you."

"It's been happening a lot. I should have slept on a towel or something."

"What you should do is see a doctor."

"I can't."

"You have to. This is no joke." Heidi swept the aspirin into the old Strawberry Cupcake trash can that had been beside her bed since she was six. "Forget those. They make bleeding worse. I'll get you Tylenol. We're going to have to take you to a doctor this morning."

Marnie hissed as a wave of agony bent her over. It passed quickly, but it had wiped out the urgency of relieving herself. She was a mess and she knew it. The question was, which was worse: her body or her mind?

"Not here," she said with one hand on the night table. "Maybe New Haven. Someplace where no one will find out."

Heidi took her by the shoulders and helped her right herself. "Fine. Anywhere you want to go. We need someone to make you better."

As Heidi led Marnie to the bathroom to clean up, Marnie thought there wasn't a doctor in the world that would ever make her better. Not after waiting too long to see the damage Dunwoody had wrought, and especially not after the horror of last night.

Not ever.

CHAPTER THIRTEEN

Chuck called Vent from a pay phone outside Merck Chemists. The town was just beginning to come alive, blue-collar workers heading to George's for bacon, egg and cheese sandwiches, the newspaper, and collecting on their bets from last night's games. Or paying up. George was the town bookie and short-order cook who made a mean breakfast on the cheap. Just don't look at the floor too hard. You didn't want to know what skittered around the old luncheonette.

"Hello," Vent answered on the third ring. He coughed hard into the phone. Chuck had to pull the receiver away from his ear.

"Let me talk to Mick."

"Who is this?"

"Really?"

"Oh, man, I'm so frigging tired. Hold on, Chuck." Vent put the phone down. Chuck heard him shuffling around his room, clearing out his lungs. A door opened and Vent tromped away. He didn't come back for over a minute. Chuck eyed the change on the shelf beneath the phone, waiting for the automated operator to tell him he needed to feed more into the slot.

When Vent returned, he said, "Dude, he's not here."

"Then where is he?"

"I don't know. I just know he's not in my house. I even checked the basement."

Dammit. First Dredd and now Mick.

"Dredd is missing," Chuck said.

That seemed to shake Vent from his stupor. "Shit, did they kill him?"

"I don't know. I don't think so. His truck was gone. But his cabin was destroyed. I went there this morning. As I was about to leave, it was set on fire. And then my car was pelted by rocks and branches. They fucked it up good."

"Did you see them? Did they follow you?"

"No, and I'm pretty sure no." Chuck had been wondering how far the Melon Heads' reach extended. Did they have sentries all along Dracula Drive? It only made sense. You couldn't maintain that kind of secretive existence without some kind of planning and preparation. Now, everywhere Chuck spied a clump of trees and bushes, he suspected there was a Melon Head peering at him through the leaves, noting his whereabouts, waiting for the moment to grab him.

"Maybe Mick went to Dredd's and they took off. Did you check his trailer?"

Chuck had been considered indestructible by everyone for as long as he could remember. Fear wasn't something he was allowed to show.

Today, he was afraid. There was no way he was going to Mick's trailer alone.

"No. Your father still have that rifle?"

Vent's old man used to be an avid hunter until his eyesight started getting bad from diabetes. He'd sold most of his guns but kept his first rifle, which had been given to him by his father. He'd often said he wanted to save it for his son, but with the way Vent was turning out, he wouldn't trust him with a slingshot, much less a rifle.

"Yeah, he keeps it in the back of his closet."

"I need you to get it."

"Are you crazy, man? Him and my mom are sleeping. I'm not going in there."

Chuck gave an exasperated sigh. "I didn't say to get it now. Wait until they're out of the house. Then meet me at my place."

He could hear the click of Vent's throat as he dry-swallowed. "You want us to go out there, don't you?"

"Yep. Only this time, we need to be ready for them."

★   ★   ★

So far, Mick had bagged two rabbits. Their bodies, curled against one another in the leather bag strapped to his shoulder, bopped against his hip when he walked. His trailer was to his back about two hundred yards to the west. The long walk from Vent's house to his rusted can of a home had taken some of the wind from his sails. His big plans would have to be adjusted to smaller ones for now. Hence, the bag of rabbits.

He wished he had something more powerful than a BB gun. If he was going to do this, he wanted to do it right.

Spotting a squirrel on a branch, its bushy tail whickering, Mick paused and lifted the gun. A BB shot out with a dull whap of air. It hit the branch and sent the squirrel scurrying higher into the tree and out of Mick's range.

"Dammit."

Mick kicked the tree. The squirrel chittered nervously. Or was it laughing at him? Maybe he should just wait here. It had to come down eventually. The nearest branch wasn't close enough for the little bastard to reach.

Nah, he was too scrawny anyway. It would be great to find a raccoon, but it's too early. If a raccoon is out this time of day, it's probably rabid. Hmmm. What would happen if I fed rabid meat to them? Would it make them sick? Maybe just crazier. I'm sure they've eaten plenty of spoiled meat. Bet their bodies have learned how to handle it.

What he needed most was to talk to Dredd, but his place was just too far for Mick to walk. After what they'd seen, he was sure there was a chance Dredd would clue him in on the rules to working with the Melon Heads. Mick saw his face last night. He was terrified. Maybe it was time for a new Melon Head guardian. Sure, Mick was scared, too, but that could change in time. He could be the reason his friends, and the town, survived. There was power in that. Power was something in short supply in Mick's life.

"Probably be happy to pass the torch to me," he said aloud. Many times out here in the woods, he was his only and best company. "He talks all tough, but he looked pretty wigged out when they attacked. I bet he shit his pants." Mick chuckled, walking as stealthily as he could along the terrain of crunchy leaves and sticks. The Melon Heads could be watching him right now, following his every move. He quickly turned around to see if anyone was behind him. The only thing back there was a cricket.

He had to see Dredd today. There were too many questions that he needed answered.

Who would take him there? Not Chuck. It was plain to see he

was mad at Mick. No way would he ever go back there. He could convince Heidi to take him. She would be reluctant at first, but he knew how to circumnavigate her walls. The only way she'd say no and stick to it is if she was still with Marnie. And Marnie looked pretty bad. Just thinking about it stoked his anger all over again.

Vent would be more than happy to do it, but he'd failed his road test twice and he'd never steal his parents' car.

Odds are, Mick would have to do it alone. He could always walk into town and swipe an unattended bike. He'd bring it back where he found it when he was done. It technically wasn't stealing.

A crow cawed as it sailed overhead. The morning's crispness was being dulled by a pall of late-season humidity. All this walking was making him sweat. Better to find a place to sit for a while and let the prey come to him. He found a white paper birch tree, its stark paleness like a beacon in a forest of muted colors. What may have been a lightning strike had split the wide trunk in half, cleaving a space that would just fit him. Mick put the bag and gun down and settled back into the cramped space. It was more comfortable than it looked, like being embraced by nature. He didn't give two shits about tree-hugging hippies, but even he had to admit it was nice.

Resting the gun on his knees, he waited. Something would come along. There were too many critters out here for him not to add to his bloody bag.

His mind kept flashing back to the night before. Sometimes he cringed. He'd seriously thought those Melon Head freaks were going to get Chuck. Other times he grinned; those first screams bursting out of Dunwoody when the Melon Heads went for him were like the best grunge tunes ever made. Kurt fucking Cobain couldn't reproduce a sound like that, or elicit so much emotion. His eyelids grew heavy as he tried to replay it all, moment by moment.

A flock of birds lining just about every branch around him woke him up. They chattered incessantly, their shrill bleats like a knife through his skull. He fired wildly into the trees to get them to piss off to another tree, and they were happy to oblige.

"Damn birds."

Something smelled bad. He sniffed the air, his nose rapidly detecting the foul smell that was coming from his bag. He looked up. The sun had shifted considerably westward in the pale blue sky.

"How long was I out?"

Extricating himself from the confines of the tree was like being born all over again, only with aching joints and muscles. He stood up, stretched, popped his knuckles and cracked his neck. His right leg had gone to sleep. Every time he moved it, a fresh onslaught of pins and needles pricked his nerves.

Shit. All he had to show for his day were the two measly rabbits. That wouldn't be enough. Not near enough. If he had money and proper transportation, he'd go to Shopwell and pick up some cheap steaks or something.

All he could do tonight was lay out his bounty and hope that if they came, the Melon Heads would see it as a sign of his willingness to cooperate with them, to atone for his sin. He couldn't trust how they would react, so there was no way he was going to seal himself up in the trailer. He saw what their fingers did to Chuck. They could pry that Airstream open like their hands were can openers.

Good thing he'd dug out that little bunker under the trailer last year when things started getting bad. No one, not even Vent, knew it was there. He'd hunker down there for the night. He could sleep a night with some bugs. It was better than the alternative. If the Melon Heads came for him, he'd hear them, but they'd never hear him.

He walked back to the trailer in better spirits.

He even hummed 'Outshined' while he walked, no longer worrying if he had enough game to offer. It would all work out in its own fucked-up way, just like everything else in his life.

The sight of the strange car parked outside the trailer stopped him in his tracks. A blue Cadillac, its top down, was parked on top of the ring of stones he'd set up so he could make fires at night. One of the quarter panels was a dull compound gray. Lights were on in the trailer.

"Who the fuck?"

Mick dropped the bag of rabbits and cocked his BB gun. It wouldn't kill a person, but one shot at close range would send a pretty clear message – get the hell off my property.

He cautiously approached the trailer, stepping lightly on the auburn leaves, trying to make as little noise as possible. Whoever was in there, he wanted them good and surprised when he flung the door open, giving him the upper hand. He cocked his ear, straining to hear a voice. All was quiet in the trailer, which made him more wary. They could be watching him right now, waiting to spring up behind him.

Just try it. Give me a reason to pop a BB in your face.

If they were people just looking for a place to hang and screw around, it would be easy to chase them off. If it was a thief, or thieves, out to rob him, it could get ugly. He was plenty nervous, not that he'd ever let anyone know. There was no one around to help him if things went south.

No matter. He'd done plenty on his own, especially over these past few months.

With just a dozen or so yards to go before he could grab the doorknob, headlights bounced off the tarnished silver trailer. Mick spun around and fired off a BB. It hit home with a metallic *ping*.

Two doors flew open.

"What'd you do that for?"

It was Chuck and Vent. Mick exhaled and aimed the gun at the ground.

"Why does everyone hate my car today?" Chuck said. When he turned off the lights, Mick saw the damage. It looked like Chuck had rolled his car down a gulley.

"You get in an accident?" Mick asked, realizing the element of surprise had flown the coop, yet relieved he wouldn't have to face whomever was in there alone.

"Not exactly."

Vent was sporting a rifle. His eyes flicked from tree to tree like a frightened bird's.

"You got an extra one for me?"

"I wish," Vent said. He nodded at the gun in Mick's hand. "You see any of them around?"

"Nah. I was hunting."

"Whose car is that?" Chuck asked.

"I was about to go in there and find out," Mick said, feeling brave now that he had backup.

"Maybe it's Dredd," Chuck said. "He could have ditched his truck." He eyeballed the old Caddy. "It's just as beat up as his truck. He doesn't look like a guy that can afford an expensive ride."

Mick didn't like that. If Dredd was here, he was sure it wasn't just to pay a nice little social call. The dude was royally pissed at Mick. Getting Dredd out of his little hidey-hole was no easy feat. This could be more serious than he thought.

"Well, at least it's not a cop. Even an undercover cop wouldn't drive around in that shitbox," Vent said. "I bet that thing couldn't chase down a go-cart."

Muffled movement from inside the Airstream shushed them. The knob started to turn. Mick raised the BB gun. Chuck took a step forward, his big hands tightening into fists, while Vent eased back toward the car, the safety net if whoever was about to open the door tried to run away.

Mick gave Chuck a solemn nod that said, *You ready for this?*

The door swung open.

Mick shouted, "Get the fuck down, now!"

The man in the open doorway had his head pointed at his feet, fumbling with the drawstring of his sweatpants. He looked up at Mick and grimaced. "Put that goddamn thing away before you blow off that acorn you call a pecker."

CHAPTER FOURTEEN

Dwight McNeil poked his pinky finger in his chasm of a belly button and dug around. He pulled out something Vent couldn't see and flicked it off his fingernail at Mick. "You morons mind telling me why you're armed? If you're expecting trouble, move that shit right on someplace else." He kicked a trio of empty beer cans out of the trailer.

Mick looked like he was about to spit nails. "Is Mom inside?"

Dwight drew in a great breath and spread his arms wide to fill the doorframe in a none-shall-pass gesture. "She's sleeping, so keep your voices down."

"Where have you been all this time?" Mick asked, not backing down. Vent noticed that Mick's finger was tapping against the trigger of his gun, though the gun was pointed at the ground.

"If it was your business, you'd know."

"You left me with no money. I could have starved to death."

Dwight looked him up and down. "You don't look like you're in any danger of that. And I'm sure you found a way to get your hands on as much of that cheap skunk weed as you could suck up."

"Fuck you."

"Come again?"

Chuck reached for Mick's arm. "Come on, let's just go."

Mick didn't break his hateful gaze at Dwight. "I said, fuck you. I'm going inside to see my mother." He tried to slip past Dwight's side. The bigger man shifted his body, bumping his chest against Mick's head and nearly knocking him down the step. Mick wiped his face with the back of his hand, visibly disgusted that he'd come into contact with his filthy body. Vent could smell the man's odor of onions and cigarette smoke from seven feet away.

"I told you to keep it down," Dwight said almost jokingly. Vent knew from experience the man could go from a smile to nuclear in a flash. "You better not wake your mom up."

Mick looked coiled to make another go, but instead he spun on his heel and stormed along the side of the trailer. He banged on the metal with his fist. "Mom! Wake up, Mom!"

Dwight's eyebrows shot up high and fast. Vent thought they would fly off the top of his head. He leapt out of the doorway and ran for Mick, cursing a blue streak. Mick flicked a glance at his approach but kept punching the trailer and calling for his mother. Dwight got hold of his shoulders, spun him around and tossed him away from the trailer.

"You little shit," he snarled.

"What are you gonna do about it?" Mick shot back.

Dwight made a fist, his lip curling.

"You wanna hit me in front of my friends? Go ahead. I dare you. You get one shot, and that'll be your last." He looked to Vent and Chuck. Vent knew he wanted them to say something to back him up. Things had gone south so fast, Vent didn't know what to say or do. Chuck could easily pull Dwight away and pin him to the ground if needed. And Vent did have the rifle. But could he even point it at another person? The way his arms felt like lead, the answer was an emphatic no. He felt like a world-class chicken and a failure.

"You think those candy-asses are going to help you?" Dwight said, both fists up, arms in a fighter's stance, circling Mick. "You should have made friends with the jocks. Everyone knows stoners are just a bunch of peace-loving pussies."

Mick lunged at Dwight. His stepfather jerked to his left, leaving Mick's roundhouse punching air. Dwight jabbed Mick right between his shoulder blades and stepped back, bouncing on the balls of his feet.

"Nice try," he huffed.

"Everyone, just stop," Chuck said.

"You keep out of it, Baby Huey," Dwight said. "This has nothing to do with you." He didn't even bother looking at Vent, as if he knew that even with a gun, he wasn't the slightest threat. Over the years, Vent had witnessed Dwight browbeating Mick every chance he got, sometimes swatting him with a backhand. He knew so much more happened when he wasn't around. He'd seen the bruises, had had late-night conversations over a joint or two about Dwight's aggressions. For all Mick had been through, he managed to retain an air of defiance, at least for a little while.

This was different. Dwight looked like he was happy to beat the living daylights out of Mick. And Mick looked ready to kill Dwight.

Mick roared and charged Dwight again. Instead of swinging, he wrapped his arms around his stepfather's waist and tried to wrestle him to the ground. Dwight staggered, spun, but kept to his feet, delivering a series of savage rabbit punches to Mick's kidneys. When the air was fully knocked out of Mick, Dwight wrapped his fists in the collar of Mick's shirt and slammed his back into the Airstream. Mick let out a pained groan as the back of his head bounced off the trailer with a metallic *thwack*.

"You have anything smart to say now?" Dwight's spittle sprayed all over Mick's face. He ground his body against Mick's, pinning him to the trailer like a butterfly to a board. "I didn't think so. Where are your friends now?" His head swiveled to face Vent and Chuck. "Standing there like old ladies clutching their purses."

Vent could hear Chuck's labored breathing and knew he was itching to jump in. It had been drilled into them since they were little kids to respect their elders. What did you do when an elder showed such blatant disrespect for you? Or when he was hurting your friend?

Dwight gave an ugly chuckle and started thrusting his hips into Mick, his face so close, when he spoke, Mick's hair fluttered from his fetid breath. "You like that, don't you, you little pussy."

"Get off me," Mick mumbled. His head lolled from side to side, his eyes barely open.

"Take it like the girl you are."

Vent watched in horror. Something snapped. What Dwight was doing was so awfully wrong. Especially in light of—

The rifle suddenly felt lighter than air. He pointed it at Dwight's writhing body. "Let him go!"

Dwight's grimy gaze slid to Vent and he sneered. "You want to shoot me? You sure you won't hit your girlfriend?"

"I said let him go." Vent's voice sounded more confident than he felt.

"Go ahead, pull the trigger."

Dwight didn't notice that Mick had regained some of his strength. The rifle shook in Vent's grip but he didn't lower it. He had to keep Dwight's attention.

Mick's limp, open hands curled.

He was about to bring them up to Dwight's chin when a woman's shrill voice screamed, "What the hell is going on here? Dwight, what are you doing? Anthony Ventarola, put that gun down right now! Have you all lost your minds?"

Dwight gave Mick a last shove and backed away with his hands up. "Whatever you say, baby. We were just messing around. Old Vent there doesn't understand our family dynamic."

Mick's mother looked like she'd aged ten years since the last time Vent saw her. Her hair had gone salt and pepper and was in desperate need of a wash and a good brushing. There were deep creases in the corners of her eyes, and she'd put on a few pounds. Her face was puffy and the T-shirt she wore was pulled tight over a considerable potbelly. Glowering at Dwight, she barely noticed her son. It took Mick saying her name for her to face him.

"You look like hell, Mark," she said. Not, hello. Not, I missed you. Not, I'm sorry for leaving you. No, *you look like hell, Mark*. And he looked like hell because of the beating he'd been given by her waste of a husband. She was the only one who ever called Mick by his first name. It sounded strange to Vent's ears.

"Nice to see you, too, Mom," Mick said. He spit on the leaves and walked between Vent and Chuck, heading for Chuck's car. "Get me the fuck outta here."

★   ★   ★

Heidi sat in the emergency room waiting area reading a *People* magazine from a year ago. There wasn't an empty seat in the house. A TV sitting atop a table on the other side of the room was playing a talk show. Sally Jesse Raphael interviewed a teen runaway and her parents. The parents were in tears. The girl, a snotty-looking bottle blonde, laughed at them every time they said they loved her.

The drive to Yale-New Haven Hospital had been long and silent. Marnie wanted to keep the radio off. She spent most of the time with her head leaning on the window, eyes closed but awake, occasionally opening them and asking Heidi if they were close. Heidi had found an old blanket in the attic and put it on Marnie's seat in case the bleeding started again. She'd forgotten all about the Melon Heads, at least for the morning. Her overriding concern about her best friend's health occupied every thought.

They'd taken Marnie in about three hours ago. Heidi was asked some questions, a few she could answer, others she thought best for Marnie to answer.

The waiting was making her crazy. Her right leg bounced a steady rhythm on her left, the magazine resting on her crossed legs. It made it hard to read the brief articles with all the words jumping about. No matter, she knew how these stories ended and didn't care.

Shifting in the uncomfortable plastic chair, Heidi looked at the clock above the reception desk for the thousandth time. She wished she'd insisted she go with Marnie when they'd called her name. A fat man wearing dirty overalls coughed into his hand on one side of her. A middle-aged woman in what had to have been a waitress outfit cradled a hand wrapped in about a hundred yards of gauze. She kept popping outside for a smoke, asking Heidi to save her seat. The coughing man watched TV, his germs spreading far and wide each time his lungs went into a spasm.

Heidi had thought it would be empty on a Sunday afternoon. She'd been dead wrong. It seemed like everybody in Connecticut was either sick or hurt.

She hoped, even prayed, that Marnie was going to be all right. Her skin had gone from pale to gray by the time they walked in the door. Marnie could barely talk through the pain. She could be in surgery right now for all Heidi knew.

Jesus, she had to get up and burn off some of this nervous energy. Heidi tossed the magazine on the uneven pile in front of her and left the waiting room. The double glass doors opened automatically. Fresh, cool air never smelled so good. She hated that weird chemical stench you only found in hospitals. She went for a quick walk, not venturing too far because she didn't want to miss the doctor when he came back.

The emergency room may have been a hive of activity, but the hospital grounds were relatively quiet. She passed by a planter bursting with wildflowers. Pretty soon they'd be dead, the fall chill crisping the leaves and sending the flowers into hibernation. Heidi looked around, made sure no one was looking, and picked a few to give to Marnie. Afraid she'd already been gone too long, she hustled back to the ER. A voice was calling over the intercom, followed by a series of chimes. The incessant chatter had been driving her crazy all day.

She looked across the room and saw that her seat was gone.

Guess the smoking waitress doesn't believe in returning the favor. Jerk.

Heidi settled for sitting on the floor, the flowers in her hand, elbows on her knees. Legs clad in different colored scrubs whizzed past her in every direction.

"Marnie Wilson?"

Heidi popped up at the sound of her friend's name. A slight Indian doctor looked around the waiting room. Heidi practically ran up to him.

"Is she all right?"

"Are you a relative?" he asked. She looked at his expression for any sign of the news to come. He had the poker face of an experienced doctor.

"I brought her in," she replied.

"Yes, but are you related?"

"I'm her sister," she said. She hoped he didn't take note that they didn't look the least bit like they swam in the same gene pool. "Now please tell me, is she okay?"

The doctor clasped his hands down by his waist. "I'm Dr. Patel. Your sister has a very serious infection. We're running a battery of tests. She's also experienced a great deal of internal trauma. I assume you know something about this?"

Heidi didn't know how much she should say. If she told him Marnie was raped, the police would be called. She wished she knew what Marnie had said. Although, from the way she'd been, Heidi was sure she'd told him very little. Her heart fluttered in that moment of silent panic.

He leaned across the small divide between them and put a hand on her shoulder. "I know this is very sensitive. Look, we took a series of X-rays and we're going to do an MRI tomorrow to get a better sense of the extent of her injuries. She's lost a lot of blood. I'm afraid there may be some lasting issues stemming from...." He was too polite to finish. "We'll find out more tomorrow."

"You mean she can't come home?"

He shook his head sadly. "I'm afraid not. If she had come to us sooner, it might be different. As difficult as it may be, you're going to need to call your parents. I'm sure they'd want to be here for your sister."

Heidi fought back tears. "Yes, you're right. Can I see her?"

"She's sedated now. We're waiting for a room to become available. Once we get her settled in, I'll have a nurse come get you. But it's important you let her rest. Her body is working very hard to heal itself. We need to give it some help." Dr. Patel was called to radiology over the loudspeaker. "I have to go. Your sister will be fine. She's in very good hands. I assure you."

He smiled and left Heidi standing in the packed waiting room, unsure of what to do next.

The doctor's words, *I'm afraid there may be some lasting issues,* played over and over in her head. Whatever the Melon Heads had done to Harold Dunwoody out in those woods, as far as Heidi was concerned, hadn't been nearly enough.

CHAPTER FIFTEEN

They searched for Dredd over the next two days, combing vacant lots and abandoned houses, hoping to see his truck. Mick crashed at Vent's house but they both had to leave in the morning for school. Vent's parents didn't trust him enough to leave him alone in the house and besides, he should be going to class. Chuck agreed. At least school was a place to stay during the day, especially Monday when it rained from sunup till sundown. Mick explained that he didn't want to have to face being berated by all of his teachers for not being around the past few weeks. He was old enough to quit and that was that.

There was no point in arguing with him. Not now. The guy had enough on his plate. Like Chuck, Mick was having a hard time sleeping. So was Vent. By Tuesday, they were bleary-eyed. Everyone just assumed they were high. Hell, they should have been getting high just to calm their nerves. But Chuck had a big advanced chem test he needed to be straight for. On top of that, they were all worried about the Melon Heads finding them. They needed to be on alert. It was uncomfortable sleeping with a knife under your pillow. Chuck kept worrying he'd stab himself in his sleep. He almost did the night before when he'd heard something moving outside his window. Jumping out of bed, he slipped his hand under his pillow and just missed slicing the web of flesh between his thumb and index finger. Turns out, it was only a raccoon bumping into the metal garbage pails. It took an hour for Chuck to settle down and fall back to sleep.

Heidi and Marnie hadn't been in class and they weren't answering their phones. That prompted a quick visit to their houses on Monday. Chuck and Mick looked in all the windows, searching for signs of a break-in or struggle. All looked fine. They were just empty.

"I'm worried about Marnie," Chuck said.

Mick tugged at his hair, lost in thought. He gnawed on the end of a Slim Jim. His mind had been elsewhere much of the time lately. "Yeah, me too."

They had no way of finding out where their friends had gone. Chalk that up to one more thing eating away at them.

At lunch on Tuesday, Chuck and Vent walked across the field to the Losers' Lair in the trees. Being in the woods was not the brightest move at this point, but there was a main road just twenty yards beyond the trees. It didn't seem like a prime Melon Head hiding spot.

"Want one?" Chuck asked, offering Vent a Marlboro. He took one and lit it, inhaling deeply.

"How'd you do in chem?" Vent asked.

Chuck exhaled a funnel of deep, rich smoke. "I don't know. I'm pretty sure I passed, but that's not gonna be enough."

"I fell asleep in social studies. Mr. Mahon threw an eraser at me to wake me up. Whole class thought it was the funniest thing they'd ever seen." He bent his head toward Chuck. "Did I get all the chalk out?"

Chuck swatted away the clinging bits of chalk dust. "That's not too bad. He once had me do pushups in front of the class while he taught. Guy's a world-class schmuck. I hear he came from a Catholic school in Florida where he got in trouble for being too handsy with the students."

"I don't doubt it."

They leaned against neighboring trees and smoked in silence. There was so much to say. Exhaustion and an undercurrent of fear had sapped them of their strength. Besides, it was nice to just smoke and not talk about Dredd, Melon Heads or their concern about Marnie and Heidi. Being in a constant state of fight or flight sucked big time.

A twig cracked behind them. Chuck pulled a kitchen knife from the inner pocket of his denim jacket. Vent grabbed a hammer he'd secreted in his boot, hiding the business end under his jeans.

"Jeez, it's only me."

Mick stepped out from behind a thick-trunked pine. Actually, it was a pair of pine trees that had somehow fused together over the decades.

Chuck felt his whole body deflate. "Thanks for the heart attack."

Mick saw the pack of cigarettes in Chuck's shirt pocket and helped himself to one. "You're welcome. Heidi or Marnie come to class today?"

"Nope," Vent said.

"I was just by Marnie's house. Still nothing. It's like they went on vacation or something."

"It's the something I'm worried about," Chuck said.

Mick toed a rock buried under the leaves. "I also did some recon by my trailer. Saw Dwight and my mom. So, I guess that means the Melon Heads aren't hanging around."

"They could have been there and just left. It's you they're after, not them," Vent said.

"It still seems weird that we're talking about the Melon Heads, knowing they're real," Chuck said.

"I liked them a lot better when they were just a stupid story," Vent said.

Chuck took note that Mick said nothing.

"I think they took the rabbits, though," Mick said.

"What rabbits?" Chuck asked.

"The day my mother came home, I was out hunting. I figured if the Melon Heads came around, I'd have something waiting for them. If they liked it, they'd leave me alone. Maybe leave all of us alone." He took a drag on his cigarette, staring across the field. Chuck felt he was leaving something out. With Mick, if he didn't want to tell you, there was no way to drag it out of him. You either had to wait or just forget about it.

"Maybe another animal got them," Vent said.

Mick flicked the cigarette butt in a high arc toward the field. "Nah. I had them in this bag. The bag was fine. If an animal had gotten into it, it would have been all messed up. It might be a good idea to find something else for them. Something bigger."

"Like what?" Vent asked.

"I don't know. A deer, maybe."

"You can't take down a deer with a BB gun," Chuck reminded him.

Mick turned to Vent. Vent put up his hands. "Oh no, I'm not lending you my dad's rifle."

"Come on, man."

"I got away with taking it out once. If I get caught, I'm dead. No way."

"I'm doing this to save our asses. You heard Dredd. They'll find us in their own sweet time. Dredd's not around anymore to feed them and whatever other shit he did for them. Someone needs to take his place. If not, we'll always be in danger. What happens when we start to get comfortable? When we start to forget?"

"There's not a chance I'm ever going to forget that night," Chuck said.

Mick tapped his own temple. "But it won't always be the first thing you think about. Sooner or later, your main concern is going to be filling out college applications. Your guard is gonna come down. That's exactly when they'll come."

"What makes you the Melon Head expert?" Chuck said. "I saw them with you. They're crazy. They're more like animals than people. I don't see them thinking that far ahead."

"I don't care what they look like or acted like that night. They're still people. And people are born predators."

"Sounded to me more like the Melon Heads picked Dredd to be their helper, not the other way around," Chuck said, taking a drag from his cigarette. "Lord knows why or how they even think. You can't just take Dredd's place and keep them from getting us just because you want to."

Peeling off the bark of a tree, Vent said, "Maybe we should be the ones hunting them."

Mick was staring at Chuck as if he wanted to say more about his plan to take Dredd's place. Instead, he turned to Vent and said, "Trust me, I thought of it. We don't have enough man- or firepower. There's too many of them."

"And who knows how many we didn't see?" Chuck said. The more they talked about the Melon Heads, the more uneasy he felt about being within the trees. He started walking toward the field. Mick and Vent followed. A couple of jocks were tossing a football down by the visitor goal post. Pretty soon the bell would ring and it would be back to struggling to pretend it was just another school day. What he wanted to do was go home, pack, and drive to the other side of the country, someplace where the Melon Heads could never find him. What was the point of doing well in school if he might not survive long enough to graduate?

"Fucking Dredd," Mick said. "He'll know what to do."

"Yeah, run like hell," Vent said. "Notice how he didn't stick around."

"He's somewhere close. I just have a feeling."

"His Spidey senses are tingling," Vent said.

Chuck smiled for the first time in days. "We could use Spider-Man right about now."

"You two are idiots," Mick said. He turned back into the tree line.

"Hey, where are you going?" Chuck called after him.

"To do something. Better than taking notes and waiting to die."

He disappeared into the gloom within the trees. They could still hear his heavy footsteps crunching through the underbrush.

"You think he'll figure out how to get us out of this?" Vent asked as they walked back to the main building.

Chuck scratched at his beard and sighed. "Knowing Mick, he'll accidentally find a way to get us killed sooner."

⋆   ⋆   ⋆

Marnie rang for the nurse. She felt like she had to go to the bathroom. The urge to pee was downright painful. She thought she was going to lose her mind.

Helen, the nice day nurse with the freckles, came to her room a few minutes later. She looked at Marnie with pity. They all did once they knew what had happened to her. What had been taken from her. "You okay, hon? How's the pain?"

"I have to pee real bad. You think you can help me to the bathroom?" She tried pushing herself up in the uncomfortable hospital bed, the over-starched sheets crinkling. Her head spun and she sagged back into the bed.

Helen tugged the sheet up to her chest. "You have a catheter, hon. It could be you're feeling pain from somewhere else."

Somewhere else. Marnie knew what that meant. The place they dare not speak of, unless it was in medical terms telling her the damage Harold Dunwoody – whom she hadn't named – had wrought.

"I know what it feels like when your bladder is about to burst," Marnie said. "If I don't get to the bathroom, I'm going to wet the bed, and then you'll have to change it. I don't want you to have to do that."

With a sweeter-than-candy smile, Helen said, "That's one thing you don't have to worry about. First, you can't wet the bed when you have a catheter. And two, I've changed more dirty sheets than I can count. What's one more?"

Marnie fidgeted. It felt like her pee had backed up to her molars. Any second now she was going to start crying, and she thought she'd run out of tears days ago.

"Then something's wrong," Marnie said.

"You know, a lot of people will still feel like they have to go. That's perfectly normal."

Marnie talked through gritted teeth. "It's not that. Can you please help me get to the bathroom?"

The nurse gave her an okay-if-you-say-so look and lifted the sheet back. Marnie looked away as she tugged her hospital gown up to inspect the catheter. "Oh my," Helen said.

"What? What's wrong?"

"It looks like there's a blockage in the catheter. Let me get a bedpan."

No sooner had Helen walked out than Heidi strode in, her arms laden with magazines. She took one look at Marnie and dropped them on the wide windowsill. "Are you okay? I saw a nurse run out of your room."

Marnie smiled through the pain. "I gotta pee so bad. She said my catheter is clogged or something."

"Here, hold my hand." Heidi cast a quick glance at the open door. "Ow!"

"Sorry."

Nurse Helen came shuffling in with a metal bedpan and medical supplies sealed in a plastic bag. "We're going to get you all fixed up in no time." When she saw Heidi, she said, "I'll only be a few minutes."

"No, I want her to stay," Marnie said. Her parents had come to see her when they first heard the news. They'd stayed for a couple of hours, conferring with the doctor and promising they'd be back tomorrow. That had been two days ago. Heidi's parents had been nice enough to let her take a few days off from school, shuttling her between Milbury and New Haven every day. Heidi was really the only family she had up here.

"Fine. Whatever makes you comfortable."

"This catheter sure doesn't."

Heidi politely looked away as Helen worked the catheter out. The moment it slipped free, a hard stream of urine tinged with blood burst from Marnie. Helen got the brunt of it, not the bedpan. When it was done, Marnie's eyes rolled up. If this kind of ecstasy was what sex was really supposed to be like, she vowed to find someone who knew how to do it right.

Heidi couldn't keep from giggling. She buried her head beside Marnie's on the pillow when Helen, her uniform dripping, threw a highly agitated look their way. It took her a few moments to compose herself, and then a smile touched the corners of her own mouth.

"Wow, you really had to go," she said. "Looks like I have my work cut out for me. Be right back."

The moment she left, Marnie and Heidi broke out into hysterical laughter. They laughed until they cried, holding on to one another, ignoring the heady aroma of urine that filled the room.

Marnie thought she would never smile, much less laugh again. She wiped a tear from Heidi's cheek. "Aren't you glad I asked you to stay?"

"It's the grossest, funniest thing I ever saw. Oh my god, her face!"

The laughter continued. It was the strangest yet most perfect distraction she could have received. It stopped her from fixating on the fact that Harold Dunwoody had forever robbed her of the ability to have children.

CHAPTER SIXTEEN

Heidi phoned Chuck on Thursday and filled him in on everything. It was difficult talking to her with his parents in the same room. They were watching *Friends*, a show Chuck thought was beyond stupid, but his parents loved. Chuck got up from the love seat and carried the phone into the dining room while the snarky guy said something that was met by canned laughter.

"When can she come home?"

Heidi sounded tense. "The doctor said maybe tomorrow. The infection was really bad. If she goes all night and tomorrow morning without a fever, I think she's good to go."

Chuck plopped into a dining room chair, the wood creaking. "I can't believe she can't have kids."

"Don't tell anyone else. And don't tell her I told you. She's devastated."

She would be. All Marnie wanted to do was find a nice guy someday, hopefully someone who didn't live in Milbury, get married and have a bunch of kids. She joked that she wasn't good at anything else, so why not spend her life barefoot and pregnant? He knew she loved kids. He saw it in her eyes every time they saw a baby in a stroller or went past a playground. She'd banked her entire future on the corny American dream of the family and house with a white picket fence. No one else would ever think that of her, but he knew it. And now that had been taken from her. His horror at recalling how Dunwoody had suffered before he died lost some of its effect on him.

"How are you doing?" he asked.

"I'm fine. I think."

"Why don't you come over and meet me in the yard?"

"I don't know. Hold on." He heard the clunk of the phone as she put it down and the squeak of her door when she left the room. She came back a few seconds later. "Okay. My parents are doing the nasty in their room. They won't miss me."

"Cool. See you in a few."

Chuck lived only a few blocks from Heidi. His yard had often been their meeting place over the years. He went up to his room, got the last joint from his stash and slipped outside while his parents laughed at the television.

He didn't have to wait long for Heidi to show up. She rode her bike into his yard and leaned it against the picnic table.

"Come on," he said, motioning with his head for her to follow him. They went out by the aluminum tool shed and huddled behind it. Chuck lit the joint, took a quick hit to make sure it would draw and handed it over to Heidi.

"Oh, I needed that," she said, resting her back on the shed wall. Chuck knew enough to not follow suit. The last time he did, his body weight put a sizeable dent in the cheap material.

"We were getting freaked out when we couldn't find either of you," he said, coughing into his fist.

"I was pretty freaked myself."

"Marnie's parents up there with her now?"

"God knows where they are. Must have found some cheap bar in New Haven. If they don't take her home, my dad says we can."

"Her parents suck."

"Always have. Why change now?"

They passed the joint back and forth until there was very little left. Chuck said, "Speaking of shitty parents, Mick's are back."

"That can't be good."

"Nope. He's staying with Vent."

"Anything with—"

Chuck shook his head. He didn't want to hear their name said aloud. "Mick thinks he can get them on his side."

"How?"

"Same way Dredd did. Or at least the way he thinks Dredd did. The dude split right after everything." He left out the part about his car being attacked and Dredd's cabin being burned to the ground. After all, he'd asked her here to help her relax.

"That's not good."

"Nothing's been good since Dunwoody put his hands on Marnie."

"At least she's safe up in New Haven," Heidi said. She hugged herself against the night chill. Chuck had a sudden urge to hold her. They'd kissed once during the summer at Missy Kapernick's kegger. They were both drunk, the kiss sloppy, and neither talked about it the next day. For Chuck, it had been a longtime wish fulfilled, although in his fantasy they were both sober and she whispered in his ear that she'd always had a crush on him. He wasn't sure Heidi saw it the same way, so he didn't press her on it.

"For now," he said.

The weed had relaxed his body but barely dulled his overactive mind. They couldn't let anything happen to Marnie. She'd been through enough. But how could they help her when they couldn't find a way to help themselves?

"You going to school tomorrow?" he asked Heidi.

"Yep. Can't wait to make up all that work I missed. That'll suck hard."

"I can help."

"And I'll take you up on that."

He told her some of the things she'd missed in class, neither of them acknowledging the much larger issue hanging over their heads. It was almost nine thirty when Heidi said, "I better get back."

"I'll walk you home."

"You don't have to."

"I'll feel better if I do."

"Okay, but I'm not putting you on my handlebars." She laughed softly.

The streets were quiet and dark. Some of the streetlights had gone out over the past week, which was nothing new on this side of town. The infrastructure was in dire need of repairs. They strolled into pools of light, followed by patches of dark. Heidi walked alongside her bike. Chuck pulled leaves off bushes and tore them into little strips, casting them to the wind.

"You believe what Dredd said?" Heidi asked when they were around the block from her house.

"Sometimes yes, sometimes no. It sounds crazy, but what I saw was absolutely insane."

"Is it weird I wish I was there with you guys?"

Chuck stopped and looked at her. "Yeah, it is weird. Trust me, you don't want to spend your life trying to un-see and un-hear what happened out there."

"I don't know. It makes me feel like I don't belong. Like you, Mick and Marnie have a different bond now. I know it sounds stupid."

They continued walking. "One thing you're not is stupid. Strange, yes. But then again, we're all freaks."

"Aw, you called me a freak. That's the nicest thing you ever said to me." She nudged him with her shoulder.

Someone darted across the street twenty yards ahead of them. They popped up in the light and disappeared in the gloom. Chuck put his hand on the bike to stop Heidi. "Who was that?"

"Who was what?"

"Kind of late for kids to be out running around on a school night."

"I didn't see anyone."

She tried to resume walking, but he held the bike in place. "Hold on."

"You're scaring me."

It wouldn't help to tell her he was scared, too. Because in that brief moment when the figure was bathed in the streetlight's luminescence, he swore he saw a head that looked much too big to be on a body that short and slight.

Fuck!

He fumbled in his pockets for any kind of weapon. All he had was his blue Bic lighter and a quarter.

"Chuck? What's wrong?"

Chuck put a finger to his lips. He turned around. Was that a shoulder that just dipped behind a Trans Am?

Was it him, or was the darkness growing, like a wine stain spreading out across a white tablecloth?

The bushes shook across the street to their left. Chuck squinted as hard as he could but couldn't make anything out.

"They're here, aren't they?" Heidi whispered.

"I think so."

He also thought they were the ones who had been knocking out the streetlights, creating the perfect place to hide in plain sight. Could they really think that far ahead?

Something skittered behind them. They spun around to catch it but were too late. Heidi grabbed his arm. She started to breathe heavily. "I want to go home."

"We're going to get you home."

He wasn't so sure he believed it.

Her house was only half a block away now. Chuck looked ahead and felt something die in his stomach. The light across the street from her house danced, as if someone were tugging on the pole – or was shimmying their way up it. It flickered for a moment and went out with the sound of breaking glass.

"Fuck."

They couldn't go forward. And they couldn't, wouldn't, make it back to his house.

"What do we do?" Heidi said.

"We stay in the light."

He could hear movement all around them. They were getting closer. Chuck grabbed the bike with two hands. If needed, he'd swing it around like an ungainly club. And he knew he'd need it. What sounded like the wet smacking of lips slithered out of the darkness.

"Scream," he said to Heidi.

"What?"

"Scream as loud as you can. And keep screaming until people start turning on their outdoor lights and coming out."

He didn't know if the Melon Heads would run away at the sight of more people or if they would just add them to the menu. It didn't matter. Right now, it was their only chance at getting out of this trap alive.

Heidi's shrill scream pierced his ears. Wow, he didn't know she had that kind of scream in her. She let loose like a horror movie starlet, her shriek ripping the night in two. It sounded like she was about to die.

She stopped for a moment to catch her breath. So far, no one in the surrounding houses had so much as flicked on a light or opened a window.

Chuck looked around incredulously. "What the hell is the matter with these people?"

"Maybe they didn't hear me."

"Anyone living in Rhode Island would have heard you."

There was one thing. The furtive movements just out of their sight had stopped. That could be equally as bad as it could be good. The Melon Heads could be preparing to attack.

"Keep going," he urged Heidi.

She drew in a deep breath and belted out a keening wail that could wake the dead. Chuck thought he saw a dark, misshapen figure scurry from behind a tree to an azalea bush to their left. Heidi kept up her scream until he thought her vocal cords would split.

A porch light popped on in the house directly to their right.

That was the first domino. Lights came on in windows and lawns up and down the street. A door opened and he saw a couple tentatively looking up and down the street.

"That's it, don't stop."

There was less strength beneath Heidi's cries, but it served as a beacon for everyone's attention.

A man's voice called out, "What the hell is going on out there?" He sounded irritated. Chuck was happy to hear him at all.

As more lights came on, Chuck heard clumsy footsteps retreating into the shadows. He couldn't believe it was working. He let go of the bike with one hand and pulled Heidi close. "You did it."

She coughed and when she spoke, she sounded like she was in the throes of a whopper of a cold. "I didn't have to fake screaming for my life."

Chuck spotted the headlights of a car turning into the road. He ushered Heidi into the street and started waving his arms. Something heavy crashed into the back of his head. He dropped to a knee, dazed.

"Oh my god, are you all right?"

He looked up into a pair of lights headed straight for him. The driver had to see them. With a quick glance at the ground, he saw the sizeable rock that had been thrown at his head. Heidi tugged on his arm.

"I don't think he's slowing down."

Chuck stood up and saw why. Several pale Melon Heads stood beside the parked cars lining both sides of the street. When the headlights hit them, they shielded their faces, turned and ran away.

The driver must have seen them too and was panicking. Heidi and Chuck darted back to the sidewalk and ran toward the nearest lit house. A woman was on her meager porch, one hand cinching her robe closed. Chuck pointed. "In there." They couldn't risk running the added distance to Heidi's house.

He looked back and the pain in his head was forgotten.

Melon Heads were running behind the car now, their rushing bodies clogging the road.

Dear god, it was an invasion!

Chuck and Heidi hit the edge of the woman's lawn. The grass was slick. She must have watered it just before sunset like so many others did every evening. Heidi slipped. Chuck latched onto her flailing hand and kept her from falling.

Until he fell.

The car was almost parallel with them.

And so were the ravenous Melon Heads.

CHAPTER SEVENTEEN

Mick sat on his haunches in the shadows, watching the Airstream. All the lights were on. Tom Jones belted out 'It's Not Unusual', the Welsh singer's voice echoing between the dense trees.

He rubbed his thumb along the BB gun's trigger guard. This wasn't safe. One of those Melon Head freaks could come up behind him and he'd be dead before he could pull the trigger. Not that a BB would do much good. At best, it would only slightly delay the inevitable.

If there were only a way to let them know what he planned to do for them. They had some ability to understand. How else had Dredd managed a peaceful coexistence with them? Mick could be just as useful to them, if not more. He'd been leaving dead animals and packaged meat he'd shoplifted from the supermarket all around the clearing. When he came back each day, it was gone. Maybe that was a sign that it was working. It was impossible to know for sure.

As much as Mick despised Dredd now, he realized their similarities. Hopefully, the Melon Heads did, too. First and foremost, it was important to find a way to save himself and his friends. Second, his future was about as dim as the darkest corners of the Airstream. Lording over the Melon Heads and keeping the town safe was a better prospect than any other of his imagined futures. From Fennerman to Dredd to Mick. It was like a succession of popes or presidents. In a weird way, it would make him special. If only Dredd were around to teach him what to do.

Dredd. Where was that bastard? Mick had spent days scouring the back alleys and woods of Milbury, though he was smart enough to steer clear of the forest around Dracula Drive. He wasn't suicidal, though he bet Chuck would disagree if he could see him now.

Come on, Dwight, you fat prick. Bring your drunk ass outside. I have a present for you.

His mother and stepfather had been out earlier. He assumed they were at a bar or maybe pawning what little they had. Money was always tight and Dwight didn't appear to be in working mode at the moment. Mick's mother sometimes waitressed at the diner, but it had been a long time since she took an order. Something about an argument with the other waitresses and how they were dividing the tips. Tact was not her forte.

No matter where they spent their day, he was there to watch them roll in about nine. The big Cadillac bumped into a tree before it came to a stop. Dwight and Mick's mother stumbled out of the car, Dwight in loud drunk-laughing mode. He slammed the trailer door shut and a minute later, Tom Jones had started. They were now midway through his greatest hits album. Mick had heard it a thousand times. It was his mother's favorite and had more skips and pops than he could count. Mick was not a fan of Tom Jones, though he could appreciate the revenge brutality of the song 'Delilah'.

"I felt the knife in my hand, and she felt no more," Mick muttered. That was pretty badass coming from some Vegas crooner who wore pants tight enough to see the wrinkles in his ball sack. Mick would have thought he was a homo if not for all the panties he got thrown at him. He bet old Tom was up to his eyeballs in free pussy.

Experience taught Mick that his mother would pass out before eleven. She drank harder than Dwight and was always the first to call it a night. Once she was snoring loud enough to scare even the bats away, Dwight would stumble out and smoke a joint, usually one stolen from Mick's stash that he spent so much time making fun of. Asswipe.

While they were out, Mick had slipped a fat blunt in his less-than-secret hiding place, knowing Dwight would find it. Now it was only a matter of waiting for him to spark up. Fuck rabbits and squirrels. If he wanted to gain the trust of the Melon Heads, and save his own ass, he had to go for bigger game. He couldn't think of anyone more worthy of their hunger than Dwight. Sure, there were others (he'd spent an hour making a list that was now tucked in his back pocket), but Dwight held a special place at number one.

The crickets were making such a racket, Mick wanted to scream at them to shut up. There was nothing peaceful about being out in the woods. He missed living in an actual house on the outer edge of Milbury. It was in a crap section of town, but at least it had honestto-god plumbing and room to move around. And he liked having neighbors and cars rolling down the street and people playing the radio and partying late into the night. It made him feel like he was part of the greater world. After his father died, no, killed himself because he was a selfish prick who obviously didn't think about the shitty life he was leaving his only child, his mother lost the house and gained a rusted Airstream and Dwight. There wasn't even any insurance money to see them through the worst of it.

Man, he wished he had Vent's father's rifle. As easy as it would have been to borrow it for the night – the freaking thing wasn't even locked up – he didn't want to take a hot, steaming dump over his friend's kindness. People thought Mick was an uncaring sociopath, but they were only half right. He chuckled softly when he thought that. Could a sociopath care, or did that negate one's sociopathy? Who the fuck cared? Labels were for adults to make them less afraid.

He checked his digital watch, pushing the little button that lit its face. Almost eleven thirty. He hadn't heard his mother in a while now. Where the hell was Dwight?

As if in direct answer to his question, the trailer door opened and Dwight came into the frame. A misstep brought him crashing to the ground. It took him a while to get back up, his equilibrium hampered by all the booze sloshing around his brain.

Mick plucked the BB gun off the forest floor and held his breath.

Mumbling to himself, Dwight took a few faltering steps while digging in his pocket. He collapsed into a lawn chair. It was a miracle the cheap thing didn't break. An orange flame flickered and died, flickered and died.

"Fugging lighter."

Mick rose from his hiding spot. He was still blanketed in darkness. Even a sober Dwight wouldn't see him.

Though the crunching of leaves was a dead giveaway.

Dwight paused and looked around.

"Whoosh there?"

Mick froze.

"Fugging animals," Dwight muttered. He worked at the lighter again. The blunt finally caught the flame and he inhaled deeply.

Just a few more hits, Mick thought. He wanted him drunk and high.

The BB would only stun him for a moment. He needed Dwight incapable of fending him off.

Dwight took another toke. And then another.

Oh yeah, he was nice and mellow now.

It was time.

Mick rushed out of the darkness and fired a round. It hit Dwight dead center in the chest. He saw his T-shirt jump when the BB slammed home.

"Hey!"

Dwight tried to jump up, but he was wedged in the chair. He ended up right back on the ground, wearing it like a tutu.

Mick pulled the trigger again. This one went wide, pinging off the trailer.

Fuck! Calm down and aim for his head.

Exhaling, Mick adjusted his aim. Dwight flailed about in the chair, not making himself an easy target.

Mick didn't hear the trailer door banging open. He was so fixated on Dwight, he'd even blocked out the irritating crickets.

He pulled the trigger multiple times, hoping one or more would get Dwight in the face.

His mother shrieked and dropped to the ground.

"Baby! Are you all right?" Dwight and the chair tipped over as he tried to reach out for Mick's mother. He landed on his side. They were face to face in the leaves and dirt.

Mick's heart went into overdrive. He dropped the gun and ran.

"Mom!"

Dwight jerked his head up and glared at Mick. "What the fuck did you do?"

Mick dropped to his knees and went to help his mother up. "Mom. Are you all right?"

As he turned her over, the light emanating from the small window above them illuminated the red hole where her right eye used to be. She felt too heavy in his arms. He shook her, trying to get her to wake up.

"Mom? Mom!"

He didn't notice Dwight extricating himself from the chair. He didn't see the blow coming until it connected with his temple, nearly knocking him out. Mick dropped his lifeless mother and rolled backward, smashing his head against the trailer.

"Look what you did!" Dwight shouted. The horror of the past few moments had instantly sobered the man. "You killed her."

"No. I didn't." Mick rubbed the knot forming in the back of his head. He was having a hard time bringing everything into focus.

Dwight felt for a pulse on her neck and wrist. He even went so far as to slap her cheek so hard, Mick winced. "She's dead."

Mick felt the world sliding out from under him.

She couldn't be dead. All he had were tiny BBs. He'd somehow shot her in the eye, and yes, the eye was gone, reduced to leaking pulp, but there's no way it killed her.

Dwight kicked him in the chest. He felt his heart stop for a terrifying moment, and then the air whooshed out of his body.

"You no good waste of life," Dwight railed. "I'll fucking kill you!"

A meaty fist clocked Mick in the jaw. Mick's face hit the ground. He tasted dirt. He tried to reach out for his mother, but Dwight stomped on his hand. He looked up at his stepfather, his vision wavering.

"Better yet, I'm just going to kick the living shit out of you. Then I'm calling the cops and I'll enjoy watching you spend the rest of your life in prison where you belong. You know what they do to guys in prison who kill their mothers? Heh. You'll find out soon enough."

Dwight brought his leg back to deliver another crushing blow. Mick did the only thing he could. He flattened himself on the ground and rolled under the Airstream. He heard Dwight's foot connect with the solid frame. A string of f-bombs followed. "Stay there like the rat you are. It'll make it easier for the cops to drag your ass away."

As hard as it was to think, Mick was sure of one thing: Dwight was in a bind. There was no phone in the trailer. Dwight would have to drive into town to call the cops. He knew the second he got in the car, Mick was going to get out from under the trailer and take off. And Dwight was too goddamn fat to get Mick out before he went for the cops.

Mick watched Dwight pace back and forth, threatening him with every step. It all became dull white noise. Whenever Mick's gaze fell on his mother's cooling corpse, a physical ache pierced his chest that had nothing to do with the kick Dwight had delivered. She'd never been mother of the year, shit, she may have been on the top ten of worst mothers in Milbury, but she was all the real family he had.

And he'd killed *her*, not Dwight.

If he ever needed proof that there was no god or justice in this world, his mother's one-eyed, blank stare was it. Dwight's cursing and rambling was just the cherry on top.

"Come out and be a man for once," Dwight said.

"Fuck you."

"You're the one who's fucked, mother killer."

Hatred boiled over in Mick. He wanted to grab Dwight by the throat and chew his Adam's apple out and spit it back in his face.

That's just what he wants you to do. He needs you out from under the trailer.

Mick bit his cheek until it bled. He welcomed the pain. It kept him focused. And he deserved it.

Dwight's goading stopped at the sound of shuffling in the surrounding underbrush.

"You bring one of your lowlife friends with you?" Dwight said. "I know you're out there. You want to share a cell with your buddy? Come on out and maybe I won't tell the cops you helped him. You'll owe me one, big time, but you won't have your shit pushed in every night when you roll over in your narrow cot."

Four sharp metallic thumps made Mick jump. He smashed his back into the underside of the trailer.

"Agh, Jesus," Dwight wailed.

Footsteps erupted from every side. Mick peered out and saw a dozen or more bare feet come rushing at Dwight.

"No! Get back! Stay away from me!"

He saw Dwight turn and run for the trailer door. Suddenly, Dwight's feet and legs disappeared. Several seconds later, his body landed on the ground. Mick had to clamp his hands over his ears to drown out Dwight's piercing screams.

In the dim light, he watched the Melon Heads gather around Dwight's writhing body like seagulls descending on scraps of food tossed off the side of a fishing boat.

"Get off me! Get off me! Please! Gaaaaah!"

One hand grabbed his bottom jaw and pulled until it cracked. It reminded Mick of the sound walnuts made when he broke them open. Fingers drove into Dwight's eyes. Another pale hand dug inside his mouth until it got hold of his tongue, yanking it out with a wet tear. The stench of fresh, hot blood hit him hard in the face. Mick thought he was going to throw up.

He caught glimpses of deformed faces and heads as they dipped into view to savage Dwight's body. Grim satisfaction bubbled in the back of Mick's mind, but the visceral terror of the feasting massacre kept him from reveling in the moment.

Any sense of victory was short-lived when the Melon Heads turned their attention to his mother.

He slammed his eyes shut as they made quick work of her, but he couldn't block out the sounds and smells of their desecration. Mick pressed his face into the soft, sour earth, crying into its embrace.

Please make it stop. Please make it stop.

He willed himself to black out, but his body and mind betrayed him.

He didn't know how long it took until the sickening sounds of their moaning and chewing and sucking stopped. They would come for him next. As much as the thought of being eaten alive horrified him, a part of him thought he deserved it. It was the only way to think when death was so near. The only way to come to any sort of peace with himself.

Any second now, he expected to feel hands wrapping around his legs and ankles, ready to drag him out.

It didn't happen.

His mother's and Dwight's bodies were lifted up and out of his field of vision. Meat and pieces of organs slipped out of them, plopping on the hard ground. The Melon Heads shuffled away.

They can't take her!

But they could. Mick was powerless to stop them.

A wide and hideous face dropped under the trailer. Mick covered his mouth to stifle the scream that wanted to rip through his throat. The Melon Head looked him up and down. Blood caked its face. It curled a lip, its tongue darting out.

"P-p-p-lease," Mick stammered.

Instead of reaching for him, the Melon Head shot back up and joined the others after gathering the loose organs.

Mick trembled under the Aistream until dawn, and even then, he was too horrified to get out.

CHAPTER EIGHTEEN

Chuck pushed past the woman at the door and pulled Heidi inside.

"What are you doing?" the woman screeched. He slammed the door shut, turned the locks and put his back against it. She started to scream.

Heidi snapped at her. "Be quiet!"

There was a loud thump at the door. Chuck flinched. He could feel the impact of something heavy as it hit the wood. He couldn't tell if it was a shoulder or a fist, but it was clear they wanted in.

"I'm calling the police," the woman said. Heidi tried to grab her, but she was fast for an older woman. She sprinted down the hall, hand outstretched for the wall phone in the kitchen. Heidi looked to Chuck.

"Let her."

"Do you want to get arrested?"

"No, but I do want people with guns to get here as fast as they can."

Outside, there was shouting and the sounds of people rushing about, doors slamming, glass breaking. A window shattered upstairs. The woman yelped in the middle of telling the person on the other end of the line that two people had broken into her house.

"We didn't break in," Heidi called down to her. "Your door was open. Didn't you see that we were being chased?"

The woman stepped out of view, the long cord following her. She was crying now. Chuck hoped she didn't grab a kitchen knife for protection.

Another whack on the door had Chuck's heart racing. Sure, he could probably hold off anyone busting through the door, but there were tons of ground-floor windows in the house. How easy would it be for one of them to break the glass and crawl through?

"The police are on their way," the woman said. "You better not come near me."

Heidi took a few steps down the hallway. "Lady, can't you hear that the neighborhood is under attack? We came in here to get away from them."

"What?" Her head popped into the kitchen doorway.

Another window was broken. It sounded like it came from the house next door. "Aaahhh!" she shrieked.

"See?" Heidi said. "It's not us you should be worried about."

"Well then, who's out there?"

Chuck shot Heidi a warning look. They could not say it was Melon Heads. That would not help their case if the police started questioning why they barged into this woman's home.

"I...I don't know," Heidi replied.

The melee started to subside. Chuck pressed his ear against the door. He caught a few retreating footsteps, and then there was silence. "I think they're gone."

Because he couldn't be one hundred percent sure, he was reluctant to stray from the door.

The woman took a tentative step out of the kitchen. She had a butcher knife in her hand.

"Please be careful with that," he said.

"Don't make me have to use it, then."

"Heidi, it's probably safer if you stay behind me."

A floorboard creaked overhead. Everyone froze, their eyes rolling upwards as if they could see through the ceiling.

A window had definitely been broken upstairs. Had one of them gotten inside? Had they staged their little siege and left so Chuck would drop his guard? Again, Chuck grappled with whether or not they were capable of such complex thought and planning.

But there *was* someone up there.

"Do you live alone?" he asked the woman.

"I'm not telling you."

When the wood groaned again, the paling of her face told him that she didn't share her home with anyone else.

"Any pets?" he asked.

She shook her head.

Heidi was behind him, holding on to his arms. "Don't go up there."

That was the last thing he wanted to do. But it was also the first thing he felt he had to do.

"What if they're waiting to find a way to ambush us?"

"Who? Who's ambushing us?" the woman said.

Chuck ignored her. "I'm just going to take a quick look. I can't sit here and wait for one of them to attack."

"I'm coming with you," Heidi said.

"No, stay here."

She gave his arms a hard squeeze. "Not a chance. We either both go, or we both stay down here. Your choice."

What he wanted to do was rush up the stairs and hope to catch the Melon Head when it wasn't expecting him. He'd hold it (he could only think of them as *it*) and wait for the police. Then, and only then, could they say it was the Melon Heads. Maybe the authorities could root them all out and in turn eradicate his, Marnie's and Mick's death sentences. It was a pipe dream, he knew it, but it gave him a sliver of hope.

Sighing with resignation, he said to Heidi, "Fine. But keep behind me." He saw the andirons by the fireplace and gave the poker to Heidi. "And take this." He opted for the shovel. Not as deadly as the poker, but he swung a mean bat and thought he could do some damage with the shovel.

He put his booted foot on the first step, testing to see if it would make a racket. One look at the woman let him know she had no intention of following them upstairs. Her hands were clasped together and pressed to the center of her chest. Her eyes went from suspicious to worried. "Be careful," she said.

Chuck gave a slow nod.

He crept up the stairs, Heidi always a step behind him. The sudden stillness upstairs seemed to him to come from someone sneaking around who knows they are about to get caught. The stairs were carpeted and made very little noise, but there were enough wood creaks to alert a Melon Head in waiting that they were coming. Pausing at the second to last step, he turned to Heidi and whispered, "Just make sure you don't hit me with that thing."

"I won't."

Odds were, she would. He couldn't promise her she wouldn't catch an errant whack from the shovel. He was shitting bricks right about now. The adrenaline bursting through his system would make him unreliable if they were attacked. That was why he wanted her to stay downstairs.

It was too late now.

They came to a narrow hallway. A small sewing room was to their right. The open door to the bathroom before them revealed pink and black tiles glowing under a nightlight. Down the hall were two other bedrooms, their doors also open. A threadbare carpet runner lined the center of the hallway.

The bathroom and sewing rooms were empty.

Or maybe not. The shower curtain was closed. And there may have been a closet in the sewing room. Perfect places to hide. He pushed Heidi gently back, urging her to stay on the stairs for a moment.

Because the hallway floor had very little padding, the wood creaked as loud as cannon fire. Chuck tensed, bringing the shovel over his shoulder, expecting a Melon Head to come rushing at him. He waited a full minute before exhaling. His next step made just as much noise, but he was resigned to having given up any shred of stealth.

Using the shovel, he yanked the shower curtain to the side. Nothing but bottles of shampoo and conditioner jammed into the four corners of the tub. The spout released a drop of water that echoed in the tiny room.

A pop of wood behind him had Chuck spinning. Heidi was heading into the sewing room.

"Heidi, wait," he whispered.

She held the poker straight out like a lance. If anyone ran to attack her, they might impale themselves in the gloom of the second floor. Chuck tried to edge around her to get into the room first, but she didn't give him an inch. Inside were a sewing machine, a wide bench and plastic drawers filled with sewing supplies. A set of curtains was draped over a drying rack. To the right of the entrance was a closet. Chuck put his finger to his lips and a hand on her shoulder. They waited, Chuck straining to see if he could hear someone breathing or shuffling in the closet. When he thought they were safe, he reached around Heidi, turned the knob and flung the door open. She charged into the closet with the poker, managing to stab a raincoat.

"Oh, Jeez," she said, shoulders sagging.

"Two down, two to go."

"I don't know how much more my heart can take."

He'd been thinking the same thing. His gaze drifted past the light coming up the stairs. He desperately wanted to be down there, bathed in light, waiting for the cavalry to arrive. Talking his way out of their jam was a bridge he'd cross later.

Feeling better that he was in front of Heidi again, he decided what the hell, why not go on the offense and try for a little surprise. He ran into the second bedroom, his footfalls sounding like thunder, Heidi's much lighter footsteps like the patter of rain on a cabin roof. He flicked the light on and scanned the room. A daybed was tucked in the corner. Chuck dropped to his hands and knees and peered under it. Nothing. Heidi had the closet open and was swinging the poker back and forth, knocking clothes off hangers.

They were both breathing heavily, as if they had just run a mile uphill.

"Clear," Heidi said.

"No monsters under the bed," Chuck joked. Heidi didn't so much as smile.

That left what he assumed was the master bedroom at the end of the hall.

He stepped into the hallway. The bedroom was pitch black.

Just great.

A police siren blared. It sounded like it was coming closer. Chuck was running out of time.

He spied the light switch on the wall and motioned with his head for Heidi to flip it. A dim, yellow light flared overhead, filling the room and hallway in jaundice.

Red and white flashing lights bled in through the window at the top of the stairs.

"Looks like the cavalry is here," Chuck said.

"Maybe we should go downstairs."

"You go. I just need to check this last room."

Now he could see the broken window in the bedroom. The curtain billowed as a breeze wafted through the shattered glass. Chuck adjusted his grip on the shovel and took a deep breath.

The sound of springs zinging filled his ears. He was hit on the back of his shoulders hard enough to drop him to the ground, the shovel falling from his grip.

Heidi screamed.

Chuck turned around, the instant ache in his shoulders warning him that something might be broken.

A Melon Head ran down the attic steps from the trapdoor in the hallway ceiling. Its eyes were as big as eggs and spread too far apart to be able to see straight. Its large head was dented on one side and bald as a cue ball. One knobby ear was set high on the side of its head, the other, this one small and round, markedly lower. Everything about its face was off, including what appeared to be two rows of crooked teeth set in an angrily red mouth.

The unfolded attic steps kept it from reaching Heidi. Instead, it stomped on Chuck's chest. His shoulder bounced off the wood floor, the pain sending flashes of white sparking into his vision and sizzling his brain. He felt the Melon Head grab the front of his shirt and lift him from the floor. Chuck brought his knee up, catching the Melon Head right where its balls should be. The creature didn't even react.

Holy shit, it's a girl!

There was nothing in that face or body that delineated the Melon Head as feminine. No, it was one hundred per cent monster.

It punched him in the jaw. Chuck felt a tooth rattle loose. He blocked the next blow with his forearm. The Melon Head dropped to a knee on Chuck's stomach, knocking the wind out of him. Chuck fought against the pain and lack of oxygen, knowing his life depended on it. Slender fingers that may have been forged from steel savagely twisted his ear and grabbed hold of his nose. He could hear cartilage starting to tear in the center of his brain.

Chuck lashed out, getting a grip on the Melon Head's large ear. He gave it a rough yank and the ear pulled free. Hot blood splashed down on his arm and hand. The Melon Head didn't so much as whimper, but it did let go of his nose and ear, only to rain punches down on his face and chest. Chuck threw his arms up, deflecting some but not enough.

There was a heavy thump, and the punching stopped. Chuck looked up and saw Heidi beating at the Melon Head's side with the poker.

"Stab her!" he shouted.

Heidi pulled the poker back and thrust it forward. The Melon Head sprang off Chuck's body, narrowly missing a skewering. It backhanded

Heidi and sent her spinning into the wall. It grabbed Chuck by the hair and started pulling him into the bedroom.

"No!" Heidi shouted. She swung the poker violently. The tip became buried in the plaster wall. She tugged and tugged but couldn't get it out.

The Melon Head dropped to its haunches, opened its mouth wide and looked like it was about to chew Chuck's face off. Foul-smelling saliva baptized his face, slipped onto his tongue. Heidi let go of the poker and emitted a raw, animal scream.

The house reverberated with the clomping of rushing feet. The Melon Head stood up straight and stared down the hall. Heidi was thrown to the side when she tried to tackle the Melon Head.

"Police!" a voice shouted.

"In here," Chuck cried weakly.

The Melon Head swiped its severed ear from the floor, turned and jumped through the broken window. Chuck heard it scrambling down the roof over the porch. A second later, the room was filled with police, their guns drawn. Heidi draped herself over Chuck. "Don't shoot! Don't shoot!"

Her body weight pushed down on Chuck's ruined shoulder. This time, he let the pain take him away.

CHAPTER NINETEEN

Marnie couldn't stop the fresh waves of guilt from pulling her under every time she looked at Chuck's sling or the slashing bruise on Heidi's cheek. Chuck's own face was a black and purple collage. His sling was secured to his torso with a strap wrapped around his midsection. In a strange way, she was glad his beard hid the other lasting marks from his confrontation with the Melon Head.

They sat on the hood of Chuck's car parked under the fluorescent lights in the parking lot outside the Shopwell supermarket. The store had just closed but lights still blazed inside as the workers set about cleaning. Marnie and her friends had been there an hour, never straying far from Chuck's battered car. A hunk of cardboard was duct-taped to the back window. All was quiet now, but that could change in an instant. The doors were left open in case they had to jump inside and burn rubber.

Vent passed Marnie the forty ounce of Crazy Horse, wrapped in a brown paper bag that all but screamed there was booze inside. Crazy Horse cost a dollar a bottle and tasted like something you'd use to clean the floor of a mechanic's garage. The malt liquor concoction packed enough punch to make it worth the pain. Marnie took a long pull, the dull buzz just starting to kick in.

It had been three days since Chuck and Heidi had been attacked. Classes had been suspended at the high school so the police could speak to every single student. Interrogate was more like it. They'd set up a so-called interview room in the gym, putting up partitions so several kids could be interviewed at the same time. The attack on the neighborhood had been deemed a wilding incident on a grander scale than the one that had made headlines in Central Park in New York a few years earlier. The residents hadn't gotten a chance to make out who was tearing up their street and houses, but they were all pretty sure it had to be kids. Naturally, every teenager in Milbury was a suspect. Marnie's interview had been short. She heard a cop say to another as she was leaving, "She looks like she can barely stand up straight. I don't peg her for this."

She'd walked out of the gym with the slow shuffle she'd adopted since leaving the hospital. Her body was mending, at least the parts that could mend, but mentally she still felt broken. She found her hand resting on her stomach off and on throughout the day, vacillating between phantom and real pain and loss.

"I still can't believe you didn't tell them," Vent said. He threw a rock into the trees lining the lot.

"Like they'd believe us," Chuck said. His voice was nasal. His nose hadn't been broken but it was swollen. He was scheduled to go to the dentist the following week to get a fake tooth to replace the one that had been knocked out. It hadn't been found. Marnie wondered if the Melon Head took it as a souvenir.

"You never know," Vent said.

"Yes, we do know," Heidi said.

"At least you guys didn't get the third degree from the cops," Vent said.

Chuck backhanded Vent in the chest. "That's because we almost got killed. I'd trade a broken clavicle for an hour of discomfort any day, man."

Vent looked at the ground, rubbing his chest. "Whatever."

"Yeah, whatever," Chuck said.

"Guys, we don't need this," Marnie said. The tension was wearing them down, whittling their nerves to gossamer threads. The fact that they hadn't been able to find Mick had been a three-ton weight pressing down on them. Marnie didn't want to assume the worst, but it was getting harder to remain optimistic. "I think we should just pick up and go."

"Go?" Heidi said. "Like, where would we go?"

"Someplace far from here."

"We have about a hundred bucks between the four of us. We wouldn't get very far," Chuck said. He winced as he made an adjustment to the sling.

"I have five hundred in a savings account my grandmother set aside for me," Marnie said.

"We can't just drop out senior year and leave our families," Heidi said.

"You don't have to. They're not after you," Marnie said with a trace of doubt in her voice. She looked at Vent. "Or you. But the longer Chuck and me stay here, the more people may get hurt, including you guys. Oh, and let's not forget they're going to tear us apart if they catch us. I've seen what that looks like and I sure as hell don't want it happening to me."

Heidi took the Crazy Horse and finished it. She tossed the empty bottle in Chuck's back seat. "I don't want to lose you."

"You're going to if we stick around too long," Marnie said.

Chuck didn't say a word. She knew he had a lot to lose no matter the choice. He was on his way to a scholarship and getting out of Milbury for good next summer. Only there was no way they were going to dodge the Melon Heads until then. Not if the Melon Heads were willing to come out in force and strafe a whole neighborhood. Chuck had to leave with her. The moment he did, he was also trashing his future, with the caveat that he at least would still have a future.

Chuck kept his cigarettes and lighter in his sling. He lit one up and blew smoke rings that quivered and broke apart as they rose into the light like tiny, fragile haloes. "How do we know if we leave that they won't take it out on our families? I can't take that chance."

Marnie hadn't thought of that. Her family wasn't anything to write home about. She knew people called them white trash. Despite all that, they were all she had. She felt like screaming.

"Maybe Mick was right. We should find a way to work with the Melon Heads," Vent said.

Marnie and Heidi had gone to his trailer the day before. The door was wide open, the inside ransacked. Heidi found splashes of blood on some leaves. Dwight's boat of a car was there but there was no sign of anyone. The whole place felt abandoned.

"You didn't see them," Heidi said, hugging herself. "You can't work with someone like that."

"Dredd did."

"I'm beginning to think he made all that shit up," Chuck said. "Sure, they left him alone for some reason and he knew all about that place in the woods. He could have just been lucky on the one hand

and curious enough to stumble on that weird teepee thing on the other. If he was able to communicate with them, why did he run? They came for him and totally trashed his place. That didn't look like they had an agreement."

A dog started barking in the night, clearly agitated. They couldn't see where it was coming from. A strip of residential homes was right behind Shopwell. Another dog joined the chorus. Marnie slid off the hood and inched her way to the open door. "Something has them spooked."

"Everyone in the car," Chuck said calmly. He cranked the ignition, taking no chances. It was hard to hear the dogs over the rumbling engine.

Marnie climbed out of the window and sat on the edge with her hands on the roof. She waited for the Melon Heads to crawl from the shadows. Heidi touched her leg. "You see anything?"

"No."

The dogs settled down. Somewhere, a screen door banged shut.

How long could they live like this? They were jumping at the sound of dogs barking. Worse still, they were afraid to go home, even Heidi and Vent. Especially Heidi. She'd attacked one of them, maybe hurt it bad. Did that put her on the revenge list? She hoped not, but how could she be sure? No one had spoken out loud about it, but Marnie worried all the time. She'd rather die than lose Heidi. She had almost lost her once already.

"Maybe I should beat them to the punch," she said to the empty lot.

"What?" Heidi said.

"Nothing. We should probably get out of here just in case."

The car rolled into a U-turn. Marnie remained sitting on the window, feeling the cool air on her face. It helped fight the burning sensation boiling under her skin as she considered all her options. None of them were good. The only sure thing was that she wasn't going to let those monsters get her. Not alive.

They drove around for the next couple of hours. It was getting late and they would eventually have to go home. Marnie wished for a freak storm or manmade catastrophe. Anything to delay the inevitable. At home, she would be alone and vulnerable. Her parents never got home before two in the morning.

Chuck popped a Poison cassette into the radio. 'I Want Action' blared from the speakers. The silly, party rock from the eighties never seemed more inappropriate.

"Turn that shit off, man," Vent said.

"You used to love Poison."

"*Used to* is the key word. Hair metal died for a reason."

"I remember when we saw their album cover at Sam Goody. You stopped right in your tracks. You even ranked them from hottest to just plain hot because you thought they were girls." Chuck's laughter filled the car. In this case, it wasn't infectious. Vent kicked the back of his seat.

"How the fuck was I supposed to know? They wore more makeup than every woman in my family combined."

"I believe you wanted to bang Bret Michaels."

"Dude, please shut the fuck up."

They went back and forth over eighties metal and nineties grunge, the Crazy Horse loosening them up. Marnie half listened to their same old arguments. Grunge wiped away eighties metal because the party was over. Grunge was the perfect backdrop to their shitty lives. Even on her best days, Marnie's soul was drawn to the haunting hooks of Alice in Chains rather than the fake cowboy hoedown nonsense perpetrated by Bon Jovi, a bunch of guys from Jersey who wouldn't know the ass end of a horse from a car muffler.

She never wanted to leave the back seat of this car, in this moment, listening to her friends talk about the same old stuff like nothing tragic had happened...or was going to happen. She leaned against Heidi and picked at the frayed edges of the hole in her friend's jeans. Only two things would have made this better: Mick and a couple of joints. Then she could truly pretend that she wasn't going to die.

"I love you," she said to Heidi.

Heidi twirled Marnie's hair between her fingers. "I love you, too. We'll figure something out. I promise."

She didn't have the heart to contradict her best friend.

Marnie drifted off to sleep, awaking when the car came to a stop. "We'll all walk you inside," Chuck said. She rubbed the corner of her eye with her knuckle. "I'll even check the closets and under the beds."

"Thanks," she said, lifting her head off Heidi's lap.

Vent led the way, followed by Marnie, Heidi and Chuck watching their backs. They lit the house up like it was New Year's Eve and methodically checked every room. Naturally, Marnie's mother and stepfather were nowhere to be seen. For once, she wished they were around.

Heidi turned on the backyard floodlights so no one could sneak up behind the house. Once they were comfortable the coast was clear, they headed back out to the car.

"Call me if you get scared or anything," Heidi said.

"I will."

"I'm serious. I can be here in like five minutes." She hugged Marnie around her neck.

"What about you, Chuck? Who's gonna check your house?"

He shrugged with his one good shoulder. "My parents are home, so it should be good. I have an axe in the trunk that I'll take with me when I walk from the car to the house."

"An axe?"

"Better than a baseball bat. Good night, Marns."

"Good night."

Vent gave her a fist pound as he walked past her. She watched Chuck back the car up and turn down the street. The night was chilly and the cold seeped past her layers of flannel. She went to close the door when a figure came up from under the porch. Marnie screamed.

"Shhh, it's me."

Mick hustled up the steps, furtively looking around. His brown leather bomber jacket had a couple of new rips. His hair was greasy and he smelled worse than usual, like he'd been sleeping in a dumpster.

"Where have you been?" Marnie asked once her heart settled down enough for her to talk.

"We need to go inside." He closed and locked the door. "Your parents home?"

Marnie swept an arm across the brilliantly lit room. "Does it look like it?"

"Guess not. I'm starving. You have anything?"

Before she could answer, he was walking into the kitchen and opening the refrigerator. "When's the last time your mother went food shopping? The seventies?" He dipped his finger in a jar of mayonnaise and licked it clean.

"We've been looking all over for you. Where the hell did you go? I was starting to think you were...you were...."

"Dead? Nah. Not yet."

Something was troubling him more than the hornet's nest they'd stirred up with the Melon Heads. He seemed manic, paranoid, and scared.

"So?"

Marnie crossed her arms and leaned on the doorway to the kitchen. She watched Mick guzzle a can of cheap, knockoff cola and gnaw on a hunk of welfare cheese that was about to turn any day now.

"I've been hiding."

"Yeah, but where?"

He waved the cheese around. "Here and there. A different place during the day and a different place each night. They're on to me. I had to keep moving."

"They almost killed Chuck and Heidi."

His mouth dropped open. "What?"

"They came like a mob and wrecked a bunch of houses over on Sycamore. Heidi and Chuck ran into one of the houses and a Melon Head was waiting for them. You didn't hear about it? It's all anyone can talk about."

"I haven't exactly been plugged into the nightly news. So, the cops know all about the Melon Heads."

She shook her head. "The Melon Heads broke the streetlights. It was too dark for anyone to see. They assume it was a bunch of kids high on PCP or coke."

He stuffed a possibly moldy slice of bologna in his mouth and washed it down with more cola. "Of course they do."

"Have you been back to your trailer?"

For a second, he looked like he was going to either yell at her or run. The moment passed and he tousled his hair. "Not in a few days. Why?"

"It's wrecked."

He gave a nervous, sidelong glance. "Maybe Dwight got in one of his drunken rages."

Marnie pulled on her bottom lip. Something about the sudden change in Mick's vibe was making her nervous. Was he hiding something? "Maybe. But it looked more like, you know, *they* were there looking for you."

"Joke's on them. I wasn't there."

It was odd how he didn't even wonder aloud if his mother was okay. Dwight he could live without. His mother, as much of a mess as she was, still mattered to him. There was something Marnie had spotted that she hadn't told the others about. In fact, she'd been waiting for a moment just like this one. "I found a pile of animal bones behind the trailer. They were stacked against the tree with the big gash in the trunk."

He nodded, chomping on more cheese, his labored breath whistling through his nose while he chewed.

"You're really going through with it, aren't you? Leaving them dead animals, hoping they would – what? Not bite the hand that feeds them? Do you know how crazy that sounds?" She wasn't sure, now that she'd asked the question, if she wanted the answer.

"Yeah," he replied with a shrug. "I was. One of us had to try something. I...I thought maybe I could take Dredd's place. It would suck, but at least we wouldn't have to watch our backs every minute of the day. I could only take down small animals with the BB gun, though. Probably was never going to be enough. Not after Dunwoody. They have bigger appetites than I can handle." His eyes glazed over, his mind drifting to what Marnie could sense was a dark, horrible place.

Marnie's arms broke out in gooseflesh.

"You're not trying to be the new Dredd anymore then?"

He was quick to say, "Fuck no. It's never gonna work. The way I see it, we either leave or we make a stand. No more running. No more hiding."

"That's easy to say," Marnie said. "There are five of us and god knows how many of them. And they're crazy. We can't fight that."

Mick hip-checked the refrigerator door to close it. Bottles rattled inside. "Maybe we can. We just need to know their weakness. Where they hide during the day."

"I don't think we're going to find the answers to that in the library. And Shaggy and Scooby don't come around here."

A nervous smile played on his lips. "That's why I kept on looking until I found him."

"Found who?"

"Dredd. I knew the fucker wouldn't go far."

"Holy crap. We have to tell everyone."

Mick shook his head. "Right now, I just want it to be me and you. I don't want to scare him off."

"I don't understand."

He walked past her into the living room. "Sit down and I'll tell you."

CHAPTER TWENTY

Chuck failed the economics test that was supposed to account for a quarter of his grade for the semester. Luckily, Mr. Murphy offered to let him retake the test next week in light of his being attacked by the wilding gang. If he only knew the truth.

He wanted a joint real bad, but he had to keep his head straight to study and be on the alert for another attack. He looked up from his textbook and into the small mirror on his wall. He looked like sun-baked dog shit and it had nothing to do with the bruises. It was all in his eyes. His body was in a constant state of fight or flight. Sleep was fleeting. He'd never felt so tired. His eyes were bloodshot all the time. Amazing how he looked stoned but, for once, he was straight as six o'clock.

The words in his book read like nonsense written by a first grader. Try as he might, nothing was getting through the thick fog in his brain.

"Screw it." He slammed the book closed and pushed his chair back from the desk. The bottle of Benadryl he'd swiped from the medicine cabinet was next to the textbook. He'd promised himself he would get some sleep tonight. What good was he going to be if he was sleep deprived?

The Benadryl would knock him out for sure. It would also send him into sleep so deep, he'd never hear trouble if it came knocking. That would be a fatal mistake.

Chuck opened a desk drawer and swept the bottle inside. He yawned and rubbed his face. Sunlight streamed through his window. It would normally be open, but he kept it locked tight now. He thought of Marnie and her idea of the two of them picking up and leaving for good. And it would have to be forever. The Melon Heads had been living in the recesses of Milbury for a long time and it would stay that way for even longer.

He looked over at the phone and considered calling Heidi. Since the attack, they'd been talking a lot. They were both scared, though he tried to keep his fears to himself. Heidi was smart, though, and he knew she saw through his BS. He could pick the phone up and call her right now and he knew she'd answer on the first ring. Something was happening between them. He wasn't that dense. This wasn't just wishful thinking. Their friendship was becoming something more. Just what, he wasn't sure. He did know what he would like it to be.

If he told Mick any of this, he knew what he'd say. "Dude, what's wrong with you? She's like a sister."

But she wasn't. Not by a long shot. Never had been. Never would. This strengthening bond between them had been the silver lining in all of this madness. He'd filled so many socks with his hurried fantasies of where all of this would lead that he was now walking in bare feet. He wasn't sure if his increased spank sessions were out of ignited feelings for Heidi or a way to burn off his nervous energy.

He picked up the phone, started to dial, and stopped.

What was the point? He was either going to leave her or die. Some choice. It would be better for both of them if things didn't go any further than they already had.

A dull throb started to build in his shoulder. If he didn't take one of the pills the doctor gave him, he knew it would escalate to screaming pain within the hour. Sometimes, he let the pain come and stay for a while because it kept him in the moment. They said he'd have to wear the sling for at least a month. There would be weeks of physical therapy after that. How had that Melon Head that was half his size and a woman (or girl...how could he know for sure?) have kicked his ass so easily and thoroughly? It was the first time anyone had ever hit him. In the past, his sheer size was enough to cut any fight off at the pass.

She beat you like a red-headed stepchild. You never even had a chance.

How would he fare against two of them? Or five? Or twenty? He'd end up just like Harold Dunwoody, torn apart like a Thanksgiving turkey.

That nightmare wasn't getting any better, either. Whenever he thought back to Dunwoody's final moments, he had to sprint to the bathroom. He'd run out of puke a week ago, settling now for painful shits that left him sweaty and drained.

Useless. He'd become pathetically useless. Hell, his brain wasn't even working. He was cracking up, that was for sure. His parents were getting worried about him. He saw it in their eyes every time he stepped in the room. They had taken to whispering to each other when he'd leave. He wished he could ask them for help, but even they wouldn't believe him. At least this new concern for his well-being had been a welcome diversion for all of the 'just say no' and 'you need to hang out with a better class of people' talks. Now, those had been uncomfortable and a little asinine, as far as he was concerned. Thank you so much, Nancy Reagan. Uptight old twat.

Sleep. He needed sleep. If he could recharge, he'd heal and maybe, just maybe, he could think straight and find a way out of this.

The big question was where could he go for a night where he'd feel safe enough to let his guard down? A hotel down in Norwalk would do, or even a seedy motel in Stamford. The problem was money. His wallet wasn't exactly overflowing with cash.

Call Heidi. She'll lend you the money.

What if she wanted to come along? His heart raced just at the thought. No, now wasn't the time for that. He needed real rest, not a night of clumsy attempts to get Heidi's bra off with one hand.

No sense calling Vent. He was perpetually tapped. He'd feel guilty taking any cash from Marnie. Besides, if he did, she'd spend the entire time trying to convince him to keep on going and never look back. It was easy when you had nothing much to look back on.

And then there was Mick. He'd find a way to pick a cheap motel door lock and get a night on the cheap. That wouldn't work, either. Chuck knew himself. He'd spend a sleepless night waiting for the police to break the door down with guns drawn.

Just. Call. Heidi.

He sighed deeply and started coughing.

And then he picked up the phone.

★ ★ ★

Marnie 'borrowed' her stepfather's Ford van, the one he used on those days when he felt like making some cash as a swinging hammer. The van had been declared off limits to her back when she was old enough to know how to use the key to open the door. She'd happily steered clear of it. What little girl would want to root around a dirty old van filled with greasy-smelling tools?

She drove it as best she could, while Mick gave her directions. The van's carburetor had some serious issues, threatening to stall every time she stopped for a light or slowed down for a stop sign. She peeked into the rearview mirror at the haphazard shelving in the back. Tools improperly stowed had been shifting around with a steady metallic clinking that was rubbing her nerves raw.

"How much further is it?" she asked.

"Couple of miles, tops. It was hard to tell because I walked it."

Mick had been busy in his absence. He'd told her how he had brazenly gone to Dredd's place two days ago, anxious to find him. The decision to go there was out of total desperation. The last place he wanted to be alone was anywhere near Dracula Drive, but it became clear it was the only place that might shed some light on their situation. The cabin had burned pretty good, but one side hadn't caught the ire of the flames for some reason. Within that sliver of still-standing cabin was a lockbox. And in that lockbox was an assortment of papers and pictures. Most important was a birth certificate announcing the live birth of Christopher James Runde in Milbury General Hospital on June 7th, 1970. The hospital was long gone and Mick was sure Chris, now calling himself Dredd, was as well. There were pictures of two boys, one looking to be almost twice Chris's age. In one, they were at a pool, waving to the camera. In another, they leaned against the garage door, looking tough. The third is what came in most handy. They sat on the porch stairs of a brown-shingled house. The number of the house was too fuzzy to make out, but the house itself stood out because of the porch swing and the diamond-shaped window in what had to be the attic. Mick had taken the picture with him and simply walked all throughout Milbury, searching for the house. He'd found it last night. It looked like no one had lived there for a very long time. Browning grass and weeds were waist high in the front yard. The front door and windows had been boarded up, though a few of the boards had rotted enough for someone to slip inside. Creeping around to the back, he detected a faint light coming from the basement.

It appeared Dredd had come home.

"Pull over here," Mick said. The little cul-de-sac was pitch black and the houses looked abandoned. Marnie wondered what had happened here to drive everyone away. The houses looked like they were on the expensive side back in the day when they'd been built. Like most of Milbury, the residents probably left when the economy tanked and no one was dumb enough to buy a place like these in Milbury, the town without a future (and not much of a past when you thought about it).

"Which one is it?"

He showed her the picture. She spotted the house right away. Of the homes in the cul-de-sac, it was in the worst shape. There were no other cars around and nary a light in a window.

Had Dredd's parents left soon after their oldest son was murdered by the Melon Heads? That's what she would do. She couldn't imagine living in a place where the ghost of her son lived in every room. Did his parents just think he was missing? A runaway? Murdered, but not by forest-dwelling cannibals? Had Dredd told them about the Melon Heads and they ran as fast and far as they could?

One thing was sure. The dilapidated house wasn't going to tell them any of its secrets.

"Come on," Mick said, practically jumping out of the car. He went to the back of the van and fumbled around until he found a hammer and a coil of rope. "You ready?"

Marnie wasn't sure she was ready for anything at this point. She was exhausted, her nerves worn to the nub from constant anxiety. The last time she'd jumped in alongside Mick on one of his bright ideas, it had led to the destruction of their lives. Was she insane for taking him out here? Possibly. Maybe it was sleep deprivation more than desperation. It would be nice to have stable adults she could lean on right about now, but so would winning the lottery or marrying Eddie Vedder. Short of that, she had to rely on her own terrible decision-making abilities.

"No," she said. "But I feel like I don't have a choice."

Mick hefted the coiled rope on his shoulder. "We don't if we want to fix this. You can wait in the van if you want. I can handle Dredd."

"Dredd has a gun. You have a hammer."

When he grinned, Marnie almost felt sorry for Dredd. "Yeah, but I'm pissed and he's just pissing his pants in that basement."

Marnie surprised herself when she followed him along the side of the house. She cast worried glances left and right, expecting a light to pop on in one of the houses and someone to ask her where the hell she thought she was going. But there was nothing in the forgotten cul-de-sac except crickets and maybe a stray raccoon or two. She followed in Mick's footsteps, avoiding the odd beer can or plank of wood. Her foot just missed a two-by-four that had been snapped in half, rusty nails the size of witch's fingers sticking straight up, just waiting to dig into the soft flesh of an unsuspecting sole. The backyard was completely closed in by a high stone wall at the end of the yard, with thick pine trees growing on its other side. Rotting fences blocked out the yards to the sides of Dredd's old house. They could do anything they wanted here and no one would see. She wasn't the first to think that. The overgrown lawn, which was more weed than grass, was strewn with used condoms, beer and vodka bottles, cigarette butts and little plastic baggies that once held weed and pills. The place was creepy as hell, more so because she knew the Melon Heads could be near.

"There," Mick whispered, pointing at a metal storm cellar door sprouting from the back of the house like the rest of the weeds. Paint peeled off the doors, which were cinched shut by a thick chain and padlock. Unlike everything else, the chain and lock looked new. "He's holed up in the basement."

"Did you see him?"

"Yep. Watched him crawl in through the window over there. I could hear him going down the steps and saw a light come on before he stuffed something against the glass. Might have been a pillow."

"And how are we supposed to get down there? I'll bet the door inside to the basement is locked up just as tight."

Mick slapped a bug buzzing on the side of his neck. He checked his palm and smeared it against his leg. "We're not going in. He's coming out."

Marnie pulled her oversized flannel shirt tight, burying her hands within the worn cuffs. "I'm not gonna sit out here all night and wait for him to leave. This place is freaking me out."

What she didn't say was that she was feeling like she was going to pass out. She was far from out of the woods from her injuries and infection. Her ratcheting anxiety wasn't making things any easier. She needed to lie down and take her pills. Though what was the sense of resting if she had a chance to save her life, her friends' lives, and didn't take it?

Mick put the hammer on the ground and cupped her shoulders. "Look, I said I needed your help. It wasn't just for the van."

She narrowed her eyes at him. In the pale blue glow of the moonlight, Mick looked as if he'd been transformed into a kid. Smoothed out by lunar glow were the worry lines that always creased his brow and the bumps of acne that reddened his cheeks and chin. He looked like the eleven-year-old Mick who would ask her if she wanted to go on an adventure, an adventure that would include a small swath of nature and a lot of imagination. She remembered games of safari played well into the night, where he was a knockoff Tarzan and she was the stranded woman who helped him find anything from a lost tribe of elephants to an ancient order of gorillas tasked with guarding a treasure left behind by Captain Kidd.

They'd changed so much since then, but they were still going on adventures. She'd come with him this far. Time to see it through.

"Just tell me what you need."

CHAPTER TWENTY-ONE

Heidi heard the desperation in Chuck's voice and was compelled to go to him. He said he needed something but wanted to ask her in person. She was worried that he was taking Marnie's suggestion that he leave town with her. She was also concerned that if he stayed in Milbury, something horrible would happen to him. Something already had, but at least he was still alive.

She checked herself in the mirror and went to the closet. She reached inside blindly and pulled out her old leather jacket, the one with the fringes on the sleeves. She'd found it at a consignment store a couple of years ago. There was a time, when she was around ten, where the only thing in the world she wanted was a fringed leather jacket. She wanted to look like Jon Bon Jovi, the coolest and sexiest guy on the planet – at least at the time. But jackets like that didn't come cheap and her parents didn't see the point in buying an expensive novelty jacket for a girl who would outgrow it within a year, both emotionally and physically.

Now you could get one for ten bucks as former metalheads ditched their leather for what Heidi called used-dads clothes. It wasn't exactly glamorous, though it did take the pressure off trying to achieve some impossible standard of beauty.

Heidi's car was perilously low on gas. She didn't think she'd be able to make it to his house and back. The last time she'd gone to the gas station, Marnie helped her reach under the seat cushions to find any spare change to get even a few drops of gas in the tank.

Dusk would be coming soon. The thought of riding her bike terrified her for good reason. Chuck could drive her back when night had fallen. It gave her small comfort as she rolled her bike out of the driveway. She propped it on its kickstand and ran to the shed in the backyard. She found her father's old, partially rusty sickle and stuffed the handle in her back pocket. Ever since he'd ditched his push mower for the gas mower, he'd had no use for the sickle. She hoped she wouldn't, either.

"Where are you going?"

Her mother startled her. A tickling breeze fluffed the bangs from Heidi's face.

Heidi froze. She knew if she told the truth, her mother would forbid her to go. Lightning, in her estimation, could strike twice. She quickly made up a lie. "I just need to go to Sammy's to copy some notes."

Sammy and Heidi were close as friends could be when they were in grammar school. Now they circled in separate orbits, maintaining an acquaintanceship that was limited to hellos and head nods whenever they ran into one another. Sammy was a brainiac who still had posters of New Kids on the Block on her bedroom walls. Heidi knew her mother would approve of her going to Sammy the dork.

"I don't want you gone long. In fact, why don't I drive you?"

That wouldn't do. Heidi said, "She's only two blocks away."

Her mother took another step down from the porch. "It's getting late. I worry about you."

Heidi rolled her eyes the way she normally would when her mother said something sappy, only this time she appreciated it more than she'd ever let on.

"How about I ask her father to drive me back?"

She smiled. "That makes me feel better. Or I can pick you up. Your father called and said he'd be late."

"Sammy's dad has that pickup truck. I can just toss the bike in the back." She took her mother's hand. "Trust me, I'll be fine. I promise I will not ride my bike alone at night." She wouldn't even ride her bike with a gang at night. She was swallowing a ton of fear just to pedal to Chuck's.

Her mother pulled her close and kissed the top of her head. Ever since Heidi's run-in with 'the wilding gang', her mother had been extra affectionate. Kisses and hugs, gestures that had faded as Heidi sped through adolescence, were doled out whenever she walked by her mom. She'd say the opposite if she were ever put on the witness stand, but she loved the added attention.

"Just be safe."

"I will."

Heidi reached behind her back and made sure her jacket covered the sickle. She hopped on her bike and headed off, turning once to wave goodbye. Her mother stayed on the step, watching her go, until Heidi couldn't see that far anymore.

The streets were busier than usual as parents came home from work. Heidi had to swerve twice to avoid being clipped by a car pulling into a driveway. She passed twin girls playing hopscotch on the sidewalk. Heidi wished she could be that young again. Things were so much easier when she was young, even though all she wanted to do at that age was grow older. Chuck's house was five more blocks away. She pedaled harder, anxious to get there before the first streetlights started to flicker on. Her eyes were in constant motion, searching for something or someone that didn't belong. The question was, if she saw a Melon Head, would she continue on to Chuck's or turn around and try to make the longer trip back to her house?

She worried needlessly, and cruised into Chuck's driveway at the same time as his parents were pulling up.

"Hey, Heidi," Chuck's father said when he got out of the car. He opened the back door to grab several shopping bags. "You came just in time."

She leaned her bike against the house and paused, confused.

Chuck's mother emerged and smiled, slipping her pocketbook over her shoulder. "He means for dinner. I'm making ritzy chicken. It's to die for."

"And at your age, you don't have to worry about it clogging your arteries," Chuck's father said.

"Your arteries are just fine." Chuck's mother playfully swatted her husband's back as he hustled past her with the groceries. Turning to Heidi, she said, "Chuck will be happy to see you. Come on in."

"Th-thanks," Heidi replied, a little out of breath and sweating more than she should. It felt as if she'd biked for ten miles, not ten blocks.

As soon as they walked in the door, his mother called up the stairs, "Chuck! Heidi's here!" She patted Heidi on the arm. "You like mashed or baked potatoes?"

Waltzing into this slice of normalcy was disorienting. For a second,

Heidi didn't even know what a potato was. She quickly regained her balance and said, "Mashed is cool."

"Then mashed it shall be. Might as well go up. I bet he fell asleep."

It was impossible not to see the delight in Chuck's parents' faces. They'd been getting all doe-eyed every time she was around since the incident with the Melon Heads. Chuck had explained to her that it was their hope he and Heidi would get closer and drift away from Mick, Vent and Marnie. That might have been part of it, but she was pretty sure there was another side to that story.

She went upstairs and knocked on Chuck's door. When he didn't answer, her heart caught in her throat. They had just talked on the phone. He sounded tired and nervous. Why wasn't he answering? His mother's high-pitched voice alone should have woken him up. Had something happened to him? Her hand trembled as she reached out for the doorknob. She knocked again.

"Chuck?"

Thank god the door didn't open with an old-time horror movie creak. Before her was his unmade bed, a stack of books on his desk, posters of Hole, Screaming Trees and Mudhoney papering his walls. But there was no Chuck. His window was wide open. Heidi rushed across the room and looked down, terrified that he had accidentally fallen – or worse. She looked down into the rose bushes on the side of the house.

"Chuck, where are you?"

The sound of footsteps above her made her flinch. Her first instinct was to run downstairs into the sounds of normal domesticity. She could clearly hear his parents talking, cabinet doors opening and closing, pots and pans clanging. The radio was on, tuned to an oldies station. 'Duke of Earl' was playing.

She backed away from the window.

Whump.

A floorboard groaned.

A flashback to what had happened at that woman's house (they later learned her name was Miriam Acosta, a recent widow with a heart problem she talked on and on about to the police) froze her in place. The steady whoosh of blood rushing in her ears threatened to drown out all other sound.

Feet shuffled overhead.

Run! I have to run!

Heidi bolted for the door just as someone was hustling down what sounded like a set of stairs in another room.

She turned toward the hallway and crashed face-first into something soft yet hard. Heidi screamed.

"Holy crap, what's wrong?"

Chuck's panicked voice managed to subdue her own flight of fear. Her nose throbbed where she'd slammed it into his chest. "Oh my god, it was you."

"You kids all right up there?" Chuck's father said.

Heidi's heart was still fluttering, making it hard to sound nonchalant. "I'm fine. I saw a spider and freaked out."

Chuck gave her a conspiratorial wink.

"No need to be afraid of spiders. It's the six-inch millipedes that should worry you," his father replied.

Chuck shook his head. "He's kidding."

They listened to his father walk back into the kitchen. He sang along, badly, with Dion to 'The Wanderer'.

Heidi and Chuck went back into his room. He gently closed the door.

"Were you trying to give me a heart attack?" she said, settling into his chair. He took the corner of his bed, the other end of the mattress lifting.

"I was in the attic looking for stuff."

"I thought…I thought…."

"I figured." He scratched at his arm under the sling. "You want me to get you a Coke or something?"

"No, I'm good. I think. What were you looking for?"

He turned on his boom box just loud enough to cover their voices. The tape warbled for a bit, making Chris Cornell sound like he was singing underwater. "I need to find stuff to pawn. Stuff my parents won't miss."

"Please don't tell me you're taking off with Marnie." Heidi's stomach dropped.

"Nah. I just need to get away for even a night and just smoke a little and sleep. I'm so tired, I'm starting to get delirious. I can't afford to be delirious now. I was hoping there'd be some old jewelry box from my grandmother or an antique I could pawn for a while. Leave it to my parents to fill an attic with junk. You think anyone would give me cash for some dusty old Christmas ornaments?"

Heidi sagged into the chair's back with relief. "Highly doubtful."

"That's what I was afraid of."

"I can lend you the money."

"I'll find a way. Thanks for coming over. I just needed to see—"

He was cut off by the kerrang of a pot hitting the floor downstairs.

Heidi smiled. "Your parents invited me to stay. She said she's making ritzy chicken. What the heck is that, anyway?"

Chuck pulled his hand over his face and tugged on his beard. "Take a chicken cutlet and simmer it in butter and cheese. It looks like a mess, but I swear, it's good."

"Sounds delicious. Hey, you mind giving me a ride back to my house later?"

"I wouldn't let you take your bike back in a million years."

A dish broke downstairs.

"What the hell are they doing down there?" Chuck said. He leaned his body toward the door.

Something smashed against a wall. The radio went silent. Chuck bolted upright and put his hand on the doorknob. Heidi was up, too, and a step behind him. "What is it?"

Thump-thump-thump. It sounded like someone body-slamming the walls. Chuck paled. Heidi swallowed hard, her throat so dry, it hurt.

"Hand me that bat," Chuck said, motioning toward the scuffed Louisville Slugger beside his bed.

He tucked the bat under his good arm and opened the door. Heidi couldn't help thinking how much protection a one-armed person with a baseball bat could offer. She scanned the room for anything that could be used as a weapon, settled on an X-Acto knife and flicked off the plastic cap.

What sounded like a muffled cry set Chuck's legs in motion. He bounded heedlessly down the stairs with the bat held over his shoulder. Heidi tried to keep up with him, mentally urging him to slow the hell down and not get them killed. When he stopped suddenly in the kitchen doorway, Heidi ran into him, nearly plunging the X-Acto knife in his back.

What she saw was a horror she could never have prepared herself for.

Chuck's father was on his back on the floor. His throat had been ripped out, revealing a raw, ragged, red hole that bubbled and pulsed with free-flowing blood. The chunk of flesh that had been there moments before sat in a quivering pile on the counter, next to the pack of raw chicken. His right leg trembled with a seizure or death spasm, Heidi couldn't be sure.

"You motherfuckers," Chuck growled.

His mother was in the clutches of two Melon Heads. One had its hand over her mouth. The other had her by the waist and was picking at her blouse, ripping buttons off with its long, dirt-encrusted fingernails. Her eyes rolled wildly in their sockets. She saw Chuck and tried to scream, but her cries were cut off by the pale, bony hand over her mouth.

The Melon Heads looked like twins. Neither had a wisp of hair on their heads. They had strange knobs on their skulls, like stumps of horns that had been shaved off. Drool hung in milky ropes from their chapped lips. She saw nothing remotely human in their charcoal eyes.

"Mom!"

Chuck swung the bat clumsily at one of the Melon Heads. It was quicker than him, rolling to its left and using his mother as a shield. The bat socked her in the elbow with a sickening crunch. Her eyes scrunched up and tears sprang from their corners.

Heidi was on the verge of hyperventilating. It was too much to bear. She spun around, lashing out with the X-Acto knife, expecting to be surrounded by Melon Heads. She slashed thin air.

Chuck wailed. "Get the fuck off my mom!"

He charged the Melon Heads. The one holding her mouth turned her head hard to the left, just a fraction before her neck snapped. Chuck stopped. The Melon Heads growled at him like angry dogs. Heidi adjusted her grip on the X-Acto knife.

"It's me you want," Chuck said. "Let her go and take me."

The one that had his mother by the waist cocked its head in incomprehension.

Heidi kept throwing glances over her shoulder, as much to watch their backs as to divert her gaze from what had been done to Chuck's father. His leg had gone still, and the blood no longer spurted from the hole in his throat.

"Come on!" Chuck shouted. The startled Melon Heads jerked back. "Take me." The bat clattered on the floor and rolled to a stop next to his dead father. Chuck threw his good arm wide. "You want me so bad. Well, here I am!"

The Melon Heads looked at the bat, then back up at Chuck in unison. His mother whimpered, trying to say something. The tendons in her neck were painfully visible.

Chuck took a step toward them. "I said let her go."

"Chuck, don't," Heidi said.

He ignored her. Instead, he found a fleck of potato on the counter, picked it up and tossed it at one of the Melon Heads. It pinged off its horrid face. The man-creature looked at him with wary curiosity.

"Come on, fucker. My friend killed one of your forest retards. You killed my dad. You still don't think we're even? Let's go. I dare you."

A Melon Head swiped at him like a cat. Chuck didn't so much as flinch. The stench of blood and sweat and fear was cloying. Heidi was sure more of them would come pouring in like a swarm of cockroaches any second now.

Chuck bellowed, "I said—"

The Melon Heads threw Chuck's mother into him, but not before giving her neck a last, fatal twist. Her neck cracked like the popping of champagne corks. She was launched savagely into Chuck. He toppled over his father's corpse, trying in vain to keep hold of his mother's lifeless body. He hit the floor with a resounding thud, awash in his father's blood. His mother rolled off his chest, her face turned up toward Heidi, a sightless eye staring at her.

Heidi screamed at the top of her lungs. She held the tiny knife in front of her. The Melon Heads ignored her. Instead, they dove for Chuck as he struggled to get off the floor. One grabbed him by the throat. The other dipped its head down and took a bite from Chuck's thigh. Chuck shrieked in agony.

They were going to tear him apart. They started working at his limbs, tugging and twisting. Chuck's bad arm was yanked out of the sling, eliciting a keening cry that rivaled the high wail of an ambulance siren. Heidi lashed out with the X-Acto, cutting a thin line across the back shoulder of the nearest Melon Head. It whipped its head around and snarled. Heidi jumped back nearly three feet. Her lower back painfully clipped the edge of a counter. The injured Melon Head went back to trying to pop Chuck's shoulder out of its socket. Chuck tried to lift himself off the floor, but the other Melon Head leapt to its feet and stomped him in the center of his chest. Chuck dropped back like a dead man.

Ignoring the pain racing up her back, Heidi stepped forward, this time burying the knife into the side of the Melon Head's neck. A bony hand quickly ripped it out. A geyser of blood burst from the hole in its neck. The Melon Head yowled, trying to hold the blood back. It glared at her with a burning hatred that could have reduced her to ash.

Heidi backpedaled, sobbing, her entire body shaking to the point where she felt as if she were coming undone. With Chuck unconscious, the pair of Melon Heads turned their attention to her. Blood pulsed between one's fingers, painting the wall in red splatters as it advanced on her.

She had to run. That meant she was going to leave Chuck, who was utterly defenseless. She knew that if she made it out of here alive and came back, Chuck would be dead.

"Help!" she shouted at the top of her lungs. "Somebody help me! Please, somebody help!"

The shrillness in her voice gave the Melon Heads pause, but not for long.

She had backed her way into the living room. The Melon Heads approached slowly, as if they knew she had no chance of getting away. Why rush a kill when you could savor it?

"Help!"

Her voice faltered at the end. Her mouth was filled with the taste of copper. The back of her leg thumped an end table. She reached out for anything to steady herself, but there was nothing to grab. She fell over the armrest of a love seat, hit the cushion and rolled onto the floor.

"No, no, no, no!"

The bleeding one scurried to her. Its hot blood spattered her chest and neck and face. Heidi turned her head away, spitting out its poisonous fluid. When she turned back to face the Melon Head, its arms were reaching out for her like a vampire in one of those old black and white movies.

The steel end of a shovel flew past her vision, hitting the Melon Head in the face with a resounding *thwang*. The Melon Head fell away from her. She felt its body hit the floor next to her. She wasted no time in getting to her feet.

"You all right?"

Vent had the shovel cocked over his shoulder, threatening to swing for the fences at the standing Melon Head. Its head bobbed between its fallen comrade and Vent, confusion and anger fighting for control on its distorted face.

"Hit it, Vent. Hit it!"

He swung, but the Melon Head jumped back. The shovel sliced through the space where its stomach had been a nanosecond before.

The Melon Head reached out to grab the handle of the shovel. Vent tugged it away and batted its hand. It cradled its hand under its armpit. The creature made a disturbing gurgling noise at him, as if it were trying to speak through wads of phlegm.

"Run, Heidi. I'll hold it back."

Heidi's sweat-soaked hair stuck to her face. "We can't. Chuck's in the kitchen."

"Fuck." Vent took another swing and missed. "Maybe we can get him and go out the kitchen door."

"How?"

"Just stay behind me."

Vent kept swinging the shovel and the Melon Head kept skipping out of the way. Heidi didn't notice they had edged around the beast until her back was at the kitchen doorway. Chuck was still on the floor. His eyes fluttered open. "Wuh?"

Heidi reached down and tugged at his good arm. The pain brought Chuck out of his stupor. "Oh, Jesus that hurts."

"We have to get out of here," she said, unable to contain the panic in her voice.

The sound of the shovel handle hitting the doorframe made her heart skip a beat.

Chuck got up, swaying a bit on his feet. He looked around the room as if seeing his murdered parents for the first time. Then he looked at Vent, keeping the Melon Head at bay with the shovel.

His damaged arm hung limply at his side. It looked like it would fall off in a stiff breeze.

Heidi pointed at the door. "Let's go."

"No." Chuck grabbed the biggest knife from the butcher block. "Vent, let it in!"

Vent looked back at them with an expression of complete bewilderment. That was enough time for the Melon Head to burst into the room, knocking him to the floor. Chuck charged, burying the knife in its taut belly. The Melon Head doubled over. Vent regained his footing and whacked it on the back of the head. The Melon Head collapsed, the impact pushing the knife past its hilt.

"Thanks, man," Chuck said. He was scarily pale and covered in sweat.

Vent saw Chuck's parents and staggered into the refrigerator. "Oh my god."

The sounds of a building commotion came from the front of the house. Heidi said, "Maybe someone finally called the police."

Chuck rushed out of the room to check the living room window. "It's more of them!"

Heidi didn't want to see for herself. "We have to go out back, now."

Chuck stomped into the kitchen. "I can't leave them." He stared at his parents, his eyes brimming with tears.

"I'm so sorry I didn't come sooner," Vent said. "I could have stopped them."

Heidi took Chuck's sweaty hand. "Look, I know this is going to be hard, but we have to leave. Your parents wouldn't want you to be killed by…by those things. They'd want you to do anything you could to survive. The only way we're going to do that is by getting out of here right now while we still can."

They may already have been too late. Who was to say there weren't dozens more waiting for them in the darkened backyard?

"Heidi's right," Vent said.

One of the front windows broke.

Chuck's good shoulder sagged. He whispered something Heidi couldn't hear. He turned and kicked the door open. He took one last look at his parents and said, "I'm sorry," his voice hitching. It nearly broke her.

The three of them scampered across the yard, waiting to be attacked. They jumped a fence, skirted around a pool, and scaled the next fence. Chuck did remarkably well for someone with one working arm. Heidi assumed it was the adrenaline.

They'd made it four blocks to the north when they finally stopped to catch their breath. In the distance, Heidi thought she heard glass shattering and wood snapping.

Vent sat with his head between his knees. "Well, now we're all in the same boat."

"What do you mean?"

"We've all killed a Melon Head. I wonder whose house is next."

CHAPTER TWENTY-TWO

Mick was banking on Dredd not remembering who Marnie was. He couldn't even recall her name when they were together. The guy was pretty burnt. He just couldn't tell if it was from drugs or a life destroyed by the Melon Heads.

He didn't like sending Marnie inside the house alone, especially not with her just recovering from the hell she'd been through. In fact, when he'd told her the plan, he half hoped she'd tell him to go to hell. Then it would be on to plan B, which is where Mick would wait outside for Dredd to come out, jump him and tie him up. Only problem with that was that Dredd was bigger and stronger than him and just might get away if he had any open space to run.

It was better to have Dredd cornered. So, plan A it was.

"You ready for this?" he asked Marnie.

She still looked sick, but there was a glow in her eyes that gave him a little comfort. "Yeah." She put her hand out and he gave her his pocket knife. She tucked it carefully in her back pocket. Mick pulled the board over the window aside so she could slip into the kitchen. He knew Dredd would hear her footsteps the second she went in. He was counting on it. He used a stick to prop the board open enough for him to look inside. Marnie snapped on the flashlight and scanned the room. Most of the cabinet doors had been ripped off long ago; the shelves, those that weren't rotted or split in two, empty. The oven door was open, and it looked like birds or other critters had once built a nest inside. There was one chair in the center of the room, the metal flecked with rust, stuffing coming out of the seat. Marnie looked back at him and gave him a thumbs up. He handed the radio through the window. She propped it on a counter and turned it on, but not too loud. Pearl Jam rocked on about a boy snapping in class. People in school used to make fun of Mick, calling him Jeremy, as if they wanted him to lose his shit. There were days he wondered what he would do if he had a gun. In the end, he decided they were all assholes and the best thing he could do was leave them in his rearview mirror. Maybe another Jeremy would come along and they would push him too far and get what they deserved.

Focus, man. He tapped the side of his head with the handle of the hammer.

Marnie made it a point to walk around, wake Dredd up if he was asleep. She propped the flashlight on the floor so the light bathed the ceiling and cascaded down into the kitchen. She took the joint he'd given her out of her shirt pocket, sat down and lit it. It was weak skunk weed, nothing that would fuck her up. She took a quick hit, exhaling a cloud of thick smoke. Marnie crossed her legs, her right nervously bobbing up and down.

"Come on, Dredd," Mick whispered. He gave his flashlight two quick bursts in Marnie's direction to assure her he was right there, watching over her.

Did Dredd play possum when stoners broke into the abandoned house for a quick smoke or screw? Mick was counting on Dredd's mercurial nature. He may have been in hiding, but he wouldn't be able to resist messing with someone.

They didn't have to wait long. Heavy footsteps clomped up the basement stairs. A door creaked open. Marnie flicked her gaze Mick's way, but then she was back, playing it cool, pretending she was on the road to getting good and baked.

"What the fuck do you think you're doing in here?"

Dredd stepped cautiously out of the basement. He had his rifle in hand. Marnie stiffened for a moment. Mick's heart stopped.

Then Marnie softened and looked at Dredd with half-closed eyes. "Can't a girl just smoke in peace?"

"Not in here, she can't."

She leaned her head back into the top of the chair. "You want a hit?"

Dredd took a step into the kitchen. "Who else is here?"

"Just the three of us."

The gun raised up.

"Me, myself, and I," Marnie said with a giddy chuckle, pretending she was already wasted.

Dredd didn't point the gun at her, but it would only take a flick of the wrist to put her in its sights. "Why don't the three of you take a hike, then."

"You own this dump?"

A disgusted frown changed his face. "Yeah, I own this dump."

Marnie took another hit. "Sorry, I didn't mean to insult you. It's better than my place, believe me. At least here my parents aren't up my ass and my uncle isn't trying to get up in other places, you know?" She ran her hand through her hair and bent over, staring at the ground as if Dredd weren't there.

"Life sucks. That doesn't give you the right to break into my place." He'd taken two more steps toward her.

"I just needed someplace to crash. I needed to get high and forget my shit for a night. I'm sorry. I didn't think anyone was here. Guess I picked the wrong abandoned house. Is the one over there totally empty?" She tilted her head toward the derelict on the left of Dredd's house. He nodded. "Cool. I'll go. You don't need to shoot me." She flashed a mischievous smile when she said the last line.

She got up and turned the tape player off. In the silence, her footsteps along the detritus-littered floor sounded like firecrackers. She took off her flannel shirt and stretched, the white wife beater she had on underneath barely able to contain her ample chest. Mick watched with disgust as the lizard-like tip of Dredd's tongue poked out of his mouth and ran between his lips.

"No harm, no foul?" she said to him. "Here, you can even have the last of this." She handed the joint out to him. It looked like Dredd had a hard time peeling his eyes off her breasts.

"Smells like shit," he said. "I have better stuff downstairs."

"Suit yourself," Marnie said. She grabbed the radio's handle and headed for the window.

"What, you don't want some?" Dredd said.

Marnie turned around. "I thought you were kicking me out."

"How about a little smoke before you go?"

Got you, motherfucker, Mick thought. Dredd didn't get out much, if at all. Mick was pretty sure the guy's balls had gone from blue to purple. Even a paranoid lunatic who talked to Melon Heads couldn't resist a pretty girl with a big rack. It made him want to choke the life out of Dredd. *You can't kill him. Not yet.*

Marnie hesitated. "I don't know."

"Come on, I don't bite."

She looked at the rifle. Dredd looked down as if it had just magically appeared in his hands. "Oh, this. Hey, you can't be too careful. I'll put it away." He headed back down the stairs. Mick used the moment to slip into the room. He squeezed himself between the kitchen door and wall, looking at Marnie. Her cool exterior had slipped to nervousness while Dredd was downstairs. She put her game face on the moment he came back.

"Look, I know it might be a little creepy going into a basement with a guy you never met before," Dredd said. He produced a massive joint from his denim jacket pocket. "So why don't we toke a little up here?"

"That's cool."

As soon as he walked past the door, Mick jumped out and swung for the back of his knee with the hammer. It connected with the top of Dredd's thigh instead. Dredd spun around, instinctively swinging. His knuckles bashed Mick in the chin. Mick dropped the hammer.

"I knew you were too good to be true, bitch," Dredd said. He stormed across the room to grab her. Mick shook the stars out of his head and wrapped his arms around Dredd's waist. Dredd didn't go down. He carried him like a running back headed for the goal line.

Marnie scooted away from Dredd, heading toward the living room. That would be a bad thing. There would be nowhere to go in there.

Mick swung wildly for Dredd's balls. Again, he hit him in the thigh. Dredd crashed an elbow down on Mick's arm, breaking his embrace. Mick's chest hit the dirty floor. He lashed out and got hold of Dredd's ankle to slow him down.

Dredd turned around, raised his boot and was going to stomp the shit out of Mick's face.

Marnie cried out as she brought the chair down on Dredd's head. He immediately went to his knees, his hands clasping the top of his head. "Fucking whore."

Mick got up and punched Dredd on the side of his face. He wobbled but didn't fall. He was about to swing again when Marnie finished Dredd with the chair. One of the legs bent and the seat broke loose from the frame. Dredd thudded on the floor, unconscious.

"That was pretty badass," Mick said, toeing Dredd with his boot to make sure he was out.

"I think I'm gonna throw up." Marnie ran to the sink and puked.

Mick got to work hog-tying Dredd. The one time he'd willingly gone to the library was to find a book on knots. He'd always wanted to hog-tie someone. "Who says dreams don't come true," he muttered as he worked the knots around Dredd's ankles and wrists. Marnie kept heaving into the sink, drawing in great gulps of air in between upchucks.

"You going to be all right?" he asked once he felt Dredd was secure.

She wiped her mouth with her shirt. "I'm fine." Even in the weak light, he could see she was about as far from fine as he was from going to Harvard. The hard part was over, though. She could sit the rest out. He'd take it from here.

"Be right back," he said, going out the boarded window and toward the van. He came back with a paper bag filled with cans of soda and the few snacks he could find in her house. Her mother was one shitty shopper.

"I couldn't eat a thing," she said, blanching at the proffered bag.

"You'll get hungry at some point," he said, cracking open a can of ginger ale. He wished it was a beer, even swill like Black Label. "Who knows how long it'll take him to wake up. You really fucked him up with that chair."

He helped her so she could sit on a counter. Dredd was trussed up in the center of the room. "So, what do we do now?" Marnie asked.

"We could finish that joint for starters."

After a couple of drags, Mick felt his nerves start to settle down. He'd been amped until his skin itched. Marnie went from looking like she needed a doctor to chilled out, which made him feel a little better about bringing her here. Dredd snored. His face was on the floor, and each heavy exhalation kicked up little swirls of dust.

They had to wait almost half an hour before Dredd came to. For a while there, Mick was worried that Marnie had clobbered him too hard and knocked his brains in. Then he'd be of no use at all. When he heard Dredd mutter, "I'm gonna kill you assholes," he leaped off the counter, a trill of relief washing over him.

Mick sat on the floor beside Dredd. "We're already dead, so your threats don't mean a thing to us." He paused and made sure he had Dredd's full attention. The man's bloodshot eye peered at him. "So don't waste your breath...Christopher."

Dredd blinked and for a split-second looked panicked. It was gone in an instant, replaced by angry defiance. "Go to hell."

"I'm sure I will. But not before you tell me a few things. Like how you came to be able to live with the Melon Heads without them killing you. Seems like a strange thing to take on after they murdered your brother."

Dredd smiled. His teeth were awash with blood. "They're gonna get you sooner or later. You know that, right?"

"They had their chance a few days ago. Instead, they took care of one of my problems for me. But they went too far and did something I'd never ask them to do."

Marnie gave Mick a curious look. He hadn't told her about what had happened to his mother and Dwight. Just thinking about that night filled him with fear, anger, sadness and satisfaction. His head had never been so fucked up.

"I'm gonna ask you again. How did you end up working with them?"

"I never worked with them." Dredd spat blood on the filthy tile.

"Okay, how did you end up working *for* them?"

"Piss off, twerp."

Mick jumped up and kicked Dredd in the ribs. His body went rigid. They heard the ropes straining to keep him bound.

"Hurts like hell, right?" Mick said. His heart was racing. "Steel-tipped boots. If you want some more, just keep not answering my questions. I can kick you in that same spot over and over until my boot comes out the other side."

Dredd was drawing in great gasps of air. His face was locked in a pained grimace. Mick figured he must have hit a nerve or something with how long it took Dredd to recover. Marnie watched it all in silence. She'd shifted on the counter and was mostly in shadow.

"What's the deal with you and the Melon Heads? Or what *was* the deal? They burned your place down. Looks like they don't want you back."

"Shit." Dredd tried to push himself up with his forehead and failed. He collapsed back to his side. "I figured they would." He narrowed his gaze at Mick. "You should be the one tied up. You're the one who ruined everything."

Marnie dropped the lighter she'd been rolling from hand to hand. When she slid off the counter to retrieve it, her face was caught in the light. Dredd's eyes went wide. "You're the one who was raped. Dammit, I knew you were familiar. Mary something. Maybe if you'd kept your legs closed, you'd be home now and not worrying about when they're gonna eat you alive."

Mick's anger rose high and fast, the instant blossoming of pressure intense enough to send him to the brink of a blackout. Next thing he knew, Marnie was pulling him back and Dredd was groaning. Dredd had a gash under his right eye that wept blood. "Stop!" Marnie said, their noses practically touching. "Or you're going to kill him."

His foot hurt from kicking Dredd and he was gasping for breath. "You don't...talk to her...you hear me?"

Dredd could only moan.

It took a while for Mick to settle down. Marnie stood by him with her hand on his chest. She led him into the living room. "I don't want to do this anymore," she whispered.

"We can't stop now."

"I'm worried what will happen if we don't."

The dark room smelled like dust and mildew. A rat chittered somewhere in the gloom. Mick checked on Dredd to make sure he hadn't found a way to set himself free.

"Look, I got mad. I promise it won't happen again."

"But will you let him go when we get what we need?"

He knew what she was implying. He was sorry for scaring her and he should have told her just that, but instead he said, "Yeah. Let the Melon Heads find him. Not my problem."

"Just...just don't do that again. Okay?" Marnie hugged herself. "You scared the heck outta me."

"I don't know if it'll make you feel any better, but I'm scared, too."

She kicked at something on the floor. "It kinda does."

"Can we go back in and get the hell out of here now?"

She led the way back into the kitchen. Mick wished he could tell her everything he was feeling but it just wasn't in him. The fact that he admitted he was scared was enough. Dredd's breathing had settled and he had stopped moaning.

"Ready to talk now?" Mick said.

"Yes," Dredd said, his eyes still closed. When he opened his mouth, Mick saw that he'd chipped two of his front teeth with his boot. What he thought would have given him some measure of satisfaction actually made him recoil.

"Start from the beginning then. What happened after the Melon Heads killed your brother? Why didn't you just stay away?"

Dredd squirmed, not to get away, but to find a way to get his face off the floor. Mick grabbed the ropes and rocked him onto his stomach and back.

"Just untie me, Mick." Dredd didn't sound like himself anymore. He sounded lost and tired.

"I will after you tell me everything."

Dredd sighed a wet sigh. Blood dribbled from his mouth as he spoke. "No one believed me. No shock there. My parents thought I'd made up a huge lie to cover up whatever Dylan had done. I cried all through Christmas dinner, but they kept telling me to calm down and tell the truth. When he didn't come back that night, they called the cops. I was sent upstairs to my room when the cops came to the house, but I snuck out and listened to them from the top of the stairs. I listened to my parents give their report and I learned a hell of a lot. Dylan had gotten this girl pregnant. She went to St. Mary's on the other side of town. He'd been freaking out ever since he asked her if she was going to get an abortion and she said no. My parents were trying to talk to her parents, but they wouldn't give them the time of day. Said Dylan was an unfortunate mistake, but they would handle it. Dylan realized he was going to be a dad and it hit him hard. My parents thought Dylan had skipped town with the girl. Her name was Sandy. That's where the cops should look first. I knew better. If they went then, maybe they would have found some blood or even his bike out on Dracula Drive. But I was just a little kid, and no one gave a shit what I thought."

Dredd seemed to relax, lost in memory. Mick knew not to interrupt. Let him talk it out.

"A day after that, they organized a search party. By that time, I'd decided there was no point in telling anyone what had happened. In fact, I stopped talking altogether. They were never going to find him. My parents, they were beside themselves. I'd never seen my dad cry before. I watched them cry for a week, holding each other as if their closeness was the only thing keeping them from flinging off the planet as it spun. And you know what? They never hugged me. Dylan was gone, but they might as well have lost both sons. He was all they could think about. And since I wasn't talking, I just kind of faded from their lives. My grandmother came to stay with us. She took care of me, but it wasn't the same. After a while, they called off the search and all that was left to do was hang up flyers all over town. I sat in the back seat while they drove around, posting those damn flyers on every telephone pole, tree and corkboard they could find. It was my job to hand them a fresh box of flyers when they ran out. We had a load of them on the floor next to me." Dredd took a deep, ragged breath.

"It took six months for the drinking to get real bad. Both of them. The marriage didn't make it another year. In their parting shot before they split, they sent me to Blanders for an evaluation. I still hadn't said a word, not even in school. I was creeping everyone out, but I didn't care. Our family was over, so why not chuck the reminder of what we once were in a mental home?"

"Jesus," Marnie hushed.

That made Dredd grin. "Jesus? He never came to save my soul, I'll tell you that much. The shrinks pulled me into session after session, trying to break down my wall. I just stared at them like they were a turd that fell out of a spaceship. That's exactly how I pictured them. It helped me stay in character. Dr. Space Turd One, Night Nurse Space Turd, Space Turd Shrink With Garlic Breath. They talked a lot of shit. In my mind, I just flipped them off, shouting, 'Fuck you!' over and over. They couldn't hear it, but I could, and that's all that mattered.

"I'd been in a couple years when this kid Tommy Aikens gets a week eval because he tried to OD on pills. At least that's what they thought. He just got some bad shit, but his parents thought an attempted suicide sounded better than OD because their son had a shitty dealer. I see him walking the hall one day in the paper slippers they give the new residents. I couldn't see myself, but I'm sure it was the first time my face changed expression in all that time. Tommy was Dylan's best friend. I'd known him all my life. He kinda scared me the way all the older kids at the time did, but he'd never wrestled me down to fart in my face or tripped me when I passed by like Dylan's other jerk friends."

Mick had to keep himself from checking his watch. It was impossible to tell if it was day or night in the sealed house. "Sounds like a real nice guy," he said, dripping with sarcasm.

Dredd glared at Mick. "He wasn't a shit like you, I'll tell you that. Anyway, we end up in the rec room and he starts telling me his story. I sit there listening like always, but now I'm itching to talk back. I look around to make sure none of the staff are watching us and say so softly he could barely hear me, 'The Melon Heads killed Dylan.' It felt funny, talking after all that time. My voice sounded different, like it didn't belong to me. My throat hurt, too. I realized saying a thing like that in a nuthouse isn't the best way to gain someone's trust. Somehow, I knew Tommy would understand. And I was right, judging by the way he got whiter than Casper's ass. He sat back in his chair like I'd just punched him in the chest. 'Why would you say that?' he says. ''Cause I saw it.' He looked guilty all of a sudden and couldn't look me in the eye no more. 'I can't believe he did it,' he says. 'Did what?' Then he got real quiet, and said, 'But then why are you here?'

"It was then I knew that my brother had told Tommy about his plan to feed me to those things. I got mad as hell, but I couldn't blow my cover. Not where people could see me. So, then I just said, 'He tried. They didn't take me.'"

Mick had been walking around Dredd while he told his story. He got to one knee so he could see his face. "How come the Melon Heads left you alone and didn't go after you?"

"I don't know. Tommy sure as shit didn't know, either. It's not like you can sit down with those maniacs and ask them. You should ask yourself the same question. Didn't they have a chance to take you and left you alone?" Dredd snorted, spitting more blood. "Who the fuck knows with them."

Marnie said, "Why was your brother going to…give you to them?"

"Tommy said that the Melon Heads would take care of your problems if you offered something in return. With Dylan, he wanted them to snatch Sandy. Fucking Dylan. He was willing to have them murder that girl and his own kid."

"How would they know to get his girl?" Mick asked.

"You give them a picture. Or actually, you give old man Fennerman a picture. He'd give it to them and they'd find her. That guy had a bond with them I couldn't come close to. Dylan and Tommy ran into Fennerman one day while out looking for a place to get stoned in the woods. They were already drunk and didn't realize they'd gone to the one place in this town you should treat like toxic waste. Fennerman liked Dylan and it was also during a drought and he needed something to give to the Melon Heads. They were growing restless. In comes my shithead brother."

"All they need is a picture and they wait for your brother's girlfriend to come around Dracula Drive?" Marnie asked.

"They're not just out there by Dracula Drive, you know. They have eyes all over town. Sandy would have just disappeared one day. As it is, she lost the baby and left for college two years later. If she only knew how close she came to getting eaten."

Mick offered Dredd a drink from the flask he had in his back pocket. Dredd's voice had been getting hoarser the longer he spoke. He had to pour it in Dredd's mouth. "What the hell is this?"

"Some old Bailey's I found in the trailer. It's that or nothing." Dredd coughed, the bitter hot booze singeing his throat. When he settled down, Mick asked, "Two more questions and we're done here. One – how did you become their watcher or whatever you were? Two – where do they stay most of the time?"

Marnie looked over at him. "Why do you want to know where they stay?"

Mick put a finger to his lips. Dredd couldn't angle his head to see Marnie. He took a deep breath and said, "Tommie told me all about Fennerman and how the old man had been a kind of gatekeeper for the Melon Heads for like, forever. The day Tommie was supposed to leave, I asked him how to get there. He drew a map on the inside of a Monopoly box. I was in that madhouse for another six years. By the time I got out, I had that map memorized. You want to hear the funny thing?"

There was nothing Mick could find even remotely funny about the story. "What?"

"I went in there sane. I was shook up and maybe had some PTSD, but I was just a normal kid. By the time I got out, I knew my brain was all twisted. What normal person fantasizes every minute of the day about meeting the man who deals with the monsters who killed his brother? Who were supposed to kill him instead? I knew it was crazy, but I was crazy. Probably still am. First thing I did when I got out was run away from home. My parents had moved to Shelton by then. I'm not sure how hard they looked for me. I could tell the day I left the asylum they didn't want any part of their damaged goods. It took me a while, but I found Fennerman. He was impressed the Melon Heads let me get that far into the woods without at least trying to scare me off. When I told him what had happened, he said, 'They must have marked you in their minds for some reason.' When I asked him what reason it could be, he just shrugged and said, 'You might as well ask me to read a shark's mind. Who knows?'"

Dredd paused and looked to Mick. "Can you please untie me? I can't feel my hands or feet."

"Talk faster, then," Mick replied coolly.

Dredd closed his eyes and recounted the rest. "Fennerman took me in, showed me their ways. Said he'd been doing it since he was marked around my age. Someone had to keep the Melon Heads happy in those woods. Sure, they sneak around town, but the woods is where they prefer to be. Out of sight, out of mind. He told me they came with the Pilgrims, castoffs in a new world that needed healthy people to build a country. If you had a baby with a birth defect, you left them to the woods. Some survived to nurture the babies. Soon enough, they were having babies with each other. The deformities only got worse with each inbred generation. They might not look human anymore, but they still have human brains. They have their own language and their own rules. The old man said he'd lived by two rules with them and things had been just fine. Feed them. And most of all, don't hurt them. They have a pack mentality and are very protective of one another."

"That we know," Marnie said. She backed into a corner of the room, wedging herself between countertops.

"Sometimes, if you fed them something special, they'd do a favor in return. I never asked them for no favors, but the old man said he'd had several people over the years brave the trip to his place to ask for something of the Melon Heads. My brother was one of them. The bigger the offering, the bigger the favor. Guess he thought I was big enough to kill a mother and fetus." He broke into a wet coughing fit, the cords on his neck protruding. At one point, his eyes started to flutter. Mick worried he'd pass out on them, so he gave him another shot of the schnapps.

"What happened to the old man?" Marnie said, soft as a mouse.

"He did what all old men do. I came by one day and he was dead in his bed. Had a smile on his face, too. We should all go like that. Way I figured it, even though it seemed like he lived a pretty hard life, if he could go out looking like that, it mustn't have been so bad. I buried him out back, seeing as he had no family or friends. House gave me the creeps, though. So I found that cabin. First night, I left a couple of big steaks hanging outside my door. I tied them up in a pretty complicated knot. They were gone in the morning, the knots all untied neatly. I knew then the Melon Heads had found me. I've been out there ever since. Now, thanks to you, I can't go back there again."

Mick was tempted to kick him again. The last thing he wanted to hear was Dredd reminding him of what he'd done...or undone. Instead, he asked flatly, "Okay, maybe you are crazy. Where can we find them?"

"You don't want to go there. Besides, they'd never let you get close. Remember, I told you they have eyes everywhere."

"You can tell me, or I can end this now." Mick pulled the Bowie knife he'd had sheathed behind his back.

Dredd glared at him. "I believe you'd use that."

"It's good to believe."

"Might as well tell you. They'll make sure you're not my problem anymore."

"So, tell us where they hide."

"I'll do what Tommy did for me. Untie my hands and I'll draw you a map."

CHAPTER TWENTY-THREE

The pain radiating up and down Chuck's arm and into his shoulder was excruciating. It wasn't close to enough to overpower the agony of seeing his parents murdered by the Melon Heads. He supposed they trashed his house just as they'd done to Dredd's, robbing him of his family and home.

They were huddled in a tool shed in a strange yard. It reeked of old grass and gasoline. They'd listened to sirens blaring off and on for several hours, way off in the distance. Things had settled down some time ago, the night ringing with cricket song. At one point, Chuck just broke down and cried. Heidi and Vent wrapped their arms around him. He was surprised at how little he cared that his friends had to watch him bawl like a baby. Then again, he'd never known loss so complete that adolescent cool meant less than nothing.

Now he had his head in Heidi's lap, his good arm hurting from lying on the hard, cold floor. Vent had somehow managed to fall asleep. Chuck was too focused on listening for anyone snooping around the shed to close his eyes for even a moment.

"I'm so sorry, Chuck," Heidi said.

"It's not your fault." He would have felt completely cored out if he hadn't had anger and despair to fill the void.

"I wonder if they're at my house now." She sounded afraid, but also as if her mind were somewhere else. It might have been shock settling in.

"I don't think so. Believe it or not, I think they're too smart to stick around this long. They know when to strike and when to retreat. They've done their damage for now."

"We have to warn my parents. I can't just let them sit there not knowing they're a target."

"We will. In the morning. I'm sure what happened to my parents will be in the news."

"But who do we tell them did it?"

Chuck thought on that a moment. "If we say it was the wilding kids, they'll ask us how we know. We'll be right back before the cops. That will get us nowhere. As crazy as it sounds, maybe we just tell the truth."

"They'll never believe us."

"We didn't think Melon Heads were real. Anything's possible now."

"Even if they did believe us, and it would take a long time to convince them, we'd have to go to Vent's parents and Marnie's, too. And even Mick's. How could we get all of that done in one day? We can't count on the Melon Heads to sit and wait for the next attack. We have to assume they'll come out every night until they get us."

"If they did that, they run the risk of getting caught. The cops will be out and on high alert."

Heidi clucked her tongue. "They'll just kill them, too. You think the Milbury PD is equipped to handle a killer horde of Melon Heads? They'd piss themselves before they ever drew their weapons."

Chuck had to sit up before his arm went to sleep. Heidi helped him, accidentally brushing against his arm and sending sparks shooting across his vision. "You know what we need?"

"The army? A tank?"

He looked over at Vent, sleeping against the lawnmower. "We need one of them."

"One of who?" He couldn't see her expression in the gloom, but he could imagine the perplexed look on her face.

"A Melon Head. If we can get hold of one, people will have to believe."

Heidi's sneakers scraped across the cement floor. "They'll just think we kidnapped some handicapped kid. It's not like they have a test to confirm someone is a Melon Head."

"So maybe we need two."

"If we came across two of them, we'd be the ones in trouble."

"I don't know. We took care of two tonight."

"And look what happened." She drew in a sharp breath, and then said, "Oh, I'm so sorry. I didn't mean it that way."

Chuck felt like crying all over again but managed to keep the tears at bay. He wasn't mad at Heidi. She was right. He was being foolish.

But when you were suddenly orphaned and homeless, you got to be as foolish as you wanted. "It's okay. I just can't run anymore. Shit, I don't have anywhere to run to. I'm sure the police are looking for me by now. I can't let them find me, either. If they stick me in some shelter or foster home, the Melon Heads will get me for sure. Maybe I'll be safe in prison if the police think I killed my parents." He chuckled mirthlessly. "Things are going real good when prison is your safest bet."

Heidi rubbed his thigh and sniffled. "This is all so fucked. How are we supposed to save everybody, much less ourselves?"

"We try your way first. It's a long shot. What do we have to lose... besides everything?"

He wished he could sound less pessimistic, but at the moment, optimism was in short supply and dwindling more by the minute. Another idea came to him, one so horrible he didn't dare bring it up to Heidi. There may come a time when he'd have to revisit it as a last resort. He prayed to god that moment never came.

⋆　⋆　⋆

They woke Vent up around dawn and crept out of the shed. Keeping their heads low, they snuck out of the yard and checked the street signs.

"Wow, we made it all the way to Wakefield," Vent said, scratching his head and stretching in the middle of the street. A squirrel spotted them and scampered across the road. It wound its way up the nearest tree, where it chittered angrily at them for disturbing its morning amble. Birds sang all around them. Chuck wanted to shout at them to shut the hell up. This was not a normal day and their normal routine was desecrating the memory of his family.

His muscles cried out for a good stretch, too, but he knew that if he tried, the pain would drop him to his knees. His shoulder throbbed to the beat of his heart, the hand on his bad arm tingling with pins and needles.

"Where do we go now?" Vent asked.

"You and Heidi are going to her place."

Heidi raised an eyebrow. "You're not coming with us?"

"I can't. If your parents see me, they'll want the police to come."

She leaned against a green Chevy, shivering from the morning cold. "Where are you going to go?"

"I need to get my car keys."

Vent chuffed. "You can forget that, dude. The cops will be all over your place for days, if not a week, especially if they don't find you. The place is a crime scene. You'll never get in without them seeing you."

"Don't underestimate me," Chuck said. He'd only gotten an hour or so of sleep, but he felt full of energy. Funny how a purpose will get a person going when they should be passed out somewhere.

"I don't like the idea of you being alone," Heidi said. She checked her pockets and found a bent cigarette in her shirt pocket. "Gimme your lighter," she said to Vent. He handed it over and she lit up, taking a deep drag. A quarter of the cigarette burned down in seconds.

"Got anything stronger in another pocket?" Vent asked.

"You have to keep your head straight," Chuck said. He hadn't clued Vent in to his and Heidi's conversation about their families being in danger. Vent wasn't one to put two and two together without a little prodding. He knew Heidi would tell him everything on their long walk to her place. Her parents were probably worried witless by now. Chuck wouldn't be shocked if they were demanding the police add her to the missing persons list, even though it hadn't been a full twenty-four hours yet. Who knows, after what happened to Chuck's family, the police might forego the regular waiting period. "And keep your eyes open. You don't want to get picked up by the cops before you get to your house."

"I will." Her eyes were glassy, either from exhaustion or a fresh sheen of unshed tears.

Chuck took Vent's lighter from her and jammed it in his pocket. "You better go," he said.

Heidi didn't move. Vent looked from one to the other.

"Seriously. We have a lot to do today. We need to get started."

"I'm worried about you," Heidi said.

"I'll be fine. It's daytime. They prefer the dark."

Heidi surprised him by pushing off the Chevy and wrapping her arms around him, burying her head in his chest. There was no way he was going to let on how much it hurt. He put one arm around her and touched his nose to the top of her head. Despite being in a shed all night and sweating like pigs when they ran, her hair still smelled like flowers.

"You better take care of her," he said to Vent.

"Why do I think you left off an 'or else'?"

"Or else," Chuck said, a smile tugging at the corners of his mouth. He didn't think it would be possible to ever smile again. Guilt overwhelmed him and the smile died before it could blossom.

"Call me if you can," Heidi said.

He tried to think of the nearest pay phone if he couldn't get in the house. It would be a long way to go. "I will," he replied, unsure if he was lying or not.

"Come on," Vent said. He tugged at her arm. Heidi reluctantly pulled herself away, tears streaking her cheeks.

Chuck watched them turn down Wakefield and onto Horner and out of sight. If he'd counted, he would have tallied seven times Heidi looked back to check on him. Once they were gone, he headed in the other direction, figuring it was about a fifteen-block walk until he got to his place. His stomach rumbled. Lord, he was hungry. *Pain and fear must absorb a shit ton of calories*, he thought. He would kill for a stack of pancakes drenched in butter and hot syrup, bacon, fried eggs and hash browns. He even knew exactly who – or what – he'd kill for that breakfast.

It was a bitter pill to swallow, settling for a mouthful of stale spit instead. Anxious to see what remained of his home, he started to jog to his street. The pain of moving too fast winded him quickly. He had to settle for an improvised power walk, listing to his bad side. A few cars passed, as did a bread delivery truck. He kept to the sidewalk, ready to hide behind a tree or duck behind a car if he spotted a cop car or any car that looked like it was an undercover unit. They'd been chased by quite a few over the past year and had never been caught when they were smoking or drinking in the park or a vacant lot. Chuck was pretty sure he knew all the local undercover cars, though they might have called in others from the surrounding towns.

He was slightly winded by the time he turned down his street. His house was at the end of the block on the right-hand side. The street and driveway were clogged with cop cars and news vans.

"Fuck me sideways." He slumped against a minivan. He'd been so fixated on the police, he hadn't even considered the news. A huge satellite dish sat atop a black van. A reporter bathed in artificial light was talking to a camera at the end of his driveway.

You got this. Don't pussy out now.

The front door was missing. As was the glass in most of the downstairs windows. His stomach filled with ice as he stared at the ruin of his house...his home. Were his parents still inside, or had they been carted away in black bags by the medical examiner? He thought he was going to be sick. He took a few gulps of air to calm himself.

Getting strength back in his legs, he cut across Dolan Avenue, went two blocks and made a right down Ramapo. The abandoned house greeted him with its weary and worn façade. The metal fence had long ago turned to rust, the gutters hanging from the roof. When he was a kid, he bought the story that an old witch used to live there hook, line and sinker. Kids gave the crumbling wreck a wide berth. If a ball or Frisbee accidentally landed in the front yard, there it stayed for eternity. It looked like a perfect place for a witch with its dirty turret, dark, deep porch and shuttered windows. Who knew what kind of horrible black magic went on inside those walls before the witch died?

Chuck was sure a whole new generation of kids were equally terrified of the place, judging by the graveyard of newish looking Spalding and Wiffle balls in the tall grass. He was tempted to find the yellow Duncan light-up yo-yo that Mick had thrown over the fence when he was mad at Chuck for being better than him at walking the dog. It was most likely still there, weathered by the elements and swallowed by the uncut grass.

The witch house seemed to leer at him. He easily dismissed his childhood fear of the place. He was about to murder a nightmare, a local legend and an eyesore.

He took a quick glance around, saw no one was looking, and kicked the door in. The wood gave way like it was made of wet cardboard. A heady stench of mold and mildew blasted him in the face. He turned away and coughed, which only hurt him more. Once he settled down, he stepped inside. The interior was dry as a matchstick. Miraculously, there were no holes in the roof. *Maybe magic had kept the place intact.* Chuck shivered.

There was a chair in the living room, covered in an off-white sheet. "That'll do."

Chuck struck the striker wheel on Vent's lighter and touched the yellow flame to the end of the sheet. It went up with a soft *whup!* Once the flames started to engulf the outline of the chair, Chuck kicked it over and sent it skittering to the end of the room. It bounced against the wall. The fire licked the exposed lathing and settled in. It didn't take long for noxious, black smoke to fill the room. He was wondering if he should light another part of the house when the ceiling took the flames like a sponge starved for water. He ducked out of the room and ran outside, coughing again and seeing not just stars but entire galaxies.

He stumbled down the rotten steps and jumped into the grass when he felt one of them starting to give way. Jogging as best he could, he made it to the end of the block, where he sat on the curb and waited. It took five minutes for the first licks of fire to poke outside the boards on the windows. Soon after that, the bottom floor of the witch's house became fully engulfed. Ten minutes later, he heard the approach of sirens. Not long after that, those cop cars and news vans came tearing ass down the street. He got up and walked casually down Ramapo so as not to elicit any unwanted attention. By the time he got to his house, it looked like a ghost town. Even the neighbor looky-loos had run off to witness the latest tragedy. There was only one cop car left in the drive. His house was virtually surrounded in yellow crime-scene tape.

Feeling slightly reckless as time was not on his side, he strode up the steps and walked right in. Nobody was in the house. In fact, he could see out the open back door. Two cops were taking a smoke break, outside the perimeter of flags stuck in the lawn. His stomach lurched when he saw the outline of his parents' bodies in tape, the linoleum tacky with blood. He was woozy for a moment and had to lean against his father's lounge chair. Catching his breath, he took in the mass destruction done to his home. Anything that was glass had been broken. An end table was sticking out of the shattered television screen. The couch cushions had been ripped open. Blinds were torn off the windows, pictures ripped off the walls. He spotted the one of him and his parents at Gettysburg, standing beside a cannon. They had taken him there for his ninth birthday. It was the year he was obsessed with the Civil War. Three smiling faces beamed up at him from behind shards of glass.

Vomit hit the back of his teeth, forcing his mouth open. He threw up on the chair, instantly angry with himself for being so weak. That chair always smelled like his father, a mix of Old Spice aftershave and cigars. Now he'd lost that, too.

Being inside the house was too much for him to take. He scanned the floor and found the bowl where they kept their keys. Chuck snatched his car keys and left, checking on the cops to make sure they hadn't heard him. He put the car in neutral, let it glide out of the driveway and keyed the ignition. He was gone before anyone noticed, crying as he sped toward Heidi's house.

CHAPTER TWENTY-FOUR

Mick drove Marnie's stepfather's van. She'd given him the keys wordlessly when they left Dredd's house. She hadn't spoken much since leaving Dredd's childhood home. In fact, the only thing she's said was, "Where did you get those?" when he took the silver handcuffs from his pocket and chained Dredd up to an exposed pipe in the kitchen. "Dwight was into some kinky shit," he'd said, shivering at a slew of bad memories. "Now you know why I spent so much time out of that damn trailer."

He had to find Chuck, Vent and Heidi. He'd called Vent's house from a pay phone and hung up when his mother answered. He wasn't in the mood to talk to any parents.

"You hungry?" he asked Marnie.

She turned to him with red, puffy eyes. She didn't look good, but she looked a hell of a lot better than she had before she'd gone to the hospital. "Not really."

"I'm starving. I'm gonna stop at a 7-Eleven. I'll get you anything you want."

"I don't think I could eat a thing."

"You have to eat. I can't have you passing out from hunger on me."

"If I pass out, it'll be from something much worse."

He turned down Main and stopped in front of the twenty-four-hour 7-Eleven. There was only one other person inside, an old guy buying lottery tickets, a coffee and a buttered roll. Mick's pocket bulged with the cash he'd taken from Dwight's wallet. It wasn't like he was going to need it anymore. Not much to buy in the belly of a Melon Head. He'd stopped short of going through his mother's purse.

He filled up two Big Gulp cups, one with Mountain Dew, Marnie's favorite, the other with a little bit of every soda on tap. The combination was a sugar and caffeine bomb with an indescribable taste. Two beef and bean burritos got a couple of minutes in the microwave. While they were cooking, he grabbed a bag of chips, can of peanuts and a handful of Slim Jims. He dropped a ten on the counter and told the clerk to keep the change. That was a first.

Back in the van, he handed Marnie the Big Gulp.

"Thanks."

She drew on the straw, literally gulping until half of it was gone. While she drank, he unwrapped a burrito and went to town. His stomach quivered at the first morsel of frozen, less-than-stellar Mexican fare. He came up for air long enough to take a sip of soda, opened a stick of beef jerky with his teeth and took a huge bite. He couldn't remember the last time he'd eaten.

"That smells good," Marnie said.

"I got one for you."

She happily took it, savoring each bite rather than appearing to go for a competitive eating record. He was done with his before she got a quarter of the way through hers. He alternated between chips, jerky and soda while she finished. When Marnie burped, they both grinned, though there was no joy in it. The town was starting to come alive around them. The doors to the 7-Eleven opened and closed every minute or so. Cars were starting to fill the street.

"Now what?" she asked.

"You want to bring the van back before your old man reports it stolen?"

"He's not my old man." She said it as if he'd accused her of killing the Pope.

"I take that as a no?"

"Let's go to Heidi's."

Mick started the van. "You mind if we swing by Chuck's first?"

Marnie hesitated, and then said, "No. Probably a good idea."

Chuck had always been the smartest and most level-headed of them. Right now, they needed a combination of Chuck's brain and caution with Mick's emotion and impulsivity.

When they got there, Mick said, "Keep your head down."

He accelerated as they passed Chuck's house. The place was a wreck and wreathed in crime-scene tape. Black smoke billowed in an almost mushroom cloud a few blocks behind it. Mick tried to take in as much as he could in as little time as it took to zoom past the house. "What the fuck happened here?"

Nothing good, that was for sure. The only positive thing was that Chuck's shit-heap of a car wasn't in the driveway. Maybe he'd gotten away from whatever had gone down. It didn't take a rocket scientist to figure out who had been there.

"Go by my house," Marnie said as she straightened up in her seat. She was worrying at a nub of a fingernail with her teeth.

"Why?"

"Just go."

She exhaled so loudly when they cruised past her house that Mick wondered if she'd been holding her breath the entire drive. He reached over and grabbed her hand. It was such a foreign gesture for him that she stiffened at first.

"You okay?" he asked.

She nodded, looking as if she were holding back tears. He understood. Even though her house and parents were equally shitty, she still didn't want to lose them. Not like this. Mick wondered if Chuck and his parents were all right...or even alive.

"Heidi's next?"

"Please."

They had to backtrack to get to Heidi's. Mick wished to hell there was an easier way to get in touch with Chuck. Not just Chuck, but all of them. He dreaded seeing what was next.

Thankfully, Heidi's house was still intact, no police to be seen. He had just started to slow down when Marnie jumped out of the van and hobbled onto Heidi's porch. The van rocked when he hit the brakes. He slammed the gearshift into park and ran after her. Her finger was about to press the doorbell when the door flew open. Heidi was crying and wasn't watching where she was going. She crashed into Marnie. Mick was there in time to catch them both.

"What happened?" he said to Vent, who was hurrying out behind her. He looked like death. As they got closer to one another, Mick's nose crinkled. He smelled like it, too.

"Heidi, come back here." Her father's voice boomed from somewhere deep in the house.

"Let's go," Heidi said, wiping at her nose with her sleeve and heading for the van.

Vent shared a look with Mick that said there was a ton to talk about. Marnie and Heidi had their arms interlocked as they went to the van. Mick got back in the driver's seat. The girls went in the back, sitting on milk crates, while Vent took shotgun.

"Chuck," Heidi said worriedly. "If he calls and I'm not there, he won't know where to find us."

"Where is Chuck?" Marnie asked.

"He said he was going back to get his car."

Mick sagged with relief. At least Chuck was still with them. "What happened at his house?"

"They came for us," Heidi said with steel in her voice. "They killed his parents right in front of him. He's hurt pretty bad, too. We have to find him."

That was easier said than done. For all Mick knew, they could be driving circles around one another, never intersecting.

While the girls talked in hushed voices with a lot of pausing to sniff back tears, Mick asked Vent, "How bad was it?"

His friend stared straight ahead with haunted eyes. "We had to kill two of them."

"Shit. You and Heidi?"

"And Chuck. There was so much blood." Mick got the feeling he wasn't just talking about what spilled from the dead Melon Heads. "We're all fucked, man. We're all fucked."

Mick had to stomp on the brakes to miss hitting a cat that darted out from between two parked cars. "At least it wasn't black," he half joked. They were way past bad luck via black cats or walking under ladders.

He checked all of their normal hang-out places. Neither Chuck nor his car were anywhere to be seen. The morning rush had given way to lunchtime. By listening in on Heidi's conversation with Marnie, he learned that she and Vent had gone to her parents and told them blow by blow what had happened at Chuck's. Mick wished he'd been there to help them. It didn't surprise him that her parents didn't believe a word of it. When the TV news showed a reporter standing outside Chuck's house, they got mad, asking her what really happened. They'd been worried sick all night and accusing her of getting high with Vent and making this story up to avoid being punished. They asked her what kind of person used a tragedy to cover up their own actions.

Heidi had screamed and cried to no avail. They asked her if she was still high and threatened to call the cops on Vent for 'kidnapping' their daughter. Heidi had begged them to believe her, because their lives depended on it. Nothing worked, and when her father picked up the phone to call the police, they ran out of the house and into Marnie and Mick.

"You talk to your parents yet?" Mick asked Vent.

"Nope. I'm not even close to ready to face them now. They're going to kill me."

"Better them than the Melon Heads."

Mick's frustration grew with every block he drove without seeing Chuck. At this rate, it would be nightfall before they even caught a glimpse of the gentle giant. There was something else to worry about. Odds are, Marnie's stepfather had reported the van stolen. They had to keep an eye out for cops. The one shred of luck on their side was that the crime scene at Chuck's seemed to have marshaled the small town's even smaller police force. They didn't see a single car at a speed trap.

At two, Mick had to get some gas. After that, he went to the McDonald's drive-thru and ordered Big Macs, fries and Cokes for everyone. Marnie and Heidi ate in relative silence while he drove. His jeans were splattered with salmon-colored special sauce in no time. Two hours later, his foot was leaning on the accelerator pretty hard. Everyone in the van but him was asleep. He turned hard down Willow Avenue and swerved hard right to miss an oncoming car. The jolt woke everyone up. Mick stopped the car and rolled down his window, cursing, "Watch where the hell you're going, asshole!"

A pale and bedraggled Chuck looked across the road at him, his car belching black smoke as it idled. "Nice to see you, too."

CHAPTER TWENTY-FIVE

They'd parked two blocks from the elementary school under low-hanging pussy willow trees. Mick led the way, finding an open window so they could sneak inside. Heidi had flashbacks to second grade and Mrs. Gatti's class. The room looked the same. She even found the puzzles she used to piece together. The one with the three pigs had been her favorite. She wondered if Mrs. Gatti was still alive. She'd been old when she taught Heidi.

Mick locked the window and jammed it closed with a wedge of wood. They found their way to the second floor where the middle-grade classes were held and where the chairs were big enough for them to sit on. On the blackboard the teacher had written: *Read Chapter 5 in your text. Take the chapter test with answers in your binder.*

"Why are we here?" Marnie said.

"This place is like Fort Knox," Mick replied, plopping onto the teacher's chair with his boots on the desk.

"Not exactly," Chuck said. "We just got in with no problem."

"That's the only window with a bad lock. No one can get in from the outside now. This place was built to withstand natural disasters. Probably a nuclear bomb, too."

"You come here a lot?"

"Sometimes, especially if it was raining and I didn't want to be in the trailer sharing the same air with Dwight."

Heidi thought her emotions had been worn to the quick, but thinking of Mick in this big, dark, kind of creepy school alone at night made her sadder still.

Mick said, "Chuck, you feeling okay?"

The pale light filtering through the tall windows highlighted the droplets of sweat on Chuck's face and neck.

"I kinda hurt, but I'll live."

"Hold on. They have painkillers in the nurse's office. Be right back."

Mick ran out of the classroom, his boots echoing down the halls. He came back breathless and holding a paper cup of water and a bottle of Tylenol. "Take two and call me in the morning."

Chuck downed a handful of the white pills. Once he'd settled down, Mick told them how the Melon Heads had gotten to Dwight and his mother. Marnie put an arm around him while he talked about watching them take Dwight. When he got to the part about his mother, he choked back tears and had a hard time continuing.

Heidi blanched. "Not you, too." She thought she was going to be sick. She didn't need further proof that her family was in mortal danger.

"Please tell me you didn't see them...do stuff to her," Vent said.

Mick flashed him an unreadable look. "I thought maybe I could change things around, take Dredd's place and save you guys." He chucked an eraser across the room. It bounced harmlessly against a window. "Now, I want to hurt them."

"Jesus, Mick," Chuck said.

Mick got quiet. "Yeah, well, at least they got Dwight out of my life." She knew there was a lot left unsaid in that.

Chuck filled in Mick and Marnie on the horror show at his house. He had to stop several times, especially once he got to the part about his parents, holding back tears. "They're not going to stop until we're all dead."

"You're right," Mick said, pacing the room now. "Though I think they're going to leave me alone, at least for now."

"Just because they didn't kill you when they did Dwight and your mom in, doesn't mean they're not just making you sweat it out a little bit longer," Vent said. He was at the blackboard, nervously breaking chalk pieces in half.

"We found Dredd," Marnie said.

Heidi felt an electric charge run through her. "You did? Where?"

"In the house where he grew up. His real name is Chris Runde. The place is boarded up. All of the houses out there are. He was hiding out in the basement. We got him to tell us stuff."

"More like tied him up and forced him," Mick said with a measure of pride in his voice. "The Melon Heads kinda choose people from time to time to be their helpers, or guardians or whatever you wanna call it. Dredd was chosen over his brother and I think they chose me, this time around."

"Chose you to do what? They murdered your mother right in front of you. That doesn't sound like a chosen person," Vent said.

Mick shrugged. "Who knows. To feed them, mostly. I get the feeling meat is meat with the Melon Heads. Maybe eating a mother is like going to a Chinese buffet to them. No big deal. At least one of our mothers. They wouldn't do it to one of their own, though."

"We are so fucked," Vent said to the blackboard, going so far as to write it in big block letters.

"We know where they live," Marnie said. "Mick had Dredd draw us a map."

Mick took the folded map out of his back pocket and laid it out on the desk. It was almost impossible to see in the dark. Vent flicked his lighter on and they gathered around.

"I can't tell where that is," Chuck said.

"You have to start here," Mick said, pointing at a big dot on the left-hand side of the page. "That's Dredd's house. They live deep in the woods, even deeper than that place where we brought Dunwoody. Fennerman, who worked with them before Dredd, had set that up as a special spot to leave them things like food and clothes. He raided Goodwill boxes every now and then and dropped off used clothes. Dredd said the Melon Heads were the ones who decorated it with that creepy stick teepee stuff."

"What kind of food did he leave them?" Heidi said. "Like, people?"

Mick nodded. "Who knows. I think mostly it was just wild game. I don't get the vibe that Dredd and Fennerman were killers. Though they would, if necessary, point the Melon Heads in the direction of someone they could take. I guess that's like leaving someone for them to eat."

Marnie wrapped her arms around herself and shivered. Heidi worried at her thumbnail.

Vent studied the map, his finger tracing the crudely drawn route to the Melon Heads' encampment. "How far are we talking to get to them?"

"They live another two miles out. Dredd said there's an old cave system out there where they hunker down. Not all of them, though. They have like sentries all over Milbury, night and day," Mick said ominously.

"Which means they'd know when we're coming," Chuck said. He sounded exhausted and deflated. "It's not like we have an arsenal and manpower to just go out there and rush them."

"We might not have to," Mick said.

"What do you mean?" Heidi asked. She was afraid of whatever plan Mick was hatching in his brain, but she was also desperate. Time was not on their side. For all she knew, her parents were being savaged at this very moment. Or Marnie's. Or Vent's. Neither option was acceptable.

Mick flicked his hair from his face. "If they're giving me a free pass, I should use it."

"You gonna walk in there and take them down by yourself like Rambo?" Vent asked, dripping sarcasm.

"I wish. No, they have a leader, like a king of the Melon Heads."

Chuck had stopped sweating and looked steadier. "So?"

Mick's façade of confidence faltered a bit, then he said, "I'm gonna find him, and I'm gonna take him."

Marnie had pulled her feet onto the chair with her arms wrapped around her legs. "I don't think they're just going to let you kidnap their leader. They'll kill you for sure. It might be better if you stick to what you wanted to do, especially now since they've let you live when they could have killed you. Try to gain their trust and work with them."

Mick flipped through the pages of a phonics textbook. He snapped the book shut and threw it on the floor. It hit with such a loud bang that everyone jumped. "You can't control them. Even if they let me in, they'll end up controlling me. We have to waste them, and we have to do it now."

Heidi knew there was no point in asking how they would do such a thing. Every way she thought about it ended with her and her friends dead.

He saw the concern etched on her face and said, "We'll figure it out. We have yours and Chuck's big brains on our side."

"I'm so done, I don't think I could pass a first-grade spelling test," Chuck said. He sagged in the chair, resting his arm on the sliver of a folding desk attached to the side.

"That's why we're here. Safety in numbers," Mick said. "We can take turns keeping watch."

Heidi thought about the state her parents must be in. On the one hand, she didn't want to hurt them or cause them any more stress. On the other, she was pissed at them for not believing her when she'd spilled her guts out. It wasn't shocking that they dismissed her. Just upsetting. It would be dark out soon. There was no way she was going back outside. The school was built in a tucked away lot, blocks from the nearest house. If the Melon Heads jumped them as they went to the van, no one would hear their screams.

"I'll take first watch," Mick said.

"I'll take it with you," Vent said.

"Nah. Take a shift with Heidi or Marnie. Watch their backs. Okay?"

Vent opened his mouth, ready to protest, and then looked at Heidi and Marnie. "Yeah. That makes sense, man."

"Let's all go down to the gym. They have these mats we can use for beds and towels for pillows. We'll bring them back in here." Mick walked out of the classroom.

Heidi looked over at Chuck. "I can bring one back for you."

He struggled to get out of the chair. "I'll manage. Besides, safety in numbers."

The four of them shuffled after Mick. Heidi stayed close to Chuck, ready to help if he got unsteady on his feet. It was weird walking through her old school. It smelled like art supplies and industrial floor cleaner. Their footsteps echoed down the hallways and stairwells, adding to the creepiness. She was positive she couldn't have done it alone. Having her friends nearby made it easier. Mick was right.

"Even a broken clock is right twice a day," she said softly.

"What was that?" Chuck asked as they walked through the gym, the wood slats cracking under their boots and sneakers.

"Nothing."

It took five minutes to find the storage room where the mats were stored and break the lock. Five more to get them up to the classroom because they had to pause several times for Chuck and once even for Marnie, whose strength was visibly flagging. They set the mats close to one another and settled in as best they could. Mick told Vent and Heidi he'd wake them up in three hours and closed the door behind him as he went to patrol the empty halls alone.

*   *   *

Crash!

Heidi popped up from the mat. Her heart fluttered as she tried to pinpoint the source of the noise.

"What the fuck was that?" Vent said, scrambling to his feet and running to the door.

"Oh my god," Marnie said. She reached out for Heidi's hand in the dark.

Only Chuck had somehow managed to sleep through the sound of breaking glass.

The three of them didn't dare move, six ears straining against the sudden silence.

"Maybe Mick was screwing around with something and dropped it," Vent said. It was entirely plausible. Heidi could just see Mick messing with the trophy case. Maybe he'd tried to get the championship trophy he'd won when he was on the baseball team in seventh grade and knocked something else over. If it was one of those glass teacher's awards that were given out at the end of every year, she could see him doing it on purpose.

The thwap of running feet, getting closer by the second, murdered that thought, that hope, before it had time to roost in her brain. Vent pulled the window shade on the door aside. "It's Mick!"

He opened the door and Mick came bounding in, his chest heaving. "They found us."

"How?" Chuck said from the floor. He rubbed his eyes with his knuckles.

"I don't know, but they just broke through the cafeteria window. I saw four of them sneak in. They went straight to the kitchen area and started loading up on all the milk cartons, stuffing them in these old-looking sacks."

"Maybe they're on a supply run," Heidi said, again pinning her hope on the hopeless.

Mick shook his head. "I think that's just a happy discovery for them. They'll be checking the rooms soon."

"What are they, fucking bloodhounds?" Vent said. He shut the door as quietly as he could so as not to alert them to their whereabouts.

Marnie had gone to the window. "I wish we'd stayed on the first floor. We could have just gone out the way we came in."

"That would also bring us one floor closer to them," Mick said.

"But then—"

Mick shushed Marnie. They could hear multiple Melon Heads running up the stairs. The sound was distorted in the empty building, so it was impossible to tell if they were on the landing below them or had just scampered up to the floor they were on. Mick looked out of the door's window. "They're not here yet. I think."

"You think?" Chuck said, keeping his voice low. "You need to know, dude."

"It's hard to see. The only light is that red exit sign at the end of the hall. If they came past it, I woulda seen them."

"What do we do?" Marnie looked to be on the verge of a full-on panic attack. Heidi pulled her close, could feel her trembling.

"We go to the roof," Mick said.

Vent's eyes went wild. "The roof? Are you out of your mind? We'll be trapped there."

They listened to doors being smashed open, chairs and tables being overturned just below them. "You want to take your chances and walk down there?" Mick said.

"Vent's right," Chuck said. "Going to the roof is suicide."

"You have to trust me on this. Follow me."

Mick didn't wait for them to voice any more objections. He walked to the door and slowly opened it without making a sound.

"What do you think?" Heidi asked Chuck. She was hit with a desperate urge to pee.

"I think Mick knows something we don't. It's not like we have another rational choice anyway."

Chuck, Heidi and Vent left the classroom. Heidi turned back and saw Marnie hadn't moved. She motioned with her hand for Marnie to follow them. Her friend shook her head. She was crying and holding on to her stomach.

"Come. On," Heidi hissed.

"I can't," Marnie said.

"Yes, you can. Just stay right beside me."

The Melon Heads sounded as if they were getting closer. Heidi had to swallow hard to get her heart out of her throat. Of all the times for Marnie to break down. Heidi told Chuck to stay and she hustled back into the classroom. "We're not leaving without you. But if you make us stay, we're all going to die."

"We're all going to die anyway."

Way too much of the whites of Marnie's eyes were visible. She flinched when Heidi went to touch her arm. "No, we're not. Only if you stay in this room." It sounded like a massive desk had been thrown against a wall. They could feel the impact through the soles of their feet.

"Girls, we have to go," Chuck whispered urgently. Vent was halfway down the hall, following Mick.

"I know," Heidi shot back. Did he think they were in here swapping stories about their crushes? "Marnie's too scared to leave."

"I'll carry her."

They were talking about her as if she wasn't in the room, which, in a way, was getting truer by the moment.

"You only have one arm."

"I'll manage." He hopped from foot to foot, anxious to get to the roof. The foolishness of Mick's plan seemed better and better the closer the Melon Heads got.

Heidi knew he couldn't manage it, especially if Marnie put up any kind of resistance. She grabbed Marnie by the shoulders and looked her square in the eye. "You coming?"

Marnie shook her head.

"Then I'm sorry." Heidi hauled her arm back and smacked Marnie in the face. The dazed, terrified glaze melted instantly.

"Hey!"

"Run," Heidi said, pulling her along. This time, Marnie didn't object. Heidi spotted the iron rungs in the wall at the end of the hall under the neon exit sign. Vent was at the bottom, waving them on like a Little League coach signaling for his player to slide in to home. They were less than twenty yards away when they heard the unmistakable sound of the Melon Heads' beating feet to the top floor. Heidi got behind Marnie and pushed her so hard, she and Chuck nearly got intertwined and fell. She whipped her head around and spied the first Melon Head shadow reaching the landing. It turned its bulbous head toward them.

"Oh shit!" Vent said, clambering up the ladder.

Chuck made Marnie go ahead of him. He siezed her by her ass cheek and nearly shot-putted her up the ladder. Vent reached down from the open hatch and grabbed her arm, pulling her the rest of the way.

"You're next," Chuck said to Heidi.

She cast a worried glance down the hall. All four Melon Heads were there, cautiously approaching them.

"You're hurt. I should go last."

"I'm hurt, which is why *I'm* going last," he said. He pushed her into the ladder. The bridge of her nose nearly collided with the rung. She grasped the rung above her, but her foot slipped off and she lost her grip. It was a fall of a mere two feet, but it was time lost. She yelped in desperation, hurrying to get a better hold.

Maybe it was her worried cry that did it. The Melon Heads suddenly broke into a run.

"Go! Go!" Chuck yelled.

He turned to face the Melon Heads, his sole good fist raised.

Heidi sped up so he would have space on the ladder. She was halfway up when she realized he wasn't behind her.

"Chuck!" she cried with such ferocity, her heart nearly broke, her throat ripped raw and bloody.

She couldn't see Chuck, but she could hear him struggling against the Melon Heads.

Heidi looked into the open hatch with the stars twinkling against an onyx sky and cried out for Mick. "They're killing him!"

"Get off me, motherfucker!" Chuck bellowed. There was a heavy thump against the wall and a Melon Head howled in pain.

Mick shouted, "I'm coming." His boots started descending the stairs, almost crushing her fingers.

Heidi jumped off the ladder, both to make room for Mick and help Chuck. She landed hard on her right ankle, rolling it in the process. She limped into the hallway and gasped at the sight of three Melon Heads grappling with Chuck, who was a full head and shoulders taller than the tallest one but at a definite disadvantage in every other way.

Heidi didn't have a weapon, nor did she have the strength to take even one on, much less three Melon Heads. She screamed like a wild and angry animal, her bellow garnering the full attention of the Melon Heads.

The trio dropped their hold on Chuck at the same time, grinned lasciviously, and pounced on her.

CHAPTER TWENTY-SIX

"No, Heidi, no!" Chuck screamed. He reached for the nearest Melon Head, hoping to get hold of its collar, but it was too fast for him. The Melon Heads wrapped their arms around Heidi and drove her to the ground. She didn't even have time to cry out.

Chuck saw that the one he'd slammed into the wall was trying to get up and join them. He kicked it under its chin and sent it to sleep.

A shadow leapt off the ladder, nearly landing on top of the pile. "Heidi!"

Mick had something in his hand. It looked like a pipe. He clubbed the backs of the Melon Heads mercilessly. He may as well have been hitting them with a broken flyswatter.

Chuck grabbed the lone clump of hair on one of the Melon Heads. He yanked its head up. The hair ripped free from its deformed skull with a sound like pulling two pieces of Velcro apart. The Melon Head howled with inhuman rage.

"Fuckers! Fuckers!" Mick bellowed, the pipe ringing every time it connected with bone. A light flashed from above as Vent came down to help with his lit lighter in one hand and a two-by-four in the other.

Heidi stared up at Chuck amidst the tangle of bodies and grasping limbs, her eyes bulging with unmitigated terror. The wounded Melon Head dove toward her face like a bird pecking at the ground. When it pulled away, Chuck's heart stopped.

Heidi's throat was gone. In its place was a gaping, bleeding hole. She desperately tried to draw a breath, the blood percolating wetly in her wound.

What happened next was a black blur for Chuck.

He was sure he shouted something, his voice alien and distant in his ears. His fingers wrapped around sweaty flesh. A heavy weight was there and then gone as he tossed a Melon Head behind him. His foot stomped on a leg, or an arm, or even a back. He couldn't be sure. He thought he saw Vent swatting the Melon Head he'd cast off Heidi. Mick kept up with the pipe as if he were chopping wood.

You'll hit Heidi! Chuck shrieked in his mind.

He managed to wrap his arm around a Melon Head's neck, yanking it from Heidi's quivering body in a chokehold.

"No! Oh my god, no!" Marnie wailed as she descended from the roof brandishing her own lighter.

Chuck locked gazes with Mick. Mick's shoulders heaved, his eyes blazing with fury. The Melon Head struggled to break free, twisting its head from side to side and batting at Chuck's arm. Chuck applied more pressure, hoping to crush its windpipe.

Then Mick did something that matched the Melon Heads in ferocity and brutality. He lunged at the captive Melon Head with his mouth open wide and bit a huge, quivering chunk off its cheek. The Melon Head unleashed a cry that could only have come from an animal. Its pain only fueled Chuck's anger. He drove his knee into the small of its back. It was getting harder to hold on as its flailing and screeching went into overdrive. Chuck used its momentum to propel it into the nearest wall. He flung the creature as hard as he could. Its nose cracked as it thumped off the wall. When it turned around to snarl at them with a ragged hole for a cheek, Vent hit it in the mouth with the two-by-four, followed by a hammering blow by Mick in the same spot with the pipe. Chuck drove his fist into its ruined face and felt the satisfying crunch of bone and squelch of wet meat. The Melon Head's eyes rolled up in its head and it collapsed onto the floor in a dead heap.

The formerly unconscious Melon Head's eyes flew open and it jumped to its feet, kicking Vent in the back and sending him sprawling. The one feasting on Heidi leapt with almost feline grace from her body to the dead Melon Head, as did the third that had been grappling with Vent. It was as if the life going out in the one sent a signal to the others, who acted in unison to gather its body. The one with Heidi's blood dripping off its chin hoisted the body over its shoulder and ran with the other two right behind it. Mick gave chase, shouting all of the things he was going to do to them when he got them. Vent followed after him.

Chuck's gaze shifted back to Heidi. Her mouth and eyes were wide open, her body still as a stone. He didn't need to check for a pulse to see if she was still clinging to life. It looked like every drop of blood in her body was on the floor. The Melon Head had devoured her throat until Chuck could see her spine. He fell to his knees beside her.

Marnie stood over them, the glow from her flashlight shaking in her trembling hand. Neither of them spoke, though they both wept, their tears absorbed by Heidi's spilled blood. Chuck had never felt anything close to the compounding grief that he was sure was going to break something vital inside him.

"Why did you come back for me?" he muttered between bone-quaking sobs.

He felt responsible for her death, the realization making him wish the Melon Heads had killed him, too. Marnie kept saying Heidi's name over and over. There was no mantra to get her back. She was gone. The Melon Heads had taken her from them with the cold cruelty of a pack of lizards.

How were they going to tell her parents?

Chuck heard the slap of feet on the bare floor and didn't bother looking down the hall. If the Melon Heads were coming back, let them do what they wanted. But when he looked at Marnie on her knees, crying as if she'd saved every tear she hadn't shed and had now set them free, he realized he couldn't let the same thing happen to her. He got up and prepared for the worst, clenching and unclenching his fist.

Mick and Vent came stumbling toward them. They dropped their weapons and bent over with their hands on their knees, gasping for air.

"They...got...away," Vent said.

Mick swallowed hard. "They were so...fucking fast."

When Marie flicked her lighter on, both boys staggered backward, as if Heidi's corpse were toxic. Vent immediately turned away and threw up. Mick stared at Heidi, burning the image of her ravaged body into his brain.

"I'm going to kill every last one of them," he said, though Chuck had the feeling he was saying it to himself rather than issuing a rallying cry. He looked at Chuck, his expression going from shock, to anger, to a cold neutrality. His face was smeared with blood. "I was gonna push them off the roof. Had perfect spots for us to hide along the ledge. We could have easily sent them over."

What he didn't say was, *If it wasn't for you, Chuck.*

Chuck couldn't speak, nor could he turn away from Mick's accusing gaze that was there one moment and gone the next.

After spitting over and over, well away from Heidi, Vent asked, "What are we gonna do? Maybe everyone will believe us now."

"Are you kidding me?" Mick said. "How can you prove a Melon Head did this to her?"

"I mean, look at her throat."

"Yeah, so? Look at that Melon Head's cheek."

Vent said, "And how do we prove that's a Melon Head? It's not like the cops have Melon Head DNA on file. We'll get busted for murdering a handicapped person."

"When do we kill them?" Marnie said, her voice so weak, Chuck almost hadn't heard her over the sound of his own breathing.

"Tomorrow," Mick said.

Chuck had no idea how they could accomplish such a thing, and he no longer cared.

Tomorrow it would be.

CHAPTER TWENTY-SEVEN

They'd tried to sleep the rest of the night on the roof. It was an impossible task. Chuck felt it was wrong to sleep while Heidi's body cooled beneath them. Marnie kept breaking out in quiet sobs. He thought he heard Vent sniffle a few times. Mick paced about the roof for an hour, checking to see if the Melon Heads would dare return. He eventually sat with his back against a chimney and closed his eyes, going still as a statue until the dawn.

When Mick woke up, he said, "Time to go."

Chuck needed Vent's help to stand. His entire body ached. He felt like he'd aged a hundred years in the past couple of days. Marnie wiped her eyes and tied her hair back. Chuck dreaded going down the ladder. He spent the entire night replaying Heidi's murder over and over, struggling hard to remember her without a throat that had been eaten away.

Mick went first and Chuck took the rear. He was shocked to see that Marnie wasn't crying. It was Vent who said, "Dude, we can't just leave her here."

Heidi's flesh had turned a color Chuck had never seen before. The tip of his sneaker touched the penumbra of blood around her. It was starting to get tacky.

"We have to," Mick said.

"We can at least cover her up," Chuck said. "Where's the nurse's office?"

"I'll take you," Mick said.

They didn't speak to one another as they went to the first floor where the nurse's office was at the end of the hall. Chuck found a neatly folded blanket in a narrow closet. When they went back upstairs, he needed Mick's help to spread the blanket over her. They stood around her for several minutes, each lost in their own thoughts. The last thing Chuck wanted to do was leave her here, alone, waiting to be discovered. Could you still be afraid after you died? How long did it take for a soul to realize it was time to move on? He thought of her ghost crying out for them not to go, weeping and trembling with unmitigated terror. His chest felt tight. Each breath was a chore.

Marnie was the first to walk away. Mick and Vent followed. Chuck debated whether he should stay. What good was he going to be for them anyway? He was a one-armed liability going on zero sleep and nearing total exhaustion. If anything, he'd only get them killed the way he had with Heidi.

Mick surprised him by stopping and turning around. "Come on."

Chuck shook his head. "You don't need me."

"Yeah. We do."

"I'll only make things worse."

"Things are only gonna get worse no matter what. We do this together. For Heidi."

Chuck took a deep breath, looked down at the small shape under the blanket, and silently said, "I'm sorry. I love you." He thought of his parents and a black hole of loss threatened to pull him under.

Mick shocked him again by patting him on the back as they walked out of the school. "We're gonna make them pay. We're gonna hurt them in ways they never dreamed possible."

The sun had cast a pink glow on the streets, the air filled with birdsong. They made their way to the van, pulling up short when they saw it had been wrecked. The hood was open, hoses and wires pulled out. The air filter was on the sidewalk. All of the tires had been slashed. Chuck noticed splashes of blood on the street.

"How the hell did they know it was ours?" Vent said.

"They have eyes everywhere," Mick said.

Were they watching them now? Chuck looked around, hoping to catch one spying on them. They may have been to the point of breaking, but he was sure their thirst for revenge would give them the strength to catch one and return the favor. All he saw was a cat slinking along the side of the school.

"They did us a favor," Mick said. "I'll bet Marnie's step-ass called it in as stolen by now. The cops'll be looking for it."

"We can't walk all the way to Dracula Drive," Marnie said. "It's too far. By the time we get there, we'll be ready to pass out."

"I'll get us a car," Mick said. "Let's get out of here."

The walk to the center of town took twenty minutes. Mick forced them all to eat again, stressing how they needed to keep up their strength for just this last day. Succeed or fail, it was all going to be over by this time tomorrow. They found a McDonald's and Chuck crammed an Egg McMuffin down his throat, each bite devoid of flavor. When Mick handed him a second one, he ate it mechanically, washing it down with big gulps of orange juice. Looking at the faces of his friends, he figured their senses were as dead as his.

A woman passed by their table with a little girl holding her hand. The girl looked at them and said, "Mommy, they smell." Her mother ushered her over to the counter, casting a look of disgust their way.

"You guys stay here," Mick said, gathering their empty wrappers and cups on a tray. "I'll be back in a half hour, tops."

"Where are you going?" Chuck said.

"To get us a ride."

"I'm coming with you."

Mick shook his head. "You'll stand out, Baby Huey. I need to keep as low a profile as possible."

Chuck pushed his chair away from the table and took the tray from Mick. "Let's go."

Mick peered into his eyes for a moment and said, "Fine. But you have to keep your distance."

They left Marnie and Vent in McDonald's, Marnie picking at the Styrofoam rim of her coffee cup, Vent tearing napkins into small pieces.

Chuck walked alongside Mick, wanting to talk to him, to apologize, to find out the architecture of his grand plan to kill the Melon Heads. Instead, he'd gone mute, every word he wanted to say getting caught in his throat. When they got to the 7-Eleven across the street, Mick pointed to a glass-enclosed bus stop. "Wait there."

Chuck obeyed like a well-trained dog. Or a zombie under the spell of a plantation owner in one of those old movies. He practically fell onto the bench, watching Mick head to the 7-Eleven.

Is he really making a stop for Slim Jims?

It was the time of the morning when people made a quick stop for coffee. Mick made sure to keep his face pointed away from people coming and going through the front door, his eyes zeroed in on the cars. Chuck saw a man in a business suit pull up in a powder-blue Buick Skylark and jump out, leaving the car running. He'd probably done it every day as he dashed for his morning coffee, thinking nothing of it. As soon as he was inside the store, Mick sprinted for the car and took off. As he passed by Chuck he shouted, "Leepee!" That was their shorthand for Lee Park, a small playground two blocks up. Chuck got there as fast as he could, which wasn't fast at all. No sooner had he walked to the main gate, huffing and puffing, than Mick pulled up with the passenger door already open. "Jump in."

Chuck kept waiting for the wail of sirens as they headed back to McDonald's. He threw worried glances out the rear window.

"No one's coming for us," Mick said, carefully obeying the speed limit.

"How can you be so sure?"

"I heard two guys talking when they were going into the 7-Eleven. One of them said, 'Did you hear about the new one?' The other guy said no, and his buddy said, 'Second house in two days. The cops better catch whoever's doing it before this whole town explodes.' I don't think it's a stretch to say the Melon Heads struck again."

Chuck's stomach fell somewhere around his ankles. "Did they say where?"

Mick gave him a stony look. "I think we both know where."

Marnie and Vent piled into the car when Mick idled by the window. Neither asked whose car it was or how Mick had come by it. What was car theft compared to being, in Chuck's mind, accessories to murder?

Vent asked, "Where we going?"

"Want to check on something," Mick said.

A few minutes later, they spotted Heidi's house. It was swarming with cops and reporters and fire trucks. The top floor was puffing gray smoke, the windows bashed in. Water dropped down the side of the house. The front door was wide open with lots of people streaming in and out, all looking as if they'd seen a ghost.

That left just Vent and Marnie with parents. Chuck turned in his seat to check on them. Both had glassy expressions, their eyes looking straight ahead but actually seeing a host of horror playing in their minds.

"Check their houses," Chuck said to Mick, leaning close to him so they couldn't hear.

"Why? They got their pound of fucking flesh already."

"Because they need to know for sure. Without that, I don't think they're going to be much good."

Mick swung onto Maple and made a right onto Balfour. Vent's house was fine. Nothing was out of order, at least on the outside. Chuck heard Vent exhale. They then made their way to Marnie's.

"Damn," Mick muttered.

The police, fire department and several ambulances were parked askew in the street. A policeman waved at Mick to turn around.

Marnie didn't react. Maybe she couldn't. All she did was say, "Mom." That was it. She took in the devastation of her family as stoically as any person could. Vent reached over to take her hand, but she kept it on her lap.

Chuck heard Mick say under his breath, "There goes that." He didn't know what it meant and didn't want to ask, at least in front of Marnie.

The next stop was Mick's Airstream. The front door was wide open. It looked like animals had been inside after the Melon Heads, searching for food. It smelled like it, too. Leaves and pine needles were strewn about the floor. Marnie and Vent stayed outside, sharing a smoke, not speaking.

"I hope they didn't fuck with it," Mick said, kicking debris aside.

"With what?"

"Dwight's little side business. Or what was left of it."

They went into the bedroom at the back of the trailer. Mick dropped to his hands and knees and crawled under the bed. Chuck stared at the shredded sheets and exploded pillows. The Melon Heads were more a force of nature than human beings. They came through houses like tornadoes with teeth.

When Mick backed out, he was clutching a cardboard box. He opened the lid and grinned at the contents. Chuck angled forward so he could see as well.

"Fireworks?"

"Everything Dwight couldn't unload by Fourth of July," Mick said.

"What are we going to do with fireworks? Give the Melon Heads a light show?"

Mick closed the lid and put the box on the shredded mattress. "It's easy to sell the little stuff like firecrackers and Roman candles and spinning stars. Everybody wants 'em. What's left is the powerful stuff. It's all mortars, M80s and quarter sticks in here."

Chuck knew all about quarter sticks, which was short for a quarter stick of dynamite or an M100. His uncle's friend had blown his entire hand off with one several years back during a drunken Independence Day party in his yard. Ever since then, there hadn't been any fireworks allowed in his family. Not that it stopped Chuck from firing off bottle rockets, though always in secret and far from the house.

"Quarter sticks," Chuck said, impressed. "How many you got?"

"A dozen. And it looks like more than that in mortars, along with some smaller stuff that still goes bang real hard and real loud." He hurried out of the bedroom, grabbed his BB gun, and handed it to Chuck. "Take this while I carry the box."

"All those explosives and you think this little gun is going to do anything?"

"Beggars can't be choosers."

They went outside, Mick not bothering to close the door. He popped the trunk and put the box and BB gun inside.

"What's in the box?" Marnie asked, exhaling a dragon's breath of smoke.

"Fireworks, but only the dangerous kind."

She just nodded, as if it were normal to return to the scene of a massacre for a box of firecrackers on steroids.

Mick slammed the trunk closed and said to Vent, "You think we can get your father's guns?"

"No."

"It's actually not a question. We need them. We need the ones at Marnie's place, but it's crawling with cops."

Vent folded his arms across his chest. "I've been gone for days. I doubt my parents are even leaving the house to go to work. How am I supposed to sneak by them?"

Mick pulled his hair back and tied it up with a rubber band from his pocket. "If you want to save them, you'll find a way. Besides, I think you overestimate how much they care."

"That was a shitty thing to say," Marnie snapped. "Take it back."

"Look, Chuck and Heidi, they had real families. The three of us, just different levels of dysfunction. If the cops are looking for the five of us, we all know who they're looking harder for."

The five of us. Chuck's chest instantly grew heavy.

When Vent didn't have anything to say, Mick got back in the car and cranked the engine.

"What the hell are we doing?" Marnie asked Chuck.

"Whatever we have to, I guess. At this point, what do we have to lose? We'll make him spill his plan right after we go to Vent's."

"We better. I'm not just walking into Melon Head territory with some fireworks. If I'm going to die fighting, I want to be able to take some of them out."

Chuck wrapped his arm around her. "You and me both."

CHAPTER TWENTY-EIGHT

There was one good thing about fear. While it had your full attention, you couldn't fixate on the pain in your body. Marnie was thankful for small favors.

She wanted Mick to drive into town so she could pick up a newspaper and see what everyone was saying. Did they still suspect that it was wild teens who had murdered Chuck's, Heidi's and her families and destroyed their homes? Were the police looking for them, or had they assumed they were dead in a ditch somewhere? Or worse, did they suspect them of turning on their parents?

She doubted anyone would care about Mick's place. Shit, she doubted many people even knew where the Airstream was located.

Mick said it was too dangerous to take the stolen car anywhere close to Main Street.

All of this was after they had gone to Vent's house and found it empty. Marnie's heart broke for him. He'd looked crestfallen. He walked through the house, touching everything as if trying to absorb every fiber into memory. He got a rifle and a handgun and boxes of ammunition. His eyes were glassy with tears as they left.

Now they were pulling up a block from Dredd's childhood home.

"You think he's still there?" she asked Mick. "Those pipes didn't seem very solid."

"I locked him up on a good one. He hasn't gone anywhere."

They went to the back of the house and through the window with the loose board, Mick leading the way just as he had all day and yesterday. So far, it had resulted in Heidi's death, her parents', and the death of Marnie's mother and stepfather. Why were they still in line with the most unstable of their group?

Because we're in chaos, and Mick thrives in chaos, she thought.

"Whoa, this place smells like mouse shit," Vent said.

Marnie hadn't noticed it before, but now that Vent had mentioned it, the smell was nearly overpowering. She hated mice – was scared to death of them. She couldn't take her eyes off the floor, searching for the nasty critters.

Mick had a flashlight in his pocket that he turned on to chase away a very small portion of the gloom.

"Where's Dredd?" Chuck said.

"In the basement," Mick said, going for the basement door.

"Hold on a second," Vent said. "If I don't take the edge off, I'm going to lose my freaking mind." He pulled two fat joints from his pocket. "I grabbed what I had left in my stash. And don't give me any shit about keeping a clear head," he said to Chuck.

"As much as I hate to admit when you're right, you're right," Mick said, flashing a look at Chuck.

"Hey, who's up there?" Dredd shouted.

Mick stomped on the floor several times. "Make him nervous."

Marnie said, "That's not cool. You know, we're the ones that messed up his life. He did what you asked him because he thought it was the right thing to do after what happened to me. There's no reason to treat him that way."

"I was just messing around."

"I'm not. Give me the keys." She stuck her hand out and waggled her fingers.

"No way. I'll take off the handcuffs when I think it's safe."

"This isn't your call. I started all this, and I'm going down to uncuff him."

She and Mick locked eyes, neither blinking.

"Dude, just give her the keys," Chuck said. "If anything, he'll be less angry if she's the one to do it."

Vent added, "The sooner you do it, the sooner I can light these bad boys up."

Mick slapped the key into Marnie's palm. "At least let me come with you."

"No."

"Then take Vent or the one-armed bandit here."

"You guys stay here," she said with a tone that she knew would have been her mommy voice when her kids acted up. Except she would never have children of her own, even if she somehow survived this day.

Dredd was sitting in a puddle of his own piss. The stench of ammonia assaulted her nose. He looked none too happy. The jarred candle they'd lit before they left was almost burned all the way down.

"Where did you assholes go? You could have at least left me a piss bucket!"

Marnie approached him slowly, as if he were a chained animal, which is exactly how he looked at the moment.

"I'm sorry. We had to do some things. My best friend was murdered by the Melon Heads. So was my family." When she said it, it sounded as if it were coming from someone else. Being a step removed was the only way to stay sane...for now.

Dredd's features softened. "Christ. I'm sorry."

"It's not your fault, so you don't need to be sorry. I'm going to take your cuffs off. All I ask is that you stay chill. My friends upstairs have guns and they'll use them."

Dredd nodded.

It took Marnie a few tries to get the cuffs to unsnap. When they finally did, Dredd threw them across the room and rubbed his wrists. Marnie backed away quickly. "Fucking things hurt."

"We're going to attack the Melon Heads today," she said.

"Hey, it's your suicide."

She swallowed hard. "You still might be able to help us."

"After what you did to me? Are you crazy?"

Marnie thought it over for a moment, and then said, "Yes, I think we are. I think we have to be. Besides, if you help us, you help yourself. I don't think you can hide down here forever, and from what I can tell, you don't have the kind of cash you need to pick up and start over someplace else."

"How the fuck do you know how much dough I have?" he said with a scowl.

"Because if you had more than twenty bucks to your name, you wouldn't be down here. You'd be in Florida or New Mexico by now."

That made Dredd grin. "You're smarter than you look."

"That's because people usually don't look north of my chest. Come on if you want to work with us and get high."

He followed her up the stairs, complaining about cramps in his arms and legs and that he was starving and thirsty as a dry well. The boys were passing the first joint around, the enclosed room filling with smoke. When Dredd put his hand out to take a hit, Mick pulled it away and said, "Who said you could smoke with us?"

"I did," Marnie said, making it clear that she was not to be questioned. It was a hard front to put up when she felt as awful, physically and mentally, as she did.

Mick huffed and reluctantly handed it over. Dredd took a drag. "Probably my stuff anyway. You got anything to drink?"

"We forgot to order takeout," Mick said.

Chuck eyed Dredd's cuff marks on his wrist. They were raw as chopped meat and raised. "Lucky for you the Melon Heads didn't come here."

"Yeah, I feel nothing but lucky," Dredd said, giving Chuck a major case of side-eye.

"At least you feel something," Vent said. "That's more than a lot of people we know can say. If you're mixed up with these freaks and alive, you're lucky as hell."

They finished the first joint and made quick work of the second. Marnie's head was nice and fuzzy, her body relaxed and free of pain. She thought if she put her head down on the filthy floor, she'd fall asleep like a baby after a bottle and be quite happy.

"Margie says you guys are planning to take the Melon Heads on in their literal neck of the woods," Dredd said, slapping his thighs to get their attention. Everyone's eyes looked like red-rimmed mirrors.

"You have to be doing this just to screw with me," Marnie said. Dredd looked at her as if she were speaking another language.

"So, how do you plan to do it? You got a tank stashed someplace?"

"How many of them are there?" Chuck asked, preempting Mick.

"How the fuck should I know? It's not like I ever took a census."

"You've been dealing with them for years. You have to have a rough estimate."

"More than you can handle, I'll tell you that much. I've never seen them all in one place, and it's kinda hard to tell one from the other. They all look like goddamn mutants."

"Take a guess."

Dredd swished his finger in his ear, pulled it out and examined it for a bit. "How does a hundred sound?"

"Fucking terrible," Vent said.

Mick punched a cabinet door, knocking it off the hinges.

"Sounds like too many," Chuck said. "You can't stay hidden that long with that many people. Plus, food would be a problem. When it gets cold, they'd need to light fires. Too many fires equal too much smoke, equals being discovered."

"You know so damn much, why'd you ask me?"

"Could they keep warm in caves?" Mick asked.

Marnie shivered, remembering when Dredd had told them about the small system of caves where the Melon Heads sometimes hid.

Chuck scratched at his face and paused. "Depends. Some caves, depending on where they lead, can be colder than the weather outside. But I guess it's a possibility."

"Then Dredd could be right."

"I take it you've never been in the caves with them?" Marnie asked.

"The only way you get in those caves is as a meal," Dredd said. "Something I'd like to avoid."

A loud pop of wood startled them. After a pensive minute, Dredd said, "Just this place rotting. If they were around, they wouldn't be subtle about it. Even they can figure out no one will hear them this far out."

"They can figure out a lot more than you think," Chuck said. "They're not imbeciles."

"Even though they look it," Mick added. He turned to Dredd and asked, "How many guns you got?"

"Two. Not enough for you to go all Ahnold on them. Believe me."

Chuck said, "Another question. How often do they come out during the day?"

"Not much. They like the night. Daytime, I think it's just sentries that stay mostly by Dracula Drive. They need a reason to come further into town. Now that you've given them one, I'm sure there's more than usual wandering around."

"What does their leader look like?" Mick said.

Dredd seemed to pull within himself. "You don't want to mess with that."

"Actually," Marnie said, "we *need* to mess with *all* of them."

"Or take out the alpha male and frighten the rest of them into leaving us be," Chuck said.

Dredd chuckled with zero humor. "Well, you picked the perfect thing to call him, because that big boy is one alpha motherfucker. He's taller than the rest, and built like a bricklayer."

"I noticed that most of them seem to be on the short side," Chuck said.

"Inbreeding. I never came across the fucker, but Fennerman told me all about him. He's a few inches north of six foot. Got a chest wide as a wine barrel. And a full head of long, straw-colored hair. If his size doesn't give him away, you'll know him by his crooked-set eyes and the huge black moles all over his face and neck. He's one ugly bastard."

"You ever deal with him directly?" Mick asked.

"Not a chance. He always hangs back a bit, lets his people have first crack at anything. Guess that's how he keeps them happy."

Marnie shivered. "I can't believe you chose to work with those monsters."

Dredd used his boot to pry up a floorboard. "You guys still don't get it. First, *they chose me*. Not the other way around. And while I was out there as barrier between them and the town, I kept you all safe. It would have gone on that way until I was the old man if I didn't let my emotions get the best of me and take you all out there."

The words struck Marnie like an anvil to the chest. Christ, he was right. The Melon Heads had been reduced to a harmless urban legend until they'd arrived at Dredd's doorstep. How many more lives would the Melon Heads ruin before they stopped them? For a moment, Marnie wondered if they should give themselves to the Melon Heads to atone for their sins. Then she realized she didn't believe in sins or hell or even heaven. Still, guilt was more powerful than any theology.

"Well, no matter what, we have to go there today, before the sun goes down," Mick said.

"Why do we have to rush it?" Vent said. "Maybe we need to think things through some more."

"Dude, by tomorrow morning, your parents will be dead," Mick said.

Vent got quiet, turning away from them. Marnie was pretty sure he'd never even punched someone before, at least until he'd batted that Melon Head in the skull at Chuck's house. He was more scared than any of them because of his nature and the fact that he still had something to lose. She reached out for him, but he pulled away.

"You coming with us?" Chuck asked Dredd.

"Not a chance."

"Are you kidding me?" Mick shouted. "You have skin in this game."

"Way I see it, if they haven't come for me yet, I might still be all right with them."

"They burned your fucking house down."

"Might have just been a message. They don't think and act like we do."

"That we get loud and clear," Chuck said. "Can we at least have your guns?"

Dredd pondered it, stepping into the pitch-black living room as if he were having a conference with someone. "I'll give you my pistol. I can't afford to lose both guns, especially because I don't think you're gonna be able to bring them back when you're done."

Mick's face flushed red and he was about to say something when Chuck put a hand to his chest to get him to calm down and said, "Fine. We'll take it."

"I don't know what good it'll do you. Unless you use it on yourself. Better that than letting them get you. You think it's gonna happen, take care of your own business. It'll be quicker, and less painful."

"Thanks for the encouragement," Vent said sheepishly.

"It's the best advice I can give you." Dredd went downstairs and came back with a .38 and a handful of bullets that Mick put in his shirt pocket.

The abandoned house was disgusting and this side of creepy, but at this moment, Marnie wanted to cling to it as if it were a beach house in the Caribbean. Mick shoved the board aside so they could clamber out the window.

"You going to wish us luck?" he asked Dredd.

Dredd spit on the floor and wiped his mouth with the cuff of his shirt. "Yeah. Sure."

Marnie interpreted it as, *yeah, I'm sure you're all gonna die.* It was exactly how she felt.

CHAPTER TWENTY-NINE

It was going on three o'clock by the time they hit the road, leaving Dredd and his decaying house behind. Chuck figured they had a little over three hours until the sunlight was no longer on their side. Sitting shotgun, he squinted into the sun as they jounced along a road in desperate need of repair, each bounce sending rolling waves of pain from his arm, down his spine and into his feet. The pain, for this moment, barely registered. He was too busy wondering if this would be the very last time he saw the sun, feel the fresh wind on his face. He wondered where the souls of his parents were and if there was such a thing as a soul. Life after death had been a topic that had intrigued him immensely a year ago. He'd read every book he could find on the subject, library hopping the neighboring towns, until he came to the conclusion that no one did or could know what was to come after a person died. The theory that he preferred over all others was that death was like living in a permanent dream.

Maybe hell was dreaming of all the worst moments of your life. If that were the case, he hoped he could somehow forget the last week.

Mick ran into a pothole big enough to swallow a motorcycle. The box of fireworks and guns thumped in the trunk.

"Careful," Chuck said.

"Not so easy on this crappy street."

"I just don't want one of those guns accidentally going off."

Getting to Dracula Drive wasn't easy. Milbury was on high alert. Every time they spotted a police cruiser, they had to make a detour. By this point, the car had to have been reported stolen. None of them had the knowledge or ability to break into a new car and hot-wire it. Not even Mick. He was more a thief of opportunity. Their only hope was that the cops were more focused on the current murder spree than some measly stolen car.

None of them complained about the longer drive. Asking Mick to get there sooner was like demanding your executioner step up the timetable to charge the electric chair. Chuck kept checking the back seat where Marnie and Vent sat leaning against their doors, heads on the windows, lost in thought.

"We sure as hell don't look like an army ready to storm the castle," Chuck said to Mick. The radio was on low, the haunting harmonies of Alice in Chains sounding like a funeral dirge.

"That's because we're stoned," Mick said, but he didn't sound very sure of himself.

Whatever high Chuck had achieved had come crashing down the moment they'd left Dredd's. He wished he could get so baked he thought he was invincible. "You really want to do this?"

"You don't?" Mick replied, his tone heavy with accusation.

Chuck thought of his parents and Heidi, Marnie's and Mick's mothers, even their evil stepdads. They owed it to all of them to get revenge and put an end to the strange Melon Heads. It would be easy to ignore them if they simply kept to themselves in the woods, harmless as woodchucks. However, as had been pointed out before, they were very much human with all of man's proclivities for destruction. Maybe it was wrong of Chuck and his friends to want to wipe them off the face of the earth. Two wrongs did not make a right.

But the Melon Heads had overstepped their bounds. Had left them basic orphans. Had robbed them of their homes. Their futures. Chuck, Mick, Vent and Marnie *also* had proclivities for destruction. Now it was a matter of seeing how far they could take those innate impulses.

"No, I do," he said.

"You scared?"

Chuck glimpsed Vent, looking pale and hollow. "Yeah."

"Good. A little fear goes a long way."

Mick made a couple of quick turns and they came to the start of the legendary Dracula Drive. He pulled the car over.

"Why are we stopping?" Marnie said.

"I need to do prep work." Mick got out of the car and opened the trunk. Chuck and Marnie followed him, Vent not acknowledging them.

Mick opened the fireworks box and took out one of the quarter sticks. It was so thick around, he needed two hands to hold it. He took out his red Swiss Army knife, which had seen better days, and cut off half the wick. "We'll need some of these to go off quick." He did the same to three others, as well as some mortars and M80s. When he was done, he took the box and the guns out of the trunk and put them in the back seat. Chuck made sure no one was around to see him transfer their cache of firepower. Not that he needed to. No one came this way. Well, almost.

When they got back in the car, Vent said, "You think they're watching us right now?"

"I'm sure of it," Mick said. "Bet they're running it down the line to alert the rest. In a little bit, they're really gonna know we're here."

They took it slow down Dracula Drive with the windows rolled up. Chuck kept expecting the first rock to ping off the car. All eyes were on the surrounding woods, searching for any sign of movement. Marnie tapped Chuck's shoulder and handed him the pistol Vent took from his house. He looked back and saw she had Dredd's .38 while Vent gripped a rifle.

"Just make sure you all take the safeties off," Mick said, eyeing them in the rearview mirror. "You don't want to come up lame when you need to shoot. Might be the last thing any of us ever do. And don't shoot while you're in the car. You'll make yourself and all of us deaf."

Chuck stared at the gun with grim finality. This was it. They were here. They could always turn back, but he knew they wouldn't. What was there to turn back for?

"I think I see something!" Vent shouted, shifting in his seat so he could press his face against the window. Mick hit the brakes and the car rocked. Everyone but Chuck turned to where Vent was staring. Chuck could easily imagine the Melon Heads setting up a diversion. He waited for them to try a sneak attack, his heart hammering.

"You sure?" Mick said.

"It was right there," Vent said, pointing. Chuck gave a quick glimpse but saw only trees.

They waited for a moment and then Marnie said, "There!"

Mick pushed back into his seat. "Just a rabbit. How can you mistake a rabbit for a person?"

Vent didn't answer.

I know, Chuck thought. *Because we're all on edge and might end up shooting each other by mistake.*

Maybe Dredd was wrong. They wouldn't have to take their own lives. They'd do it to each other instead.

Mick eased the car forward. Sunlight slanted through the wild canopy of trees. It looked peaceful, almost serene. Taking in his surroundings and trying to reconcile it with what was to come was like standing on a boat amidst a swollen sea and gazing at the steady, immovable dock. It made him unsteady. Odds are, if he had to step out of the car now, he would stumble and fall.

They came to the turn to Dredd's cabin and stopped short of the charred home. Chuck rolled the window down a crack, taking in the heady sc ent of burnt wood. No one made a move to open their door.

"See any rabbits?" Mick joked. Chuck assumed it was to settle his own thrumming nerves. They turned this way and that, seeking any sign of a hiding or approaching Melon Head.

"They won't do a thing while we're in the car," Chuck said. "They won't even throw rocks this time. What they want is us out of the car where we're vulnerable."

Mick popped his lock open. "Well, then I aim to please."

Marnie said, "Wait!"

He was out the door with his BB gun in one hand and a mortar in the other.

Chuck grabbed a lighter from the glove compartment that he'd found earlier while checking things out. He stuck it in his bad hand, his finger just able to get a grip on it. "One of us needs to be able to light the fuse."

Mick nodded solemnly. He spun in a tight circle, searching the woods. Just like the first time they'd come here, the forest was dark and silent.

Marnie and Vent came out next. Marnie tried to hold on to the box of fireworks but didn't do a very good job of it. Chuck stuck the pistol in his waistband, fully aware that he was one wrong move away from blowing his balls off. "I've got it," he said to Marnie.

"No, I'm fine."

"You are until it falls."

He tucked the box under his arm, the fireworks slamming together and making him nervous. He had a loaded gun pointed at his privates and an armful of TNT. Not a good combination.

"I hate this place," Marnie said.

"We all do," Chuck said.

With a faraway look in her eyes, Marnie recited the Melon Heads song every kid in Milbury knew by heart.

Dare to walk,
Down Dracula Drive,
In day or night,
You won't survive.
They wait in trees,
And hide below,
Hungry for people,
Too blind to know.

"Yeah, well, we're not blind," Mick said. "We know exactly what those fucks are capable of."

Marnie shivered, her eyes sweeping the trees.

A light, wavering breeze had some of the higher leaves clacking.

When nothing came running for them, Mick stuck the mortar in his back pocket and got the map from inside the car. He unfolded it on the hood. Chuck looked at it from across the hood and realized it was best to come around so he could see it straight on and do his best to memorize the route.

"That map sucks," Vent said, barely giving it a look because he was too busy scanning the woods with the rifle ready to go.

"He's no cartographer for sure," Chuck said.

"Cart-what?" Mick said.

Chuck grinned despite their situation. "Map maker, for the simple."

Mick half smiled back. "Hope that big brain of yours doesn't weigh you down."

He lifted his sling a few inches from his body. "I have this for that."

"How far do we have to go again?" Marnie asked worriedly.

"Too freaking far," Vent said.

"Mile and a half, maybe two," Mick said. Chuck heard him say under his breath, "If we make it that far."

"We will."

Mick looked surprised, as if he wasn't aware he'd spoken that last part out loud. "You guys ready?"

No one said a thing. It wasn't the time to lie and say yes. Nor was it the time to back out and say no. From here on, it would be a fight to survive. At least now, they were bringing it to the Melon Heads rather than running and waiting for them to strike.

Mick took the lead with the map in hand. Marnie went next, followed by Chuck lugging the fireworks and Vent at the rear, walking backwards for the most part. They crept past the scorched cabin, the remaining leaves on the ground charred and brittle. The smell reminded Chuck of campfires with his family when he was young, his mom helping them make s'mores while his father drank cold Schlitz beer from a can, making the kind of jokes he never would at home when he was in full dad mode.

It seemed to take forever for the cabin to be far enough behind them that they could no longer see it. At the rate they were going, they wouldn't get to their destination until well after nightfall. At that point, the game would be over. For them.

Mick must have read his mind when he said, "Goddamn. I wish we could have stayed in the car. This is gonna take forever."

"Dredd said this is the quicker route. If we brought the car, they'd hear us from a mile out. Maybe we can surprise them."

"I wouldn't bet the house on that," Marnie said.

Aside from being hyper-vigilant of any Melon Heads around them, Chuck was also concerned about Vent and his rifle. He was spooked, as were they all. "Keep your finger on the trigger guard."

"Um, yeah. Yeah. I got you."

Mick held up his arm and they stopped. After a few breathless moments, he said, "You all hear that?"

"Hear what?" Marnie said.

"Nothing. Absolutely nothing. They're here, all right."

"Wish they'd show themselves," Vent said.

"They see the guns," Chuck said. "That'll keep them away. For now." *But for how long*, Chuck wondered. They must know the power behind a rifle, having spied on hunters in the past.

Mick took a step and stopped. He took three more and stopped. Chuck knew what he was doing. He was trying to trick the Melon Heads and radar in on where they were hiding by the sound of their footsteps.

Chuck whispered what was going on to Marnie and Vent. "Keep doing it," he said to Mick.

It took three more times before they heard the snap of twigs to their left. Mick pointed to a tree that had a split trunk fifteen yards away. He motioned for Chuck to open the fireworks box and took out an M80. It wasn't going to mangle a Melon Head, but it would make a hell of a statement.

We know you're there.

Mick turned his back to light the fuse. He waited until the sputtering flame had consumed most of the wick, and then he threw it at the V-shaped tree. The M80 went off just as it was sailing through the V like a football through the uprights. The bang sounded like thunder in the quiet forest. It was followed by a terrified screech. A Melon Head sprang from his hiding place, hands clamped over his ears. He was pale as death, his bony skull sprinkled with dry tufts of black hair. He wore torn jeans and, of all things, a New York Yankees T-shirt. The absurdity was not lost on Chuck.

Mick fired his BB gun after the fleeing Melon Head. He landed one on the back of its neck, and the Melon Head was forced to take its hand from its ear and grasp for the source of the sudden pain. "Can you get him?" Mick said to Vent.

Vent followed the Melon Head with his rifle and shook his head. "He's running too fast."

"Shit. We can hope he's deaf now," Mick said. "At least for the rest of the day."

"One maybe down, who knows how many more to go," Marnie said. "Doesn't sound too hopeful, does it?"

Chuck thought it certainly didn't. He was about to say just that when a Melon Head sprang from behind a cluster of bushes on their right. It looked like a woman with long, wild hair filled with crushed leaves, pine needles and twigs. She went straight for Marnie, tackling her to the ground and growling like a wild animal. Vent turned the rifle toward the Melon Head. The only problem was that she was intertwined with a struggling Marnie.

"Don't shoot!" Chuck and Mick shouted in unison.

But they were too late.

CHAPTER THIRTY

The rifle went off, the bullet just missing Marnie and the Melon Head. Instead, it kicked up a divot of dirt and leaves. Vent looked like he was going to try again. Chuck ditched the fireworks box and grabbed the rifle out of his hand.

"Get her off me!" Marnie screamed.

She had one hand on the throat of the snarling Melon Head, the other trying to push her off. The Melon Head snapped her jaws open and shut, eager to get a piece of Marnie's face in her dripping maw.

Mick jumped on the Melon Head's back and locked his arm around her neck while pulling her back. They rolled off Marnie. Mick couldn't believe the strength of the Melon Head. She was under five feet and thin as a starved dog, but it felt like she was made of solid muscle. He tightened his chokehold. She threw her arms back, swatting at his face and trying to claw at his eyes. Her fingertips were black with filth, her long nails he was sure filled with infection should she dig them into his flesh. She used her legs to push him onto his back. He struggled to maintain his hold on the howling she-beast.

He was really worried she was going to get away when Chuck and Vent each grabbed an arm, helping to pin her down. She headbutted Mick, clipping his cheekbone. The sudden shot of pain blinded him for a moment. When he recovered, he saw Marnie standing over the Melon Head. She was holding a lit M80.

"I'm sorry," Marnie said, jamming the M80 in the Melon Head's shirt. "Let her go and get the hell away!"

Chuck and Vent dropped her arms. Mick pulled his arm from her neck and rolled as far as he could go. The Melon Head sprang to her feet, howling with what sounded like terror. She clawed at her shirt. Mick was sure the lit fuse burned like hell.

The Melon Head had just turned to run away when the M80 went off. She was jolted off her feet and went stiff as a board as she fell backward, her arms splayed out. She hit the ground hard, knocking the base of her skull against a gnarled, exposed tree root. A crimson stain blossomed on her shirt.

Mick got to his feet and stood over the motionless Melon Head.

"Is it dead?" Vent said, standing on the other side of the body.

"If she keeps bleeding like that she sure will be," Mick said. He gazed at Marnie. "That was pretty badass."

She didn't look like she felt the same. "God, that's awful."

She was looking at the hole in the wild woman's shirt, the edges blackened by gunpowder. Within the hole, they could see right into the Melon Head's exposed guts.

"She was gonna eat your face off," Mick said.

"Yeah. I know. But...."

"We better get moving. Daylight's not staying around longer today just for us," Chuck said.

They trudged on, Mick hoping there were other Melon Heads who'd witnessed what they'd just done. *Run and tell everyone else that we're not to be fucked with!* The rest of the way wasn't going to be easy. In fact, it would most assuredly get worse and worse. But it felt good to draw first blood.

Mick kept checking the crudely drawn map. They followed a narrow game trail that was rife with briars and low-hanging branches. The gnats got thicker the further they went. He had to keep his mouth closed tight to avoid sucking in a hundred of them. They were biting the hell out of his face and ears. No matter how much he swatted at them, they wouldn't leave. Marnie looked especially miserable. She was terrified of bugs. He gave her credit for not losing it. Instead, she kept plowing through them, keeping close to his back.

They wound their way through the game trail until they were plunged into a false twilight. The air was cooler, going on cold, in this part of the woods. It was like swimming in a lake and coming across a cool current, dimpling your skin with goosebumps for that brief moment you sluiced through the unseen wave.

"At least it's too cold for the bugs," Chuck said. "I know all the tree cover would lower the temperature, but this seems almost supernatural." He exhaled and produced a short-lived trail of vapor.

Mick looked at the map. "Dredd said it doesn't last long. Just stick to the trail."

It was dark but not too dark to make their way, though it would be easy for the Melon Heads to hide in plain sight. Mick felt as if hundreds of eyes were on him. The back of his neck tingled, anticipating a Melon Head to reach out of the gloom and grab him. He wanted to set fire to everything, both for the heat and the light.

Mick spun around at the sound of pounding feet on the loamy ground.

There was a brief flash of light as Vent's rifle went off. Mick saw a bulky Melon Head wielding a heavy branch throw its arms out and fall to the ground.

"You get him?"

Vent and Chuck approached the fallen Melon Head with care. "He did," Chuck said.

"Are you sure?" Marnie asked.

When she went to see for herself, Chuck stuck his arm out. "Don't look, Marnie. It's bad. He got it in the face."

"I wasn't even aiming," Vent said. He sounded like a kid who just got in trouble for breaking a window.

"Just imagine what will happen when you do aim," Mick said. It sounded callous, but he needed them to be ready for anything, not filled to the gills with guilt every time they took a Melon Head out. Yes, the Melon Heads were still people and even hardcore soldiers had a hard time killing the enemy, but it was now a matter of us or them. They were going to see a lot worse than a Melon Head with its face blown off. If they were lucky.

"I don't like it here. Let's get through this as fast as we can," Marnie said, pushing Mick in the back to get him moving. He was happy to oblige.

They heard more heavy footsteps, except this time it was almost impossible to determine where it was coming from. Mick's mouth went dry. "They're flanking us."

There was definitely more than one Melon Head in the darkness with them. And now they weren't even trying to be sneaky. Why bother when they had the deep shadows on their side?

Mick handed Marnie the map and dug into the fireworks box. He took out a mortar and stuck it in the ground, loosely so it would take to the air. He lit it and backed away. "Get ready for the light show."

The wick crackled, and seconds later the mortar zipped into the trees with a keening whistle. It smacked into a high trunk, just like Mick hoped it would, and exploded. A dazzling display of red and blue sparks rained down on them.

Within the sudden burst of light, Mick could see the Melon Heads that had managed to surround them. Most were crouching on the ground, stunned by the mortar that continued to birth an array of sparks. He counted five, one of them apparently a child.

"Come on!" He grabbed Marnie's hand and ran, casting a quick glance behind him to make sure Chuck and Vent were doing the same. The branches around the sizzling mortar caught on fire. It couldn't have gone any better. As the flames grew, the darkness shrank. The Melon Heads hadn't bothered to look their way, their attention focused on what was going on above them. Mick wondered if some of them were momentarily blinded as well, especially if they had been hiding out here, waiting for them, their eyes fully adjusted to the dark. Now, it was a matter of getting out of this virtual chamber of horror and into the light.

Mick's boots smacked into rocks and raised roots, but he managed to keep on his feet. Marnie's palm was sweaty. He wasn't about to let her go. He spotted a light up ahead, maybe fifty yards away. Mick whooped. "We're almost there!"

Chuck huffed behind them. He'd never been much of a runner. And he was pretty banged up.

"Keep up with us, buddy," Mick said.

"I'm...trying."

All around them were fallen, misshapen trees covered in thick carpets of moss. It looked like something out of a fantasy movie. He spotted the first Melon Head poking its head out of a large knothole in one of the tree trunks, its extrication nauseatingly resembling Nature herself giving birth to a tainted offspring. The Melon Head slipped out, glided along the moss and jumped to its feet.

Leaves rattled overhead. Mick saw a shadow leap from one branch to another. He shot wildly into the trees as he ran. They had to get the hell out of there.

"Look out!" Marnie shouted.

Mick didn't see the Melon Head slithering toward him like a snake until it grabbed his leg and pulled him down with a hard jerk that nearly dislocated his ankle. He kicked at it, but it moved too fast, disappearing back into the dirt and leaves.

More and more Melon Heads were emerging from their hiding places, blocking the way out.

"Vent!" Mick said.

A bullet zinged close enough to Chuck, it sounded as if a bee had zipped noisily by his face. He dropped to his knees. Vent fired again, though this time, the Melon Heads didn't stand there like sitting ducks. They disappeared as suddenly as they had appeared.

Mick dragged himself along the damp ground, his ankle throbbing. He and Chuck exchanged a worried glance, and Chuck got behind Vent to watch for any Melon Heads coming up behind them. The fireworks box was open, some of its contents on the ground. Mick grabbed another mortar and lit it.

"Get out of the way," he said to Marnie. She looked back and jumped to the side. Sparks burned his hand as he held on to the mortar until a split-second before takeoff. The mortar blasted forward in an unsteady line, hitting near the knothole. It bloomed into a cascade of fiery white that was so bright it hurt his eyes. A slew of Melon Heads exploded from their hidey-holes, whooping and yowling. It was like going into the primate house at the zoo and scaring the living hell out of them. They ran from the sparkling display. Vent tried his best to take them down now that he had good light, but they moved with such startling agility, he may have winged one at the most. No matter, the path to get out was now clear. Mick staggered to his feet and scooped up the box and ran. He didn't need to tell his friends to follow.

There was movement all around them, but it seemed as long as the mortar continued to burn, the Melon Heads were too frightened to attack. It had just started to fizzle out when they hit daylight. They stopped to look back.

"Holy shit," Chuck said.

In their panic to escape, they hadn't heard the dozen Melon Heads trailing after them. The mortar burned itself out, which meant the rest were about to join their ranks.

"Guys, help me," Mick said. He handed a mortar to Chuck and Vent, chewing most of the wicks off and spitting them out. He handed Marnie the lighter. "Light 'em up."

She went down the line, wincing every time the flame took. Chuck's was the first to go. It sailed to the left and then up, igniting somewhere inside the forest cavern. A curtain of sparkles rained down the exit. Mick's went next, a straight shot that must have lanced a Melon Head, judging by the pained cry that echoed out to them. Vent's took a wicked turn and didn't make it inside, though it did dive into the ground just outside the exit.

Mick's forearm felt as if he'd been stung by a nest of hornets. The sparks had burned a multitude of red dots into his skin. Chuck and Vent were flicking their hands, shaking off the pain. Mick grabbed Vent's rifle and fired a few rounds into the blistering madness inside the cavern. He smiled when he heard the Melon Heads shriek.

"That should hold them."

He hastily covered the box and was about to run when Chuck said, "Where's Marnie?"

He looked all around. There was no way she'd go off on her own. "Marnie!"

Chuck and Vent started calling out for her as well.

"Goddammit, where did she go?" Mick said, his stomach filling with lead. If something happened to her....

"I don't think she went anywhere," Vent said, pointing at the ground. Her boot and gun were there, but that was it. "It looks like she was taken."

CHAPTER THIRTY-ONE

Marnie's abduction had taken all the wind from their sails. The only shred of luck on their side was the fact that the Melon Heads hadn't stormed from the darkness after the mortars shed their last spark.

They must know, Chuck thought. *Maybe all of this was one big distraction so they could grab any one of us. Why did it have to be Marnie?* He didn't think she'd been intentionally chosen. It was probably just a matter of opportunity as she watched them send the mortars into the darkness, unaware that a Melon Head was nearby, waiting.

"What do we do now?" Vent asked. He looked like he was about to cry.

Mick tossed the rifle back to him. "We keep going."

"But we can't just leave her."

"We're not...leaving her," Mick said. His chest was heaving and his eyes looked crazed. "If anything, they'll take her to their camp."

"And if not?" Chuck asked.

Mick turned his head and spit. "Then we have one more reason to kill every last one of them, now don't we?"

Chuck would have worried about Mick's anger making him reckless and getting them killed, but he'd gone into this assuming most or all of them were never coming back. It would be impossible to search these primeval woods for Marnie. She could be anywhere. It would be full dark before they traversed even one-twentieth of the overgrown acreage. All he could do was hope she was still alive and hadn't been brutally murdered and eaten. Just the thought of it made his legs go weak.

They picked up the pace now, anxious to find where the Melon Heads stayed and face their own mortalities. Every now and then they called out for Marnie, never really expecting to hear her call back to them. Chuck was sure there were Melon Heads near them, watching them, reporting back in whatever strange language they must have had that they were coming. Any tribe, for lack of a better word, that could plan and prepare like the Melon Heads surely had some form of speech. Chuck wondered what it sounded like. He was sure it would haunt his nightmares.

For sure, he and Mick and Vent were running headlong into a trap. Fuck it. There was no turning back now.

"What I wouldn't give for an Uzi," Vent said, his eyes wide as golf balls.

"I'd rather have a tank," Chuck said.

Mick, who was running with the map held in front of him, didn't say a word. Chuck flashed to the grisly sight of Mick biting off the Melon Head's cheek back at the school. He could only imagine what Mick would do to one now if he could get his hands on them. His savagery might make the Melon Heads look like purring kittens. As much as they needed his fury, Chuck worried about how they'd put a stopper on it should they accomplish their mission. If Mick had been destined for a life in prison like everyone said, he was doomed to an asylum now.

Maybe they all were.

The trees had thinned out on the path and Chuck was alarmed to see that the sun was starting to wane. What time was it? None of them were wearing a watch, so they would just have to guess, which was less than ideal. Judging by that sky, time was ticking by faster than a jackrabbit fucking.

"Any more…obstacles like the one…back there?" Chuck said, huffing. There was no way he'd be able to run back the way they'd come.

"I don't think so. At least Dredd didn't point any out, other than saying we'd never get this far."

Chuck didn't know whether he should take that as encouraging or not. As long as Marnie was missing, nothing was encouraging.

Mick suddenly stopped. Vent and Chuck pulled up, immediately bending over with their hands on their knees, trying to catch their breath.

"Why'd you…stop?" Vent said.

"Because I can hear you guys wheezing."

Mick looked like he was forcing himself not to pant. His cheeks were red as pepperonis.

"We really need to stop smoking," he said.

"Just cigarettes," Vent said, coughing and spitting into the leaves.

"Let me see the map," Chuck said. Mick handed it over. It was little better than chicken scratch, with notes scrawled at the bottom in a doctor's handwriting. He couldn't make out a word and had to hope Dredd had told Mick what he'd written. If he was reading the map correctly, they were three-quarters of the way to the Melon Heads' camp. Or village. He didn't know what you would call a place where deformed monsters dwelled.

A lair seemed more like it.

Mick was looking off into the distance, the hinges of his jaw bulging. Chuck stuck the map in his sling and dropped his hand on his friend's shoulder. "We're going to find her."

Mick sniffed hard and wiped his nose with his sleeve. "Yeah, but will she be alive?"

"She will be."

Chuck wished he felt as confident as he sounded. Mick rubbed his thumb along the side of the gun Marnie had been carrying. He had tied the lace of her boot to his belt loop. "She'll need it to walk back home," he'd said.

"The caves won't be far," Chuck said.

"Dredd said some of them are just holes in the ground and we have to be careful. He thinks the Melon Heads cover them loosely, using them as traps for game and anyone who's dumb enough to go out this far."

"So, basically, we won't know if it's a trap until we fall in one," Vent said.

"Kinda looks like that, yeah."

"Just great."

It was the kind of thing Mick should have shared with them earlier so they could have brought some rope just in case one of them fell in. Normally, Chuck would have said something at Mick's failing to mention such a vital fact. Not today. There was no time for fighting with one another. They would cross that bridge – or trap – when they came to it.

"I'm good to go," Chuck said, though he was most definitely not.

"Me, too," Vent said.

Mick took a deep breath. "Home stretch, guys."

"Home stretch," Chuck said.

There was a little more pep in their step now, but they were extra cautious about falling into a hole in the ground.

Ten minutes in, they came to a pile of sun-bleached bones stacked upon one another. The skull of what looked to be a deer sat atop the pile, the dark, empty eye sockets staring at them.

"Well, that didn't just happen on its own," Mick said.

"That's a lot of deer," Vent said, walking around the free-standing collection.

Chuck tilted his head, scanning the bones. As he looked closer, a tingle of dread wiggled its way up his spine. "That's a human femur," he said, pointing. "And those look like finger joints."

"Let me see," Mick said, squatting down to get a closer look. "How do you know?"

"Unlike you, I went to biology class. I can't be totally certain, but those are a mix of animal and human bones."

"Why the fuck would they stick them out here like that?" Vent asked nervously.

"To scare people away, dummy," Mick said. He stood up and kicked the center of the pile. Bones rattled together, scattering all over the forest floor. Mick wasn't done. He stomped the deer skull with the heel of his boot, shattering it to bits. "Now they know we're not scared. Maybe when they see this, it'll scare them instead. Fucking inbreds."

"Uh, guys," Vent said, staring ahead of them.

Similar bone mounds lined the trail as far as they could see. Resting on top of each one was a skull from a different type of animal. Chuck tried to figure out which animal was which as they walked, Mick demolishing each with a measure of satisfaction. There was a possum. A rabbit. That small one had to be a squirrel, looking lost amidst the larger bones. There was a dog. Was it a stray, or had the Melon Heads snatched it from someone's yard? When he saw the human skull, he pulled Mick back. "Wait. Not that one."

"Why not?" Mick was sweating, wet strands of hair clinging to his face.

"I don't know. Out of respect for the dead, I guess. It just doesn't seem right."

"I'll bet there are human bones in all these piles. What makes this one so special?"

Because this one was looking straight at them. Because this skull might belong to one of their parents. Chuck saw the nicks and gouges along the bone, signs of the Melon Heads scraping the flesh off with crude instruments.

"Just leave it be," he said, moving Mick forward.

Mick considered the mound for a moment and Chuck was sure he was going to kick it down. Instead, he turned away, tromped to the next one, and delivered a back kick that dropped bones on the trail.

"This is starting to freak me out," Vent said. "I mean, look at how many bones there are."

"It either means there are a lot of Melon Heads out here, or they've been collecting them for a long, long time."

"Or both." Vent gingerly toed the bones aside so they could pass through. "Man, what I wouldn't give to be in statistics class right now. I'd be thrilled to be taking a test I didn't even study for, you know what I mean?"

"Yeah, I do." A moment like this made you wish for all the mundane and irritating things that you normally dreaded or complained about. All of them were preferable to this. Chuck promised himself that he would never bitch about having to do anything again when they made it out of here. He was also self-aware enough to realize that it would never hold. It was like that day or two after attending a funeral, when you appreciated life more than usual. Not long after, everything went back to normal, appreciation for each moment lost in the jungle and jumble of life.

The trail took a hard right, the trees getting denser with less space for bone mounds. Mick dipped behind a tree and out of sight. Chuck and Vent hurried after him. A bird took off from a tree limb, giving them both a start.

"It's just a pigeon," Vent said.

Chuck looked up and saw the pigeon flying in a ragged circle over their heads. It was the first live animal they'd spotted since they left Dredd's cabin. "I wonder why it's here. You think Dredd screwed up the map and we're getting farther from them?"

Vent raised the rifle and followed the pigeon's erratic path. "You can train pigeons." He pulled the trigger. The pigeon spun in the air and dropped like a stone. The gunshot echoed through the woods. "Probably one of theirs."

"That was some shot."

"My dad used to take me skeet shooting, at least until he couldn't afford it anymore."

"Well, the Melon Heads know where the fuck to find us now," Chuck said.

Vent gazed at the area where the pigeon had fallen. "I'm pretty sure they've known all along. I hope I was right. Nice to take something from them instead of the other way around."

Mick had come running back to them, puffing hard. "Where are they?"

Vent said. "Chill out. It was only a pigeon."

Mick almost looked disappointed. "Oh. Come on, you have to see this. You're not gonna believe it."

Chuck's chest tightened. He wasn't anxious to see what fresh hell awaited them.

When he turned the corner of the trail, he almost fell to his knees.

CHAPTER THIRTY-TWO

The first thing Mick thought when he saw the towering pyramid of bones was, *there's no way I can knock that sucker down*. It stood at least twenty feet high, with what looked to be hardened mud packed between the bones to keep the whole thing from collapsing in on itself.

"Are you kidding me?" Vent said in a hushed tone reserved for churches.

It was impossible to miss the vast number of human skulls embedded within the walls. Mick figured they had to have raided an entire cemetery to make such a thing. If it wasn't for their situation, he would have been in awe of it.

Chuck hadn't moved since it came into view. He stared up at the pinnacle with his mouth slightly open. Vent kept his rifle pointed at it as if it could spring to life at any moment.

"Pretty fucking sick, right?" Mick said. "How many people you think they had to kill to make it?"

Finally breaking from his paralysis, Chuck slowly approached the pyramid. "No animal bones. This is something sacred. If you ask me, I'd say these are their bones. Look."

Mick got close enough to touch it. Instead of seeing the whole structure, he concentrated on parts of it. Yes, those were human skulls, but they were misshapen human skulls. Melon Head skulls. "You think this is what they do with their dead?"

"I think it's a strong possibility."

"I wonder if they eat them, too," Vent said.

"If there wasn't enough food for everyone, why not?" Mick said. This entire time, he had been able to think of the Melon Heads as something outside of his own species. A withering branch of some family tree that nature had long determined to be a failed experiment. But seeing this made it difficult to think they were anything other than human. Some of the skulls were bleached white, especially those on the side exposed to the sun. Others were yellowed with age, some covered in verdant moss. The pyramid of bones had a palpable aura about it. This wasn't just a monument of death. It was ancient. How long had they been living out here?

Vent had cautiously crept around the pyramid. He called out, "Over here!"

Mick and Chuck ran to him. He was pointing the barrel of the rifle at the triangular opening at the base. "It's hollow inside."

"A pyramid *and* a teepee," Chuck said. "Bizarre."

Inside was dark as night. Anything, or anyone, could be inside.

"You got something inside this box that doesn't explode?" Chuck asked Mick.

Mick opened the box of fireworks. There were some scattered sparklers at the bottom. He wondered how they even got in there. You could buy sparklers at the corner store. Dwight only specialized in the illegal stuff. Lighting one was harder than it should have been, the old powder reluctant to take the flame. "When I throw this inside, be ready."

"Ready for what?" Vent said.

"For something to come out." Mick wasn't just thinking of Melon Heads. Who knew what animals could be lurking inside? He flipped the sparkler inside and quickly lit another.

Within the flickering light, they saw a vast collection of random things. Mick spotted a rusted bicycle, one that must have been popular back when his parents were kids. There were clothes and broken pieces of furniture, chairs and a pile of blankets.

"What's that over there?" Vent asked. They crowded the entrance now that they hadn't been rushed by a Melon Head or angry critter.

Something glowed yellow at the other end of the bone pyramid. "Looks like a trumpet," Chuck said.

Mick saw a snare drum, the head perforated, next to the rusting instrument. There was a hat rack beside it with old-time bowler hats resting on each peg. The sparklers started to die out. Mick lit the four left in the box and replenished the light. He dared to step inside. It stank like diseased soil. He buried his nose in the crook of his arm and threw a sparkler to the other end of the teepee. "Oh man."

The further the eye went from the entrance, the older the jumble of items became. Some of the rotting bric-a-brac had to be turn of the twentieth century or older. There was even a collection of bayonets and muskets. He stepped closer to an old steamer trunk that was left open. Inside were crumbling black and white pictures of stoic men and women and creepy kids all dressed like little girls.

The sparklers died and he was encased in utter darkness. He spun around, desperate to see the light at the entrance. His heart went into an instant gallop. Chuck and Vent were waving at him to come to them.

"You okay in there?" Chuck said.

"Yeah, I'm fine." He didn't feel fine at all.

"I'm coming in with more light."

"We should get going," Vent said.

"Just hold on," Chuck said.

Mick listened to his friends moving around outside, each footstep crunching leaves.

Chuck had to duck to walk inside. He held a thick, dry branch, a small flame sputtering at its end. "Best I could do for a torch. They make it look a lot easier on TV." Mick saw his eyes go wide. "Whoa. Look at all this stuff."

"You coming in?" Mick asked Vent.

"I'll keep watch out here." He crinkled his nose. "Smells like dog shit in there."

Chuck hustled over to a bookshelf. "Here, hold this." Mick took the makeshift torch while Chuck ran his fingers over the spines of the moldy books. He took one out and opened it, grabbed the branch so it was close enough for him to see the pages. "Copyright 1907. It's a book about wilderness survival." The pages crackled as he turned them. "Look at this, all you ever needed to know about knots." He closed the cover and put it back, searching through the others. "This explains a lot."

"What does?"

Mick sensed time slipping away. They needed to get to those caves. But something about this place told him they shouldn't discount it too quickly.

"All these books on this shelf are about Ancient Egypt." Chuck went through book after book, all of them illustrated with pictures of pyramids, tombs, the great Sphinx, buried treasure and hieroglyphics. "Man, are these old." The spine of one book gave way, splitting down the middle. "All the other books are on a bunch of random topics. Looks like the Melon Heads from way back were fascinated by Egypt. That explains the pyramid shapes they construct."

Mick didn't like the sound of that. "You mean they can read?"

Chuck shrugged. "Maybe. Or maybe some can. There's even a possibility that they used to, but the ability died out bit by bit, though I wouldn't put some basic reading skills past the current ones. All I know is, this place and all this stuff has been here for a long fucking time."

"You guys coming out or what?" Vent asked nervously. "We're losing the sun."

"Just a minute," Chuck said. He walked in a crouch even though there was plenty of headroom for three Chucks to stand atop one another. Shifting burlap sacks aside, he bent down and reached inside a thick stack of mismatched items. He pulled out a full native Indian headdress. The feathers were lacking, and what remained was filthy. Chuck brought it close to his face to study it. "I don't think this is a replica."

Mick huffed. "No way they've been around that long."

"Why not? Hell, for all we know, they are Indians, or maybe part Indian and part white man."

"What?"

"You think either side was happy if the two got together and made babies? No way. Medical care was nonexistent back then. Just being born was a long shot, much less being born without something wrong. Suppose the Melon Heads are the offspring of Indians and the settlers? They weren't accepted by the tribe or the white settlements. So, they chucked them out here and hoped nature would take care of the rest. Isn't that one of the legends?" He was clearly getting excited. Mick wasn't sure why, since knowing their origin wouldn't help him get Marnie back or wreak his revenge.

"Kinda close. So what? It's obvious those freaks think this place is special. Let's show them how special we think it is." He took a quarter stick from his pocket, one with a normal fuse, lit it and tossed it amidst the junk pile. "Come on," he said, grabbing Chuck by the arm.

"Are you crazy?"

There was no time to argue and Chuck was no dummy. He followed Mick out of the bone pyramid as fast as they could both run. The quarter stick went off the moment they stepped outside, the boom so loud it nearly deafened Mick. They were peppered with shrapnel that bounced off their backs.

Mick brushed himself off and looked at the still-solid pyramid. "Huh."

He took two more quarter sticks from the box and jammed them between pairs of skulls while Chuck told him to stop. Vent was too busy looking like he was about to piss himself to care.

Mick lit them and ran.

The three of them hopped over a fallen log and ducked. Mick could feel the explosion reverberate from his feet right through the top of his head. He poked his head up and was greeted with success. The side of the pyramid quaked, bones slipping into the twin holes that had been punched through the wall. The top of the pyramid swayed for a moment and it started to crumble. The whole thing came down in seconds, the clattering of bones sounding like monster teeth gnashing under the bed on a stormy night. Mick shivered, a primal wave of fear taking control for longer than he would have liked. Bone dust and smoke hovered over the fallen pyramid.

"Holy crap," Chuck said. "If the Melon Heads didn't want to kill us before, they do now."

Mick cleared his throat and arced a wad of spit that hit the edge of the bone pile. "Fuck them." He turned to see if Vent appreciated the display of sacrilege. He wasn't there. "Vent, did you run away?"

Chuck shot to his feet. "Where is he?"

When Mick looked down and saw Vent's rifle, he knew exactly where he was. "They got him, man. They fucking got him."

And then there were two.

If Mick thought the odds of four against a village of maniacal Melon Heads were daunting, this took it to absolute zero. The realization was actually liberating. What did you have to lose when you already lost?

Chuck spun around on his heels. "How? He was right next to us.."

"They move like ghosts," Mick said, pointing at the rubble of antiquity and death. "But I can tell you one thing. They didn't get far." He picked up Vent's rifle and made sure it was loaded.

Chuck pointed between a pair of crooked saplings. A ghost of a shape dropped to the ground and out of sight.

"Want to bet there's a cave entrance right there?" Chuck said.

"Either that or that Melon Head is a frigging magician."

"That has to be where they took Vent."

No shit, Sherlock, was on Mick's tongue. For a brainiac, Chuck could be dense when it came to things outside of books. "That's exactly where they want us to go. I'm not falling for it."

Chuck grabbed his arm. "Are you crazy? We're not going to just sit here while Vent is so close. We have to get him."

"And get picked off by minions? No way. We need their leader. We just crushed his temple or whatever that was. Let them come to us."

"I'm going for him." Chuck stormed off, taking the pistol from his sling and leaving the box of fireworks behind.

"Hey, wait!"

Mick jammed some fireworks in his pockets and chased after Chuck as he plodded toward the saplings.

"Just hold the hell up!" Mick shouted. To his shock, his friend listened to him.

"What?"

"I'll show you."

Mick got ahead of him. Five feet before the saplings, he stopped and held up his hand. He tucked the rifle under his armpit, took out his lighter and touched the flame to the long wick of a quarter stick. They had plenty of time to edge around the trees and find the leaf-littered jagged hole in the ground. Cooler air wafted up from the crack in the earth.

"You wanted to just drop in there and fight them off so we could get Vent back, right?" Mick said softly.

"Yeah," Chuck replied breathlessly.

"This will make is easier."

When the wick was almost gone, he dropped it in the hole. It detonated an instant after if dipped into the darkness. Dirt spewed from the hole like lava from a volcano. A grain of grit wedged itself in the corner of Mick's eye. He twisted away, rubbing at it with the heel of his palm.

Even his pain couldn't distract him from the intense wails of pain emanating from the fissure. It was like finding the entrance to hell and quaking at the lament of multitudes of lost souls. The horrific cries didn't sound as if they came from human throats.

"That's what was waiting for you," Mick said. The vision in his left eye was blurry. Every time he blinked, it felt like he was pushing a shard of glass deeper into his eyeball.

Chuck spit dirt from his mouth and wiped it from his beard. "How did you know they were waiting for us?"

"Maybe I'm starting to think like them." The thought chilled him. Had he been living in the woods, just like the Melon Heads, for too long? Was this why they had 'chosen' him? He was pretty sure he'd been un-chosen by now.

"But what if Vent was right down there with them?"

"Then we did him a favor."

Chuck glared at him. "You can be pretty goddamn cold."

Mick's nostrils flared and he felt his cheeks burning. "Fuck you. Vent is my best friend. I don't know about you, but I'd rather be killed quickly than get torn apart by those things. Vent would feel the same." *So would Marnie*, he thought. Just thinking about her stoked the flames of vengeance in his heart.

They stared at one another until Chuck turned away first. He didn't see the Melon Head struggling to get out of the hole. It was missing an eye, the socket blasted red and raw, the tip of its nose somewhere down in the hole. Its lone eye rolled toward Mick and it bared its yellow, jagged teeth. Mick lifted the rifle and shot it in the other eye. The Melon Head slipped out of sight, but not before painting the leaves scarlet.

Chuck had jumped five feet sideways at the sound of the rifle going off. He stared at the now empty hole. "Christ."

Mick cocked an ear toward the fissure. "There's more down there. Can you hear them?"

"All I hear is ringing in my ears."

"We could stay here and take a few out. It'll be like playing whack-a-mole."

"And while we're playing, it'll get darker and darker and we'll be no closer to finding Marnie and Vent and taking the rest of them out."

Hearing Chuck say that made Mick realize how monumental the odds were against them.

Before he could say something morbid and flippant, a pair of Melon Heads sprang from the hole as if there was a trampoline underground. One wrapped its arms around Chuck and sent him skittering into a tree. The other saw the rifle in Mick's hands and went into a crouch. It was one ugly bastard. Its eyes were half-lidded and askew, one drifting up near its forehead, the other down by its cheek. It had a wide, flat nose and the worst case of chapped lips in human, or Melon Head, history. White flakes of skin covered its mouth. Mick looked down and saw the Cabbage Patch Dolls T-shirt and stained gray sweatpants. The Melon Head swiped at the air between them, growling like an angry cat.

"Yeah, I'd be pissed too if I had to wear that shirt." It sprang from its haunches. Mick's shot burrowed a hole in its throat. The Melon Head flipped backward and dropped stone-cold dead on the ground.

Mick turned to a struggling Chuck, who was repeatedly bashing the Melon Head in the head with his forearm, but it still wouldn't let go. The creature snapped at Chuck's neck, just missing taking a bite from his Adam's apple. Mick sprinted the distance between them, jammed the barrel of the rifle under its arm and pulled the trigger. It jumped off of Chuck, howling in high-keening agony. It ran headlong into the brush and disappeared from view before Mick could finish it off.

Chuck was bent over from breathing so hard. "The moles never whacked back at the fair," he said, huffing.

Mick kept his eye on the underground cave entrance. He didn't hear any more shuffling around. "You okay?"

"No."

"Me neither. I don't think they're going to try that again. Game over."

"They're too intelligent to keep coming out like lemmings. I say we get the map and keep on going."

"Yeah." Mick considered dropping an M80 into the hole just for laughs. If another one of those things was down there, its ears would be ringing louder than Chuck's. Then he considered how many other hiding places were potentially out here and realized he didn't have any fireworks to waste.

They went back to get the box and map. The collapsed bone mound was still smoking.

"Coulda made a lot of money selling that shit to an antique store," Mick said.

"Museums would have wanted half of it."

Mick grinned at the destruction. "Not anymore."

Chuck clapped him on the back. "Nope. Let's go."

The sound of a gun being cocked behind their backs had Mick spinning on his heel, ready to shoot. If the Melon Heads had guns, they were done for.

He wasn't expecting this.

"Hello, boys."

CHAPTER THIRTY-THREE

Chuck couldn't believe he was happy to see Dredd. He was a warm body and he had a gun, which was enough to make Chuck want to whoop with joy.

"I thought you weren't coming," he said.

"Yeah, well, I changed my mind. Looks like you're a regular two-man wrecking crew." He motioned the rifle at the demolished bone pyramid. "That mustn't have been easy. I used to think about all the hurricanes and such that thing withstood. And it was made by *them*. Kinda makes you think it didn't take a genius to build the pyramids. At least back in old Ancient Egypt, you guys weren't around to make a mess of it all."

"You knew about it?" Mick asked. He didn't seem to be as happy as Chuck was to see Dredd.

Dredd nodded, his eyes roving over the destruction.

"Then how come you didn't put it on the map? Seems like a pretty big thing to miss."

"Maybe because it wasn't important," Chuck said to Mick.

"You think *that* wasn't important?"

"You had me hogtied, asshole," Dredd said. "We weren't exactly on the best of terms."

Mick looked at Dredd's rifle, which was still pointed right at him. "I guess we're still not."

Dredd looked down as if he hadn't realized he was holding a weapon. He shifted it so the barrel faced the ground. "Sorry about that. Can't be too careful. I didn't see your faces when I came up on you."

"You know a lot of Melon Heads his size with their arm in a sling?"

Chuck didn't like the way things were escalating. Why did Mick look like he wanted to kill Dredd? "Guys, just take it easy."

"Yeah, Mick, cool your jets. I came to help you. We're in the same sinking ship. I figured if you don't make it, I'm next and I'll have to do it alone."

"They took Marnie and Vent," Chuck said. "You think they killed them, or would they take them somewhere?"

Dredd scratched his head. "You never know. Though I suspect if they wanted to kill them, they'd do it right away, especially if it was in front of you. They don't mess around, especially when they're hungry."

A soft breeze rattled the crisping leaves in the deadly quiet woods. It sounded like thousands of teeth chattering. Chuck clung to the hope that his friends were still alive somewhere. Now they had to find them.

He wasn't sure Mick had blinked since laying eyes on Dredd. A look of distrust was painted on his face.

Mick said, "Okay then, fearless leader, lead."

Dredd shifted on his feet, started to walk, and turned back. "I don't think I like the idea of having you behind me, Mick-O. Side by side would be better."

Mick made a barely noticeable shrug. "Fine by me. Chuck, can you take the box?"

"Sure."

It was awkward going now as Mick and Dredd struggled to never let one get in front of the other. Sometimes, the game trail narrowed and they had to squeeze together like the Three Stooges wedging their way through a doorway. It would have been comical at any other time.

"Are we getting close?" Chuck asked.

"Won't be long," Dredd replied.

"How many times have you been out here?"

"Just once." He looked back at Chuck. "It's the kind of thing you never forget. You'll see for yourself if we make it back."

If we make it back.

That should have instilled more fear in him, but the words hit him like blank rounds from a gun. Back was funerals for his parents and Heidi, being grilled by cops, school that seemed like it no longer mattered and a future that had been fucked seven ways to Sunday. Back was nothing, other than the satisfaction of knowing they had accomplished what they had set out to do and saved their friends to boot. That moment of glory would be short-lived. And then what?

No, the words only made him sad for a life that he never got a chance to live.

"How many'd you kill?" Dredd asked.

"We're not keeping score," Chuck said.

"I'm sure Mick is."

Mick didn't answer him. He didn't even so much as glance at him.

"I heard a pretty big boom and then another smaller one and some shooting. You have a shootout at their pyramid?"

Chuck pushed a branch from his face. Gnats, attracted to his sweat, were forming a second skin. "Mick blew it up when it was empty. Then we found some hiding in this hole in the ground. What was that pyramid, anyway?"

"I always think of it as a kind of school. It's where they store anything they find and then study it, but not like we do. They had shit from a long, long time ago in there. I don't know if they find it just digging around, or if they've been out here all this time and steal stuff when they can. If that's the case, they've been here for centuries."

Centuries. Long enough for settlers to come in close contact with the native people, destined to create something new and terrifying.

Chuck said, "I'm surprised none of them came when Mick blew it up. There were a bunch behind us in the dark woods."

Dredd jumped over a log with Mick in tandem. "That just means you surprised them. They don't know what to do yet, but they'll figure it out. If we let them."

"They're going to be pissed."

"That's putting it mildly. Insane is more like it. You just destroyed what I figure is the cultural center of their hive of freaks. Not to mention their graveyard. Which means we better find them fast. You boys think you got enough firepower to blow them all sky high?"

Chuck was pretty sure they didn't. It wasn't worth speaking it aloud.

They walked in silence for another ten minutes. Chuck kept throwing looks at the darkening sky. He figured they had an hour of daylight left. Would an hour be enough? It would have to be.

"Hold up," Dredd whispered. He hunkered down behind a moss-covered boulder. "I think that's it right over there."

Chuck followed where he was pointing. The trees and brush grew very close together here, so it was hard to see much farther than twenty feet. In the murky distance, Chuck spotted a wisp of gray smoke coming from the ground. "Is that the cave entrance?"

Dredd nodded. His expression was anxious and dire. "More like the doorway to the caverns below us. You have to climb down to get inside. It looked pretty narrow the one time I saw it."

"Did you go inside?"

"Hell no. They may give me special privileges, but I'm not one of them. That's Melon Head-only territory."

Chuck lifted the lid off the fireworks box, depressed to see how much it had emptied since they'd set out. "You think we could cave it all in?"

"You could, but that's only one entrance. I've spotted others in the area. I expect there's a maze of tunnels down there they can just run to and get out."

Mick finally broke his silence. "Then how do we get their leader?"

"You don't."

Mick turned to Dredd with fire in his eyes. "We have to. It's not like we have a choice. Is he down there or not?"

"Usually, yes. But he's surrounded by guards, or at least the stronger freaks that never leave his side. You have to kill them first."

Mick licked his lips and said, "How many?"

"That I don't know. Maybe six. I think it changes. You have them on high alert now. They're gonna go all out to protect him."

A bee buzzed Chuck's ear. He had to stop himself from slapping at it. He checked the bullets in his gun. Five. Mick was probably lucky if he had a bullet left. He hoped Dredd came fully prepared.

Mick slipped around the boulder and crept closer. Dredd and Chuck tried to keep up with him. They stopped now and again, pausing to see if they'd been detected. If this was the spot where the Melon Heads lived, it was awfully deserted. Though now Chuck could clearly see where the smoke was coming from. There was a rise in the forest floor with an open jack-o'-lantern mouth spewing smoke. What there wasn't was a Melon Head in sight. Chuck took a quarter stick from the box and squeezed it, waiting.

"Where are they?" Chuck said. The Melon Heads couldn't all be out searching for them. He looked down, imagining hundreds of Melon Heads scurrying just beneath them like angry moles.

"Fuck if I know," Dredd said. He rested the barrel of his rifle on his knee and aimed it at the ragged chasm.

Mick suddenly stood and stepped behind Dredd, pressing his rifle on the back of Dredd's head. "What did you tell them?"

Dredd tried to turn around, but Mick pressed harder against his skull, keeping him from moving his head. "What the hell are you talking about? You can't tell them anything, man. Now get that fucking gun away from me."

Mick pulled the hammer back instead. "You came from the wrong direction."

Chuck said, "What are you talking about?"

"He came from this direction. If he'd been following us, he would have approached from the other side of the pyramid. He'd gotten here before us. Probably warned them, too. So, what's waiting for us, Dredd?"

Dredd's finger inched down toward the trigger. Chuck kicked the rifle out of his hands.

"You're making a big mistake," Dredd said to Chuck.

"We've been making a lot of mistakes the past week," Mick said. "What's one more?"

"I'm not the enemy. We're on the same side in this."

Mick sneered. "So you tell me."

Chuck didn't hear the Melon Head in the trees until it had fallen on top of Dredd, piledriving him into the dirt. The Melon Head grazed Chuck just enough to knock him down. It jammed its knees into Dredd's back and punched him in the neck. Chuck tried to get up and slipped. He lashed out with his foot, but his heel skipped off the Melon Head's hip with little effect.

"Get it off me!" Dredd wailed. The Melon Head delivered a series of savage rabbit punches to his ribs, knocking the wind out of him.

Mick flipped the rifle in his hands and swung it like a baseball ball. The wooden stock made a loud thunk as it connected with the creature's bare skull. The Melon Head raised a fist to hammer Dredd, and then the arm went limp, followed by the rest of its body. Blood leaked from its ear as it slumped. Dredd was quick to flip himself over, his hand going to his neck. Chuck saw a red fist mark that took up the entire side of Dredd's neck.

Dredd stared at Mick. "Happy now? Do I have to get killed before you realize I'm not your problem?"

Mick looked like he was about to hit Dredd with the rifle, but then he reached out to help him up.

"I'd say thank you, but I wouldn't really mean it," Dredd said.

"I still don't give a shit what you say," Mick said.

"Then we're all in agreement and on the same page," Chuck said. He kept glancing up into the trees. If there was one Melon Head, there had to be others. He felt like setting off a mortar into the thickest cluster of branches and leaves just to see what shook out. "What's our next move?"

Mick looked back at the cave opening. "We get their attention. Help me with this one."

They dragged the unconscious Melon Head through the brush and to the entrance of the cave. The feral man was clad in filthy rags and smelled like eons of hot excrement. "Leave it here." He grabbed a mortar from the box, laid it on the so-called doorstep of the cave, aimed into the darkness. He lit the fuse and stepped away. The mortar exploded with a shower of sparks, its scream echoing as it zoomed into the depths. Flashes of light strobed in the cave when it exploded. Mick straddled the wounded Melon Head's back and slipped an arm around its neck. He stared at the opening, waiting.

"They like the whole eye-for-an-eye thing so much," he said. "Maybe they'll think twice just to save old stinky here."

A commotion of excited guttural grunts and cries seeped from the cave, along with the sound of shuffling feet after the fireworks display stopped. They were coming. Chuck and Dredd had their weapons ready.

When the first Melon Head appeared, Chuck nearly lost his resolve. Its naked flesh was so pale, it must have never seen the sun. It walked on all fours, a brutal cleft palate bisecting the bottom half of its face. It had white, sightless eyes and a mouthful of rotted teeth, each one Chuck assumed ripe with infection. It was on a leash made of vines.

The Melon Head holding the leash emerged, followed by several others, each with barrel chests, though small in stature. Their fingertips swayed past their knees, their arms corded with muscle and looking as if they could easily crush a man.

Last to come out was the largest Melon Head Chuck had seen. He knew in an instant this was their leader. The alpha male. He was nearly as tall as Chuck and less deformed than the others. If you had dressed him in modern clothes and cut the mat of hair growing from different spots on his head, he might almost pass for human.

Almost.

His eyes were set too far apart and hard, his jaw overly large and square, like a caricature of a WWF wrestler.

More, lesser Melon Heads, men, women and children, clambered out after them, all with vicious looks on their faces. They wanted to rip Chuck, Mick and Dredd apart. Chuck wasn't entirely sure what was stopping them.

In all, Chuck counted thirty-three Melon Heads at the cave entrance. He knew there had to be more in the woods. He could practically feel them at his back.

Both sides glared at one another for what seemed an eternity. Mick locked eyes with the leader, engaged in a standoff. Chuck looked at the quarter stick and lighter he'd stuffed in his sling. It was one of the sticks with the very short fuse. If he lit it now and tossed it at the leader and his guards, would it go off fast enough to kill or at least maim them?

How would the others react? Would they run from the grisly display or toward him, Mick and Dredd?

Just wait, he thought. *See who makes the first move.*

He didn't have to wait long.

CHAPTER THIRTY-FOUR

The Melon Head holding the leash (this one was wearing an old-time zoot suit with more holes than a wedge of Swiss cheese) dropped it to the ground. That set the animalistic Melon Head in motion. It galloped toward Mick with a wild, unsteady gate, ropes of saliva spewing from its awful mouth. Mick jumped off the captured Melon Head's back a split-second before the feral one was on top of him.

Instead of attacking Mick, it sniffed at the unconscious Melon Head, nudging it with its nose. When it didn't react, the feral Melon Head opened its mouth and tore into the back of its neck, ripping a wad of flesh free. It gobbled it down like a seagull ingesting fish guts and went back for more.

"What the fuck?"

Mick grabbed his rifle, ready to shoot the feral Melon Head in the back.

So much for having a hostage.

The only thing to do now was to hit them with everything they had.

He whipped around to Chuck. "Light 'em up!"

Chuck dropped the box onto the ground and worked at the lighter.

Mick shot the feral Melon Head in the chest just as it was leaping for him. It rolled on the ground in agony. The Melon Heads let out a collective whoop of tribal outrage.

The first mortar zigzagged into the heart of the gathering. They deftly avoided it, the firework smacking into the dirt and going off, showering the Melon Heads' backs with painful sparks.

Mick aimed for one of the guards, the one with a head that looked as if it had once been staved in by a pipe, and got it right in its open mouth. Teeth, bits of tongue and cheeks flew in every direction. He quickly pulled the trigger and caught another in the throat. It dropped to its knees, clasping the spurting hole.

The Melon Head leader stood tall while the others jittered about in a panic. Even the other guards seemed confused and frightened. Chuck lobbed an M80 that exploded right at the feet of the leader. He jumped back, wincing and clasping his ears when it went off. Mick aimed at a Melon Head wearing an off-white dress sporting a mosaic of black stains. He pulled the trigger and nothing happened. He was out of ammo. The female Melon Head ran in an arc, looking to catch him from the side. He turned to Dredd. "Shoot it!"

Dredd looked as if he'd awoken from a dream into a nightmare. He shook his head to clear his brain and pulled the trigger. The shot went wide, pinging off a tree. The Melon Head raked her nails across Mick's face just before she tackled him. He hit the ground hard and saw Chuck holding on to a lit mortar, flames singeing his arm. Just as it was starting to screech, he let the mortar go. Mick didn't see where it went because he was too busy trying to keep the Melon Head from eating his wounded face. He punched her in the nose, feeling the cartilage crack beneath his knuckles. The Melon Head smiled, sniffing back blood before it dropped from her nostrils onto his face. She went for his throat this time, but his forearm blocked her path to an easy meal.

"A little help," he said, struggling. A pair of M80 detonations told him Chuck was still busy hurtling fireworks at the mob.

The Melon Head's head suddenly snapped back. Dredd had his fingers wrapped in her hair. He tossed her aside, delivering a savage kick to her midsection.

Mick clambered to his feet. "Fucking shoot her!"

He then turned to see that the other Melon Heads were fast approaching. Several were down, others having either run off or back into the cave. He ran to Chuck. "Gimme your pistol!"

It was in Chuck's sling. Mick looked for the leader, who was smart enough to hunch down now at the sight of the gun, and fired again and again. Melon Heads clapped their hands on entry wounds, blood spraying in every direction. But try as he might, Mick couldn't get a clear shot at the leader. When the bullets ran out, he grabbed the last two quarter sticks in the box. After jamming one in his back pocket, he bit half the fuse off the other, lit it and ran at them. That seemed to stun them into paralysis for a precious moment. He could hear the crack of Dredd's rifle at his back. A mortar caught a Melon Head in the stomach, driving it backward, firing off in its open guts.

There was just one fugly guard between Mick and the leader. He leapfrogged over it with a level of agility he'd never had before. The leader opened its mouth to shout something either at Mick or to its minions. Maybe it was a cry for help. No matter. Mick stuffed the firework into its maw hard enough to feel its jaw crack. As he jumped away, it went off, turning the leader's head into a red mist.

Mick hit the ground and let out a war cry. The leader's big body stood for a moment, wavering on its feet, arms twitching. It dropped to its knees and fell forward, the impact forcing a copious splattering of blood from the hole where its head used to be. Mick swore he would never eat ketchup again.

Silence settled over the battlefield.

Mick stood over the corpse, turning to the Melon Heads gathered around him. None of them dared to make a move.

I did it! I fucking did it!

What would happen next was a mystery, but he knew he had to take advantage of the situation and assert his dominance.

He looked over at Chuck, who had paled considerably.

Dredd caught his eye and grimaced. He pulled the trigger and it simply clicked. "I don't suppose you'd let me reload."

Mick had no idea what he was talking about, and then it hit him. Dredd had just tried to kill him.

"What the fuck, bro?"

Dredd chuckled. "I bet you think you're King Shit right now. Well, you might want to save your celebrating for the afterlife."

Melon Heads sprang from the bushes and grabbed Chuck. He fought them briefly, but there were just too many. In seconds, his face was pushed in the dirt, eight arms and legs pressing down on him.

Dredd strolled up to Mick. "That's not their leader. In fact, he was nothing but a big, dumb worker bee. Good job taking out the help."

Mick was about to remind Dredd he'd been attacked and had shot at them, when he realized the attack hadn't hurt him much and he couldn't remember any of Dredd's shots hitting their mark. "You set us up."

"More like found a way to make amends and save my ass." He took Mick by the shoulders and spun him around. A salt-and-pepper-haired Melon Head woman stood at the entrance. She wore a suit made of bones, her long hair draping over the yellowed rib bones encasing her own torso. She looked strong yet soft, a leader and the embodiment of a woman. Her face was severely disfigured, everything just out of place so it appeared as if her features were melting off the bone. Dredd put his lips to Mick's ear, his hot breath whooshing into the center of his brain. "That's their leader. And you, my good buddy, are fucked."

★   ★   ★

They were grabbed by the Melon Heads and ushered before the leader. Mick's legs were kicked out from under him and he was made to kneel before her. Chuck looked woozy beside him, having taken a potshot to the head.

Mick tried to look the leader in the eyes, but hers were too far apart, too uneven to lock on to. Her eyes were cobalt blue and clear as day. Her suit of bones rattled as she approached him.

"What did you do to our friends?"

She looked down at him with a cold indifference.

"I told you I'd bring them to you," Dredd said. Mick wanted to kill him. "I'm true to my word."

He looked like a kid expecting a reward for washing the dishes. Dredd seemed to avoid even glancing at Mick and Chuck, now that his deed was done. "They broke the rules and should be punished. I've accepted my punishment. I'll rebuild my cabin and be your watcher. You'll see."

The leader regarded him for a moment, and turned back to Mick.

"You're a real piece of shit, Dredd," Mick spat.

"At least I'll be alive. Say hi to your mom and stepdad."

Mick tried to break free, but he was held down fast. He watched Dredd start to walk away. Several Melon Heads stepped aside so he could go through. The sight made Mick sick to his soul.

"I hope you die!" Mick shouted after him. Dredd didn't turn around, but he did give him the finger as he made his escape.

"How could he do this?" Chuck said.

"He can and he did and I hope there is a hell, even though I'll be in it, too. Maybe I can kick his ass when I see him again."

The leader had been holding a long bone in her hand the whole time. She smacked it once against her bone breastplate. A pair of Melon Head males tore off after Dredd. When they grabbed him, Dredd stuttered, "W-w-wait! I did what I was sup-supposed to do! Please. P-p-please!"

Mick couldn't help from shouting out, "Kill him!"

They punched Dredd in the solar plexus, taking out any fight he had in him. Then they dragged him back and threw him on the ground. Each of his limbs was grabbed by a Melon Head. Dredd, once he got his breath back, wailed and pleaded. A dozen or more Melon Heads children pounced on him while the adults held on. The kids tore at his clothes, popping buttons and ripping fabric, until his chest and stomach were bare.

That's when they started digging.

His flesh gave way like Play-Doh under their long-nailed fingers. Dredd's cries hit an ear-quaking crescendo as they reached inside his torso, pulling for prime, squishy hunks of meat and organs. In no time, they'd hollowed him out. His mouth was left wide open, his eyes rolled back in his head.

Chuck started to cry. "They're going to do the same thing to us. Jesus fucking Christ. I don't want to die like that."

Mick couldn't think of anyone who would.

The leader had watched the evisceration with a smile on her crooked lips. Now that it was over, she trained her gaze on Mick and Chuck.

"I'm so sorry," Mick said.

"I know," Chuck said.

The leader smacked the bone again. Mick lashed out but was held firm. "No! No! No!"

Chuck was lifted to his feet, as was Mick.

They weren't being thrown to the children.

They were being led to the cave. Seconds later, they were carried into utter darkness, the stench of blood all around them as the children followed.

CHAPTER THIRTY-FIVE

There were candles everywhere, nestled in candleholders placed within any jagged crevice that could hold them. Chuck felt his knees start to give way several times as they were marched down a long and winding tunnel. The Melon Heads held him up most of the way, which wasn't easy considering his size. Mick had grown silent.

So. this was the end. Murdered by deformed freaks in the bowels of the earth. Chuck wished he could fight, but his body, soul and mind were spent. What was left was grim acceptance.

The tunnel system reeked of human waste, sweat, rancid earth and rotting food. It got worse the further they ventured. Chuck wondered if it was toxic. He started to hope it was; that way the fumes would kill him before the Melon Heads could.

"Hey, Mick."

His friend was just ahead of him.

"Mick."

The Melon Heads tightened their hold on him. What was more pain at this point?

"Yeah," Mick finally replied. He sounded irritated, as if Chuck had derailed his train of thought.

"You remember that championship game when we were on the Tigers?"

"What does that have to do with anything?"

Chuck was punched for talking, but he kept on. "We were down by four in the bottom of the ninth and we'd totally given up. You got all mad and started yelling at everyone on the bench, calling us a bunch of losers for quitting. Coach screamed at you, said, 'Sit the hell down, you misfit!' Remember that?"

"I do...hungh!" Mick was punched in the gut.

"We won the game. It took a misfit like you to get us to win the game."

"This isn't Little League, man."

Chuck was going to reply, but a hand was clamped over his mouth and nose. For a panicked second, he thought they were going to choke him. He found he could breathe out of one nostril. It stayed that way the rest of the walk.

They eventually came to a chamber filled with musty furniture. The floor was covered in animal pelts. With the warm candlelight, it almost looked comfortable. Chuck and Mick were thrust into padded chairs and ropes were tied around their chests and legs.

Mick cocked his head toward him. "At least we can die sitting comfortably."

"Speak for yourself. This is killing my arm." Chuck tried to find a way to alleviate the throbbing agony, to no avail.

Across from them, Mick spotted a pile of bones placed upon what looked like a makeshift altar. Resting atop that pile was a large human skull. The skull had a mane of straw-colored hair that spilled down into the carefully placed collection of bones. The edges of a blackened, shriveled scalp peeked from under the hair, the wig itself affixed to the skull with thick, iron nails.

"I think that's the head cheese Fennerman told Dredd about," Mick said to Chuck, motioning with his head toward the bones.

"Doesn't look like he's done any leading in a long time."

"I guess the biggest Melon Head gets the prize."

A more elaborate chair was dragged from the dark corner of the chamber and set before them. The female leader sat, the bones clicking and clacking. She leaned forward, staring at them, the others around her doing the same.

"Hello, beautiful," Mick said mockingly. If she didn't understand the words, she comprehended the tone. He was rewarded with a sharp backhanded smack that spun his head.

The absurdity of the moment triggered a comforting flow of gallows humor in Chuck. "What do we do now? Staring contest? I can tell you, I'm pretty good at it. Just tell me which eye to look at."

That only seemed to confuse her. He was not smacked for his indiscretion.

"No fair," Mick said. "He's being just as much of a douche."

Mick and Chuck caught one another's eye and shared a fatalistic smile.

"Any chance you can let us go and call it even?" Chuck asked. One of the Melon Heads kept smacking its lips, turning Chuck's stomach. He did not want to end up in that mouth.

"I'm not leaving without our friends," Mick said coldly.

The Melon Head leader stiffened.

"Where...the fuck...are they?" Mick said.

Chuck didn't want to remind him they were probably in the stomachs of the Melon Heads.

The leader leaned forward as far as she could and sniffed Mick from head to toe. There was something animalistic in the gesture, a wolf taking in its prey. Chuck decided there was no point talking. They were ants trying to communicate with an anteater.

"If you're going to kill us, just hurry up and do it," Mick said. "I really don't give a shit anymore."

When the leader shot up from her chair, Chuck flinched. She made a strange clicking sound with her teeth and several Melon Heads scurried to the other side of the chamber. They returned carrying two thick wooden poles. Tied to each were Vent and Marnie. They were bloody and bruised, their heads lolling on their shoulders. Dried blood was crusted all over Marnie's chin and neck.

Both looked very, very dead.

"You motherfuckers!" Mick shouted, fighting against his bindings.

The poles were placed on either side of the leader's chair, held in place by her deformed subjects. While Mick raged, Chuck stared hard at the chests of his friends. It took an interminable while, but he detected movement.

"They're alive!" he said. "Mick, they're alive!"

The leader's face broke into a lopsided grin, as if she were happy that she had them all in one place.

"Let them go," Mick seethed.

She tilted her head to him the way a dog does to its owner when it's told something it can't understand. Then she plucked a bone that had been sharpened on one end from her armor and used it to pick Vent's head up, the point close to piercing the soft flesh under his jaw.

His head tilted slightly and he groaned. She smacked his cheek hard and his eyes flew open.

"Vent," Mick said.

Vent's eyes rolled in their sockets and it took a while for him to find Mick and focus. "They got you, too?" he said despondently.

"Looks like Milbury is going to have to find a new gang of stoners," Mick said.

"I don't wanna die." Fresh tears trailed down Vent's face.

"I know, buddy. I know."

Next, the leader grabbed Marnie by the hair and tugged hard enough to wake her up. Marnie's first words were, "Get the fuck offa me!"

She saw Chuck and Mick and sagged with defeat. "Oh, god."

Chuck was sure if there was a god, this entire scenario would not be possible.

"We're sorry, Marnie," Chuck said. "We tried."

Her lips trembled but there were no tears.

Now there was only the wait for the inevitable.

Chuck kept expecting the leader to call the cannibal children to finish them off. Instead, there was a heavy silence.

"Do your worst," Mick said.

The leader stood, grabbed something behind her neck and the armor of bones clattered to the floor. The sight took Chuck's breath away. Beneath that terrible cloak and beneath a face that barely resembled a human was a perfect body with full, dark-nippled breasts and long legs that belonged on a dancer. Her stomach was fit but not flat, the mound between her legs hairless. Chuck's brain reeled at the juxtaposition.

She approached Mick, her breasts dangling by his face.

She gestured toward herself. And then at Vent and Marnie.

"What?" Mick said.

She repeated herself with a flurry of gestures. Mick shook his head. "Yeah, you're naked and they're tied up. What the fuck do you want me to do?"

He struggled when she grabbed the back of his head and pulled his face into her vast cleavage. He whipped his head back and forth, struggling to break away. Chuck watched in horror as she propped one foot on the arm of Mick's chair, easing his head slowly downward.

Mick fought wildly to break free.

"Mick, calm down," Chuck said, not sure if his friend could even hear him.

He was inched closer and closer to her vagina, the reek of it wafting over to Chuck. It hit Mick as well, because he started to gag. She thrust herself into his face. Mick opened his mouth and bit down hard. She hit him with a heavy fist in the side of the head and backed away. She grabbed a bone from her armor on the floor and swiped it across Vent's throat. A red grin opened up on his flesh. Blood audibly spurted from the opening wound, bathing Mick in his best friend's hot life force.

"No!" Marnie screamed. Chuck cried out, thrashing in the chair, hoping it would break.

The Melon Head leader let the last gout of blood hit Mick in the face. She rubbed her bitten privates. With another clack of her teeth, two Melon Heads untied him and dragged him away. Mick never made a move against them or tried to utter a sound. He'd been shocked into submission...or a kind of near death.

Chuck and Marnie called after him until the leader and everyone else had left the chamber, leaving them alone with Vent, the patter of his blood hitting the floor drowned out by their sobs.

CHAPTER THIRTY-SIX

Mick was roughly thrown onto a bed of sheets and blankets that hadn't been cleaned since Nixon was president. He tasted Vent's blood. It stung his eyes and filled his ears until it sounded as if he were underwater.

The Melon Head leader stepped inside the room, a side chamber made by nature, not man.

She quickly got on the bed and straddled him, her weight pinning him down. He barely saw her. He kept replaying Vent having his throat slashed over and over in his mind.

She moved just enough to fumble with his jeans. He didn't protest as she pulled them off, followed by his underwear.

He'd never been smart, but he knew what she wanted.

He had been chosen, all right.

Maybe she realized the clan had become too inbred. That there would be no future if things kept on going the way they were. Genetic mutations would only get worse, more debilitating, until they were nothing but a collection of mentally incapacitated cripples.

That's where he came in.

She fumbled with his cock, roughly tugging on it. He remained soft as warm butter. What other way could he possibly be? She grunted with obvious dissatisfaction.

Mick turned his head, unable to continue looking at that horrendous face. How long would she try to get blood from a stone until she killed him? It couldn't come soon enough.

As she rubbed herself on him, he saw his crumpled jeans. The quarter stick poked out of his pocket.

I could....

He reached out for it but was too far away. The leader hadn't noticed.

Mick had never had sex, despite what he told his friends. One thing he never thought he'd have to do is fake it during his first time. It looked like this would be his last as well.

He grabbed her hips and tried to squirm under her. She responded by growing hotter on his limp crotch.

Just a little more.

Mick touched her breast, eliciting a coo of pleasure that was both feminine and animal. It made him sick. He willed himself to get hard, but it just wasn't happening. He needed to make her think this was going to happen, to keep her focused on the areas between their legs.

It only took a couple of minutes to move her enough so he could grasp the quarter stick. The lighter dropped from his pocket.

Think of Marnie.

He conjured up a vision of Marnie atop him, gloriously nude and wanting him. His cock immediately responded. The leader sensed it and jammed it inside her, groaning and drooling.

The image of Marnie blinked away and he stared into the face of the Melon Head.

No! Don't look.

He closed his eyes. Slowly, Marnie came back to him.

He wished he'd told her how he felt. Then again, by not doing so, he'd saved himself a painful rejection. Of course, that would have been a lot less painful than this.

The Melon Head leader started to build a rhythm, her hips grinding into his. Mick needed to end this.

He put the firework and lighter in one hand, reached behind her and transferred the lighter to the other.

It was simple. He'd light the quarter stick, grab onto her so she couldn't break free, and wait for it to blow a hole in her back. It would take his hands, and his life, with it, but he'd been ready to die anyway. There never had been a future for him, even before their run-in with the Melon Heads.

His thumb flicked the lighter. He'd have to guess where the wick was. This could take some time, not that he was in danger of finishing any time soon.

His hands jounced up and down and now he didn't even know if the lighter held the flame. He felt himself start to soften.

Marnie. Marnie, I always loved you. I hope somehow you know that.

He flicked the lighter again.

Wait.

Marnie.

If he killed the leader now, what would become of Marnie and Chuck? They would be killed, more than likely.

"Fuck!" he shouted. The leader mistook his aggravation for ecstasy. Mick chucked the quarter stick and lighter aside.

I can save them. It'll be worse than dying, but I can save them.

The Melon Heads needed him. If the leader needed new offspring, she had to keep him alive. And if he was more than compliant, maybe he could be her equal. Or if not equal, at least less than a sire or subject.

He squinted his eyes closed and let her take him, take everything from him, and when it was over, he whispered, "Marnie," into the filthy pillow.

★   ★   ★

The same routine was repeated for what felt like days but was probably only one. Mick was red and raw and exhausted. He'd been brought food and water, only eating food from cans or packets and not the bowls of red gruel that he was sure was the remains of Dredd.

When he could no longer perform and the leader was lazing beside him, he got up and left the room, walking unsteadily back to the main chamber. She let him without dragging him back, proof that he'd made the right decision. He was hers now. He belonged to the entire Melon Head community. He could be their hope for a future. That thought didn't fill him with an iota of pride or satisfaction.

Chuck and Marnie were still tied up, both asleep.

Several Melon Heads were in the room with them.

"Go away," Mick said, swiping at the air so they got the point. To his amazement, they skittered out of the chamber.

It was hard untying their knots with numb fingers. Everything was numb now. Even his brain. It was a miracle he'd come this far.

"You're alive," Chuck said, waking from his stupor. His voice was weak and dry.

"I'm kinda hard to kill," Mick said. Chuck looked down at his nakedness. Mick didn't care. He was way past that. "Help me with Marnie."

This time, Chuck undid the knots while Mick held on to Marnie. When she was free, she fell into his arms. Her eyes fluttered open. "Am I dreaming?"

"Not in this place," he said softly. "Only nightmares here. You and Chuck go. Dream someplace where dreams matter."

"What do you mean?" She was groggy, rubbing at the sores on her wrists.

"Let's get out of here," Chuck said, grabbing on to them both.

Mick pulled away. "No. I have to stay."

"No, you don't."

Mick nodded slowly. "I kinda do."

"We're not leaving you down here," Marnie said.

"No choice. Now go."

Neither moved. "We can't," Chuck said.

"Yes, you can. They won't bother you."

"How can you know that?" Marnie asked.

He thought of the horrible ordeal he'd suffered all through the night and the many more to come. "I just do. You have to trust me. You trust me, right?"

"Not really," they said in unison.

That made Mick laugh. Not a happy laugh. Just one of fondness for the way things used to be.

Marnie took his hand. Her hand was so cold. "Come on. You're not staying down here."

"I have to. It's the only way. Trust me, I wish there was another."

"But why?"

"They need me. And while I'm with them, I can maybe keep them under some kind of control. Hopefully. Besides, no one's gonna miss me. No one ever would."

Chuck put a beefy hand on his shoulder. "I will, you stupid idiot."

Marnie opened her mouth to say something and buried her head in his chest instead, her tears hot and welcoming. He waited for a bit and willed himself to separate from her. "We'll see each other again. I promise. But for now, I need you to get the hell out of this place. Please. For me."

He looked to Chuck and his friend nodded with understanding. Chuck put his arm over Marnie's shoulder and led her out. She kept throwing pleading glances Mick's way, each look an arrow in his heart.

And then they were gone.

He sat on the leader's throne, his feet atop her bone armor. Melon Heads quietly filtered into the room, staring at him with fascination.

He felt like screaming until something vital burst in his brain.

CHAPTER THIRTY-SEVEN
Milbury, CT – 2000

"You sure you want to do this?"

"Yes, I'm sure."

Chuck turned the enormous pickup truck onto the old Dracula Drive. The sign demarking it as Wainscott Road was gone, but they all knew what this place was.

Marnie chewed on her fingernail and looked out the window. She couldn't remember the last time she'd been this nervous.

No, she could. It was that last time they'd been out here.

Since then, she and Chuck had gone through hell together, growing close enough to marry but not to truly love one another like a traditional husband and wife. The scars were too deep to heal, their true love for those they left behind trapped underneath the wounded tissue.

"That's it, I think." She pointed at the overgrown turn to Dredd's old cabin. The truck was scraped by branches. It sounded like nails on a chalkboard.

The cabin was gone now, though there were some planks of wood still visible. Nature had reclaimed the land.

The stumps where they'd sat to hatch out their plan to get rid of Harold Dunwoody were still there, though. Chuck parked the truck, grabbed the assault rifle he kept in the cab and got out.

"Come," she said, holding his hand and leading him to a stump.

It was still so quiet out here. She bet if she pushed the leaves from the ground, she wouldn't even find a single ant.

They sat and they waited. Chuck thrummed his fingers on the weapon. Marnie folded one leg over the other and bounced it in a heavy metal rhythm.

"He may be gone by now," Chuck said after an hour.

"Maybe."

"Any time you want to go."

She patted his thigh. "I know. I also know you want to wait a little longer, too."

"I do."

They waited some more, and the sun started to head westward.

Marnie was about to go to the truck for some water when she heard rustling. Chuck jumped to his feet with the rifle at the ready. Her heart trip-hammered until she felt dizzy.

Low-lying branches of a tree parted.

Mick emerged, older, his hair down to his waist, deep wrinkles around his eyes and mouth that made him look as if he'd aged twenty years. He was very skinny now, to the point of emaciation.

But he was smiling.

"You came," he said.

"We knew there would be eyes everywhere," Chuck said. "Figured you might want this." He handed his old friend a box of Slim Jims. Mick's eyes shimmered at the sight of the salty beef sticks.

"You remembered."

"I remember everything, bro. Everything."

Mick turned to Marnie with a beatific look in his eyes. "You're so beautiful."

"Hello, Mick," she said, choking on his name. Her vision blurred with tears. "How have you been?"

"Busy. Very busy. There's someone I want you to meet."

More rustling, and then several small children gathered around him. They all had his hair and they were beautiful. Their faces, the shapes of their eyes, gave them away as being special, different. Marnie's heart shattered. She barely registered the adult Melon Heads that had come out to witness the reunion.

One of the children, a little girl of about four, came bounding to her and wrapped her little arms around Marnie's leg. Marnie ran her fingers through her coarse, dirty hair. Her tears fell into her hair.

"She's beautiful," Chuck said.

Mick stared in wonder at Marnie and the girl. "She should be. Her name's Marnie."

ACKNOWLEDGEMENTS

Growing up in New York, so close to Connecticut, we knew all about the Melon Heads. Or at least we thought we did. This was before the internet and easy access to all the information in the world. I mean, I was getting my facts from the collection of Peanuts encyclopedias my mother bought at the Finast supermarket. No matter, we feared the Melon Heads and were glad they were another state away. I roamed with a bunch of boys in the woods as often as possible, spending days in abandoned houses and construction sites at the reservoir. We were always hoping to come across a monster, at least in theory. I truly believe if anything the least bit menacing came across our path, we would have burned rubber on our Mongoose bikes as we rushed home to our mommies.

Now, we didn't have Melon Heads, but we did have the tribe of killer albino dwarves that wielded machetes and would attack you if you went down Buckout Road in White Plains or dared to spend the night in the abandoned Sisters of St. Francis facility in Yonkers. (That's what we called that creepy place, though it might have been called something else entirely. New condos reside there now, where the rent is scarier than any creature.) Why did they have to be albinos and dwarves? Where did they get all those machetes? Who the hell knows? What I did know is that they were real, not like Bigfoot and UFOs, and they were right in my goddamn backyard. Me and the boys talked a big game about searching for them, but you can bet your bottom dollar nothing ever came of it.

I always thought of them as the New York cousins to the Melon Heads. Now, my Monster Men buddy Jack is a Connecticut kind of guy, so when I was contemplating what to write next, I thought, What would make Jack get all tingly? It was either Melon Heads or

Dudley Town. That man loves him some Dudley Town. Since I had come up with a title before the story concept (kind of like the movie magic revealed in Ed Wood), it leaned more toward a Melon Heads-inspired kind of terror. Oh, what was the title? *They Eat People*. My editor didn't like it. My wife thought it would piss readers off who thought they bought a zombie book. As in all things, I deferred to them because they're right.

As I get older, I find myself getting more and more nostalgic. I was a total metalhead in the eighties, complete with long hair, leather jackets with fringes, spurs on my boots, you name it. I can't convey the beauty of the party that was the eighties. Just glorious. Then I graduated college and there was a war and the economy was in the tank and the party was definitely over. In came grunge rock, and literally overnight, we were wearing dirty flannels and getting depressed and angry right along with Alice in Chains, Nirvana, Pearl Jam, The Screaming Trees, Soundgarden, Hole, Stone Temple Pilots, you name it. Man, that was a fucking scene. There may never be another like it. It was dark, dudes and dudettes. Real dark, but it had a beyond great soundtrack. Writing *Misfits* was my way of going in the time machine and reliving those years. And why *Misfits*? Aren't we all misfits? Some more than others, for sure, but the whole world is full of people struggling to belong somewhere and feeling like they're just a half-step (or more) removed from the lane they desire to cruise within. Mick, Marnie, Chuck, Heidi and Vent are the misfits who knew what they were and embraced it, who gave the finger to those who tried too hard to fit in. My friends and I have a little bit of each and every one of them in us. Thank god.

Big martini thanks to my editor, Don D'Auria, a man who is somehow as ageless as he is priceless. I spent what seemed like a lifetime hoping and praying I'd get the chance to one day work with him, and now I get to spend the rest of my time on this rotating sphere of insanity calling him not just editor, but friend.

Thanks to my mother, I was provided the perfect place to write, alternating between the yard on sunny days and the basement when the season changed. She still reads everything I write, which is why I tend to get a lot more side-eye now. Without her, there is no me, so there are folks who will thank her and some who will question her life decisions.

Jack Campisi is the yardstick by which greatness is measured, handier than a pocket on a shirt and a bad motor scooter and mean go-getter. I had you riding shotgun in my head the whole time I wrote this little yarn.

Huge ups to my A-team of beta readers – Kim Yerina, Shane Keene and Rich Duncan. You are the best. Seriously. If you're not my target audience, I don't know who is. If you gave me the thumbs down, this book would be on the scrapheap. Thank you for taking the time out to read it and let me know what worked and what needed work.

Last but not least, thank you to my wife, Amy, who puts up with the highs and lows of an artist (that's what I call myself to have my shortcomings, outbursts and misfit thoughts excused) and I think loves me for them. Every time I trundled off to write, she would ask, "Which book is this one? Is it the slasher killer one, or the one with the, whaddya call them, big heads?"

Okay, so my wife is the penultimate thank you. I always wanted to put 'penultimate' in a book. Thank you, readers, hellions, horror-loving maniacs and even you 'normies' who were cajoled into reading a book about cannibal Melon Heads. I hope you enjoyed your time on Dracula Drive. I invite you to come again, because there will be more. Oh, so much more....

FLAME TREE PRESS
FICTION WITHOUT FRONTIERS
Award-Winning Authors & Original Voices

Flame Tree Press is the trade fiction imprint of Flame Tree Publishing, focusing on excellent writing in horror and the supernatural, crime and mystery, science fiction and fantasy. Our aim is to explore beyond the boundaries of the everyday, with tales from both award-winning authors and original voices.

•

Other titles available by Hunter Shea:

Creature

Ghost Mine

Slash

Other horror and suspense titles available include:

The Wise Friend by Ramsey Campbell

The House by the Cemetery by John Everson

Hellrider by JG Faherty

Sins of the Father by JG Faherty

Boy in the Box by Marc E. Fitch

The Toy Thief by D.W. Gillespie

One By One by D.W. Gillespie

Black Wings by Megan Hart

The Playing Card Killer by Russell James

The Siren and the Specter by Jonathan Janz

The Dark Game by Jonathan Janz

Will Haunt You by Brian Kirk

We Are Monsters by Brian Kirk

Hearthstone Cottage by Frazer Lee

Those Who Came Before by J.H. Moncrieff

The Mouth of the Dark by Tim Waggoner

They Kill by Tim Waggoner

•

Join our mailing list for free short stories, new release details, news about our authors and special promotions:

flametreepress.com